WANTING MAGGIE

"Oh, Maggie," Aaron whispered as his hand moved up her neck to fondle the side of her face. "Why did you come into my life?"

"You mustn't . . ."

But the words died on her lips when his fingers touched her mouth and his other hand went to her waist, pulling her closer.

The first kiss was hard and hot and powerful. He was dying for the taste and feel of this woman. Nothing had ever been so good as having Maggie in his arms, his mouth on hers. . . .

The Right Wife

BEVERLY BARTON

KENSINGTON BOOKS
KENSINGTON PUBLISHING CORP.
http://www.kensingtonbooks.com

KENSINGTON BOOKS are published by

Kensington Publishing Corp.
119 West 40th Street
New York, NY 10018

All Kensington titles, imprints, and distributed lines are available at special quantity discounts for bulk purchases for sales promotion, premiums, fundraising, educational, or institutional use.

Special book excerpts or customized printings can also be created to fit specific needs. For details, write or phone the office of the Kensington Special Sales Manager: Attn. Special Sales Department. Kensington Publishing Corp., 119 West 40th Street, New York, NY 10018. Phone: 1-800-221-2647.

First Electronic Edition: June 2014
eISBN-13: 978-1-60183-279-5
eISBN-10: 1-60183-279-6

First Print Edition: June 2014
ISBN-13: 978-1-60183-280-1
ISBN-10: 1-60183-280-X

Published in the United States of America

Chapter 1

"Get your filthy hand off her," Maggie Campbell said. "How dare you accuse Daisy of stealing your watch?"

"Look girlie, you stay out of this. Your nigger stole my watch, and I intend to search her," the red-faced, little pig-of-a-man shouted.

"I'm not going to tell you again, you stinking idiot, get your hands off of Daisy!"

"Please, Miss Maggie," the pale-eyed young Negress said, her womanly body trembling with fear. Clean but terribly worn clothes covered her alluring body, and slender, bare feet revealed her poverty. Her fair maize skin, ebony hair, and huge, almost iridescent blue eyes bespoke of a beauty that once would have sold at a high price.

"Shut up, gal." As he spoke, her accuser pulled the black woman closer to his rotund body. He turned to the redheaded girl who was pointing her finger in his heavily bearded face. "Just what you going to do about it, huh? I say this gal stole my watch, and I got a right to search her for it. You take those two brats and get on the train. I'll send this 'un on after I get my watch back."

Maggie moved closer, pulling on her servant, trying to free her from the tight embrace of her captor. The man's grasp loosened when Maggie's tug caught him off guard. Daisy staggered, barely catching herself before falling.

The disturbance on the loading platform attracted Aaron Stone's attention. He noticed that a small group had gathered around the heavyset, bearded man, the slender Negress, and the auburn-haired girl. Two youngsters, by looks obviously the screaming redhead's brother and sister, stood by her. Their tense, young faces seemed to be warning one and all not to interfere. The tall, lanky boy, who appeared to be about sixteen, moved in closer as if ready to pounce.

Aaron took a deep draw on his cigar as he stepped down onto the platform, walked a few yards, and stopped at the edge of the small assembly.

Aaron's green eyes moved over the angry redhead whose full breasts were heaving in tantalizing movements as her anger steadily increased. The small rose attached to the bodice of her dress attracted his attention, the crimson petals brilliant against the pale blue background.

"Damn you!" the fat, little man hissed, grabbing Maggie by the wrists. "Maybe *you* stole my watch. Maybe I need to search *you.*"

"Stop it!" Maggie's boyishly brave brother yelled. "Let her go."

"You're an awful man," the small girl said. "You better let my sister go or I'll bite you."

"Let me loose, you fat, old goat," Maggie said, just as her foot rammed into his shin.

Momentarily stunned, he released Maggie, but, before she could move, he grabbed her around the waist. Just as Maggie aimed her knee, the boy jumped on the man's back, the girl bit into his fat hand, and the daring Negress whacked him in the head with a tiny case. Within seconds, their attacker lay on the platform cursing loudly while Maggie Campbell and her troops gathered their belongings.

Aaron could not contain the chuckle rumbling from his chest. He had seen many a sight in his thirty years, but nothing to match the spectacle of this feisty redhead and her unlikely entourage. She looked far too young to be on her own. She looked far too poor to have a servant. He found the incident amusing and the girl intriguing. She certainly was not a well-behaved young lady. Her actions had been those of a wildcat, not a tame, little tabby. Aaron knew his beloved Eunice would have been shocked senseless. Never would she have degraded herself by becoming embroiled in a struggle to protect a darky servant girl.

The scarlet-faced man got to his feet and stormed toward his assailants. "You better stop, you little slut, you and that nigger of yours. I got police friends. I'll have you in jail. Huber Smith ain't nobody to rile."

Maggie didn't slow down. She kept walking, but the black girl stopped.

"Miss Maggie, go 'head and let him search me. Then he'll know I ain't got no watch."

Maggie stopped. "I will not allow that . . . that . . . animal to touch you. He knows you didn't steal his watch."

"Please, Miss Maggie, I don't want to cause you no trouble." Tears filled Daisy's huge, blue eyes.

"Flibberation!" On Maggie's lips the word became a curse.

What prompted him to interfere Aaron would never know, but the impulse to be Miss Maggie's champion overcame his better judgment.

"Mr. Smith." Aaron's deep voice froze the other man to the spot and equally immobilized the small crowd of onlookers.

Smith's keen, black eyes darted up at the big man who had called his name. "Sir?"

"I think perhaps you have delayed this young . . . er . . . lady long enough. I, too, have friends in Chattanooga. The mayor and I have shared a brandy at the Stanton House on more than one occasion."

"Look here, sir, this colored gal stole my watch, and I intend to search her."

"Mr. Smith, being a man of the world myself, I can understand how the dark charms of this quadroon might tempt you, but this is 1885. Since her mistress is unwilling to allow you the privileges you desired, I suggest that you quietly drop the matter." When Aaron smiled, his handsome face hardened. His stance tensed and he turned to Maggie.

"May I have the honor of escorting you aboard your train, miss?"

"Miss Campbell, Miss Margaret Campbell. And thank you, but we can board the train without any more help."

Maggie looked up at Aaron and the whole world seemed to fade away. He was far from the first handsome man she had ever seen. In Grovesdale, there had been men of all shapes, sizes, and ages. She had even had a steady beau before Pa died. Benny had been handsome, in a youthful sort of way, and every bit the gentleman this big, blond man was, probably more so. She attributed the giddy, sinking feeling in her stomach to her unwilling attraction to the handsome stranger.

"It would be my pleasure to help you, Miss Campbell."

Maggie trembled. She wasn't sure whether she was trembling outside or just inside. Lordy, he was big. Bigger than Pa and Pa had been a tad over six feet.

Aaron held her eyes with his. She didn't look a day over eighteen with that smooth, flawless complexion and innocent gold eyes. Just looking at her made him restless with a need he hadn't felt in years. Not since he had been a randy boy. She might not be a well-bred lady, but she certainly was a rare beauty. He knew he should say good-bye and good luck, and get the hell away from her before he made a fool of himself.

"Where are you headed, Miss Campbell?" he heard himself asking against his better judgment.

"We're going to Tuscumbia, Alabama," Maggie said as she began walking. She motioned for the other three to follow.

"I happen to be a new resident of that area." Aaron smiled when he saw the momentary pause in her step. He decided it was fate. Somehow this redheaded witch was going to cause him trouble.

"Then perhaps we will see you there, Mr. . . . ah . . . Mr. . . ." Maggie flushed. She did not want this aggressively arrogant rogue to think she was trying to become familiar.

"Stone. Aaron Stone," he introduced himself, knowing that, although Maggie feigned indifference, she was as interested in him as he was in her.

Remaining a few discreet steps behind, Daisy and the children kept pace with the fast-moving Maggie. All three were avidly listening to the ongoing conversation between the titian-haired tigress and their golden rescuer.

"Thank you for your assistance, Mr. Stone." Maggie tried to sound genuinely appreciative without being coy. If there was one thing that she hated, it was sugary-sweet women who batted their eyelashes and spouted asinine nonsense like "Oh, dear me."

"Perhaps I should accompany you and your party on the remainder of the trip," Aaron said, dumbfounded by his inability to leave this girl. "It's unfortunate that some older male member of your family couldn't see you safely to your destination."

Aaron Stone knew he was unwanted and probably not needed, but, for some perplexing reason, he could not bring himself to walk away from Miss Maggie Campbell. At thirty, he was too old to be infatuated with some winsome girl, even if she were the most beautiful creature he had ever seen. She was definitely the wrong woman for him. Woman? She wasn't much more than a girl, a hot-tempered, unladylike, poorly dressed girl.

"Look, Mr. Stone," Maggie said, "although I appreciated your help, I do not appreciate your persistence. All appearances to the contrary, I, sir, am a lady. And ladies do not encourage acquaintances with strange men."

"Well, I'll be damned," Aaron laughed. "Pardon me, miss." His jade eyes scanned her shabbily attired body. "I simply thought that your party might be interested in traveling to Tuscumbia in a private car. I happen to have one at my disposal."

He had never known a woman who could resist the lure of wealth. Why should this beautiful ragamuffin be different? Even his own mother had sold herself to the highest bidder.

"We have our tickets, sir. Paid for with good, honest money." Maggie's quick steps increased in speed.

"What makes you think my money is bad, Miss Maggie?"

"Intuition, sir. Intuition."

Aaron slowed his stride to a standstill, watching as the Campbell clan headed toward the passenger car. Determined not to follow the sassy miss, he counted the reasons he should not pursue his baser instincts. She was too young, too poor, too ill bred, and too independent. That type made a good mistress, but a bad wife for a man seeking to overcome his own unsavory past.

He probably would have been able to turn around and go in the opposite direction if Maggie hadn't stopped just as her siblings boarded the train ahead of her. She stood there with those big gold eyes staring at him as if she'd never seen a man before. Damn, if she didn't stop looking at him, he wouldn't be responsible for his actions.

He walked the few feet separating them while she watched his approach, not moving when he reached out and took her small hand into his giant clasp.

"Miss Maggie." He wanted this woman. He wanted her badly.

"Mr. Stone, I . . . I . . ."

"I don't want you to leave with a bad impression of me." Her hand felt warm and soft, yet strong, as if she were capable of hard work. He wanted to pull her hand to his lips to open her palm and stroke it with his tongue.

"Please, let me go." She jerked her hand away, tingling from his touch.

He stood motionless, watching while she practically ran up the steps to board the passenger car.

"Good-bye, Mr. Stone," the wide-eyed child, who was a pale, petite version of her older sister, called from the open window of the Memphis and Charleston railroad coach. "We'll see you in Tuscumbia."

He looked up in time to see Maggie jerk back the waving hand of her young sister and hastily close the window. Amused green eyes met molten gold ones, as unconscious invitation and acceptance passed between them.

Maggie tried to settle into her seat, but fidgeted nervously as she stole quick glances at the scattering of other passengers seated around her. She knew that soon the mighty steam engine would move the train forward, propelling her into an adventure of the new and unknown. She did not want her sixteen-year-old brother, Micah, or her ten-year-old sister, Judith, to be aware of her uneasiness. They were depending on her to be strong. Since Pa had passed on this last winter, the young ones looked to her for guidance, even though Micah tried hard to be the man of the family.

"Why can't Daisy sit with us?" Judith turned backward, her knees resting on the cushioned bottom of the seat. Her large hazel eyes boldly inspected the passenger car's interior and the interesting human specimens settling in for the long ride.

On the walls, small gaslights were attached every few feet apart. At one end of the wood-paneled coach stood a cold, potbellied stove, an empty brass cuspidor overturned beside it.

"Daisy has to ride in the colored car, Judith," Maggie said, personally wishing that Daisy were by her side. "Things aren't that different back home. It's just that out in big cities, things are done more proper."

"Is it proper that Daisy has to ride in a different car from us?"

"Yes, Judith, it's the proper thing." Maggie didn't approve of the way things were, but she had learned to accept them. Poor little Jude was only a child, with a child's rosy outlook on life. Maggie knew it was hard for her to understand why things were the way they were.

"Would it not have been proper for us to ride in that private car with Mr. Stone?"

"Judith Campbell, will you please sit down," Maggie laughed, barely stopping herself from swatting her young sister's backside. "The proper thing is for a lady to sit on her bottom, facing forward, and not sit on her knees gaping at strangers."

"I'm not gaping. I'm showing an interest in what's going on around me."

"Sit down, Jude, and quit acting like some ignorant farm girl," Micah said. Having settled in the seat facing his sisters, he crossed his legs and relaxed.

Judith spun around and practically fell into the seat, a self-satisfied smile curling her pink lips. "There, is that better?"

"Let's all try to behave as if we've had some raisin'. Aunt Tilly and Uncle Chester will expect good manners from us." Maggie knew that her siblings dreaded the thought of living with their mother's brother and his puritanical wife. She had grave misgivings herself.

"Does Daisy like being colored?" Judith seemed intent on straining her sister's nerves to the breaking point.

Sympathetically eyeing the inquisitive girl beside her, Maggie said, "Daisy accepts her lot in life. She knows that the good Lord put us all here for a purpose, whatever our color."

"I wonder what that handsome Mr. Stone's purpose is?" Judith sighed, a dreamy expression on her pretty little face.

"I'd bet his purpose is to drink hard liquor, make easy money, and bed as many willing females as possible." Micah's face brightened with laughter, his raw-boned features almost gaunt.

"Micah James Campbell!" Maggie pretended shock, praying silently that no one had overheard her brother's tasteless comments. Aunt Tilly would have an attack of the vapors if she heard such language. "Anybody could tell he's a man of the world, a man used to getting his own way," the boy said.

"Lord only knows what a man like that did to make the money to afford the kind of life you're talking about." Maggie refused to believe that Aaron Stone would play a part in her life or the lives of her siblings. Surely Aunt Tilly would shun a man of his type. Maggie was powerfully certain that he hadn't been born a gentleman.

"I don't see that it makes much difference how a man gets rich as long as he does." Micah's words reflected his own unhappiness with his poverty-stricken life.

"Don't talk such nonsense," his older sister said. "You know that Cousin Wesley has great hopes that you will follow in his footsteps by joining the ministry. A true man of God has little chance of becoming rich."

"I don't want to be no preacher." The rangy, auburn-haired youth twisted in his seat, positioning himself to face the window. The morning breeze cooled his heated face, which had flushed scarlet beneath his healthy Tennessee tan.

"Is being a preacher a proper thing to do?" Judith asked.

Maggie's head began to throb. Was her dream of a better life for Judith and Micah just that, a dream? Would she be able to curb the adventurous streak that ran so deep within her brother? Would she ever be able to make a real lady of the bubbly, constantly curious Judith?

Micah refused to acknowledge either Judith's question or the existence of his two sisters. Maggie knew he would sulk for a while, perhaps even think about being in cahoots with the likes of Aaron Stone. No doubt, that rogue could teach her little brother all sorts of improper things.

"I don't think I'd like being married to a preacher," the younger girl said thoughtfully. "You could never do anything fun. It'd all be a sin."

"Please don't talk like that in front of Aunt Tilly," Maggie told her talkative sister. "She sets great store by sin and salvation."

"I wish we didn't have to live with Aunt Tilly. She sounds like such a sour old—"

"Oh Jude, honey. We should be grateful that Uncle Chester and Aunt Tilly are offering us a home. We'll just have to mind our P's and Q's, that's all."

Maggie was willing to do almost anything to give her family a chance for a better life than a future struggling on a sharecropper farm in Tennessee. Pa's death had left them with little money and no hope of improving their lot.

"I promise I'll try to be good, Maggie."

"I know you will, honey. And remember that I'll always be there for you and Micah."

"And we'll always be there for you."

"First thing I plan to do is talk to Aunt Tilly about your schooling. You can't be a proper lady without book learning."

"But you can read and write. Why, you're one of the smartest people I know."

"I've got common sense," Maggie corrected. "I'm a good, honest, hardworking girl, but I'll never be a real lady. It's not in me, but it is in you, and I intend to see you get your chance."

"Oh, Maggie."

"My God, Aaron, what a little hellcat this Maggie of yours must be." Thayer Coleman's loud laughter filled his private railroad car. "I regret that you were unable to persuade her to join us."

"I don't think she's really a hellcat. She was just trying to protect her servant girl. I'd do the same thing for Phineas. And Maggie's not your type, old friend," Aaron told the other man as he glanced meaningfully at the voluptuous brunette lounging across the car.

Thayer smiled as his dark eyes caressed the scantily clad woman. "Verda can be amusing, but no different from other creatures of her type. I think your little Maggie Campbell would prove to be quite a challenge for a man."

"I'm not interested in challenges anymore," Aaron said. "I'm ready to settle down."

"How boring. Lord, the very thought of settling down with a woman scares the hell out of me."

"I'm six years older than you. I've also met a very suitable woman."

"Eunice Arnold will bore you to tears. I'll wager that within six months of taking vows with that suitable lady, you'll be looking for one of Loretta's hot-blooded whores to warm your bed." Thayer ran a hand over the coarse, black stubble covering his jaw. "I need a shave and another drink."

"Dammit, Thayer, you don't need a wife like Eunice. I do. If I'm ever to gain a respectable place in society, I've got to make a good marriage. With the right wife, people won't ask as many questions about my past."

Thayer poured himself another shot of whiskey from the imported crystal decanter. "Shall we drink to respectability?"

"It's a little early in the day for me," Aaron said.

"Is it really morning?" Thayer gulped down the burning liquid and laughed again. "Maybe I should get some sleep. When I wake up, it should feel like morning."

"Good idea. I'll wake you when we stop in Huntsville. It should be lunchtime by then." Aaron could almost taste the scrumptious fried chicken and mouthwatering peach pie in the box lunches that were sold at the depot there.

"Make sure Verda is dressed by then," Thayer said. "She's disembarking in Huntsville. You want to visit your sister for a while, don't you, sweet thing?"

Verda shrugged, her huge breasts shaking from the slight movement. "Don't make me no never mind. If I ain't welcome at my sister's, I got other friends there. Men friends who'd be more than glad to see Verda again."

"Good. Good. Then that's settled." Thayer rested his shot glass on the small oak bar. "You probably wouldn't enjoy Tuscumbia anyway."

Aaron felt the sudden movement of the train and knew they were under way. He wondered what Miss Maggie Campbell thought of the passenger car. This was probably her first train ride. Was she excited? Afraid? Why the hell should he care? He had to put that beautiful little witch out of his mind. Proposing marriage to Eunice should be uppermost in his thoughts.

"You going on to Tuscumbia with Thayer?" the luscious Verda

asked as she placed her half-nude body beside a partially aroused Aaron.

"I've got business to attend to." He wanted Verda to leave him alone. Even though he and Thayer had shared a woman on more than one occasion, he had no intention of slaking his desire for a virginal redhead with this overripe whore. Last night he had enjoyed their flirtation, but he had momentarily lost his taste for soiled goods.

"Why don't you put off that business? I got friends in Huntsville. We sure could have us a good time." Verda's bare foot stroked Aaron's ankle and gradually moved up the calf of his leg.

He wondered if Maggie's feet were pale and soft. How would it feel to have her toes tickling his skin?

When the seductive hussy reached out to touch his chest, Aaron caught her slender wrist, stopping her abruptly. "I'm not interested."

Verda smiled, shrugged, and slowly removed her womanly body. Aaron looked out the window, completely ignoring her departure, wishing he were in the passenger coach with the Campbell clan.

Why are the Campbells going to Tuscumbia? he wondered. Did they have relatives there? What if Maggie were going to meet a future husband? Aaron knew it shouldn't matter to him. If he had suddenly become so enamored of the idea of bedding a virgin, there were more likely candidates available. He was so certain that Maggie was a virgin, he'd bet his last dollar on the fact. Virginity was something that even the prestigious Eunice Arnold couldn't lay claim to. Of course, her lack of innocence was quite proper since she was a widow.

Marrying Eunice would be a step in the right direction, just as buying the old White Orchard plantation had been. He pictured himself as a country gentleman with a genteel mate and several well-bred offspring. He hadn't told Eunice anything about White Orchard. When he proposed, he wanted it to be an extra surprise. By the time they were lawfully wed, restoration of the manor house should be complete.

Intrusive thoughts of shimmering gold eyes and glorious red hair filled Aaron's mind. Mile after mile passed as he sat gazing out the window of Thayer Coleman's private railroad car. All the while he fantasized about making love to an ill-bred, outspoken girl who could mean nothing to him but trouble.

Having made this same trip on many previous occasions, he recognized the outskirts of Huntsville. He had been so engrossed in his own thoughts he had forgotten to make certain that his friend's current mistress was dressed and ready to disembark.

After standing slowly and taking a long, much-needed stretch, Aaron looked across the car and saw a fully clad Verda watching his movements.

"Just looking, honey. Just looking." Her voice had a soft, almost childlike quality to it. "It's a pity we ain't going to get to know each other better."

Aaron reached over and gently nudged Thayer. His friend grunted and turned over. Aaron tried again, more forcefully the second time.

"What the—" Thayer grumbled sleepily.

"We'll be in Huntsville in about fifteen minutes." Aaron grinned. At this precise moment, his young friend looked like a grouchy child needlessly awakened from a sound sleep.

"Make sure Verda gets off," Thayer mumbled.

"He's so charmin' when he's drunk," Verda said. "Don't worry none about me, honey. I'll get myself off and get a boy to take care of my bags."

"Good," both men said simultaneously.

"I'm getting off for a walk," Aaron said. "Think I'll get a box lunch. Do you want me to get one for you, too?"

"Hell if I know." Thayer sat up and ran his fingers though his thick black hair. "My head is pounding and my stomach is churning."

"I'll get two. You'll be starving before we reach Tuscumbia."

Maggie was thankful that Judith had finally worn herself out and fallen asleep. Micah, still sulking, seemed to be absorbed in watching the quickly passing scenery outside the window.

She wondered how long the train would be stopped in Huntsville. She had heard some of the other passengers talking about getting off for lunch. She supposed they'd just have to eat the cold biscuits she had wrapped and placed in her bag before leaving Grovesdale last night.

She'd bet that Mr. Aaron Stone wouldn't be eating any cold biscuits for his noonday meal. She wished that she could stop thinking about that damnable handsome rogue. Every time she closed her eyes, she could see his face, hard and strong, like something chiseled out of granite. Every time she gazed out the window, almond-shaped green eyes stared back at her. She could not let this unwanted attraction change any of her plans. Even nodding hello to him would mean trouble.

Before the train had actually stopped, the hustle and bustle taking place on the loading platform outside alerted Maggie that they had arrived. The sudden jolt awoke Judith, who wiggled restlessly. The child opened her huge, blue-green eyes and smiled up at her sister, on whose lap her strawberry-blond head lay nestled.

"Where are we?" a sleepy Judith asked. "We can't be in Tuscumbia already, can we?"

"No," Maggie told the girl who sat up and looked outside. "We're in—"

"Huntsville!"

"Lower your voice, heathen," Micah said, giving his little sister a look of warning.

"I've got biscuits in my bag if either of you are hungry," Maggie told them. "And I've got a little jug of water too."

"Oh, look there," Judith said, jumping to her feet and leaning across her sister in order to reach the window. "It's Mr. Stone."

"What?" Without thought, Maggie looked outside, searching for the big, blond man. Her heart raced out of control. *What is wrong with me?* she wondered. *What kind of a spell has that man cast on me?*

She could barely see the depot for the crowds of people swarming about, men and women, black and white. Dozens of wagons, buggies, and carriages were lined up at the far end of the one-story structure. When she lowered the window, the aroma of food flooded the railroad coach, as the sounds of the sellers' voices carried through the air.

"Hey there, Mr. Stone," Judith yelled as loudly as she could. "Hey, it's me. Over here."

"Jude, will you please hush up," Maggie said nervously, wondering what she would say to Aaron Stone. What would he think of her, of her sister? *Oh, Lord, don't let him hear Jude,* she prayed silently.

"He heard me." The child beamed with delight. "Look, he's coming over here."

Maggie stole a glance, her eyes devouring every inch of the rugged giant making his way through the crowd. His lean, square face was clean-shaven. His mouth was big and wide, his lips thin and straight as they parted in a generous smile. His teeth were pearly white against his weather-darkened skin.

Oh, those eyes, Maggie thought, *those hypnotizing green eyes.* Deep-set eyes that slanted upward were surrounded by the longest straw-brown lashes she'd ever seen on a man, and the thick brows were an even darker brown.

Wavy, golden hair curled about the collar of his fancy white-linen shirt. Maggie had the irresistible urge to run her fingers through that tawny mane.

He was a big man standing alone, but in a crowd, he towered over others like a giant oak tree in a forest of seedlings.

Judith, leaning across her tense and aggravated sibling, stuck her fiery-gold head out the window. "What are you doing getting off in Huntsville? I thought you were going all the way to Tuscumbia with us."

Aaron had heard the pretty little girl's shouts before he spotted her smiling face. He made his way through the crowd and stopped below the window out of which half the child's petite body hung precariously.

"I'm stretching my legs and buying a box lunch." He noticed that Miss Maggie was deliberately looking the other way. "Would you care for a lunch, Miss Campbell?"

Maggie did not want to face him. She jerked on Judith's skirt, trying to pull the child back inside and avoid any further embarrassment. "Please sit down, Jude," she whispered.

Ignoring her sister's plea, Judith continued to hang dangerously from the window. "What's in a box lunch?"

"The very best fried chicken." Aaron could see the look of mouthwatering hunger on the girl's face. "Please take mine. I can purchase another before the train pulls out," he said, holding the food container.

Just as Judith reached for the lunch, she lost her balance. With Maggie and Aaron both watching but neither able to prevent the disaster, Judith Campbell fell out the window. Instinctively Aaron dropped the meal and caught the child. She shrieked with fear and relief, then looked up into the face of her astonished rescuer.

"My God, Miss Campbell," Aaron said after his heart started beating again. "You do have a unique way of getting a man's attention."

Frantically Maggie made her way outside the coach and stepped down from the train, holding up the skirt of her dress with one hand to better maneuver the steps. A glimpse of frayed cotton petticoat and scuffed black shoes disclosed her circumstances even though her dress was fashionable and well tailored.

"Maggie's going to kill me dead." Judith laughed as she watched her sister approach, her blazing red hair flying about her shoulders.

"Leave Miss Maggie to me," Aaron said. "I've always had a way with the ladies."

"That's what Micah said." The child still lay cuddled in his huge arms when Maggie confronted them.

"I assume Micah is your brother." Aaron pretended to ignore the older girl. "And just what did he have to say about my success with the fair sex?"

"Judith!" Maggie warned.

"Micah said that he bet you had bedded as many willing females as possible," the little girl quoted quite guilelessly.

"Did he indeed." Aaron hadn't enjoyed himself so much in years. Sneaking a peek at Maggie, he could see the pink flush of shame covering the beautiful girl's face. "And what made him think that?"

"Because we figured you're a—" Judith started to explain when Maggie's hand covered her mouth. Judith twisted and turned, indicating to Aaron that she wanted down, all the while mumbling beneath the restricting hand.

Once on her feet, Judith pulled away from her sister, obtaining revenge by finishing her comments. "We figured you're a hard-drinking man who's made a lot of easy money and uses it to get things done your own way."

Please Lord, Maggie prayed, *let me die right now.* Of all the stupid, childish things her sister had ever done, this had to be the worst. What would this man think of the Campbells? What could he think but that they were ignorant Tennessee trash?

Amusement lit his ruggedly perfect face as laughter built deep within him, vibrating his chest and finally erupting into such loud guffaws that those around him stopped to stare.

For the second time in one day, the Campbells had acquired a crowd of onlookers. With her head held high, Maggie grabbed Judith by the arm, paying no heed to Aaron Stone or the people being entertained by their actions.

Not saying a word, she simply glared at her young sister, her yellow cat-eyes glowing with rage.

"I'm coming. I promise." Judith pulled free and reached down to retrieve the lunch that Aaron had dropped onto the wooden platform. "Thank you for saving my life, and thank you for the lunch."

Aaron's amusement subsided enough for him to reply, "You're quite welcome. It was not only my pleasure, but obviously the pleasure of this entire assembly."

"We will see you in Tuscumbia, won't we?" Judith asked as she rejoined Maggie, who immediately ushered her onto the train.

"Most certainly, Miss Campbell, most certainly." Aaron looked directly at the younger girl first, then raised his eyes to the older, who had been able to refrain from taking one last glimpse in his direction.

Maggie didn't wait until they reached their seats before chastising an unrepentant Judith.

"How could you? Of all the dumb fool things to do. What on earth will Aunt Tilly think if she hears about this?"

"Fiddlesticks. Who's to tell her?" Judith disregarded her sister's concern as they moved hastily down the aisle, other passengers looking, laughing, smiling, and whispering at the quarreling girls.

"Promise me that you won't encourage friendship with that man."

"I like Mr. Stone. And I think he likes me."

"Oh Jude."

"He likes you, too. I can tell. He looks at you all funny-like."

"You mustn't say such things. Men like Mr. Stone look at women all the time. It doesn't mean a thing."

"She's right, Maggie," Micah said. "The way Mr. Stone looks at you means a great deal."

Flaming tresses swayed with the movement of her shaking head as Maggie denied her brother's accusation. "I want both of you to hush up right now. And promise me that neither of you will have any more to do with that man. And for heaven's sake, don't breathe a word of this when we arrive in Tuscumbia. You know that Cousin Wesley has a very important reputation to uphold."

Neither sibling spoke. They exchanged knowing glances that infuriated their older sister.

"If we're to have any chance of a better life, then the two of you have to help me." Maggie knew they were too young and unaware of how their actions could be misunderstood by truly genteel people. People not used to Tennessee hill folk.

"We're going to help. Just don't expect us to change into different people overnight." Micah's voice was so deep, so richly baritone that most people took a second look when they heard him speak. Being such a tall, skinny fellow made others view him as a mere boy.

"I'm sorry to be so hard on you both, but I love y'all, and I can't bear to think how bad things could be for us if we can't fit into the life that Aunt Tilly and Uncle Chester have."

"I promise I'll try real hard to behave better," Judith said. "But I like Mr. Stone, and I won't lie and say I don't want to get to know him better."

"All right. All right. I give up." Margaret Mary Campbell knew that all the Campbells were a stubborn, single-minded lot who usually chose to do things their own way, which was, most often, the hard way.

Once settled in her own seat and ignoring the chatter of curious passengers, Maggie tried to dismiss everything from her mind but the promise of the bright future that lay ahead. Mile after mile of Alabama passed outside the train window, acre after acre of month-old cotton, stretch after stretch of woods flowing into verdant grasslands. Maggie was fascinated by the way mountains gradually became smaller and smaller, and finally transformed into hills. Alabama, even the northwest section, was mostly flatland. She wondered if she would miss the beautiful mountains of her native state, knowing in her heart that she already did. She had been born and raised in Grovesdale, a farming community nestled snugly in the foothills of southeastern Tennessee near the great river. She had a deep-rooted love for the earth, an appreciation for the bounty it could produce, and a reverence for the power of nature.

She knew that she had to put the past behind her and forget about the life she might have had farming the land with a husband like Benny. She had to prepare herself and her family for life in town, with a small plot of ground behind Aunt Tilly's house where she could plant a vegetable garden and a few flowers. Perhaps, she could plant a rosebush to brighten all their lives. There would not be a husband for her, at least not for a long time. Not until she had fulfilled her promise to Pa.

She smelled the tangy aroma of fried chicken seconds before she heard lips smacking with enjoyment. She opened her eyes and turned toward the tempting smell. Judith crunched busily on a crispy wing while Micah demolished a meaty leg.

"It's delicious, Maggie. Want a piece?" her sister asked between bites.

"Don't try to talk with your mouth full, honey. You could get choked," Maggie said. "And no, thank you, I'll eat my biscuits. I wouldn't touch a morsel bought with that man's money."

Several hours later, Maggie almost regretted that she had not overcome her pride and feasted on chicken and fried peach pies. By the time the train backed into the Tuscumbia station, she was hungry, tired, and far more apprehensive than she would allow anyone to know.

"It's not near as big as Chattanooga," Judith said. "But it sure is pretty. Look at all the trees."

"They even got a hotel." Micah gazed up the street where the three-story brick building stood.

"We're stopping!" Judith squealed, jumping quickly to her feet. "Is Cousin Wesley meeting us? I don't see him."

"How would you remember what he looks like? You were just a baby the first time you saw him," Micah said.

"I was nearly six years old, thank you. I saw him when his ma married Uncle Chester."

"Tuscumbia," the porter called. "Fifteen minutes."

The Campbells gathered their few meager belongings, preparing to depart. Three other passengers hurried ahead of them. As soon as Maggie stepped into the fresh air, she breathed deeply, thankful to be away from the smell of tobacco and sweat that had permeated the train.

She scanned the small crowd near the street. An assortment of people scurried here and there all around the old wooden passenger and freight station. She looked up the street to her left, getting her first close-up view of the town. An elegant hotel was situated on the right-hand corner of the next street, and beyond that lay tall buildings, wooden sidewalks, blossoming trees, and endless stretches of dirt streets.

From behind her came a gentle voice, oddly familiar. "Dear Cousin Margaret, I presume?" the immaculately groomed gentleman asked as all three Campbells turned to stare at their cousin-by-marriage.

Wesley Peterson stood almost six feet tall, his young body soft and flabby like that of a woman long past her prime. His brown hair was thinning on top, revealing a slight bald spot. His face and features were large and round, from big, silvery eyes to fleshy double chin. His black suit and white shirt had obviously been tailor-made to accommodate his wide girth.

"Cousin Wesley," Maggie said, allowing him to take her hand. "It was so good of you to come to meet us."

"I have a buggy." He nodded toward the carryall awaiting them. "Your uncle wants us to stop at the store for a few minutes before I take y'all home."

Maggie glanced beyond Wesley and saw Daisy, who was toting a large cloth valise and a small case. "Oh, Cousin Wesley, there's Daisy."

Wesley turned, prepared to meet what he assumed was an acquaintance of his cousin, only to be duly shocked at the sight of the comely Negress.

"Who is this person?"

"This is Daisy," Judith told him. "She lives with us."

"Daisy's been with us for a good many years," Maggie said. "We could hardly go off and leave her."

Wesley's huge, round eyes glared at the servant girl. He rubbed his chin, cleared his throat, and grunted. "I see. I see. I'm sure Mama can make use of her. We can bed her down with Auntie Gem."

Judith watched the busy activity at the station as people went about their routines. Fascinated by the fancy railroad coach at the end of the train, she noticed two tall, well-dressed men disembarking, their laughter filling the air. The big blond threw down his cigar, crushing it with his boot heel.

"There's Mr. Stone," Judith cried. "I'm going to run over and say good-bye, and thank him again for the chicken."

"No, Jude," Maggie said, but too late. Her young sister was halfway to her destination.

"Mr. Stone?" Wesley asked. "Not Aaron Stone? My dear Margaret, surely this is not the type of person with whom you would associate?"

"No, of course not," she told her stunned relative. "I'll just go fetch Judith, and we can be on our way."

"Perhaps I should," Micah said.

"No," Maggie told her brother. "You help Daisy get our things in Cousin Wesley's buggy while I get Jude."

Aaron saw the flash of honey-red hair as the running child neared him. Slightly winded when she stopped in front of him, Judith Campbell took a deep breath and smiled up at the laughing man.

"My, my, Miss Judith, hasn't your sister told you that young ladies do not run through a crowd of people?"

Judith knew he was teasing her, so she responded in kind. "And gentlemen never correct ladies in the presence of others."

"This must be the baby sister," Thayer Coleman said.

Judith took notice of the dark stranger standing beside Aaron Stone. He was not quite as big as the golden-haired giant, but he was very muscular and beautifully handsome.

"Miss Judith Campbell, may I present Mr. Thayer Coleman."

"How do you do?" Jude knew her polite response would have done her sister proud.

"Jude, you come back here, right now." Maggie's hushed voice could not disguise her anger.

At the exact moment Maggie Campbell waddled between her sister and Aaron Stone, a gun fired. The sound alerted everyone of the happening, but Maggie was the first to realize that the blond rogue beside her had been hit. He slumped against her when the bullet entered his chest and blood began oozing from the wound. He was far too heavy for Maggie to hold, so she went to the ground with him in her arms.

"My God!" Thayer said.

"Get help." Maggie cradled Aaron against her, her hands trembling as she touched him. "Get a doctor. He's been shot!"

Chapter 2

Maggie, totally unaware of what was happening around her, held Aaron tightly. Her farm-girl strong arms clutched him with a tenacious grip. He could not die. She would not let him die!

"Maggie . . ." Aaron's voice echoed in her ears. "What . . ."

"Hush now," she crooned as if to a hurt child. "You're going to be all right."

"Cousin Margaret!" Wesley Peterson gasped when he made his way through the throng of curious bystanders and saw his relative on her knees, the wounded man in her arms.

Micah moved up behind Judith, placing a protective arm around her. She turned into his arms as he lifted her.

"Oh, Micah, Mr. Stone's been shot," Jude said. "Who would do such a terrible thing?"

"I don't know who he is, Jude," Micah said, soothing her with tender strokes on her back. "But some men caught him before he could run away. He's a big ugly fellow with a long beard."

"Miss Campbell." Thayer Coleman placed his large hand on Maggie's shoulder. "If you'll let go, these men will carry him up the street to the Parshall House."

Maggie raised her head. Her topaz eyes, filled with fear, met Thayer's, and they shared a sense of mutual concern. Maggie liked and trusted this young man immediately. She knew he was Aaron's true friend.

"I've sent a boy to fetch the doctor," Thayer told her when he noticed she had not loosened her hold. "I've sent for Dr. Cooper. He's a fine physician."

"He'll be all right," Maggie said.

"Of course I'll be all right," Aaron said. "I wish . . . oh, hell . . ."

"You are in pain," she said with tears in her eyes.

"Margaret, I'm afraid I must insist you remove yourself from that man at once," Wesley said. "Whatever must people be thinking?"

"I've been hurt worse," Aaron told her, trying to smile. His right hand jerked, clutching at his chest, his finger inching inside his vest pocket to stroke the gold watch nestled there. "You go with your folks and come and see me when I can appreciate being in your arms." Even though dazed by the pain, he could make out the bulky silhouette of the man speaking to Maggie. Who the hell was he? Surely not a would-be husband. "Get her away," he told Thayer.

"Come on, Miss Campbell," Thayer said, gently prizing her arms from Aaron's body. "These men are going to take him now."

Thayer helped Maggie to her feet, his strong arms steadying her as she stumbled. Three big men moved quickly, lifting Aaron. Maggie gasped and reached out for him when she saw his blood-soaked clothing. Her fingers touched his once-white linen shirt, the crimson stain leaving its mark on her white skin. The men walked on, hurrying up the street.

As Thayer walked away, Wesley stepped forward, taking both of Maggie's shaking hands into his meaty ones. "Let me get you to the buggy, Margaret."

"I want to go see about Mr. Stone," Judith said from her perch in her brother's arms. "Please, Maggie. We can't leave him now."

"I'm all right," Maggie told Wesley. "I've never fainted in my life."

"Maggie!" Judith claimed attention as her brother set her on her feet. "Let's get on over to that hotel."

"Nonsense, child," Wesley said, already tugging Maggie away from the station, prompting the other Campbells to follow. "I'll send someone later to inquire about Mr. Stone's health. This entire incident has been totally improper."

"Maggie, please," Judith pleaded.

Maggie was torn between necessity and desire. She wanted to go worry and pray in secret. This was not something that could be kept from Aunt Tilly, and she was sure to demand an explanation.

"Cousin Wesley is right," she told her little sister. "We hardly know Mr. Stone."

"But—"

"Hush now."

"We do know Mr. Stone. He helped us in Chattanooga."

"I said hush. We'll talk about all this later."

When they got to the buggy, Micah and Daisy loaded their meager belongings. Wesley reached out to assist Maggie, but stopped suddenly, his cool gray eyes inspecting the front of her pale blue dress.

"My dear girl," Wesley said, hesitating to touch her. "I'm afraid your dress is ruined. Mother will be quite displeased. Perhaps you should change at the store before I present you at home."

"Oh." Maggie looked down at her bloodstained dress, her hand smoothing the damp bodice. She opened her palms, staring at the mixture of dark dried and moist red blood covering them. *How much blood did he lose?* she wondered. *Too much? How long will it take for the doctor to arrive?*

A rather loud ruckus near the station gained Judith's attention as she settled into her seat on the buggy, Daisy beside her. Jude jumped to her feet, climbed on the seat, and stood gazing toward the group of men struggling with a burly, gray-bearded ruffian.

"What are they doing to that man?" she asked. "Who is he? Did he shoot Mr. Stone?"

Micah, stepping into the carryall, turned to the questioning child. "I don't know who he is, but he's the one who did the shooting. They must be holding him till the law comes."

Maggie raised her foot, braced herself, and climbed into the buggy without waiting for Wesley's assistance. She might have stood there all day before he could have overcome his disgust at her appearance enough to help her.

"That's Rube Whitcomb," Wesley told them as he sat down, taking the reins in his wide, smooth hands. "He's some of that bunch moving into Sheffield looking for work."

Wesley adjusted the reins, motioning the horse, which began trotting down Railroad Street. Behind them lay the old station house. Bellows of smoke coming from the steam engine clouded the clear sky. Ahead lay rows of two-story brick buildings occupied by merchants, the local newspaper housed in the corner building.

Wesley slowed the buggy as a large carriage careened around the corner, nearly colliding with them. Everyone tensed with the expectation of collision, and sighed with relief when disaster was avoided. Daisy quickly jerked Judith into her lap. Thick swirls of dust flew upward, covering all of them with a fine layer of dirt.

Maggie coughed several times, then turned around to check on Jude and Micah and Daisy. Seeing that they were unharmed, she tried to smile before turning back around. So much had happened to her family today that she was certain none of them could endure another calamity. When she had received Uncle Chester's letter the month after Pa died, she began making plans. She'd been forced to sell what few possessions they had in order to buy their train tickets, but she had been so sure that coming to Tuscumbia to be with her mother's relatives could help her keep her promise to Pa.

Meeting Mr. Stone at the railroad depot in Chattanooga ruined everything. He did not fit into her plans. But if he died . . . She didn't want him to die. She wanted him to live. She couldn't bear the thought of what might be happening to him this very minute. He was little more than a stranger. His welfare shouldn't mean so much to her. *Oh, why did I meet him?* she wondered. *And why did all of this have to happen?*

"Why would this Whitcomb man shoot Mr. Stone?" Maggie asked, knowing she would probably only whet Cousin Wesley's curiosity by inquiring.

"I have no idea," he said, but was apparently eager to continue the conversation. "Whatever acquaintance y'all might have with that man, I wouldn't mention it to Mama."

"I understand." Maggie's eyes caught sight of the Parshall House Hotel. She wanted to jump from the buggy and rush inside to find Aaron. She had the strangest sense of urgency, as if he needed her, as if he were calling to her. As they passed the hotel, it was all she could do not to turn around and continue staring.

"Well, I don't understand," Judith said, pulling free of Daisy and bracing her arms against the back of Maggie and Wesley's seat.

"Sit back, heathen," Micah said. "I heard some men saying that they'd sent for the town marshal. It seems that fellow's got a daughter who's been after that black-haired man who was with Mr. Stone. It was him that Whitcomb fellow aimed to shoot. Mr. Stone just got in the way."

"But why did he want to shoot Mr. Stone's friend?" Judith asked.

"I heard them whispering and laughing about it," Micah said. "It seems Mr. Stone's friend had his way with the gal, and her pa didn't take kindly to it."

"My word, Micah," Wesley said. "Is this a proper subject to be discussing in front of the ladies?"

"I don't suppose so," Micah agreed, but finished his tale all the same. "They said the daughter isn't any kind of lady. They said she was a—"

"Micah!" Maggie warned.

"Most regrettable," Wesley said. "Sally Whitcomb is, unfortunately, one of God's poor creatures who has allowed her body to lead her into a life of sin. Stone and his friend Coleman have quite a reputation with women of her sort."

"Do you know Mr. Stone?" Maggie wanted to know more about the man who had mesmerized her, whose emerald eyes had looked into her heart and claimed it.

"He's been around here for about a year," Wesley said. "No one knows where he came from or how he acquired his fortune."

"He's rich," Micah said. "See, what did I tell you?"

"He's making investments in Sheffield," Wesley said. "Coleman purchased land back last year when they had the big three-day auction and sold off lots cut from the old Winston and Habbeler cotton fields. They say the two of them have money in the Alabama Improvement Company and the Sheffield Land, Iron and Coal Company too."

"Is Mr. Coleman rich too?" Judith asked. "And is he married?"

"Why yes. Thayer Coleman is one of the wealthiest young men in the county, and from one of the finest old families. Unfortunately, he seems to be trying to single-handedly ruin their good name." Wesley shook his head in a display of sorrow and condemnation.

"Is he married?" Judith repeated her question.

"No," Wesley said. "He's a bachelor and quite a hell-raiser, if you ladies will pardon my saying so. Why do you ask, Cousin Judith?"

"Well, I'm mighty glad he's unattached because I plan to marry him," Jude Campbell said.

"Oh, dear Lord," Maggie whispered prayerfully.

Wesley Peterson smiled, creating deep dimples in his pudgy, pink cheeks. "Well, Judith, it's well and good that you plan to marry one day, but I'd not set my cap for Mr. Coleman."

"Why's that?" Jude seemed genuinely puzzled. "Don't you think he'll have growed out of his wild ways by the time I'm a woman?"

"Will have *grown* out of his wild ways," Wesley corrected. "Mr. Coleman will most certainly marry one of his own kind. I'm afraid, dear little cousin, that we are but simple God-fearing people and can never attain the social position to which Thayer Coleman was born."

"Maggie's going to make a lady out of me," Judith told him. "I guess I'll be one of his kind then."

Ignoring any more foolishness from the child, Wesley stopped the buggy in front of a small, two-story building set between rows of other similar structures. Above the front door a sign read GOWER GENERAL STORE.

"Oh, my. Oh, my," Wesley groaned.

"What's the matter?" Maggie searched the man's face, suddenly void of any color. She followed his glazed stare in the direction of the sidewalk.

There, in front of the store, stood a short, obese woman with her tiny, fat fists planted squarely on her wide hips. Her steel-gray hair was slicked tightly back into a huge bun at the nape of her chunky neck. Her eyes, as coldly silver as her son's, declared her outrage before she spoke.

"Is it true?" Mathilda Gower asked as her round, taffeta-clad body waddled closer to the buggy. "Dear Mrs. Stanford had her boy drive me here as soon as we heard. Auntie Gem's little grandboy ran all the way from the station with the news."

"Calm yourself, Mama." Wesley departed the carryall quicker than an agile child, and hurried to his mother's side. "You must not overexcite yourself."

"Is it true?" Mathilda yelled, then caught herself behaving improperly, and lowered her voice. "Gem's grandboy said that Mr. Stone had been shot and lay dying in the arms of a beautiful redheaded woman who had just got off the train to meet Mr. Wesley. Tell me it was not our Margaret."

"Mama," Wesley said, trying to console the raging woman.

"There girl." Her sharp gray eyes inspected every inch of Maggie as she pointed a finger at the young woman. Sighting the scarlet stains defacing Maggie's blue dress, her aunt gasped. "Merciful Lord, Wesley, I do believe this is all too much for my poor heart." She swayed, clutching the bodice of her black dress.

"Let me help you inside," her son said.

"Yes, dear boy, please do. Poor Chester was too ashamed to come outside. His own dead sister's child!"

"Come, Mama." Wesley assisted his mother to the entrance of her husband's store, and then turned to the Campbells. "Please come in, cousins. We will work through this tragedy with the Lord's help."

Micah hopped down to the street, reached up for Judith, and deposited her on the sidewalk before turning to offer Maggie assistance. But she and Daisy were already on the street, standing silent and unmoving.

"Is that the kind of gentleman you want me to become?" Micah asked.

No one responded. Maggie took a deep breath and looked around. Uncle Chester's store was well situated on Main Street. Her pa had spoken highly of his wife's older brother. He'd always said that the man had done well for himself.

"I don't want to live with her," Judith said.

"Hush up," Maggie said, taking her sister by the hand. "Micah, you stay here with Daisy and our belongings. We may be looking for a place to stay the night."

With that said, she and Jude marched into her uncle's general store. Once inside, they both stared, amazed by the vast supplies that lined the numerous shelves and the variety of fruits and vegetables displayed in a center aisle. The whole room reeked of an earthy sweet aroma. The sound of unnatural quiet in the store was broken by the hum of a stray fly that had entered with the Campbell sisters. Maggie gazed upward where stalks of bananas hung from the ceiling. Huge wooden barrels flanked the corners of the counter, and a much-used chopping block stood near a front window.

Mathilda Gower was seated in a cane-bottomed chair, her excess flesh hanging over the sides. Her son held a dipper filled with water to her lips as he fanned her with a folded piece of paper.

Chester Gower met the girls at the door, embracing each in turn and bestowing a light kiss on their cheeks. If it had not been for the familiar brown eyes, Maggie would not have recognized her uncle, so much had he changed in five years. His once brown hair had grayed and thinned to baldness, his always slender frame was slumped and skinny, and his once healthy fair coloring had yellowed to a sickly pallor.

"Come in, girls," he said.

"Then we're still welcome?" Maggie whispered.

"Tilly will calm herself eventually," Chester assured his nieces as he led them farther into his establishment. "The news that Mr. Stone had been shot has spread like wildfire. And, of course, er . . . hmph . . ." He cleared his throat as he wiped his perspiring hands on the long, white apron covering him from chest to knees. "How ever did you make his acquaintance, Maggie?"

"It was all my fault, Uncle Chester," Judith said, her hazel eyes filled with tears.

"How so, child?" her uncle asked.

"I went over to say good-bye," Jude replied. "And to thank him again for the fried chicken."

Realizing by her uncle's expression that he was bewildered, Maggie spoke. "We had a bit of trouble boarding the train in Chattanooga. Mr. Stone was kind enough to help. We didn't see him again until we stopped in Huntsville since he was riding in his friend's private car."

"That's when I fell out the window," Judith added.

"What?" Chester strangled then recovered quickly after he coughed a few times.

"It wasn't Judith's fault. Mr. Stone was offering her his box lunch, and when she reached for it she fell."

"I see. I see," Chester mumbled as he neared his wife, who sat quietly while her son continued fanning her. "The girls have explained their acquaintance with Mr. Stone, my dear Tilly. It was all quite innocent. Once we tell everyone, there should be no problem."

"Indeed," the hefty Mrs. Gower said. "Within minutes after her arrival in town, your niece is involved in an incident that will be a topic of conversation for months, perhaps for years."

"I fear you exaggerate, Mama," Wesley dared speak. "The gossipmongers will weary of this in a few weeks."

"Don't be foolish, Wesley," his mother admonished. "If it were common ruffians involved, I would agree, but not when it involves important gentlemen like Mr. Stone and Mr. Coleman, and the niece of a renowned merchant of Mr. Gower's standing."

"Aunt Tilly." Maggie approached the older woman.

"Yes?"

"We're so pleased to be here and grateful that you'd have us."

"It was our Christian duty. The Lord commands us to care for our own."

"Yes, but thank you all the same. And I'm awfully sorry about what happened."

"You know a young girl's most precious possession is her reputation. Lose that and you have nothing. Lusts of the flesh must be overcome for they are tools of the devil. Evil begets—"

"Tilly," Chester interrupted. "The girl has done nothing wrong."

"Do you promise to have nothing else to do with that man?" Mathilda asked, taffeta rustling with the movement of her heavy body as she struggled to stand.

"I . . . I . . ." Maggie stammered, knowing she should agree to the request. But agreeing would be a lie. She knew she must see Aaron Stone again, if only once, to see with her own eyes if he were dead or alive. Somehow she had to persuade Aunt Tilly that it was the proper thing to do. "I feel my moral duty to inquire about Mr. Stone. After that, I see no need to further any acquaintance with him."

"There is no need for you to inquire personally," Mathilda said. "Wesley can go. After all, it would be proper for a minister to attend the . . . er . . . the sickly."

"Please, Aunt Tilly," Maggie said. "This is something I feel I must do."

"I shall go with her," Wesley told his mother. "Perhaps it would be best. It might show the town that Cousin Margaret has nothing to hide."

"He's right, Tilly," Chester said. "The girl would most certainly prove herself an innocent party by attending upon Mr. Stone in Wesley's presence."

"You're possibly right, Mr. Gower," his wife said. "Go then, and do it quickly. I'll have Mrs. Stanford's boy take me home to rest before supper. Bring the others when you come, Wesley."

"Yes, Mama."

For the second time in less than an hour, Maggie found herself riding down Railroad Street, right past Commercial Row, but this time she was stopping at the Parshall House instead of leaving the railroad station. Her small hands lay in her lap, her fingers clutching at the material of her skirt. She knew she must have looked a sight with no ribbon tying back her hair, her one good Sunday dress ruined by crimson stains, and her entire body dusted with grime. She wondered if the combination of sweat and dried blood was something only she could smell. Pa had set great store by cleanliness. He would sure enough have told her that she needed a bath.

But a bath would have to come later when she joined the others at her uncle's home. Right now, she had to see Aaron. It was plumb crazy to care so much about a damned fool stranger. The man didn't mean a thing to her, and she was sure she didn't mean anything to him. A man like that could have his pick of women. No doubt, every well-to-do mama in town had set her sights on the wealthy Mr. Stone, hoping he might marry her daughter.

After this one last time, she would have to keep away from him. He could mean nothing but trouble for her. Aunt Tilly had come mighty close to sending them packing. Dear Lord, what would she have done? They couldn't go back to Grovesdale. There was nothing to go back to. The land Pa had sharecropped had already been rented out to other folks.

She would have to find a way to appease Aunt Tilly's wrath, but keeping on that woman's good side was going to be hard. Maggie knew that all three of the Campbells had a problem with holding their tongues. She was well aware of her own fiery temper and outspokenness. She would have to force herself to come to terms with these sins. She wasn't too sure how well Micah and Jude would handle theirs.

Wesley hitched the buggy in front of the impressive Parshall House, helped Maggie down, and walked with her to the entrance. Upon entering the lobby, they saw Thayer Coleman sitting on a long, oak bench, his head in his hands.

"Mr. Coleman," Maggie called as she approached him.

He turned his dark head, his black eyes recognizing the beautiful woman speaking. "Miss Campbell?"

"We've come to inquire after Mr. Stone," Wesley said.

"Where is he?" Maggie held back the tears, trying to keep from begging this man to take her to Aaron immediately.

"He's down the hall," Thayer said. "The doctor is still with him."

"Is he hurt real bad?" Maggie had to know.

Thayer smiled at the lovely woman. He couldn't ever remember seeing anything quite as perfect as the angel who stood before him, her eyes gleaming like topaz stones. "I'm sure he'll live. Aaron's tough. He's lived through worse."

"Could I . . . that is, would it be possible . . ."

Wesley cleared his throat loudly, giving her a stern, disapproving look.

Thayer stood, his tall frame towering over a five-foot-five-inch Maggie. "You'll be the first to see him when Doc Cooper comes out."

"Thank you," Maggie said.

"Of course, I shall accompany her," Wesley said.

"Of course, Reverend Peterson." Thayer's dark eyes glared at the man mockingly. "Even in his condition, a rascal like Aaron might ravish Miss Campbell."

"My dear sir," Wesley said. "Such talk is unnecessary."

"I want to see Mr. Stone," Maggie told the two men. "With Cousin Wesley, with both of you, or alone. I don't care."

"I assure you, Miss Campbell, that you will see Aaron." Thayer smiled sheepishly at the good reverend.

"I feel that your passionate display of concern is uncalled for, Cousin Margaret," Wesley said.

"Dear Reverend Peterson, surely you have taken no offense at Miss Campbell's concern for my friend?" Thayer asked.

"I don't need you to do any pretty talking on my behalf, Mr. Coleman," the titian-haired girl snapped. "No doubt, it was some of your pretty talk to that Whitcomb gal that got your friend shot."

"Margaret!" Wesley's voice vibrated with shock.

"A body couldn't help but wonder," Maggie said. "Micah told us that he overheard some men talking about how her pa tried to shoot you and accidentally hit Mr. Stone. I figure you sweet-talked your way into trouble."

While Wesley stood there mortified by his cousin's comments, Thayer Coleman threw back his head and roared with laughter.

A bare-chested, bandaged Aaron Stone sat propped up against several feather pillows, resting in the big double bed. His thick, golden hair was mussed and his bronzed face was a bit pale, but he'd felt worse. He wanted a cigar, but knew Doc Cooper would veto the idea.

"Well, am I going to live?" he asked.

"Unfortunately, it would appear that you are," Dr. Cooper said jovially. "A couple of days' rest and you should be as good as new."

"A couple of days? I've got things to do. I haven't got time to lie around in bed."

"Well, you'll rest for tonight. That shot I just gave you would put a mule to sleep. And it looks like that's what you're trying to be, a stubborn mule."

"You calling me names, Doc?" Aaron guffawed, and then grunted when a sharp pain ripped through his midsection.

"You were damned lucky that fool Whitcomb was such a poor shot," Dr. Cooper said.

"Actually, I'd be better off if he were a better shot. He was aiming at Thayer. If he'd hit his target, Thayer would be laid up here instead of me."

"Well, if you boys would quit messing with the likes of Sally Whitcomb, you wouldn't have half-crazy fathers putting bullets in your chest."

Aaron laughed. "Talk to Thayer. I've already decided to put my evil ways behind me. I'm planning on settling down one of these days soon."

"Well, well. Wouldn't be the Widow Arnold, would it?"

"Now that'd be telling."

"So it would. You get some sleep. I'll be around tomorrow to take a look at you."

Dr. Cooper closed the door quietly behind him and walked down the hall to the lobby where Thayer Coleman was waiting.

Seeing the doctor enter, Thayer met him. "How is he?"

"Damned lucky."

"He's going to be all right, then?" Maggie asked.

Thayer remembered his manners. "Dr. Cooper, may I present Miss Margaret Campbell. Of course, you already know our esteemed Reverend Peterson."

"Miss Campbell." The doctor nodded. "A few days' rest and he'll be fine. I'm counting on you to keep him here and in bed, Thayer. He lost quite a lot of blood. That old revolver of Whitcomb's did a nasty job on Aaron's insides. A few inches higher and he'd have a bullet in his heart."

"Can he have visitors now?" Thayer asked.

"Well, maybe for a few minutes. I just shot him with enough painkillers to make him sleep till morning."

"Go ahead, Miss Campbell," Thayer said. "He's in room six. Down the hall and to the right."

"Thank you," Maggie said as she turned to find her way down the corridor, not waiting for Wesley.

Her cousin quickly followed but was stopped by Thayer Coleman's muscular body planted squarely in the hallway entrance. "I give you my word, as a Coleman, that Miss Campbell will be safe. By the way, Reverend, just what connection do you have with her anyhow?"

"Margaret is the niece of my dear stepfather, Mr. Chester Gower," Wesley said. "Her father passed away this winter, and, of course, Mama insisted that, since she and Micah and Jude were Mr. Gower's dearly departed sister's children, it was our Christian duty to provide a home for the orphans."

"Hmm ... mmm ..." Thayer knew Maggie Campbell and her

family would have a hard time adjusting to people who lived such a strictly proper life as Mathilda and Chester Gower did. And Reverend Peterson? My word, the man was considered saintly by the townfolk.

Aaron's eyelids felt heavy, and it was becoming a struggle for him to keep them open. He couldn't figure out why Thayer hadn't come in to check on him. He supposed Doc Cooper and Thayer could be having a drink to his recovery, but doubted the busy doctor could spare the time. *Maybe Thayer has gone to check on Maggie Campbell,* he thought. He'd asked his friend to do just that before the doctor ran Thayer out of the room.

He knew she had left with that holier-than-thou preacher. He'd heard rumors about that man, whispered words from some of Loretta's girls. What was the not-so-saintly reverend to Maggie? Aaron could never picture a woman like her betrothed to a popinjay like Wesley Peterson. A girl like Maggie needed a man, a real man to initiate her into the pleasures of lovemaking. More than anything, he wanted to be that man. He had had more than his share of women over the years, whores and ladies alike, but he had never wanted anyone the way he wanted Maggie Campbell.

He had to get the notion out of his head before it became an obsession. He had no place in his life for the beautiful redhead. He had to think of his plans for the future . . . White Orchard . . . a country gentleman . . . a genteel wife . . . well-bred children . . . Eunice Arnold. The highly respectable Widow Arnold was his future wife, not some seductive farm girl with hair like a hot July sunset and eyes the color of pale amber crystal.

God, but he was sleepy. And his chest hurt. But the pain was not nearly as bad as an agony from the past, one he well remembered. The night Phineas had come into his life. The night the big black man had saved him from a gang of unsavory, knife-wieding cutthroats, in a New Orleans barroom.

Maggie stopped outside of room six. She wanted to see Aaron again, to know that he was alive. It was foolish to be here, foolish to need to see a man who was practically a stranger, foolish to long to keep him safe from all harm.

She had never before felt this peculiar attraction to a man. It was wrong, probably a sin, to have such wanton feeling. A woman should never think about kissing a man, touching a man. Not unless he was her husband, and then, only if he made the first move. She could remember Ma and Pa kissing. They had kissed a lot, so it had to be all right for married folks. She knew there were wifely duties a woman performed. When she had been courting Benny, Daisy had tried to tell her about such things.

She could not allow herself to fall in love with Aaron Stone. She had made Pa a promise, and nothing or nobody could stand in the way of its fulfillment. Judith was going to become a lady, even if it killed all of them in the process. And Micah would learn to be a gentleman of sorts, with an education and an occupation that Pa could be proud of. Meeting Aaron now had been a cruel trick of fate.

Maggie knew she had to think of her plans for the future. A fine husband for Judith, a respected position for Micah, a home and a husband for herself . . . eventually. It would be years before she could think about marriage, and then it would have to be to a simple man who would want a simple woman like her. There could never be a place in her life for a man like Aaron Stone.

But for now, she would go in and say hello, and tell him that Judith had been greatly worried about his health. She would see with her own eyes that he was alive and well, and then she'd say good-bye and that would be that end of it. Cousin Wesley could take them home, and they'd begin their new life in Tuscumbia.

Her hand trembled on the doorknob as she turned it, opening the door slightly. She peeped inside before entering, and saw Aaron, eyes closed, lying peacefully in the big, oak bed, and the feather pillows in disarray, one resting above his head. Against the high, ornately carved headboard.

"Mr. Stone?" Her voice cracked with emotion. She wanted to rush to him and at the same time she wanted to run back down the hallway and flee the hotel.

There was no answer. She tiptoed into the room. "Mr. Stone, are you awake?"

No reply came. She moved quietly to the bed, standing silently staring down at Aaron. He was a very big man. Even reclining, he dominated the room. The sheet had slipped below his waist, revealing the unbuttoned top of his Nankeen trousers and the broad expanse of his naked chest.

My, but he is a beautiful man, Maggie thought. His body was hard and muscular, and covered with a layer of dark golden hair that appeared brown in the dim light coming from a nearby oil lamp.

She moved so close to the bed that her knees brushed the side. "Mr. Stone, I'm so glad you're going to be all right."

Aaron was breathing deeply, his body relaxed in sleep. Maggie reached out and touched his arm, her eyes inspecting the white bandage that strapped his chest. He felt warm, but not so hot that she worried about a fever. She moved her fingers to his face, touching his strong jaw. She wanted to kiss him good-bye, but instead she allowed her fingertips to brush across his full lips. He sighed and moved, readjusting his big body. Maggie jerked her hand back, holding her breath, afraid she had awakened him.

Within minutes, he settled himself and was resting again. Maggie knew she couldn't stay there just staring at him. She had to go before Wesley came looking for her.

Just as she reached the door, she heard the sound of Aaron's groggy words. She didn't understand what he was saying, but knew he was talking in his sleep. Again he mumbled something incoherent, and then, quite clearly, she heard him say, "Maggie."

Her heart skipped a beat as she stood in the doorway looking back at the drugged man who had just called her name.

"Good-bye," she whispered, tears of regret falling from her sad eyes. "Oh Aaron . . . good-bye."

Chapter 3

Bright springtime sunshine had replaced the shadows of dawn, and somewhere in the distance a rooster crowed. The smell of fresh coffee and hot biscuits filled Maggie's nostrils when she entered the kitchen with an armload of dirty clothes. Wesley sat at the square kitchen table, his Bible opened and a cup of well-sweetened coffee in his hand. Since his mouth was filled with the last bites of a jam-covered biscuit, he was able only to nod at Maggie as she breezed through the kitchen and onto the back porch.

Daisy sat in a straight-backed, pine chair at the edge of the porch, her slender fingers gripping the pole of a churn as she moved it rapidly up and down.

In the yard, Auntie Gem, an ebony-skinned old woman, stood over two huge cast-iron pots filled with hot water and heated from the fires beneath them. The smell of smoke, lye soap, and buttermilk made for a strange combination.

"Bring your things on here, Miss Maggie," Auntie Gem said. "I done finished with the Gowers' washing."

Maggie and Daisy exchanged smiles, knowing they had both taken an instant liking to the small, energetic woman. Maggie walked across the backyard and handed Auntie Gem the clothing.

"Is Mr. Wesley still in my kitchen?" the old woman asked, sorting the clothes and, one by one, dropping them into a pot of boiling water. Taking the long, wooden batting stick propped against the shed, she poked and punched until the clothes submerged into the soapy wash-water.

Maggie laughed. "He just finished off another biscuit. That's the fourth one since breakfast an hour ago."

"Land sakes, that man's always underfoot eat'n and munch'n," Auntie Gem said. "I don't reckon Miz Gower come down yet."

"Why no," Maggie said. "Is she ill this morning?"

Auntie Gem chuckled, deepening the heavy lines in her dark, aged face. "Miz Gower's always sickly. She can't make it downstairs till the sun's high in the sky. I just reckoned she might be down to give you your orders for the day."

"She did that last night," Maggie said, smiling. "I'm to see our clothes get washed, make all the beds, help Jude wash dishes, and dust everything in the house, the—"

"She done put Mr. Micah to work too, ain't she?"

"Yes, he's to go to the store every day and help Uncle Chester until we can save up enough money for his schooling."

Maggie joined Daisy on the porch, taking a seat beside her. They both observed Auntie Gem as she hummed, her work-hardened old hands busy at their task. Her black dress had faded to charcoal from repeated laundering, and her long gingham apron was already stained from morning chores. Around her heart, she wore a dark scarf under a ragged calico bonnet.

"Is there enough room for you both in that shed?" Maggie nodded toward the small, one-room building close to where Auntie Gem was working. Although the structure was sturdy and well kept, it badly needed a fresh coat of paint.

"Auntie Gem's a good soul," Daisy said. "Ain't much room, but it's clean. She tried to get me to take the bed, but I told her I was fine on that pallet on the floor. Don't worry about me none, Miss Maggie. You take care of yourself."

"I'll speak to Uncle Chester about getting you some kind of bed. You can't sleep on that dirt floor come winter."

"What about you and Mr. Micah and Little Jude? That Miz Gower seems like a mighty hard lady."

"Aunt Tilly's a mite high strung, and I'm afraid she has different plans for us than I do, but I aim to speak to her today."

"What you planning on saying?"

"I want to find a way to earn some money. I know Aunt Tilly won't pay a cent on educating Micah and Jude, so it's up to me."

"How's a young gal like you going to earn any money around here?"

"As a seamstress," Maggie informed the other woman. "I made over all Ma's things for you and me and Jude. Look how good that dress fits you."

"I know you got talent in your fingers, and you was a real wonder with your ma's old sewing machine, but—"

"No buts," Maggie said.

Daisy continued churning as Maggie looked over her own handiwork, admiring the way the blue and green calico dress clung to Daisy's slender curves. She knew she could be a seamstress. She made everything she and Jude and Daisy wore, many items constructed from her ma's wardrobe. She had even made most of Pa's and Micah's shirts.

"Cousin Margaret," Wesley called from the doorway.

Maggie turned, seeing Wesley's large frame, dressed in a dark suit and tie, filling the opening. "Yes, Wesley. I'm out here with Daisy."

"I thought you might care to join me in the back parlor," he said. "I know you read and write, so I thought perhaps you could assist me with notes on my Sunday sermon."

"Of course, Wesley."

"Good. Good. I've already asked Cousin Judith to join us for Bible reading and a morning prayer. She can finish her chores later."

"Aunt Tilly wanted the dusting finished before noon."

"No problem. A half hour of her time will suffice."

Maggie and Judith sat side by side on the velvet settee, listening to Wesley's prayer. His voice carried loudly through the stillness of the small room, his flowery words evoking a sense of reverence.

Jude, head bowed, hands folded, eyes tightly squeezed shut, fidgeted in her seat. Her henna-gold locks, plaited in two long braids, hung down her back. Her blue cotton dress, with several discreetly hidden patches, covered her petite frame from high-collared neck to full, frayed hem.

Maggie silently said "amen" to Wesley's prayer and listened as he began to read from Psalms. Ever so slowly, her mind wandered, and she began her own heartfelt prayer, heard only by God:

Please let Aaron be well and fit. Keep him safe always. Let Micah be a big help and please Uncle Chester down at the store today. Help Judith to keep her tongue and remember her manners. Look over Daisy, for she has no one else to protect her. And Lord, give me strength and patience so I can keep my promise to Pa.

Maggie was busy clearing the dishes from the dining table while Mathilda Gower, dressed in brown muslin, sat sipping a cup of sassafras tea.

"Please tell Auntie Gem to fix me some more tea, Margaret. I do believe it has already restored me this morning."

"Of course, Aunt Tilly," her niece said, hurrying toward the kitchen with a handful of dirty lunch time dishes.

Just as she was returning with a fresh pot of tea, Maggie heard the front door open, and sounds of talk and laughter came from the foyer.

Judith bounced into the dining room with a smiling Thayer Coleman by her side.

"Good morning, ladies," he said. "Beautiful day, isn't it? May is quite a glorious month."

"He does talk so pretty, don't he?" Judith said.

"Doesn't he," Maggie corrected, in a whispering voice, looking from the handsome, well-dressed man to her open-mouthed aunt.

"My . . . my dear Mr. Coleman, to what do we owe this honor?" Mathilda asked, obviously surprised by the young man's appearance in her dining room.

"Well, Mrs. Gower," Thayer said. "I was on my way to see Miss Maggie, on a mission of mercy, when who should I see swinging on your gate but little Miss Judith, who most graciously invited me in."

Mathilda glared at Jude, her silver eyes issuing a warning to never again play on the gate. "You're calling on Margaret?"

"Yes ma'am." Thayer turned to Maggie. "I'd appreciate it if you could come down to the Parshall House and see Aaron."

"I—" Maggie started to reply.

"Mr. Coleman!" Mathilda gasped, her fat hand gripping her throat in a gesture of shock. "You must admit that such a request is highly improper. My niece is, after all, a young lady under my protection."

"I assure you, I meant no offense," Thayer said. "I'm well aware of what an upstanding young lady your niece is. I'm simply here hoping to call upon her Christian heart to be of assistance to a wounded friend."

"How so, sir?" Wesley Peterson asked as he strutted into the dining room and stood behind his mother's chair.

"Now, son," Mathilda said, "please let us hear Mr. Coleman out."

"Again, sir, I ask how can Cousin Margaret attending upon Mr. Stone be of help to him?" Wesley's fat cheeks reddened as his thick fingers grasped the wooden rounds of his mother's high-backed chair.

"I'm afraid we're having a rather difficult time keeping him in bed as the doctor requested," Thayer said, carefully gauging the mother's and son's reactions. "He refuses to eat a bit, demands his cigars, and has been abusive to those of us who only want what's best for him."

"Why, pray tell, would you expose Margaret to such a vulgar display of temper?"

"I thought perhaps a pretty face and a soft voice might be more persuasive. I assure you that I would accompany Miss Campbell there and back. And she could even bring along her servant. I believe that would be proper."

"Oh, my, my," Mathilda said.

"I beseech you, Mrs. Gower, on behalf of a friend who needs some Christian kindness." Thayer bestowed his most charming smile on the reluctant Mathilda.

"I think this entire matter is quite improper," Wesley said. "Cousin Margaret, do you wish to see Mr. Stone again?"

"I do," Judith said.

Maggie's heart screamed yes. Oh, yes, she wanted to see Aaron. He was a stubborn fool not to follow the doctor's orders. He could worsen his condition by getting up and out so soon. "If I can help Mr. Stone, perhaps it is my moral duty to do so. Do you agree, Aunt Tilly?"

All eyes turned to Mathilda, awaiting her response.

"Wesley, fetch Daisy from the kitchen," Mathilda said. "She will accompany Margaret. I expect you, as a gentleman, Mr. Coleman, to advise one and all of my dear niece's benevolence in this matter."

"But of course," Thayer said. "All of Tuscumbia will know of her kindness and your generosity in sparing her for a few hours."

"Mother . . ." Wesley hesitated before daring to question his mother's judgment. "Are you certain about this?"

"Fetch Daisy!" Mathilda said. "Of course, I'm certain. Hurry up. We don't want to keep Mr. Coleman waiting."

"I want to go too," Judith said.

"Nonsense, child," her aunt said sternly. "You have no place on this charitable trip. You will be assisting me this afternoon."

Judith sulked, but knew better than to talk back to her authoritarian aunt.

"Should I change my dress?" Maggie asked, looking directly at Mathilda.

"No, no," Thayer said. "You look lovely, Miss Maggie. We do need to hurry before Aaron does himself any more harm."

"Of course," Maggie said, but she couldn't help worrying about her appearance. The dress she wore had been made from the same cloth as Judith's pale blue percale and was just as grayed and faded. Quickly untying the strings, she folded her apron and placed it on the mahogany buffet behind her.

Daisy joined them, looking nervously from one white face to another.

"We're going down to the Parshall House with Mr. Coleman to see after Mr. Stone," Maggie told the wide-eyed servant.

"Yes'am, Miss Maggie."

"Mrs. Gower, I promise to return your niece safely home as soon as she has soothed the wounded lion." Thayer smiled, his black eyes twinkling like onyx diamonds.

"We shall be pleased for you to call upon us again at anytime, Mr. Coleman," Mathilda practically cooed. "We're pleased to be of service to you."

"I shall forever be in you debt, madam." With that closing remark, Thayer hurried Maggie and Daisy to the front door and out on the porch.

Maggie knew that Wesley followed them to the door. She could feel his cold, gray eyes piercing into her back as she walked down the steps and toward the street where Thayer's open carriage awaited them. She knew that Wesley did not approve of her visit to Aaron. Was he suspicious? Had he guessed the truth about her true feelings?

Thayer opened the iron gate for Maggie, and she rushed quickly to the carriage, Daisy only a step behind. Standing there by the horses was an enormous black man who stepped forward to help Maggie into her seat. She was as impressed by the immaculate newness of the well-tailored suit the man wore as she was by his vast size. He immediately turned to assist Daisy. Maggie noticed the way his dark eyes explored her servant from head to toe. She wondered what Daisy thought of this handsome buck.

"This is Phineas," Thayer said. "He's Aaron's man. Been with him over ten years. Isn't that right?"

"Yes, sir." When Phineas smiled, his thick mustache curled upward. "I been looking after that man since he weren't much more than a boy."

Thayer seated himself beside Maggie and motioned to Phineas that they were ready.

"It will probably be best if you go in Aaron's room without me," Thayer said. "One look at me and he's liable to start throwing things. I'm not sure he's forgiven me for missing the bullet."

Maggie stood outside of room six, feeling hesitant about knocking. Running her hands down the skirt, she smoothed her dress and tried to calm her nervous trembling. Wishing she had taken time to change, she looked down at the blue percale that had been cut from the endless yards in one of her mother's full-skirted dresses. The material had been slightly worn and faded long before she fashioned it into two dresses, one for herself and one for Jude. She supposed it was just as well that she hadn't changed. Aaron had already seen her in her Sunday best, the dress she could never wear again because it was hopelessly stained with his blood.

Taking a deep breath and uttering up a prayer, Maggie knocked on the dark wooden door. Her knock was so light that she knew no one could have heard it. Her second try was more forceful.

"Go away!" Aaron's angry voice blasted through the door.

"Mr. Stone," she called out, her voice quivering. "It's Maggie Campbell. May I come in?"

There was no reply, but Maggie could hear the sound of shuffling movement quite clearly. Suddenly the door swung open, revealing a half-dressed Aaron Stone glaring down at her.

"Well, well, Miss Maggie," he said. "To what do I owe the honor of this visit?"

"I . . . er . . . I . . ." *What am I doing here?* she wondered. It was obvious that he wasn't happy to see her, that he didn't want her here.

"How did Thayer persuade you to come?" he asked, his green eyes glowering with resentment.

She stood there in the doorway, speechless, her soft pink mouth slightly ajar, and her honey-gold eyes gazing up at him in awe. She had never seen anything like the big man whose near nakedness hypnotized her.

Aaron stood bare-chested and barefooted, an impressive six feet three, his huge arms planted squarely on each side of the doorframe. The stained bandage circled his middle, and the upper expanse of his broad chest was covered with an abundance of thick, sandy hair. His long, muscular legs were encased in a pair of unbuttoned trousers hanging loosely about his slim hips.

"Well, don't just stand there gaping," he said. "Either come in or leave."

When he turned back into the room, Maggie stepped over the threshold and closed the door, unsure if she were doing the right thing. She knew it was very improper to be alone with a man in his hotel room, but where this man was concerned, she seemed to have lost all sense of reason.

He slumped on the edge of the bed, a frown marring his handsome face as he groaned.

Maggie moved farther into the room, going immediately to the bed. "You've hurt yourself with so much activity, Mr. Stone. You should be in bed."

Reaching out toward a box of cigars on the bedside table, he winced with pain, but stifled a grunt before it reached his lips. "Damn. Hand me a cigar."

"Please get in bed, Mr. Stone."

"I want a cigar!"

"You're apparently in pain, so you should lie down," Maggie said. "Has the doctor seen you today?"

"He's delivering a baby. Thayer wanted to call in another man, but I told him that I didn't need a damned doctor."

"Sit down on the edge of the bed. I'll check your wound and put fresh wrapping on it. Mr. Coleman said that Dr. Cooper left the necessary things."

"How did Thayer bribe you?" Aaron asked, still sitting on the side of the bed.

"He simply asked if, as a Christian kindness, I would attend you," Maggie said, reaching for his box of cigars just as he did.

She took the box in her hand, eyeing it and then him. "Where did these come from?"

"Phineas brought them."

"You shouldn't be smoking in your condition."

"Dammit, Maggie, I'm not dying of consumption. I'm recovering from a minor bullet wound."

She looked on the dresser near the window where a covered tray had been placed. "Please," she tried to reason with him. "Let me change your dressing, and feed you lunch, and then we'll discuss the cigars."

"You're a hard woman," he said teasingly. "So you've come to care for me out of the goodness of your heart, have you?"

He looked up at the beauty standing above him, noticing the free-flowing mane of her fiery curls was neatly subdued into a bun atop her head.

"Well, get on with it. Change the cursed dressing. But I warn you that I'll yell if you strip away my hair."

Her eyes focused on his chest, and her fingers itched to touch the abundance of golden curls. She had never felt a man's chest, never experienced the desire to explore a masculine body, and had never longed to be held in strong arms.

Removing a pair of small scissors from Dr. Cooper's package, she clipped away the bandage, which had stuck around the wound. When she hesitated, Aaron jerked it away, moaning slightly. Maggie moved quickly, taking the soiled cloth, doctoring the puckered, discolored wound, and applying fresh dressing.

Aaron held his arms up, out of the way, until she finished. He lowered his arms over her head, holding the back of her neck with both of his hands, pulling her face downward. He wanted to thank his ministering angel with a kiss, but she struggled to free herself.

"Be still, Maggie girl," he said. "You'll hurt yourself trying to pull away."

"Please, let me go."

"All I want is a kiss."

"No."

"One kiss."

"No," she said, but ceased to struggle as she felt his hands loosen their grip about her neck and move slowly down her shoulders, down her arms, stopping at her wrists.

"Why have you knotted your hair up today?" he asked, his hands moving to her tiny waist.

"Aunt Tilly feels it highly improper for a woman my age to wear her hair loose. I should have known better, but Pa always liked it hanging free except for a ribbon tied around it."

"Your pa was a man with good taste." Aaron smiled as he held her about the waist with one hand and reached upward with the other to touch her hair. "I like the way you wore it yesterday."

"I . . . had . . ." Maggie whispered unsteadily, acutely aware of his potent nearness. He smelled of medicine, sweat, and maleness. "I had lost my ribbon struggling with that awful man in Chattanooga."

"Who's this Aunt Tilly?"

"Mathilda Gower," Maggie said. "My uncle Chester's wife."

"Oh, yes, the mother of the reverend."

"Yes."

"Good God! You're not blood-related to that idiot Peterson, are you? You're just a cousin-by-marriage."

"Why, yes." Maggie did not understand why Aaron seemed so

upset that Wesley was not a blood relation, nor did she understand why he had insulted the other man by referring to him as an idiot.

"You haven't come here to marry the good reverend, have you?"

The question stunned her so much that she was speechless. Aaron's hand tugged at the twist of her hair. His long, broad fingers threaded through its thickness, loosening the tightly coiled mass, freeing it to fall about her shoulders.

"Oh," she gasped as one big hand encompassed the back of her head, pulling her face down next to his.

"You're too much woman for a man like that." His voice was deep and low, caressing her with words. "Answer me, beautiful Maggie."

"I . . . I . . ." she stammered, feeling the breath from his lips touch her face. "No. I've not come here to marry Wesley. We've come to live with them in order to have a better life."

His lips hovered over hers, the warmth heating her mouth as he spoke. "You have a glorious mouth. The kind of mouth a man dreams about."

His lips touched hers, and the world began to spin around and around for Maggie as she clutched Aaron's shoulders. Fear and longing coursed through her while he continued the gentle kiss.

When he released her mouth and looked into her dazed eyes, she tried to speak. "Aaron . . . Mr. Stone, please."

"Please what, Maggie love?"

"Please let me go. I'm not your love."

Observing the fear in her amber eyes, he took a deep breath and released her. "Fetch my lunch, Miss Maggie. I've suddenly developed a ravenous appetite."

Maggie straightened, turned around, and walked to the dresser where she uncovered his meal. "It looks inviting," she said as she returned to the bed, tray in hand. "Do you need help getting back in the bed?"

"Is it necessary for me to go back to bed?" he asked, grumbling. "I can manage the tray like this."

"Please."

"Say, 'Please, Aaron,' and I'll oblige you."

Maggie fumed. He was the most exasperating man she had ever known. "Please, Aaron."

Cautiously, he eased his large body into the bed, leaving the covers wadded at the foot.

"My arm is a bit stiff," he said, raising it slightly while a frown appeared on his face. "See?"

"What can I do to help, Mr. Stone?" She stood by the bed, hands demurely at her sides. She seriously considered throwing the plate in his face.

"Aaron. Remember to call me Aaron. Now that we're friends, you can feed me."

Maggie eyed him suspiciously, looking from him to the tray, and then back to him. She decided that she'd been a fool to have come, and was an even bigger fool to stay.

"Sit down." He patted the bed.

Seeing no better way to accomplish the task, she obeyed, seating herself on the edge of the bed. She picked up his spoon and dipped into a portion of peas. She put the spoonful of peas into his open mouth. He began to chew slowly.

"Hmm . . . mmm, good," he mumbled. "More."

Overcoming the desire to jab him with his own fork, she complied, silently angry. Maggie fed; Aaron ate, bite by bite, mouthful by mouthful, until he'd cleaned his plate. She held a coffee cup to his lips as he drank. When she lowered the cup, he took it from her, placed it on the tray, and clasped her hand in his.

"Thank you, Maggie." Aaron pulled her hand to his lips, tenderly kissing the top.

"You're welcome, Mr. . . . . Aaron."

"How long can you stay?"

"I've stayed too long already," she said, wishing he would release her hand so she could leave. "Mr. Coleman is waiting for me. And Daisy and your Phineas are still outside, no doubt."

"I don't want you to go." He pushed the tray to the far side of the bed and reached for Maggie. She gasped loudly when he pulled her into his arms.

"No, Aaron. No."

"Yes, Maggie. Oh, yes."

His arms tightened about her, crushing her soft breasts against his uninjured side as he lowered his head and took her mouth with his. Gone was the tenderness of the earlier kiss, the gentleness of reason. He ravished her sweet lips. His tongue, hot and wild, circled feverishly around her closed mouth, coaxing, prizing. He caressed her back, and then grasped her hips in his big hands. He shifted her half on top of him as he forced her lips apart, whispering hoarsely, "Open your mouth, my love."

When she obeyed, he thrust inside, stroking her tongue, exploring her softness. Slowly, almost reluctantly, her own tongue responded, easing into his mouth, dueling sweetly with his.

The kiss deepened and intensified. Maggie had never known such mindless pleasure. Her mouth throbbed from his assault, but pleaded for more as it met his with equal passion. Innocent and unknowing, she could not understand what was happening to her body. Why did her breasts feel swollen, her nipples tight? Why did her blood feel like fire coursing through her veins?

Aaron's lips moved to the pale softness of her neck, his tongue sliding downward until it reached the barrier of her collar. His breathing uneven, he whispered against her ear, "I want to touch you."

She buried her face against the hard muscles of his big shoulder, a hot ache filling the secret depths of her femininity. Her fingers inched upward into the thick whorls of his tawny chest hair, and a sensation of heated longing shot through her body, hitting her womanly core.

Just as he reached to unbutton her dress, his hand stopped, resting against the quivering pulse in her throat. Aaron's befuddled brain barely registered the sound of voices in the hallway until they were right outside his door. He did not want to stop kissing the responsive woman in his arms, but, when he recognized Thayer's voice, he knew he must.

"Please, Eunice, wait," Thayer said as Eunice Arnold thrust open the door of Aaron's room.

"I must see Aaron," Eunice said in a shrill voice.

Just as the Widow Arnold pranced in, yellow parasol in hand, Aaron pushed a stunned Maggie out of his arms. Perplexed, but quickly recovering, she jumped up from the bed and turned to face the intruders.

"Aaron, my . . ." Eunice halted midsentence when she saw the beautiful blushing redhead standing by Aaron's bed.

"Please come in, Eunice," Aaron said, groping for the covers at his feet. Seeing his dilemma, Maggie tugged the covers up to his waist.

"Eunice, may I introduce Miss Margaret Campbell," Thayer said. "She was kind enough to administer to Aaron's needs since Dr. Cooper was unavailable. Maggie, Mrs. Eunice Arnold."

"Are you a nurse?" Eunice asked.

"No," Maggie replied, taking a long, leisurely look at the tall, elegant woman who stood eyeing her rather contemptuously.

Eunice Arnold was at least five feet nine, with a body as willowy as a young girl's. Her fine, white-blond hair was parted in the middle with a row of curly bangs gracing her forehead. She looked every bit the well-dressed lady in her French-gray faille with an accordion-pleated underskirt of yellow silk and a waistcoat trimmed in velvet. A black felt hat decorated with a yellow ostrich feather adorned her head.

"Pleased to meet you," Maggie blurted out as she practically ran to the door. "I have to go. Aunt Tilly's expecting me."

"Wait, Miss Maggie," Thayer called as she rushed past him and out into the hallway, almost knocking over a small walnut table.

Thayer looked at Aaron, who nodded in a silent plea. Thayer excused himself and followed Maggie, not catching up with her until he reached the lobby.

Just as Thayer spoke her name again, Wesley Peterson walked through the front entrance. Ignoring Thayer's call, she walked straight to the reverend.

"I was beginning to worry, Margaret," Wesley said, taking her hand. "Why, you're trembling, my dear. Is something wrong?"

"No," she answered in a weak voice. Summoning all her courage, she smiled. "I'm afraid I'm not accustomed to men like Mr. Stone."

"He didn't—"

"No, no. He's just a bit rough-spoken," Maggie lied, wanting to be as far away from the Parshall House and Aaron Stone and his fine lady friend as she could get. "Take me home, Wesley."

"Of course, Cousin Margaret," he said, escorting her outside to where Daisy and Phineas stood waiting.

For one brief second, Maggie turned backward, catching a glimpse of Thayer standing at the hotel's entrance, his black eyes filled with concern.

Chapter 4

Over a week had passed since Maggie's flight from the Parshall House, but, try as she might, she could not forget one moment of the last day she had seen Aaron Stone. Her feelings for the man alternated hourly, ranging from bitter hatred to what she assumed was unrequited love. On this warm June afternoon, Maggie's thoughts kept wandering back to the very instant Aaron's lips had first touched hers. It had been such a gentle kiss, but the feeling it had induced in her had been so wild they had set her head to spinning. She had begun to resent the man because he had invaded her mind and heart so thoroughly that Micah was accusing her of being love-struck.

"Margaret." Mathilda Gower moved about the room like a butterfly despite her heaviness. Maggie had soon learned that Aunt Tilly's health and agility had little to do with her body. She was well and happy whenever it suited her to be so. "I was telling Alice how becoming this lavender jersey will look on her. Don't you agree?"

"Yes, certainly." Maggie had her doubts that the material was suited to Mrs. Alice Mobley's rather bony body or sallow coloring but the lady was her first customer now that Aunt Tilly was allowing her to take in sewing. "Since I've adjusted the pattern, I'm sure it will be a fine fit, Mrs. Mobley."

Alice smiled, and the warmth in her expression changed her pale, plain face into a pleasantly pretty one. Maggie liked her aunt's friend, whose husband practiced law in Tuscumbia and twin daughters attended the Deshler Female Institute. She envied the Mobley family their happy, secure life. "I shall return on Wednesday for the fitting, dear. Tilly has praised you highly. I understand you've made her a lovely new dress this past week."

"Indeed," Mathilda confirmed, a plump hand patting her niece's shoulder. "I shall have it on at church Sunday. It is the most beautiful gray cashmere, and the jacket is trimmed in black. It's a perfect match for my gray straw bonnet."

"Margaret, I'm so pleased you and your brother and sister have joined our community." Alice Mobley's voice was loud and clear, each word thoroughly enunciated, indicating that her origins were not Southern. "I'm sure you will grow to love Tuscumbia as much as my family has since our arrival fifteen years ago."

"I'm sure we will," Maggie said as she methodically folded the yards of material her aunt and Mrs. Mobley had inspected. "Please come on Wednesday. And if you wish, I can see your daughters on that day to adjust the pattern for them."

"Most definitely," Mathilda invited. "You must all come over. I'll have Auntie Gem bake a batch of tea cakes."

"We shall be here." Alice nodded good-bye as Mathilda escorted her from the small, second-story bedroom where Maggie had set up the sewing machine that Uncle Chester had brought down from the attic and proudly presented to her. Maggie treasured the machine all the more for knowing it had belonged to her uncle's first wife, who had died along with their only child in the yellow fever epidemic of '78.

Once her aunt and their guest were gone, she sat down on her small bed, smiling serenely because she was filled with a sense of hope and purpose. Aunt Tilly had been in complete accord with Maggie's desire to earn money of her own, and had even praised her plans to pay for Micah's and Judith's schooling. Her aunt had actually gone on and on about the virtues of honest labor, and exhorted her nieces and nephew to work hard, obey God's commandments, and keep spotless reputations in the community.

Maggie's plans were beginning to come together nicely. Micah had adapted well to work at the general store, and his intelligence and conscientiousness greatly pleased Uncle Chester. Judith, though still too outspoken and curious, was putting forth an effort to conform to Aunt Tilly's strict rules. Daisy never complained. Luckily she liked and worked well with Auntie Gem and was enjoying being paid court by Phineas, who had stopped by twice during the past week. Maggie suspected that Daisy was very attracted to the big man.

Maggie had neither seen nor heard from Aaron Stone, and she had to admit that she had foolishly hoped to have some word from him. Thayer Coleman had sent a handwritten message by Phineas earlier in the week, thanking her for her kindness. She should be grateful that the man was ignoring her existence, especially after what had transpired between them at their last meeting. The thought of lying wantonly in his naked arms, while his hungry mouth devoured hers, had caused her several sleepless nights. She had been in the bed with him, had allowed him intimacies only a husband should have known, and then had been shoved from his embrace when the Widow Arnold appeared.

She had learned more than she wanted to know about Eunice Waite Arnold, the elder daughter of Henry Waite, prosperous lawyer-landowner, whose ancestors had moved to Alabama from Virginia half a century ago. Eunice had money, breeding, and a place in local society. Her marriage to John Arnold, a wealthy young cousin to Thayer Coleman, and his untimely death had elevated her to the highest echelons of respectability in Colbert County.

Wesley and his mother seemed to know the most intimate details of their neighbors' lives, and were genuinely piqued that they had no information on Aaron Stone's past. The air of mystery surrounding him seemed to fascinate the local citizenry. All they appeared to know was that he had a great deal of money. That he had purchased the old White Orchard plantation near Barton, and that he would probably marry Eunice Arnold before the end of the year.

Maggie had told herself over and over again that she had no right to be jealous. A few stolen kisses did not mean commitment to a man like Aaron. He probably didn't think of her as a lady who deserved his respect. After all, she hadn't so much as protested when he'd pulled her into his arms and across his virile body. If she had been a lady, she would have screamed for help instead of responding so shamelessly. She knew Thayer Coleman was aware of what had been going on, and she was sure that Mrs. Arnold was suspicious. If Aunt

Tilly were to ever learn the truth, it could mean the end of everything. No doubt, she would condemn Maggie as a harlot.

She hoped she never saw Aaron Stone again as long as she lived. He could bring her nothing but heartache and trouble. If he would stay away from her, she knew that eventually she would forget him. Forget the sight of his handsome face and muscular body. Forget his earthy male smell. Forget the hot sweetness of his mouth when her tongue had explored it. Forget the caressing sound of his deep voice whispering, "I want to touch you."

"Cousin Margaret," Wesley called, his stout body framed in the doorway of her room. "Judith and I have finished with her reading lesson for today, and I thought you might join me downstairs for some tea."

Standing quickly to greet him, Maggie smiled at her cousin-by-marriage. "That sounds quite nice, Cousin Wesley. There are a few things I wish to speak to you about."

After straightening the skirt of her gray muslin dress, she joined Wesley at the door, her fingers reaching out to touch the sleeve of his coat. "First, let me thank you again for taking the time to help Judith with her reading and Micah with his arithmetic."

"It's been my pleasure," he assured her as he placed a fleshy hand on top of hers. "I derive pleasure from seeing you happy, dear Margaret."

"Oh, Wesley," Maggie's voice lowered. She was touched by his concern. "You're such a kind man. You've helped us all so much."

His plump hand squeezed hers gently. "I'm growing quite fond of you, you know. I hope you don't object."

How could she answer him truthfully without hurting his feelings? For over a week now, he had done everything possible to make her feel welcome and at home. He insisted on teaching her siblings until she had acquired enough money to pay for their special schooling. He often smoothed his mother's ruffled feathers when any one of the Campbells said or did something that upset her, and Judith seemed destined for that purpose. He even saw to it that Daisy had a cot to sleep on. Indeed, Wesley Peterson was a saintly man.

"We're all fond of you, too," Maggie said, smiling at him sweetly.

After clearing his throat and patting her hand, he asked, "Shall we find Auntie Gem and order that tea?"

"Oh, yes," she said, following his lead down the short hallway.

"Judith's a very bright girl. You did a fine job teaching her the basics."

"Well, I just used the *Blue Back Speller* and *McGuffey's First Reader* that my ma used when she taught me," Maggie said, as they slowly proceeded down the stairs.

"She seems well versed in the Holy Word, also."

"Oh, yes. Pa was mighty stern about our Bible reading and prayers."

"As well he should have been. I shall instill a love and respect for our Heavenly Father in my sons and daughters one day if I am so blessed."

They entered the back parlor, which Wesley used as his study. Just as he had spoken of his future children, he turned to face Maggie. "You will make a fine mother. You've proven your worth with Micah and Judith's care."

She didn't know what to say. She was certain that he was giving thought to the idea of her being the mother of his children, but she simply could not picture him as the father of hers. Even more, she could not imagine sharing the marriage bed with Wesley. Perhaps if she had not met Aaron Stone, perhaps if the awful man had never kissed her, she wouldn't constantly compare dear Cousin Wesley to that notorious cad.

"Speaking of Judith and Micah," Maggie said, seating herself in a pine rocker near the window. "I will need to know the cost of those schools you mentioned. For Jude, do you recommend the Deshler Institute or Miss Anna Pybas's school?"

"Both are fine." He took a seat in the large oak chair at his desk. "The cost is twelve dollars a month with Miss Pybas. It's possible that arrangement can be made for you to exchange your sewing skills for part of the tuition."

"Oh, that would be wonderful."

"As for Micah, I highly recommend sending him to Brother Larimore in Florence. Tuition for a twenty-four-week, January-to-June term is one hundred and thirty dollars."

"Oh, my," Maggie said, realizing how unlikely it would be for her to make that much money.

"January is over six months away," Wesley said. "I shall, of course, be willing to assist you in making payment."

"Oh, no," Maggie said, her golden eyes flashing with objections. "I could never accept your money."

"Perhaps by January, I will have persuaded you to change your mind."

Wesley rang the bell for Auntie Gem, but when there was no reply after several summonses, he excused himself to go to the kitchen.

Maggie was glad that Wesley liked her, but she did not want to encourage anything more. Marrying him could solve most of her problems, but she refused to ruin both of their lives in order to keep her promise to Pa. There had to be other ways to give Micah an education and see that he was set up in a well-paying, respectable profession. But how would she ever come up with enough money to educate both her siblings? Jude just had to become a lady, one who would be able to choose any fine gentleman she wanted for a husband.

Pa had regretted not being able to do more for them, but after Ma died he had never been the same. Mary Campbell, with her beautiful smile and happy laugh, had enriched their poverty-stricken lives. Never once had Maggie heard her mother complain about her lot in life. And she could have. She had been born the daughter of a prosperous blacksmith and sister to a now-successful merchant. Her entire life had changed when she had run off with wild, redheaded Jimmy Campbell to live a life of drudgery on a Tennessee farm.

Maggie wanted a better life for them all, but she would not marry a man she didn't love in order to do it. Her parents had been poor, but even as a child she had known that they were deeply in love. She could remember the way her ma looked at Pa. Her eyes would go all warm and soft as if she were about to cry, but they were filled with love. And Pa would touch Ma with such tenderness. A hug around the shoulders. A pat on the hand. A caress across her cheek. Maggie wanted a man to love her like that. Stupidly, she had dreamed of Aaron Stone being her true love.

She knew she was half in love with the man already. Why couldn't her foolish heart beat faster when Wesley looked at her, spoke her name, touched her. Why did it have to be Aaron? Wesley would be far more suitable as a mate. He was kind, helpful, respectful, and would most certainly offer marriage before trying to make love to her.

Aaron Stone was a man practically betrothed to another woman, a man who would never offer marriage to a girl of Maggie's circumstances. He had flirted with her, toyed with her emotions, and made unseemly advances, with no thought of her good name. He was a dangerous man, one to be avoided at all costs.

Thayer Coleman leaned back in the brown leather wing chair and downed the last drops of coffee from the Haviland cup. Aaron Stone sat across from him in an identical chair, puffing on a cigar while he gazed distractedly out the long, narrow window of his friend's town house library.

Aaron like the comfortable camaraderie he shared with the younger man whose hospitality he had been enjoying for eleven months now. The two men had met five years ago at the Point Clear Hotel on the gulf when Thayer had been a young pup of nineteen, eager to sample all of life's forbidden fruits. Aaron had been a willing teacher, and soon the two men were sharing wine, women, and adventures. Besides the two of them only Phineas and Thayer's family knew the bitter secret that had brought them together.

Aaron stretched out his long legs, crossing his black-booted feet at the ankles. "I received a message from Buckley in Anniston. He thinks our visit last month proved our determination to have a say in the way things are done down there."

"I received a message concerning our trip too." Thayer chuckled, remembering all the dances he had shared with a blue-eyed enchantress. "It was a sweet note from Miss Eloise."

"Should I be jealous?" Aaron laughed, tossing his cigar butt into a nearby brass spittoon. "After all, I did dance several times with the lovely Miss Eloise the night of the Anniston Inn's grand opening."

"She was the belle of the ball," Thayer said. "However, I was the lucky man allowed to call on her the next day."

"I think her mother was impressed with your name. She had known your parents, hadn't she?"

"Oh, yes. Mrs. Stafford couldn't say enough about Colonel and Mrs. Coleman."

"I can think the lady had marriage in mind for you and her daughter."

"I can think of a worse fate." Thayer smiled, the memory of Eloise's delicate china-doll face flashing through his mind. "In a few years, I might be inclined to marry."

"The time comes for all of us. You're young yet. You need to bed whores and raise hell a few more years."

Thayer laughed, reaching to pour himself more coffee. "I should think you'd reconsider marriage to Eunice after meeting Miss Maggie. And after getting shot by Sally's pa, you shouldn't be encouraging me to bed more whores."

"If you'd stay with the ladies at Loretta's, you wouldn't have irate fathers trying to kill you and hitting me by mistake."

"I'll keep that in mind." Thayer grinned, his dark eyes full of mischief. "Now about our lovely Miss Campbell."

"Our?"

"If you're not interested, I am." Thayer noted the tightening of his friend's square jaw and saw the slightest glint of anger in his green eyes.

"Maggie isn't the girl for either of us," Aaron stated, uncrossing his long legs and standing his big body facing the window. He would not allow himself to think any more about that redheaded witch who had haunted his dreams and tormented his every waking moment. "I spoke to the marshal about Whitcomb. He thinks we have to press charges and go through a trial, or the man will be after you again."

"Old Whitcomb is crazy," Thayer said, his black eyes narrowing to a squint. "Sally may be sixteen, but she's been whoring for years. She told me she had her first man when she was twelve. Can you imagine? She wasn't much older than little Judith Campbell."

"Hell," Aaron said, turning to face the other man. "I don't want to hear any more about the Campbells. Leave well enough alone."

"Why don't you admit that Maggie stirs your blood like Eunice never has?"

"Dammit, Thayer, a man wants more from a wife than a good roll in the hay." Aaron's big hand ran through his long, tawny hair. "I need a wife who can give me social position and respectability."

"I was born with everything you want so badly, my friend." Thayer placed the cup on his desk and looked up at his agitated companion. "I would exchange it all for the right woman. Especially a woman like Maggie."

"You don't know what you're talking about. No matter who you marry, you'll always be a Coleman."

"And no matter who you marry, you'll always be Richard Leander's bastard."

If any other man had dared refer to him in such a manner, Aaron would have been tempted to call him out, or, if in a black mood, would have killed him on the spot. But Thayer was his best friend, a man who would never defame him. He knew the words had been spoken to force him to reconsider the decisions he'd had made.

"Eunice need never know the truth about my past. She seems willing to accept me at face value."

"You'd want to share the rest of your life with a woman to whom you couldn't tell the truth about yourself?"

"You've been against my courting Eunice from the beginning. Why? Is it because her husband was your cousin?"

"Damn stupid question," Thayer snapped. "John Arnold was a fine man. The perfect match for Eunice. He was charming, soft-spoken, and gentle. An undemanding, young boy. You're far too much man for the widow. You'll scare the hell out of her on your wedding night."

"I have the good sense to know not to treat Eunice like a whore."

"I happen to know, on the word of some married men, that the happiest marriages are the ones where the wives enjoy their duties as much as their husbands do."

"Who, pray tell, is your source?"

"Martin, for one."

"Martin!" Aaron said. "Your brother-in-law actually spoke about your sister in such a manner?"

"I admit he was drunk at the time he was extolling Reba's womanly talents."

"She would have his hide nailed to the barn door if she knew."

"You'll have a chance to tell her," Thayer told his friend who had just walked to the window, something outside catching his attention. "They're all coming to Silver Hill for the summer."

"Martha too?"

"Of course, Mama will be with them. Now that Reba is carrying her third child, she wanted Mama to stay with her for a while."

"It will be good to see your family again," Aaron said as he watched Phineas outside in the backyard where he stood talking to Daisy.

"They're your family, too. They will accept you, if you'll accept them."

Aaron had no family, except Thayer's. He had no parents, not brothers, no aunts and uncles eager to accept him.

Since the day his mother died when he was sixteen, he had been alone. Perhaps he had always been alone, even before Louise Stone had been killed in August of 1871 when an explosion had wrecked the *Ocean Wave*, a steamer on which she and her lover had booked passage. When Aaron had visited Point Clear five years ago, parts of the wrecked steamer could still be seen on the bay shore at low tide. Although he had known where she died, how she died, and with whom she died, he had waited nearly ten years to visit the site and seek revenge.

There had been no revenge, only a bittersweet regret when he found out all the truths that had been a mystery to him for so many years. Martha Coleman had given him his birthright, and it had made him determined to acquire the respectability and social position always denied him. He had already made a small fortune, mostly by unscrupulous and often illegal means, when he met the Colemans. Since then, he had invested his "ill-gotten gains" in timber, cotton, steamboats, and the new steel industry.

"What seems to be fascinating you outside the window?" Thayer asked, standing, but still unable to see around his friend's big body.

Moving slightly, to allow Thayer full view of the backyard, Aaron replied, "I was watching Phineas. He's taken quite a liking to that Daisy girl. I've never seen him so smitten."

"You have to admit that she is a beautiful creature," Thayer remarked, watching the lovely Negress as she smiled at the huge black man holding her hand. "I dare say Phineas is in love. Surely you understand how he feels, having been smitten so recently yourself."

"Leave it be, man!" Aaron hissed through clenched teeth.

"Deny it all you want, but I've seen the way you look at her. And I was there at the train station when you had to be prized from her arms."

"The girl was in shock. A wounded man had just fallen on her."

"Tell it to somebody who didn't walk in on the two of you the day I tried to keep Eunice out of your hotel room."

Aaron could feel a heated flush creeping up his neck. He refused to admit any feelings for Maggie Campbell, neither to himself nor his best friend.

"She's the most beautiful woman I've ever seen, and that's all there is to it. I have no feeling for her other than lust, and even you would know that she's hardly the type I can bed and forget."

"I'll wager that you can't forget about her anyway." Thayer put a hand on his friend's big shoulder. "You owe it to yourself and Maggie, and even to Eunice, to find out what your true feelings are before you propose to the wrong woman."

"Just what are you suggesting?"

"I think you should become better acquainted with Miss Maggie. I'll bet that once you know her better, you'll be wanting to spend the rest of your life with her."

"Dammit, man, she is not the woman for me."

"Are you afraid to find out?"

"What?"

"You heard me." Thayer eyed the taller man, whose entire attention was focused on him. "I'll bet you can't spend an afternoon with Miss Maggie without trying to make love to her."

"Is that a dare?"

"Yes."

"What are you betting?"

"Mmm . . . mmm . . . Let me see. How about my new spider

phaeton? Take Maggie for a ride in it tomorrow. I'll be a gentleman and take your word as to whether I win or lose."

"It's a bet." Aaron reached out, taking his friend's hand in his strong clasp.

"This is a perfect time to court Miss Maggie since Eunice is away at Bailey Springs with her mother."

"I'm not going to court Maggie."

"How long are Eunice and Mrs. Waite going to be gone?"

"Just till the end of the week. Eunice felt a week away at the spring would help Mrs. Waite's condition."

"Poor Henry Waite," Thayer sympathized. "He's one lone man in a household of females. Weak, complaining females, at that. Are you aware that Eunice is hoping I'll take an interest in her sister?"

"Henrietta is a lovely girl," Aaron said, knowing that Eunice's younger sister was a plain, sickly girl whose main redeeming quality seemed to be her sweet disposition.

"I prefer more colorful beauties like Eloise Stafford and Maggie Campbell," Thayer said, smiling thoughtfully. "Someone like little Judith will be one day, with that mane of fiery gold hair and those enormous blue-green eyes. Can you ever see a man taming either of the Campbell sisters?"

"A man could die trying," Aaron said. He did not want to think about taming Maggie because that conjured up visions of their two bodies intimately entwined while he drank his fill of her lusciousness. Lord, but she would be sweet, sweeter than anything he had ever known. He could remember her lips, soft, hot, moist. He knew her womanly core would be the same, and the thought of being inside her had been torturing him night and day.

"Tomorrow is Sunday and the perfect day for a gentleman to go calling." Thayer's eagerness was evident in the timbre of his slow, Southern voice. "Right after dinner tomorrow, we'll pay a visit on the Gower household."

"You appear to have a plan," Aaron said. "We will probably need one. No doubt, Miss Maggie has no desire to take a buggy ride with me."

"Have no fear, dear friend. I do indeed have a plan. You will have the whole afternoon to be alone with your temptation."

"Come tomorrow night your new phaeton will be mine."

"If you lose, Aaron, I want you to postpone asking Eunice to marry you for three months."

Aaron gasped, his green eyes shooting jade fire. "What?"

"Is it still a bet now that you know my terms?" Thayer asked.

Aaron hesitated. Surely he could resist one pretty redhead for a few hours. Couldn't he? "It's still a bet."

Chapter 5

The sun's warmth touched Maggie's face as she leaned back against the tree trunk. Bubbly and out of breath, an equally happy Judith laughed as she caught up with her sister. Dropping to the ground, she looked up at Maggie.

"It was fun playing catch, wasn't it?" Jude smiled, her lightly freckled nose curling as her eyes squinted against the sun's bright glare.

"I'm far too old to be playing with you," Maggie laughed. "Micah thinks he's too old. That's why he's enjoying lemonade on the porch with Uncle Chester."

"You'll be even older when you have children of your own, and I bet you'll play with them."

"Yes," Maggie sighed, feeling more relaxed and content than she had since their arrival in Tuscumbia. "I suppose I'll be a most improper mother running around playing games with my little ones."

"You'll be the very best mother ever," Judith said, her tiny fingers plucking at the grass surrounding her. "Just look at all the practice you've had with Micah and me."

"Oh, dear." Maggie tried to hide her smile as she slowly lowered herself to sit beside Jude beneath the old oak tree. "I've done a terrible job of raising you. Look at yourself, sitting here in your Sunday dress playing in the grass."

"I'm looking for four-leaf clovers."

"Jude?"

"What?"

"I'm very proud of you." Maggie wanted her young sister to know that she was aware of the effort she was making to follow all the strict rules and regulations of Mathilda Gower's household. "Wesley says you're doing good in your schoolwork. He thinks you're a very smart girl."

"He likes you, Maggie. I mean, he likes you in that special kind of way."

"I know." Maggie was well aware of Wesley Peterson's feelings for her. He was a perfect gentleman, attentive, caring, and so kind to her and her family. She knew that eventually he would ask her to marry him, if Aunt Mathilda gave her blessings.

"You don't like him that way, do you?"

"No, Jude. I don't." Her life would be so simple if only she did love Wesley. Perhaps she would consider marrying him, without love, if she had never met a particularly handsome, green-eyed lion.

"He wanted you to go with him to visit all the sick people and shut-ins this afternoon, didn't he?"

"Yes. I'm trying not to lead him on. I like him, but I could never marry him."

"Hey, you two," Micah called from the side porch of his uncle's two-story, white house where they sat together enjoying the peace and beauty of a sunny June Sunday. "Looks like we've got company coming."

Both girls looked from their brother to the gate, and then to the road where Aaron Stone and Thayer Coleman were stepping down from a two-seated cabriolet. With the carriage top down, the soft leather upholstery gleamed in the bright sunlight, and a spit and polished Phineas sat perched on the driver's seat. The two men were dressed in their dark Sunday church suits, high-collared white linen shirts, and derby hats. Just as Maggie caught sight of Aaron, he removed his hat and tossed it into the carriage.

"Maggie! Maggie!" Judith could hardly contain her excitement. "It's Mr. Stone and his friend, Mr. Coleman. What shall we do? Why do you suppose they're here? Oh, Maggie."

"Calm yourself, Jude," her sister scolded as she rose to her feet in one quick and quite unladylike movement. "It's possible that they're here on some business with Uncle Chester."

"It's Sunday," the child said. "You only pay social calls on the Lord's Day."

"Get up and let's go see what's going on." Maggie's heart was racing wildly. Just a glimpse of Aaron had turned her stomach inside out. What was he doing here? Didn't he have the decency to stay away from her?

"Should I go upstairs and wake Aunt Tilly?" Judith asked as she jumped up from the ground and brushed the grass from her tan muslin dress. She hated the garment, but Aunt Tilly had given Maggie the material to fashion them both a suitable Sunday dress, so she didn't dare complain.

"No, you mustn't disturb her."

"She'll be greatly disappointed if she doesn't get to greet Mr. Coleman." Judith said the man's name, mocking her aunt's speech and manner.

"Jude!" Maggie fussed. "Don't make light of Aunt Tilly's respect for other people's importance."

"Look," the hazel-eyed child whispered, tugging on her sister's arm. "Mr. Stone is walking toward us."

"Then let's go meet him and invite him to join us on the porch." Maggie wanted to run to the man who was leisurely approaching her, a friendly smile softening his rugged face.

"Hello, Miss Maggie," Aaron said as he stopped directly in front of her.

"Good afternoon, Mr. Stone."

"Hey there." Jude stepped from behind the older girl.

"Well, hello, Miss Judith. Don't you look pretty today." Aaron tried to focus his attention on the child, but he could not take his eyes off of Maggie. That marvelous red hair was confined in a bun atop her head, but stray tendrils framed her face and neck, begging a man to curl his fingers about them. Her plain, tan dress fit every curve of her upper body to perfection, drawing his attention to the lush swell of her womanly breasts.

"Won't you join us for lemonade?" *Why are you here?* she thought. *Please don't look at me like that. I hate you for making me feel this way. Why aren't you with your precious Widow Arnold?*

"I'd be delighted." *You aren't happy to see me, are you, Maggie?*

Why do you have to be so beautiful? I want to take you in my arms and kiss the breath right out of you.

As they joined the others on the porch, Maggie heard Thayer Coleman asking her uncle's permission to take her family for an afternoon carriage ride.

"I would deem it an honor to give the Campbells a tour of Tuscumbia," Thayer said. "What better time for a ride than a Sunday afternoon?"

"Of course, they have my permission, Mr. Coleman," Chester Gower assured his visitor. "It's so kind of you to make the offer."

"Please sit down, gentlemen," Maggie invited as she entered the porch. "Let me pour some refreshments."

Both men obliged, taking seats and accepting tall glasses of sweet lemonade.

"Are we really going for a carriage ride?" Judith asked impatiently.

"Jude," Maggie said, her amber eyes darting a silent warning. "I'm afraid it wouldn't be possible. Micah has been invited to the Stanfords' today."

"Just because I'm going over to Hollis Stanford's to play paddle cat doesn't mean you and Jude shouldn't go on and enjoy the ride," Micah said.

"It wouldn't be proper to go without you." Maggie was trying desperately to find a way out of accepting Thayer's invitation. She did not want to go riding with Aaron Stone at her side for hours.

"Nonsense," Uncle Chester said, smiling. "What could be more proper than for these gentlemen to take the two prettiest girls in Tuscumbia for a Sunday ride?"

"What would Aunt Tilly say?" Maggie hoped that the mention of his wife's name would make her uncle reconsider.

"You leave Mathilda to me," he told them. "Go and enjoy yourselves."

"Come on, Maggie," Judith said. "I want to go."

"I'm sure Wesley would not approve." Maggie knew that Wesley would be upset because he was already suspicious of her attraction to Mr. Stone. He would, no doubt, assume that she had been eager to spend the afternoon in Aaron's company.

"Wesley is far too busy administering his holy duties to concern himself with an afternoon's entertainment for you," Chester informed his niece.

"I'm going," Jude declared.

Thayer laughed at the girl's determination. If his plan worked, he would be spending the next few hours in the child's company, and suddenly the idea appealed to him greatly. He found her a constant source of amusement and fascination.

"I . . . I really see no need." Maggie was afraid, afraid of Aaron and even more afraid of her own feelings.

"Please, Miss Maggie." Aaron took her hand, and immediately realized that she was trembling. She wanted him as badly as he wanted her, and she was fighting the unwanted attraction with all of her strength.

"A short ride," Maggie finally conceded. If she continued to resist, Uncle Chester might wonder why.

Within ten minutes, bonnets on and light shawls draped about them, the Campbell sisters were sitting in Thayer's carriage. Although Jude had not taken her eyes off Thayer and was gaily chatting away, Maggie sat silently by Aaron, her gaze downcast.

"I thought we'd begin our tour with a trip to my house," Thayer said, watching Judith squirm in her seat, her big eyes focused on him.

"Have you lived here all your life?" the child asked.

"We've had the town house since I was a boy," Thayer said. "But I grew up at Silver Hill."

"What's Silver Hill?" Jude asked.

"It's my family's plantation down toward Cherokee," he answered, wishing he could show the magnificent mansion to the little girl. "Actually, part of the acreage is in Alabama and part is in Mississippi."

"Can I see Silver Hill someday too?"

"We'll plan on it. My mother and sister and her family are coming for the summer. I'll invite you and Miss Maggie down to meet them. I have a niece named Rachel who's six. I think you two would like each other."

"Why do you think that?"

"Because she's an adorable little hellion destined to break a thousand hearts just as you are, my dear Judith."

"Am I your dear Judith?"

"Jude!" Maggie's shocked voice startled her sister, whose huge aqua eyes misted with tears.

"Here we are," Thayer said as Phineas stopped the cabriolet in front of an impressive red-brick house with a raised portico, four Doric columns, and winding stone steps on each side of the veranda.

"Oh, my goodness." Jude was in awe of the stately mansion, her eyes devouring the sight as Thayer assisted her from the carriage.

"Shall we go inside for a grand tour?" Thayer suggested, leading a willing Judith up the herringbone brick walkway.

Aaron disembarked and turned to help Maggie. Their eyes met and locked for a brief instant before she looked away. His big hands reached out for hers. When they touched, he groaned silently, longing to pull her into his arms.

"Before we join them," Aaron said as he helped her down, "I'd like to show you something."

"What?" Maggie knew her voice sounded weak, but she could not help it. The very nearness of this giant of a man was destroying her senses. She did not trust him.

"Over here," he told her, leading her a few yards up the road where another buggy stood. "This is Thayer's new phaeton. Isn't it a beauty?"

Maggie had to agree. The fashionable blue vehicle, with brass mounting and a skeleton rumble seat, boasted intricately curved iron body loops from front to rear. "It's lovely."

"Come on," Aaron suggested. "Let's try it out."

With no time to protest, Maggie was lifted and seated in the phaeton, a quick-moving Aaron at her side. "What do you think you're doing?" she asked him.

"I'm taking you for a Sunday afternoon ride, Miss Campbell." Aaron pulled the reins, and the horse began a slow trot.

"Stop this buggy right now!"

"Stay calm, Miss Maggie," Aaron said. "What if someone were to see you acting so unladylike?"

"That's what I'm afraid of," she said. "I'm afraid that someone will see us alone together and start a vicious rumor."

"Is that what you're really afraid of?" Aaron asked, looking at the truth evident in her vivid topaz eyes.

"I want to keep my good reputation. Being seen alone with you could very well ruin it."

"Is my own reputation so bad that being seen in my company is shameful?" Aaron hissed. How dare this little nobody be embarrassed to be seen with him?

"Please stop the buggy and let me out," Maggie demanded. How dare he treat her like this, as if her good name meant nothing to him. He was just a money-grubbing rogue who was trying to improve his lot by marrying a socially prominent widow.

"We'll ride to Sheffield," he said. "More people can see us that way."

"Why you blackhearted—"

"Now, now, Miss Maggie," Aaron said as he increased the buggy's speed. "A lady never uses such language."

"And you know all about ladies, don't you, Mr. Stone? Does Mrs. Arnold not object to all the ladies in your past?"

"Being a real lady herself, Mrs. Arnold would never speak of my past liaisons with the type of ladies you've mentioned." No, Aaron knew that Eunice could never bring herself to discuss a matter as delicate as his past sexual encounters, but not ill-bred Maggie Campbell. She was obviously jealous of both his past women and the Widow Arnold, and she certainly had no qualms about debating the issue.

"Then Mrs. Arnold may be a lady, but she is a foolish one." Maggie wanted to slap his face. She hated him and every "lady" he had ever bedded.

"How so?" Aaron asked, noticing several onlookers as the phaeton headed down Main Street.

"Any woman thinking of marriage should want to know everything about her future husband." Maggie wanted to know about Aaron, his past and present. She wanted to be able to understand the kind of background that had created a man so determined to keep his past a secret, even from his future wife.

As they rode out of town, Aaron nodded friendly greetings to several people whose curious stares riled Maggie even more. Aaron's determination to antagonize her outweighed his concern that this leisurely afternoon ride would soon be the talk of the town. He would have to think of some way to explain it to Eunice because he was certain word would reach her the very minute she returned.

"Did you have to go straight through town?" Maggie snapped. "And why did you call attention to us by speaking to everyone?"

Aaron did not reply, knowing his silence would further irritate his companion. He knew that the best way to win his bet with Thayer was to make Maggie so angry that she would keep her distance. An irate woman would be less seductive and easier to resist.

The short ride to Sheffield seemed endless to Maggie. She had never felt so miserable. The beautiful June Sunday had been ruined by Aaron Stone's ungentlemanly actions. She could not understand why he had bothered to whisk her away if all he wanted to do was make her angry.

"This is Sheffield, Alabama," Aaron announced, slowing the phaeton almost to a standstill.

Maggie looked down an endless stretch of wide dirt street lined with newly planted trees. She could see only one large building and a scattering of small structures, but it was apparent that construction was under way, and there was a sense of anticipation in the air.

"That's the Cleveland Hotel," he said.

"It looks rather odd, doesn't it? A three-story hotel and a row of little buildings practically all alone out there."

"Yes, I guess it does," he agreed. "But they built the place a couple of years ago for the engineering crew and potential investors. That row of small buildings beside it are offices and business houses."

Aaron motioned the horse forward, and they rode farther up the street, gradually leaving the wide, graded avenue to enter a small, bumpy road.

"Thayer and I have invested money in Sheffield, so we're expecting a bright future for this town. It's close to the Tennessee River, and, a few miles back in the hills, there's an abundance of iron ore. Then to the south, there's the Warrior coal fields."

"I plead ignorance, Mr. Stone," Maggie said. "Just what does that mean?"

Aaron smiled, thinking how unladylike it was to question a man about his business. "It means that Sheffield, England's namesake, should become a great industrial city."

"You have important plans for your future, don't you?"

"Yes, I'm a wealthy man, Miss Maggie, and I intend to be even wealthier. I've purchased an old plantation at Barton where I plan to live and raise fine sons and daughters."

"With the Widow Arnold as your wife?"

"Eunice Arnold is a genteel lady," he said as he maneuvered the buggy along the narrow path leading through a thickly wooded area. "She's everything I need in a wife."

Maggie felt a pain so intense shoot through her body that she had to fight back the tears. He wanted his wife to be a lady, and that was one thing Maggie knew she could never be.

"I want Judith to grow up to be a lady," Maggie said, disclosing one of her dearest wishes. "When the time comes for her to marry, I want her to have her pick."

"That's a fine ambition, Miss Maggie," Aaron said, stealing a glance at the beautiful woman beside him. The muted beams of tree-filtered sunlight struck her hair, turning it to flame. The fast, wind-blown ride had loosened it so that more strands hung free. Her creamy skin glowed with the vibrancy of youthful health. He had never wanted to touch a woman so badly in his entire life.

"I'm taking in sewing so I can have enough money to send her to Miss Anna Pybas's school." Maggie had to keep talking, had to keep thinking about Jude and Micah and their future because, otherwise, she would shatter into hundreds of little pieces. She must not think about Aaron married to another woman, loving another woman. "Wesley thinks it's a good start. He's offered to help me send Micah to Brother Larimore's in Florence, but I intend to find a way to come up with the money on my own."

"Do you have Micah's future planned too?"

"Only partly," she admitted. "I promised Pa to see Micah got an education and was set up in a profession. I kind of had the ministry in mind, but Micah is not too taken with that notion."

Aaron laughed heartily. He had never known anyone like Maggie Campbell. "And what about you? What plans do you have for yourself?"

"After I see to Jude's and Micah's futures, I want a home and a family of my own. I want a plot of land where I can grow vegetables, and flowers, and strong, healthy children."

"And what do you want in a husband, Maggie?"

"I want a good man who'll love me." She didn't dare look at Aaron because she knew the desire she felt for him was written plainly across her face. "I want a man I can work alongside, and talk to, and laugh with."

"You don't want money or social standing?"

"No. I'm a plain woman with simple, honest needs."

"You don't want much from this life, do you, Miss Maggie?"

"Oh, but I do," she corrected. "What I want is so rare that very few people ever get it. I want contentment, Mr. Stone."

Aaron could not reply. She had struck a nerve deep within him. Contentment. He had never been content and never expected to be. If he could marry Eunice and fulfill his personal dreams, he would be satisfied, but because he could never reconcile the past with the present, contentment was an unattainable goal.

"Before you, Miss Campbell, is the mighty Tennessee River." Aaron loved to come riding down here by the river. There was such a sense of peace pervading the place, gentle water rolling on and on for miles, tall trees and green grass, insect and bird songs, endless blue sky, and the smell of springtime rebirth.

"Oh, it's beautiful," Maggie said as he stopped the phaeton. All around them nature had painted a canvas of growing verdancy. It was like being cocooned in a lush green nest with an azure canopy.

"White Orchard is close to the river," he said, finally daring to look at her.

She turned, smiling at him. "White Orchard?"

"The old plantation I bought."

"What a lovely name."

"There's row after row of pear trees, and in the spring, acres of white blossoms cover the land."

"I'd love to see it." She spoke without thinking, and immediately wished back the words.

"You'd love it, Maggie." White Orchard was a place where a woman like Maggie could plant her flowers and have her vegetable garden, and raise beautiful children. His children. No. Damn her, he could not allow himself to think such thoughts. Eunice would be the mother of his children, but the image in his mind was not the Widow Arnold's slender frame. It was titian-haired Maggie Campbell's body swollen with his child.

"I . . . I'm sure I would. Perhaps . . . maybe you'll bring me some pears. I make awfully good preserves, and my pear pies are better than apple pies."

"I'll most certainly bring you all the pears you want." Aaron's big hand reached out slowly, his thick fingers hesitantly touching her folded hands as they rested in her lap. One finger began to rub methodically back and forth across the top of her hand.

"Thank you." Maggie was barely able to gasp the words. The moment he touched her, a tingling sensation passed through her, leaving her weak and trembling.

He should never have touched her. It had been a deadly mistake in judgment. He could feel the tiny tremors racking her body. His fingers gradually moved up her sleeve-covered arm, stopping at her long, lovely neck.

"Please don't," Maggie pleaded. Even though she longed for his touch, she could not allow his advances. She wanted him to go on touching her forever, but nothing would be forever with this man.

"Oh, Maggie," Aaron moaned as his hand moved up her neck to fondle the side of her face. "Why did you come into my life?"

Tears had formed in her eyes and were threatening to spill. She swallowed back the flow, pain clutching at her insides. "You mustn't . . ."

But the words died on her lips when his fingers touched her mouth and his other hand went to her waist, pulling her closer. Of their own accord, her lips kissed his fingertips, igniting an all-consuming passion within her. The touch of her moist lips against his flesh incited him to action, his mouth quickly replacing his fingers.

The first kiss was hard and hot and powerful. He was dying for the taste and feel of this woman. Dear God, nothing had ever been so good as having Maggie in his arms, his mouth on hers.

She flung her arms about his neck, responding with equal fervor, as wild for this joining as he was. Her body was racked with spasms of desire, as feverish excitement spiraled downward to the very core of her womanliness.

Each kiss became deeper and more urgent as his wet tongue thrust into her waiting warmth. He tasted faintly of cigar and lemonade, but potently of male muskiness. She strained closer to his huge body, her own tongue shyly responding.

When her tongue touched his, he groaned in his chest and crushed her to him with a force that rocked them both. His mouth spread kisses all over her face, his tongue drawing a moist line along her neck to her ear.

"I want to touch you," he whispered heatedly into her ear as his big hand moved over her breast, enfolding it gently. When he squeezed, she moaned. "So full and round and soft," he breathed against her neck.

"Aaron, we mustn't—" Somewhere in the back recesses of her mind, Maggie knew she should stop this before it went any further, but her surface senses refused to listen.

"Let me look at you, my love," Aaron pleaded, his fingers slowly loosening the front buttons of her dress.

As he unbuttoned the dress bodice, his mouth played with her ear, covering it with warmth, his tongue darting in and out, then circling it with tantalizing strokes. Maggie tried to stop his hand, but he brushed her efforts aside. "I promise I won't hurt you."

He eased the dress from her shoulders and lowered it to her waist. When she struggled against him, he pulled her back into his arms, pressing her swollen breasts against his granite-hard chest. The thought of looking at Maggie was driving him insane. He was being pushed beyond reason by his uncontrollable desire for this hot-blooded woman who smelled of female need and sweet springtime.

His mouth took hers again as his hand reached up to massage her breast, his thumb flicking slowly back and forth across her protruding nipple.

"Aaron." She breathed his name against his shoulder as he lifted her into his lap, and his hand moved inside her camisole, above her corset, to grasp her heated flesh.

"I want to see you and taste you." He feathered kisses across the top of her breasts, his tongue plunging into the valley between as his thumb continued its administrations to her nipple.

Maggie's body jerked with passion, her bottom squirming against his legs. She could feel the hard, swollen manliness against her buttocks, and his big hand clutched her by the waist, pushing her lower body up and down against his need.

Just as his other hand delved beneath the camisole, Maggie cried out and buried her face in his chest. "What are you doing to me? I feel so strange."

"Does it feel good, Maggie?" His voice was softly seductive. "Do you like my hand on your body?"

"Oh, yes!"

"My God, Maggie!"

Aaron was so absorbed in making love to the willing woman in his arms that he tried to ignore the disturbing noise rumbling in his ears. But as the sound of horses and riders grew louder, he forced himself to listen. Human laughter and animal hoofbeats broke loudly into the riverfront stillness.

"Not now," he cursed. "Dammit, not now."

"Oh, Aaron," she cried out. "Someone is coming."

He reached to help her pull up the bodice of her dress. She quickly redid the buttons as he moved her out of his lap and onto the seat. "I'm afraid your hair is a mess."

She tried to no avail to rearrange the mass of curls hanging around her shoulders. She couldn't think. She could barely react to the abrupt cessation of a passion like she had never known. All she wanted was to cling to Aaron, to beg him to love her.

"Leave it," he snapped angrily, guilt and frustration controlling him. He wanted Maggie Campbell with a fervor that could destroy them both and ruin all his plans for the future. He had to alienate her in order to keep her out of his arms.

"Well, I guess I lost my bet with Thayer," he told her flippantly.

"What?" Her mind hardly functioned enough to understand what he said. Her bewildered body was still in charge.

"Thayer bet me his new phaeton here that I couldn't spend an afternoon alone with you without trying to make love to you." Aaron had to hurt her in order to protect himself. "I guess he was right. A man can't resist a girl who's as hot for loving as you are."

The sound of flesh striking flesh reverberated through the peaceful quiet when Maggie's hand made bold contact with Aaron's cheek.

"Please take me home, Mr. Stone."

"Certainly, Miss Campbell."

Chapter 6

Maggie stood up and stretched to relieve the aching muscles in her sore back, closing her tired eyes to rest them. Sewing every day for the past week from six o'clock until after noon had put a strain on her young body. She was not only sewing for Mrs. Mobley and her twins, but for several neighbors and Aunt Tilly. Although the pay was meager and the work hard, Maggie was determined to continue for the sake of Jude's and Micah's educations.

She leaned her head back against the wall, groaning as she grasped the sides of her back and began massaging.

"Miss Maggie," Daisy called out from the hallway where she stood holding a tray. "I've got you somethin' to eat. It's done nearly two o'clock."

"Please bring it in, Daisy," Maggie instructed as she cleared a small, material-covered table. "Sit it down here."

"It ain't much," Daisy sighed. "I do declare I thought that Mr. Wesley was going to eat everything we cooked."

Maggie inspected the tray when the woman set it down, realizing that she was indeed quite hungry. "It looks good."

"Just beans and cabbage and corn bread. Mr. Wesley ate all the blackberry cobbler."

"This is fine. Thank you."

"Miz Gower's sending me down to the store for a few things. Is there anything I can get for you?"

"Not for me," Maggie said, sitting down to her meal. "But see if Uncle Chester will send some stick candy for Jude."

"Yes'am."

"Oh, by the way, you wouldn't be planning on stopping at Mr. Coleman's, would you?" Maggie picked up the glass of milk and drank slowly, enjoying the rich taste.

"Why, Miss Maggie, whatever do you mean?" Daisy laughed.

"Is he a good man, Daisy?"

"Yes'am," the blue-eyed servant girl said. "He's a fine man that wants a wife and children. He said Mr. Aaron done deeded him twenty acres of White Orchard land and plans on him overseeing all the farming done on that place."

"I see." Maggie could not bear to hear the man's name. She had neither seen nor heard anything of Mr. Stone in the five days since, angry and silent, they had ridden home from the river.

"Oh, my goodness," Daisy gasped. "I done nearly forgot. There's a lady downstairs to see you. A Miz Eunice Arnold. She come just as I started up there with your food. She says she wants to talk to you about sewing for her."

The last person on Earth Maggie wanted to sew for was the Widow Arnold, the future Mrs. Stone. She wondered if the woman had been told about the newsworthy Sunday buggy ride. No doubt, some eager friend had rushed to tell her the moment she returned from her trip.

"Tell Mrs. Arnold she may come up here to my sewing room."

"Yes'am."

"And Daisy."

"Yes'am?"

"If she stays too long send Jude upstairs."

"Yes'am." Daisy giggled as she exited the room.

Maggie had tried to put Aaron Stone and their disastrous last encounter out of her mind, but she kept reliving every moment. Some nights she had awakened in a cold sweat, her body hot and hungry for his touch. He had aroused desires in her that only he could fulfill.

"Good afternoon, Miss Campbell." Eunice Arnold stood in the doorway, serenely elegant in a dress of black taffeta with an underskirt and sleeves of blue and mauve silk print.

The woman had a way of always making Maggie feel plain and drab. "Hello, Mrs. Arnold. Won't you come in?"

"Yes, thank you." Eunice smiled, her expression sugary sweet.

"How can I help you?" *Flibberation!* Maggie decided the woman must spend a fortune on hats because perched on Eunice's perfectly coiffed head sat a Dolly Varden hat accented with pink roses and mauve ties. But having a wealthy father and being the widow of a rich man, Mrs. Arnold probably never gave a thought to money. The clothes she was wearing today would more than pay for Micah's school tuition.

"I've heard so much about you since Mother and I returned from Bailey Springs that I decided I simply had to drop by," Eunice enlightened her suspicious listener.

"And what have you heard about me?" *Do you know that Aaron drove me through Sheffield and down to a private spot near the river? Do you know that he started making love to me, and I let him? Do you know that I love the man you're going to marry?*

"That you're a marvelous seamstress, of course," Eunice answered, scanning every inch of her rival's body, but avoiding making eye contact.

"You want me to sew for you?"

"Possibly." Eunice came into the tiny sewing room that doubled as Maggie's bedroom. "While Mama and I were enjoying a delightful stay at the springs, Papa returned from New Orleans. He brought some lovely material for us. Some exquisite Chinese crepe and yards and yards of a very lightweight foulard."

"Do you already have a seamstress here in Tuscumbia?" Maggie inquired. "I wouldn't want to take your business away from somebody else."

"Mercy no!" the refined Mrs. Arnold gasped as she looked about the small room, spotting a meal tray and crinkling her nose at the offending smell of boiled cabbage. "I have a dressmaker in Atlanta and one in New Orleans, but for more simple things, I thought you might suffice."

"Do you think so?" *For more simple things, huh? You ... You bitch! Why are you really here? Are we talking about sewing, or are we talking about Aaron?*

"I realize how young and inexperienced you must be, therefore, I would never ask you to take on something complicated, something only an older and more experienced seamstress could handle."

"How kind you are to consider my lack of ability, Mrs. Arnold,"

Maggie said, the softness of her voice misleading. "But you have been told wrong if you think my being eighteen means I'm not able to compete with an older woman."

Eunice's platinum head snapped around, her brown eyes finally colliding with the candent glint in Maggie's golden stare. "You certainly would not dare to compare yourself to m-my other seamstresses?"

"No. But I do know my own worth. I know what I have to offer may not be as fancy as your New Orleans or Atlanta dressmakers, but I am reliable and less expensive, and my clothing is well made and fits the wearer perfectly."

"You certainly are confident for an illiterate sharecropper's daughter, Miss Campbell."

"As I said, Mrs. Arnold, I know what I have to offer." Maggie wanted to scream that her pa had been able to read and write as well as anybody, but she would not give this woman any more explanations. She knew it was unlikely that she would ever sew a stitch for the widow.

"Several of the ladies at the springs were wearing some charming little day dresses," Eunice said, as if no insult had been given. "Perhaps I could arrange to stop by tomorrow afternoon and bring the foulard and describe one of the simple dresses I want."

"If you wish."

"I don't suppose you've ever been to Bailey Springs, have you, Miss Campbell?"

"No."

"We went, of course, for Mama's health. Dr. Moody is convinced that there is great medicinal value to the water there. We would have remained for a longer stay to enjoy the string band and the excellent stables and the tenpins alley, if I hadn't been so eager to return to Aaron."

Maggie remained silent, simply staring boldly at the other woman.

"Of course, you're acquainted with my dear Aaron," Eunice said, emphasizing her close relationship with the man.

"Yes. I've made Mr. Stone's acquaintance."

"He's quite the ladies' man, you know?"

Maggie continued to stare silently, the beginnings of a smile forming on her lips. The widow was warning her off. That meant she was afraid of losing dear Aaron.

"Of course, men are expected to run a bit wild before settling down," Eunice said.

Is the explanation to herself or to me? Maggie wondered. "You're not worried about his other women?"

Eunice's high, shrill laugh betrayed her. "Mercy no. When the time comes, Aaron will marry a lady. I intend to be that lady. All the others are simply amusing little dalliances which mean nothing to him."

"You seem very sure."

"I am." Mrs. Arnold smiled, but her lovely face had lost its color, and there was tension in her gentle voice.

Maggie wanted the conversation ended. She conceded that she was no rival for this woman, but the longer Eunice Arnold talked, the more determined Maggie Campbell became to fight for the man they both wanted. "I'll see you tomorrow, then?"

"Oh, yes," the widow said. "But, no doubt, I will see you at the Brush Arbor meeting tonight?"

"Of course. Cousin Wesley will be speaking."

"A dear man, Brother Peterson. A fine catch for any young woman."

"Will Mr. Stone be with you tonight?" Maggie refused to discuss Wesley Peterson's desirability as husband material with this . . . this . . . lady.

"Unfortunately, Aaron has business he must attend to tonight. I shall be with my parents. I'm sure you have heard of my papa, Mr. Henry Waite?"

"Aunt Tilly speaks very highly of him."

"Well, yes." Eunice scanned Maggie, a patronizing sneer beneath her pleasant smile. "I must be off. Aaron is expecting me to stop by on my way home, and I wouldn't want to disappoint him."

"No, you wouldn't."

Mrs. Arnold turned to go. "Please continue with your . . . lunch. I can see myself out."

Maggie stood rigidly still, the anger within her reaching the boiling point just as she heard the front door slam closed. Her hand swept across her bed, sending pins, scissors, pattern pieces, and yards of material flying in every direction.

"Damn her," Maggie screamed through clenched teeth. "You haven't won yet, Mrs. High and Mighty Arnold."

The early night sky was alight with after-sunset colors. Orange and crimson melted into streaks of gold, and shades of pink cast an unearthly glow on the surroundings.

In a clearing, illuminated by numerous coal oil lanterns, stood a large arbor covered with boards and brush. Inside were split log benches and dirt floors spread with straw. The smell of earth and hay and newly cut wood permeated the air, and the sound of hundreds of human voices destroyed the quiet stillness of the woodland.

Back home in Grovesdale, Maggie's family had attended the yearly Brush Arbor meeting held after the crops had been laid by and before gathering time. Folks from miles around would come to hear the visiting preacher's long nightly sermons. Maggie wished Pa could be here, for he dearly loved a good revival.

Cousin Wesley had asked her to look her best tonight because he wanted to introduce her to Brother Osborne, the visiting minister who would be sharing the podium with him in these two-night services. She felt obligated, because of Wesley's many kindnesses, to try to please him.

Maggie watched as Aunt Tilly and Uncle Chester disappeared into the huge crowd milling around and about, slowly assembling in the arbor. She hugged the borrowed navy fichu about her shoulders. She was trying not to be nervous, but her navy-and-white gingham dress was new, the matching navy straw bonnet and wrap a loan from her aunt. She had never felt quite so dressed up in her entire life. If only Aaron could see how nice she looked. But it was Wesley who would compliment her appearance tonight.

"Looks like everybody in the whole town is here," Micah said, tugging on the stiff collar of his starched shirt.

"I haven't seen Mr. Coleman or Mr. Stone, either one," Judith said.

"Men like them have better things to do than listen to a couple of Bible spouters holler about hellfire and damnation," Micah told his young sister.

"Flibberation!" Maggie said. "They're the kind that need to hear a good sermon most."

"Look, there's Wesley." Jude waved at their cousin. "He's coming over this way."

Just as Maggie turned, Wesley took her hand. "Margaret, my dear. I'd like you to meet Brother Osborne."

The elderly, white-haired man smiled and shook hands with each Campbell in turn as they were introduced. "We have great hopes for Brother Peterson. He is such an inspired speaker, and his good works in this fair city are abundant."

"We're much beholden to Cousin Wesley," Maggie said. "His kindness has been a blessing to my family."

"I understand young Micah will be attending school in Florence with Brother Larimore this winter," the preacher said.

"Why, yes," Maggie said, noticing the frown marring her brother's boyish face. "That is, if I can save enough money to pay his tuition."

"Wesley said you were a hard worker," Brother Osborne said. "A commendable trait. Most helpful in a minister's wife."

Brother Osborne didn't seem to notice the sudden silence because he was quickly drawn away by others eager to meet the visiting evangelist. Wesley smiled, patted Maggie's hand, and whispered that he would see her later. Then he humbly followed his guest.

"Let's see if we can find a seat inside," Maggie said.

"Looks full to me," Jude said.

The three Campbells began making their way through the crowd, smiling, nodding, and speaking to new friends and acquaintances. Tuscumbia had proven to be a friendly town, most of the local citizenry warm and welcoming. Maggie had decided Aunt Tilly was right. If they worked hard and maintained spotless reputations, she had a chance of keeping her promise and securing a bright future for all of them.

"Maggie," a familiar voice called.

"Hello, Mrs. Mobley," Maggie greeted her best customer, a lady with whom she was forming a friendship.

"You look lovely tonight," the older woman told the younger.

"We've got matching dresses," Jude said, eager for attention.

"So I see," Alice Mobley laughed. "You look lovely too, Judith."

"Is that your husband?" Jude asked, pointing to the stocky, brown-haired man sitting up front near the preacher's podium. "I saw him with the twins."

"Yes, that is my Clarence. He's an elder, you know," Mrs. Mobley explained, a twinkle in her eye. "That's why he's in the amen corner."

Judith giggled but quieted instantly when Maggie nudged her with a well-aimed elbow.

"I must get to my seat." Alice Mobley, looking rather fetching in her gray-blue crepe dress and white lace shawl, gently squeezed Maggie's hand. "It was good seeing you."

After much searching, the Campbells found an empty space on the next to the last back seat, and were in place only seconds before the song leader began the first hymn, "Amazing Grace."

Only a few people had their own hymnbooks. Most of the congregation sang from memory, having recited the words countless times since childhood.

Maggie listened to the voices blending in unharmonious praise to the Lord, but the words and feeling were so real that the imperfection was made perfect. Her own sweet soprano joined in the singing as did Jude's and as did Micah's bass.

Song after song filled the night air, carrying the message of hope and salvation to all of God's creatures. The crowd, filled with the spirit, welcomed Brother Wesley Peterson as he stood before them praying fervently. Many amens were heard at the closing as silence filled the arbor when the good reverend began delivering his message.

Maggie became absorbed in the sermon, inspired by every word. Her concentration was broken by the feel of Jude's fingers thumping on the side of her thigh. Finally she glared at her sister, questioning her rudeness with a disapproving look. The little girl seemed to be examining the people seated several rows in front of them across the aisle. When Jude nodded her head in that direction, Maggie followed her gaze, and suddenly stiffened. There sat Eunice Arnold.

Maggie had known the other woman would be here, but she had hoped to avoid seeing her. No doubt, the stately older couple at her side were her illustrious parents, Mr. and Mrs. Henry Waite.

Maggie tried to look away, but she couldn't. Her curiosity overcame her better judgment. Wasn't it best to know one's enemies? Eunice appeared to be as perfectly groomed as always, radiating an air of wealth and breeding. Maggie decided that the color purple was very ugly. Of course, that decision had nothing to do with the fact that Mrs. Arnold's dress had a polonaise of lilac Indian pongee print with a basque and sleeves of purple silk. Nor did the fact that a purple silk bonnet adorned the other woman's head have anything to do with Maggie's sudden dislike of hats.

She became so absorbed in thoughts of the Widow Arnold that Maggie missed the end of Wesley's sermon and was able to grasp only bits and pieces of Brother Osborne's enthusiastic message. Eunice Arnold had the respect and admiration of every Tuscumbia citizen. Her family was considered one of the finest in the state, almost as prominent as the Colemans. She had been born and bred to be the perfect wife for a rich gentleman. She was beautiful, intelligent, cultured, and well educated.

How could a girl like Maggie compete? She possessed so little in comparison. A pretty face and a quick mind were hardly equal attributes. Maggie knew herself well, good qualities and bad. For some men, men like Wesley Peterson, she would make a better wife than Mrs. Arnold. But not for Aaron Stone. If he wanted a lady with social standing and a highly respected lineage, Eunice was indeed perfect. Maggie was a good woman capable of giving much to a man, but no one would ever be impressed by the fact that she was James Campbell's daughter.

After three hours of singing praises of the good word, the meeting closed to the strains of "Blest Be the Tie That Binds." Maggie sang, her voice steadily growing louder as she tried to clear her mind, praying to the Lord to forgive her for allowing her thoughts to stray to worldly matters.

When the crowd dispersed, Maggie decided not to try to make her way to Wesley. She could see him at home later. She knew that he and Brother Osborne would stay until the last sinner had left. Aunt Tilly had suggested that the Campbells stay for a while after the meeting and enjoy the fellowship of the congregation's other young folks while she and Uncle Chester rode on home. Maggie looked forward to the long walk on this warm June night. She wasn't used to having a buggy. Back home they walked nearly everywhere, using the wagon for hauling things and on long trips.

Questioning her siblings, Maggie found that they were as eager as she was to leave and enjoy the solitude and family companionship of their walk. Saying good nights and good-byes a dozen times over, they finally made their way past the densest areas of the crowd when Maggie spied Eunice Arnold, surrounded by the town's most prominent ladies. Staring a minute too long, Maggie caught the other woman's attention. Brown eyes clashed with gold ones as superiority fought with determination, the victor uncertain.

"Let's go." Micah tugged on his older sister's arm, drawing her out of her dazed state of mind.

Immediately the Campbells found the path to the road and headed for home. Carriage after carriage passed them, and many people on foot walked ahead of and behind them. The three of them talked and laughed and reminisced about back home in Tennessee and happy times when Pa had been alive.

A Whitechapel buggy pulled out from a small side road, the driver stopping directly in front of the Campbell family, riveting each person's attention to the trim black vehicle. Inching closer, Micah could see that the top was folded down, making the driver instantly recognizable.

"It's Mr. Stone," the boy said, surprised by the man's appearance.

Maggie's heart stopped. She couldn't breathe.

"Hey there, Mr. Stone," Judith said. "What are you doing here?"

"I was waiting for Maggie," Aaron admitted.

"Really?" Jude asked.

"Why were you waiting for Maggie?" Micah asked in a protective, brotherly way.

"It's all right, Micah," his older sister said. "You and Jude walk on ahead. I'll catch up after I talk to Mr. Stone."

"Let me drive you home, Maggie," Aaron said. "I think we need some time alone to talk, don't you?"

"I'll walk, thank you."

"I don't think you want your brother and sister to hear what I have to say."

Micah tensed, but did nothing when Maggie agreed. "You take Jude on home. I won't be long."

"Maggie?" her brother asked, questioning her judgment.

"Go on now," Maggie told him. "This is something I have to do."

Begrudgingly Micah walked on, pulling a wide-eyed Judith behind him as Aaron stepped down to assist Maggie into his buggy.

They both sat in silence for several minutes after the buggy started moving. She was so close to him that her shoulder kept bumping against his arm as they rode along. Maggie suspected that he had ended his business tonight with a drink because the smell of whiskey was strong in the air around him.

"Would you have any objections if Phineas were to marry Daisy?" Aaron asked.

"What?"

"Phineas wants to marry Daisy," he repeated.

"Oh, I see."

"Are you agreeable?"

"Of course," Maggie snapped. "If Daisy wants to marry him, it's fine with me."

"Phineas is a good man. He'll take good care of Daisy."

"And she'll make him a fine wife."

"I've never known Phineas to care so much for a woman. He's obsessed with her."

"She loves him, too. They should have a god life." Maggie envied Daisy. She had found the right man, and nothing stood in the way of their happiness.

"Phineas saved my life when I was just a boy," Aaron said. "I owe him a lot."

Maggie simply nodded, wondering if Aaron intended to share this special memory with her, but when he said nothing else, she remained silent.

"Maggie . . ."

"I saw Mrs. Arnold. She was at the Brush Arbor meeting tonight."

"Yes, I know."

"Why aren't you taking her home?" Maggie wanted him to deny any plans to marry Eunice, to deny any feelings for the other woman.

"I'll see Eunice tomorrow night. I'm taking her to a performance at the opera house. Tonight, I need to see you, to work things out between us."

"What things?"

"I owe you an apology for last Sunday." He knew that he owed her more than a mere apology. Few ladies would ever forgive a man for the type of behavior he had displayed.

Maggie said nothing.

"Everything that happened was entirely my fault," he said.

Still Maggie said nothing.

"I know you're an innocent young girl, and that I've taken advantage of your feelings for me."

Maggie gasped.

"Don't try to deny it," he warned. "I know you are as attracted to me as I am to you. I've never been so besotted with a woman before in my whole life."

"Oh, Aaron."

"I want you, Maggie Campbell. I want you so badly that I wake up at night in pain. You're all I can think about."

Maggie smiled and reached out to touch his big hand holding the reins. "Oh, Aaron. I feel the same way."

From the feel of his broad hand, she was aware of his entire body stiffening. "But it's wrong, Maggie. We can't act on our feelings. I like you too much to take advantage of you again."

"But—"

"I could never offer you marriage. You're a fine woman, and, if things were different—"

"I'm not good enough for you," Maggie cried. "That's what it is, isn't it?"

"No," Aaron denied. "God, no! I'm probably not nearly good enough for you. I'm a rich man's bastard, his beautiful, young mistress's illegitimate son."

"Aaron." Tears filled her eyes, her small hand covering his once again.

"I've just given you secret information about my past that half this town would kill to know." He wasn't sure why he had blurted out the truth that way. Very few people were ever privy to his past. "I trust you not to spread it around."

"No one will ever know from me."

"I'm very rich, Maggie," he said bitterly. "But all the money in the world can't buy a man respect. The right wife can."

"Eunice Arnold?"

"Yes, Eunice," he admitted. "She can give me everything I've always wanted."

"Yes, I can see that."

"I won't allow anything to stand in my way. Not even my desire for you, Maggie."

"I understand," she said. "If all you're willing to offer me is an affair, then, you'd destroy my dreams as surely as I'd destroy yours."

"I want us to be friends."

"Friends?"

"Avoiding each other will only make us want each other more," he reasoned. "If we can learn to be friends, then I think we can control these other feelings we have."

"Maybe you're right."

"I want you to spend the day with me tomorrow."

"What?"

"As friends," he told her. "I want to take you to see White Orchard. I know you'll love the old place." While forming this idea, he had never once thought about the fact that Eunice had never seen the plantation, even though he had bought it to be their home once they were married.

"Aunt Tilly would never allow it."

"Think of some way to get out of the house," he suggested. "Tell her you're going to a friend's house. That won't be a lie."

"Aaron, I don't think I can."

"It's important to me," he said, turning to face her for the first time during their conversation.

She thought she would drown in the depths of his emerald eyes, so hypnotic was his stare. "I'm not sure this is going to work, our being friends."

"Yes, it will. It has to, or I'll go insane." He wanted to take her in his arms, but knew she would say that friends didn't react to one another that way.

"I—"

"We will work on it," he said, stopping the buggy in front of the Gower house.

"This isn't another bet you've made with Thayer, is it?"

"God, Maggie," he groaned, pulling her into his arms. "Forgive me. Thayer was trying to be a friend, trying to prove a point. Sometimes he knows me better than I know myself."

It felt so right being in his strong arms that Maggie snuggled closer, her arms circling his neck. "This being friends isn't going to be easy, is it?"

"No," Aaron moaned, his lips hovering hesitantly over hers. "Damn, Maggie, what are we going to do?"

"We're going to be friends," she replied, touching his lips with a quick kiss. "Very good friends."

He returned the kiss, gentle and sweet. She responded, her mouth parting slightly as she whispered, "Kiss me good night, friend."

His mouth covered hers, and his tongue entered her welcoming warmth. Somewhere in the back of his mind, he knew that friends never kissed like this, but it didn't matter. Nothing mattered but loving Maggie.

She broke away, ending the heated kiss. Stunned, he gazed into her amber eyes, so filled with desire.

"Maggie . . ."

"Good night, Aaron. I'll try to get Aunt Tilly's permission to go with you tomorrow."

"Good night, Maggie. Send me word."

"Yes. I will."

She stood on the porch and watched him drive away, wondering if she had made the right decision. She knew Aaron Stone could never be just a friend to her because she loved him too passionately. She had to have all or nothing.

Chapter 7

"Where is Daisy?" Maggie asked, watching Auntie Gem place kindling wood in the cook stove.

"She's ... uh ... she ain't feeling none too good this morning, Miss Maggie." The old woman did not look up from her task.

"Is she sick?" Maggie asked.

"Yes'am."

"What's wrong with her?" Maggie's concerned voice sounded overly loud in the early morning quiet.

"She just ain't well. That's all."

"I'll go see about her myself," an aggravated Maggie said, turning toward the kitchen's back door.

"No, Miss Maggie, don't do that," Auntie Gem pleaded, reaching out a hand toward the door.

"Why not? What's wrong?"

"Oh, Miss Maggie," the old servant groaned. "She ain't out there."

"What do you mean? Where is she?"

"Gone."

"Gone?"

"Yes'am." Auntie Gem's worried black eyes met Maggie's, a plea for understanding radiating from them. "She left early. Before daybreak."

"Where did she go?" Maggie demanded. "And why?"

"She done gone over to the Coleman place."

"Has she run off to be with Phineas?" Maggie laughed. "Oh, Auntie Gem, you had me worried. I thought something was bad wrong."

"She ain't run off to be with Phineas," Auntie Gem whispered, looking about the room as if afraid of being watched. "She ran to him to get away . . ."

"To get away from what?"

The old woman, head bowed and voice barely audible, cut her eyes toward the inside door where Wesley Peterson stood staring at the two women. "She won't come back."

"Auntie Gem, tell me."

"I done said too much," the elderly servent said, returning to her chore.

"Good morning, Margaret," Wesley greeted her solemnly, a weariness in his gray eyes.

"Morning," she replied. "Wesley, something's happened to Daisy. She's run off to the Colemans'."

Maggie noticed the deathly pallor of her cousin's face and the quick exchange of glances between him and the old woman.

"Do you know something about her leaving?"

"My dear Margaret, why would I concern myself with the comings and goings of a servant girl?" Wesley asked sternly.

"There's something very wrong here, and I intend to find out what," she told him.

"No doubt, she's gone to her lover. They're all like that, you know. They have no control over their animal instincts."

Maggie looked at him as if she had never seen him before in her life. Even knowing he could be sanctimonious at times, she had never heard him sound quite so judgmental.

"They mate like dogs," he said. "Out where anybody can see them. They'll burn in hell, mark my word."

"Auntie Gem said she ran off to Phineas because she was scared," Maggie said, stunned by his outburst. "Why would she be afraid?"

"How would I know? Perhaps Auntie Gem can tell you."

They both turned to the old woman who continued working as if she hadn't heard a word.

"Auntie Gem?" Maggie said. "Please tell me."

The servant looked up, shaking her head. "I don't know nothing."

"I'll go to Mr. Coleman's and find out myself," Maggie told them.

"That would be highly improper," Wesley snapped.

"I'll ask Uncle Chester's permission. I know he hasn't left for the store yet."

"Margaret, you concern yourself much too much with that nigger when you should be thinking about your own reputation," he said bitterly.

"What are you talking about?"

"Did you think no one would tell me?"

"Tell you what?"

"That Aaron Stone brought you home from the meeting last night."

"And what if he did?" She knew that she had reason to feel ashamed, but refused to allow this man to humiliate her.

"One of my own flock came to me, in front of Brother Osborne, to relay the news."

"Mr. Stone and I are friends," Maggie told him. "There was nothing improper about our buggy ride."

"Mother will be greatly displeased."

"I'll talk to Aunt Tilly and explain as soon as I return from Mr. Coleman's."

"You mustn't go."

"I'm sorry, Wesley, but I must."

Phineas opened the door, his dark eyes void of emotion, his clothes rumpled, and his face unshaven.

"Where is she?" Maggie asked, walking past him into the foyer.

"She's in my cabin out back." The huge black man closed the door and turned to face Daisy's mistress.

"Why did she run off?" Maggie questioned. "Auntie Gem wouldn't say anything except she ran away because she was scared."

"She's afraid of somebody, Miss Maggie," he replied. "She's been beat something awful."

"Oh my Lord, no!"

"Auntie Gem helped her get over here. She was beat so bad she could hardly walk."

"Who did it, Phineas?"

"I don't know, Miss Maggie. She won't tell me nothing. She's scared half to death. Wouldn't even let me touch her at first."

"Have you called a doctor?"

"Me and Auntie Gem doctored her up," Phineas explained. "Ain't no bones broke."

"I want to see her."

"Yes'am," he replied. "I'll show you the way."

Maggie eased open the door to the two-room dwelling at the back of the Coleman mansion. The closed curtains prevented daylight from entering the darkened room where Daisy lay in a bed, her slender form huddled into a ball.

"Daisy?"

"Please go away, Miss Maggie," a soft, broken voice answered.

Maggie looked behind her, up into Phineas's face. "I'll see her by myself."

"Yes'am," he said as Maggie slowly made her way across the dimly lit room.

"Daisy, who beat you?"

"Go away, Miss Maggie."

Maggie inched closer to the bed, reached up to open the curtains of a nearby window, and took a good look at the golden-skinned woman.

"Oh, Lord," Maggie cried, staring at the woman's swollen face, bruised eyes, and cut lip. "You tell me who did this!"

"I didn't think I'd ever get beat again," Daisy mumbled.

"Who was it?" Maggie asked again, shock and anger consuming her.

"When your pa brought me to your farm, he said wouldn't nobody ever beat me again."

Maggie sat down on the bed, taking the woman's trembling hands. "Who beat you like this, and why did they do it?"

"Silas used to beat my ma all the time," Daisy said, her blue eyes glazed with remembered fear. "He was a mean old nigger. He took me my first time when I was just a little girl. Oh, Miss Maggie, I fought him. I tried to make him stop."

Maggie grasped Daisy's face, her fingers holding the woman gently. "Who? Are you talking about Silas or the man who beat you last night?"

"He killed my ma."

"I know, Daisy. I know Silas beat your ma to death."

"I told him I didn't want him to touch me," Daisy cried, huge dry sobs racking her body.

"What else happened?" Maggie feared the answer. "Did he do more than beat you?"

"He said I was the devil's seed," Daisy moaned. "He said I was evil, that all women are evil."

"Oh, Daisy."

"Don't tell Phineas. I'll tell him in my own good time."

"I want you to tell me who did this."

"It don't matter, Miss Maggie. Ain't nothing you can do about it."

"Surely, if I tell Uncle Chester and Wesley, they could see that the man is punished."

For several minutes Daisy remained quiet. "He was a white man."

"Oh." Maggie knew that there was nothing that could be done under the circumstances. Even if Daisy were to accuse the man to his face, no lawman in the state would arrest him.

"Miss Maggie, you be careful."

"Why do I need to be careful?"

"That's all I can say. You just be careful."

Puzzled, but understanding enough not to demand more of an explanation, Maggie replied, "All right, I will."

She sat on the side of Daisy's bed until the servant girl drifted off to sleep. When she opened the cabin door to leave, Phineas met her.

"She's asleep," Maggie said.

"I'll stay with her. I'm going to take care of her. If I ever find out who did this to her, I'll—"

"Hush, Phineas," Maggie warned. "Think what you will, but hold your tongue. I've heard that there are those who kill black men just for talking."

"Yes'am."

"I'll come every day," she told him. "If Daisy needs anything, send for me."

"Yes'am, Miss Maggie. I'll sure do that." Phineas entered the cabin, leaving Maggie standing alone in the backyard.

Deciding that there was no reason to reenter the Coleman mansion, Maggie looked for a path to the front of the house. Tall shrubbery on each side seemed to block any entry into the front yard, but a passageway to the side beckoned her attention. Following the opening, she soon found herself approaching the carriage house and stables where a tall, golden-haired man stood stroking a Tennessee Walker, soothing the animal with sweet words.

Maggie wanted to run back, but realized it was too late when Aaron turned around and smiled at her.

"Well, good morning, Miss Maggie. Have you come for our trip to White Orchard?" His smile warmed his roughly handsome face.

"I came to see about Daisy," she informed him, her heart beating wildly just from the sight of him.

"Would she tell you who beat her?"

"No," Maggie said. "But it was a white man."

"I thought as much."

"Why?"

"Daisy is a beautiful woman. A beautiful Negro woman. There are men who can't resist the temptation." Aaron patted the sleek stallion's neck.

"You know, don't you?"

"That she was raped as well as beaten? Yes, I suspected as much. So does Phineas. If he ever learns the man's identity, he'll probably kill him."

"He loves her very much, doesn't he?" Maggie hoped that love would help Daisy survive this horrible thing, this reminder of a nightmarish childhood and an inhuman stepfather.

"Phineas is a man who loves well and hates well," Aaron said.

"I'm leaving her in good hands then. I have to get home. I have sewing to finish before going to the meeting tonight."

"Don't go," he said, reaching out to take her small hand in his. "Stay and let me take you to see White Orchard today."

"I can't. Aunt Tilly would never give her permission."

"Don't ask. I'll send a messenger to say that you're staying here with Daisy all day. No one need know."

"Wesley knows you brought me home from the meeting last night. He was very displeased. I'm sure he'll tell Aunt Tilly."

"He's jealous."

"Yes, I know." Maggie pulled her hand free, moving close to the black horse. "Is he yours?"

"Thayer's. Mine are already at White Orchard."

They both stroked the horse, their fingers touching, their eyes meeting.

"I want today with you, Maggie Campbell," he confessed. "If we never have a time alone again, I want today."

"It would be wrong."

"Yes, it probably would."

"Wesley will be hurt. Aunt Tilly will never forgive me."

"They need never know. We'll leave now, and go by a back road until we get out of town."

"I can't." Even as she was refusing, Maggie's heart was relenting. She wanted to spend the day alone with Aaron. She wanted to see his new home.

"I'll send a boy with a message saying that you can't leave Daisy until her fever breaks."

"What fever?"

"The fever that will keep you here, but will keep Mathilda Gower and the good Reverend Peterson away."

"Oh, Aaron," Maggie gasped. "What if Daisy were to need me while I'm gone off with you?"

He brought her hand away from the horse and upward to his lips, kissing it tenderly.

"Daisy will sleep all day and all night," Aaron said. "I sent to Dr. Cooper for some morphine. Phineas has probably already given it to her."

"Morphine?"

"She was badly beaten. She's been in terrible pain."

"Who would do such a thing?"

"Put it out of your mind," Aaron advised, coming around the horse to stand directly in front of Maggie. "The time may come when Daisy will tell us. Until then, there's nothing we can do except take care of her."

"She warned me to be careful, but wouldn't say anything else. Why should she do that?"

Aaron pulled the trembling girl into his arms as she began to cry. She snuggled into his comforting embrace and allowed the tears to flow freely. His big hand stroked her as gently as he had the stallion, his whispered words soothing her.

"Don't be afraid, sweet Maggie."

"It's . . . it's someone I know," she wept. "It's someone I'd never suspect, isn't it?"

"Probably," he agreed. "But whoever he is, he'd think twice about attacking a white woman."

She stood there, enfolded within his strength, safe and secure, a woman with the man she loved. "Send the message. I . . . I want to go with you to White Orchard."

Aaron's Whitechapel Buggy gleamed a shiny black in the bright morning sunshine, the silver mountings reflecting the light like polished mirrors. The soft summer breeze caressed Maggie's face, blowing tiny strands of titian hair into her eyes. The horse galloped speedily down Memphis Pike, jostling the passengers within the buggy as it moved mile after mile down the unpaved roadway.

Maggie felt so alive, so free, and so happy to be at Aaron's side. She wanted this day, even if there could never be another. Even if he married Eunice. She needed the memory of one perfect day spent with the only man she would ever love.

Aaron ran his fingers through her hair, loosening the pins holding it in place. He smiled as the fiery mass began to fall free. She shook her head, a swirl of red curls circling her face. She laughed, loving the feel of her long hair flying about her.

"I love it down, Maggie mine," Aaron said.

She laughed again, moving closer to his side.

He adored the way she laughed, so honestly, so spontaneously. The sound excited him. He knew what a passionate woman she was, a woman capable of experiencing life through all her senses. He thanked God for this one day alone with her.

"Is it a long way to White Orchard?" she asked.

"It'll take a few hours to get there. It's past Barton, not too far from Cherokee, near the river."

"Oh, Aaron," she sighed. "Near the river?"

"There's nearly two hundred acres, Maggie. It's near a lot of things."

"I love the river," she told him. "Grovesdale wasn't far from the river. Sometimes Micah and I would watch the steamboats. I always wanted to ride on one. So did Micah."

"I own a steamboat."

"Really?"

"Really," he said. "I promise you a ride on her someday."

"Where is it now?"

"On its way to Chattanooga. When it returns, we'll board her and come downriver to Chickasaw, disembark, and take a buggy ride to Cherokee, and then on to White Orchard."

It was only a dream, one they would share today, but one that would never become a reality. She would never ride on Aaron's riverboat or come again to see his plantation. Today was all they would ever have.

"What's her name, your steamboat?"

"The *Chattanooga Belle*."

"The *Chattanooga Belle*," she repeated.

Maggie looked out at the world around them seeing that it was mainly farmland, knee-high cotton everywhere. She loved the sight of the growing crops, of the fields, bursting with life. Even knowing that they were moving away, she had planted flower seeds and had been able to see them break through the earth before they left Grovesdale. She had longed to dig up her ma's red rosebush and bring it with her. Instead, she had picked a rose and pinned it to her dress. Aaron must have loved the land as much as she did if he planned to make his home in the country instead of in town. She wondered how the Widow Arnold would like living so far away from the mainstream of Tuscumbia society.

As they rode along, Maggie could see a scattering of vast woodland areas filled with tall cedars and pines, and hickories, as well as maples and oaks. The red clay earth gave way to richer soil in many places, but the russet dirt was predominant along the path they were traveling. She couldn't help but think of what a beautifully colored dye could be made from that clay.

In the distance she saw a wagon stopped on the roadside, a short, stocky man standing by the horse.

"Are they in trouble?" Maggie asked.

As they drew nearer, Aaron replied, laughing, "Not anymore."

Out from behind a thick cluster of bushes a few yards from the road ran three children, the boy hastily buttoning his breeches.

Maggie smiled as she watched the children run toward the big farm wagon where their mother sat on the seat holding a tiny infant in her arms.

"Good morning, Mr. Gibbs," Aaron called out. "How are you doing?"

"Doing well, Mr. Stone," the man responded, a warm smile appearing under his reddish-brown mustache. "I don't think you've met Mrs. Gibbs, have you?"

"No sir. I haven't had the pleasure," Aaron said, nodding courteously to the pretty, black-haired woman who simply smiled in reply.

"And these are our children," the proud papa introduced. "My eldest son, Eddie, and my youngest, Walter, there with his mother. The girls are Bessie and Susie."

"You've a fine family, Mr. Gibbs," Aaron assured the gentleman. "May I introduce Miss Maggie Campbell."

"Ma'am," Mr. Gibbs said.

Maggie exchanged a smile with Mrs. Gibbs as her husband helped his offspring into the back of the wagon. Waving good-bye, the wagon's passengers headed toward Tuscumbia as the buggy's occupants moved westward toward Cherokee.

"How do you know Mr. Gibbs?" Maggie asked.

"He lives at Barton. He has a big farm there. He runs a gristmill and a cotton gin out toward Mount Mills. He's one of the most respected men in the area. His wife's uncle, Dr. Chisholm, is a dentist in Tuscumbia."

"Do you know everybody in Colbert County?"

"I know everybody of any importance in the whole state, my dear Miss Campbell."

White Orchard had been built in a broad, fertile area on the northern edge of a two-hundred-acre plantation. The sight of the enormous

Greek Revival house took Maggie's breath away. On a small rise overlooking the Tennessee River, the white mansion, with her six square pillars and a complete upstairs veranda, stood regally against a backdrop of blue sky and green trees. Crepe myrtles and flowering almond bushes grew in profusion, undoubtedly the work of a long-dead gardener.

"It's beautiful," Maggie sighed, closing her eyes and breathing deeply. The smell of the earth and river and flowering plants assailed her senses.

"What do you want to see first?" Aaron asked, helping her down from the buggy.

"I don't know," she said. "Let me just peek inside, then I'd like to see the pear orchard. We can come back to the house for a complete tour later."

"I'll show you the hall and the front parlor first. They're the only rooms completely finished."

"All right," she said, her arm entwined in his as they stepped onto the veranda and entered the house.

They stopped momentarily in the spacious central hall where a crystal chandelier hung overhead and a spiral, hand-carved staircase rose to the second floor.

"There are fourteen big rooms in here," Aaron bragged. "Can't you just hear the sound of children filling this house?"

"Oh, yes," Maggie said. If only she could give him those children and fill this house with her love.

"Come see the parlor," he coaxed, leading her forward. "The ceiling is sixteen feet high, and the mantel over there is black marble imported from Italy."

The parlor extended the length of the house, the center broken by two freestanding columns that supported three broad arches.

Maggie had never been in such a huge house. She suddenly felt very out of place.

"What do you think of the room?" Aaron wanted her to like his house.

She looked around, noticing the white velvet carpets embossed in pink flowers. She was afraid to step, afraid her feet would soil their perfection.

"It's . . . it's magnificent." What else could she say? It would be a perfect house for a woman like Eunice Arnold who was used to such splendor.

"Do you like the parlor suite?" he asked. "It's carved rosewood."

Maggie's eyes moved over each elegant piece of furniture upholstered in satin damask. Aaron, standing behind her, put his arm around her body, pulling her back against him. She had to keep reminding herself that this man belonged to another woman, a woman whose presence was already alive in the quality furnishings of the parlor.

"It's all beautiful," she said, turning in his arms. "Let's go outside and walk. I want to see the grounds, especially the orchard."

He responded to her request by immediately escorting her outside, and, hand in hand, they began walking.

"The man who built this place had a wife with a passion for pear trees, so he planted an entire orchard for her. She named the place."

"Oh, Aaron, smell the air. Look at the trees and flowers. Everything grows here."

"Maggie. Maggie. You make me feel so alive."

"We are alive, Aaron. Feel how alive." She twirled around and around, the blue sky turning into a mass of blue cotton before her dizzy eyes. Laughing, she fell into Aaron's strong arms, her lips boldly seeking his. Lifting her from the ground, her feet dangling, he returned her sweet kiss.

"Show me the orchard now," she said as he set her back down on her feet.

The orchard was only a short distance behind the house, so they walked, Maggie stopping now and then to touch a tree, to listen to a bird, to look at a wildflower, to smell the aroma of country life.

"It's more beautiful than the house," she told him as they entered the orchard, tree after tree after tree planted in perfect rows. Like leafy green pyramids, the trees peaked into the clear, blue sky, a few late blossoms scattered among the budding fruit.

"You love the earth, don't you, Maggie?"

"I'm a country girl, a farmer's daughter."

"This place is perfect for you," Aaron said. "It's as if it's been waiting for you." He had furnished the parlor with Eunice in mind, but it was Maggie's face, her wide amber eyes, stunned by its elegance, that he would always see there.

"The land perhaps," she said, "But that house is far too fancy for me."

"You're fancier than you think you are." He pulled her into his arms, his lips brushing her forehead.

"No, I'm not. I'm not fancy at all."

"Then I don't want fancy," he said. "I want you."

"Aaron?" She pulled backward, trying to free herself from his embrace, but he held her securely within the strength of his arms.

"I'll stop whenever you say, but please, Maggie, let me love you just a little." His mouth covered hers, wild and sweet and hungry for loving.

Still capable of rational thought, Maggie did not resist. She told herself that she would never be with him again, never know the feel of his body, the taste of his mouth. Today was all she could have, and she intended to take it.

The kiss continued, growing deeper and harder and hotter. Her arms circled his neck as he lifted her into his arms, and their lips clung together as they looked into each other's eyes.

"I won't hurt you, Maggie mine," he reassured her as he knelt, lowering her to the ground beneath a large pear tree.

She could feel the grass and leaves covering the hard earth beneath her, and she gloried into the feel of his big body hovering over her. He rolled her to her side as he lowered himself beside her.

"You're so beautiful."

"So are you," she whispered, her fingers touching his face, stroking his thick eyebrows.

One finger moved lovingly down the length of his nose, slowly circling his full lips, stopping to slip inside as his mouth opened. The moment his lips closed around her finger, Maggie began to ache with longing, and, when he began gently sucking, a tingling sensation burst within her.

She looked at his handsome face, so hard and strong, his deep green eyes smoldering with desire. She ran her hand down his throat to the open collar of his linen shirt, her fingers plucking at the dark golden hair she found there. He took her hand, showing her that he wanted her to unbutton his shirt. She obeyed. His sweat-dampened chest begged for her touch, the swirls of masculine hair beckoning for her fingers.

"Touch me," he pleaded, his eyes devouring her.

Her hand rested on his hard chest. His breathing quickened when her slender fingers glided through his hair. Maggie loved the feel of him. She wanted to go on touching him forever. She wanted to know how he would taste. He smelled of sweat and tobacco and sunshine. When her lips touched his naked chest, she heard a tortured groan erupt from within him, and then suddenly, she found herself flat on her back, a hungry, aroused giant leaning over her.

His mouth took hers with a feverish urgency that had her emitting tiny sounds of pleasure. His mouth felt so right, as if it had been created for the sole purpose of kissing her. The memory of his other kisses flooded her brain heating her with demanding need.

His tongue touched hers, coaxing a response. She could feel the wild beating of their hearts as his chest pressed down on her breasts. Wantonly she began to explore his mouth, imitating his caresses.

Aaron's body was trembling when he ended the kiss. He gazed down at her beautiful face. He had never seen a woman as exquisite as Maggie Campbell with her fiery red hair falling about her shoulders and her yellow cat-eyes staring up into his with such yearning.

His big hand slowly unbuttoned the bodice of her faded blue dress, untied the ribbons of her cotton chemise, and pushed it apart to reveal the high, round mounds of her breasts. The nipples, still hidden beneath the chemise, strained against the muslin. Aaron lowered his head, taking her into his mouth. Maggie jerked convulsively, mewing like a hungry animal as he suckled harder, his hand coming up to clasp the other breast.

Wild with need and impatient with the barrier of her clothing Aaron ripped the chemise apart, exposing Maggie's breasts fully to his view. Her chest rose and fell with the force of her ragged breathing tantalizing him beyond endurance. Both of his big hands reached out, covering her firm flesh, and Maggie moaned.

He buried his head between her breasts, his mouth seeking and finding one jutting pink diamond as his hands moved under her hips and pulled her into the urgency of his lower body. The taste of her warm sweetness was driving him wild.

"Oh, Maggie, you taste like heaven."

She couldn't reply. Feeling helpless against her own womanly urges, she simply lay there letting him derive his own pleasure while giving her such delicious enjoyment. She was so lost in a sensual haze that the thought of right or wrong had left her mind. All that mattered was loving this man and being loved by him.

"I want to love you," he groaned against her neck as his fingers replaced his lips on her body. "I've never wanted anything so much."

His lips joined hers, hot and hard and demanding, his body rubbing rhythmically against hers as she squirmed beneath him. She wanted something, needed something that she knew instinctively he could give her. She put her arms around him, her hands clutching the tense muscles of his back, fingernails raking his flesh, urging him on.

Aaron had bedded women for years, had known passion and fulfillment, but nothing as all consuming as this crazed desire he felt for his wild Maggie. If only Eunice could set him afire this way. If only she inspired such lust. If only she responded to him so amorously. How would he ever be able to settle for a timid, lukewarm relationship with the woman he planned to marry after knowing ecstasy with Maggie? Once he had bedded her, he'd never be able to give her up.

"I'll never be able to give you up when I marry Eunice." The words were a mere whisper against her swollen lips, Aaron unaware that he had spoken.

When his mouth sought hers again, she turned her head, avoiding his kiss. He felt the tenseness in her body and sensed her withdrawal.

"Maggie?" Dear God, had he given voice to his thoughts? Had she heard him?

"Please, Maggie."

"Let me go!" she hissed. "Get off of me now." The pain was almost more than she could bear. She had yielded to this man, forgetting that he intended to wed another. She felt dirty and ashamed.

Aaron rolled to his side, releasing her. He lay there watching her get up and rearrange her clothing, buttoning her dress and brushing away the grass and leaves clinging to her skirt. He was having a difficult time calming his raging senses, his aching male body.

Maggie left him lying under the trees in the pear orchard while she ran back to the house. Finding the buggy, she jumped in and motioned the horse to a fast pace.

Aaron came around the side of the mansion just in time to see the buggy going out of view, far up the country road. Realizing that she could easily get lost this far away from town, he rushed to the stables, hoping to find one of his horses inside instead of in the pasture.

Maggie had no idea where she was going. She simply had to get away from Aaron Stone. She loved him, but she hated him. He wanted her, perhaps even loved her, but not enough to give up his dream of marrying the Widow Arnold in order to gain respectability. He had no right to think that he could use them, expecting their love and devotion when he would be cheating them both. How could she have been so stupid? She had come so close to ruining her own life and destroying any chance for a good future for Micah and Jude. She had to get away from Aaron and stay away from him. He was far too dangerous to ever be alone with again.

When Aaron finally caught up with Maggie, he saw that she had stopped the buggy near the covered bridge crossing Buzzard Roost Creek. She was sitting there with her head in her hands, her body jerking with sobs. The sound of her crying tore at his heart. He had never wanted to hurt her, but he had. He had allowed his own selfish passion to overwhelm his sense of morality. Maggie Campbell was an innocent young girl who loved too well, too honestly. He knew now that they had no choice. Their only hope was to stay away from one another.

Maggie looked up when she saw Aaron stop the big palomino and dismount. They looked at each other, her eyes red and puffy from crying, his crazed with worry and regret. He hitched his horse to the back of the buggy and climbed up to sit beside her.

"I'll take you home," he said, grasping the reins.

"We can't be friends," she told him.

"I know."

"You mustn't ever try to see me again."

Chapter 8

Maggie hoped that she could slip in the back way, through the kitchen, and find Auntie Gem before facing Mathilda Gower. She knew her aunt would be furious because she had supposedly spent the day caring for a sick servant when she had so much unfinished sewing to do.

She did not want to talk to anyone, but knew that the old black woman would have to be her contact to Daisy. She could not return to the Coleman house and risk seeing Aaron again.

The buggy ride back to Tuscumbia had been a slow torment, both of them silent the entire trip. When they arrived at the Colemans', Aaron tried to talk to her, to apologize, but she left quickly, refusing to listen. What had happened today had happened, and there was nothing she could do to change it. If there had been any doubt as to whether she could ever pass for a lady, her actions at White Orchard had ended them. She had acted like a trollop, allowing the immoral instincts of her body to get the better of her. At first, she had felt dirty and ashamed, but now she realized that those feelings were a result of Aaron's treatment of her and not from any regret at her own wanton actions. She loved Aaron Stone and had wanted to express that love in the most natural way.

"There she is," Mathilda said, her fat body blocking the hallway as Maggie approached. "About time you got home."

"I'm sorry I was gone so long," Maggie said sincerely. "I sent a messenger."

"You sent a lie!" Dark and enormous, his gray eyes icy cold, Wesley Peterson stood behind his mother.

"What?" Maggie could see that mother and son had no intention of letting her pass.

"You have not been at the Colemans' nursing that nigger gal," Mathilda spit the words out as if they were contaminated. "You were gone off with Aaron Stone. God only knows where."

"And doing God only knows what," Wesley said, his jowled face flushed with anger.

Maggie had no idea how they had learned the truth, but she knew it meant her damnation. She had to think of some way out of this mess. She had lost Aaron, she could not lose everything else, too. "Please, Aunt Tilly, let me explain?"

"How can you possibly explain such deplorable behavior?" the older woman asked. "Wesley has tried his best to defend your unladylike actions time and again, but even he cannot condone this."

"Please," Maggie cried. "I didn't . . . we didn't . . ."

"Have you no shame, girl?" Mathilda roared, her pudgy finger shaking in Maggie's face. "You have disgraced us and humiliated poor Wesley."

"No, please. I haven't," Maggie told them.

"To think that my son was considering the possibility of proposing marriage to you," Tilly moaned, clutching at her heart. "What ever will Brother Osborne think when hears of this?"

"But how . . . who?" Maggie wanted to know who had seen them and given away their secret.

"I'm afraid I had to be the bearer of these sad tidings," Eunice Arnold said, moving into view as Wesley and his mother moved aside to allow the handsomely attired widow to pass. "I felt it my Christian duty to let these good people know that they have a harlot living in their midst."

Maggie, stunned by the woman's presence and venomous words, stood silently, trying to make sense of what was happening to her.

"You see," Eunice smirked, "the whore is no longer denying her sins."

"Don't call my sister a whore!" Micah Campbell's deep voice startled everyone.

Maggie leaned on her brother as he came from behind to stand by her. "Jude?"

"I made her stay in the kitchen," Micah whispered, placing a strong arm about his sister's shoulder. "We heard the shouting when we came in."

"You've thrown yourself at Aaron since the day you met him," Eunice said. "I suspected the truth about you from the first when I caught you in Aaron's room at the Parshall House."

"You're jealous of Maggie," Micah said. "You're afraid you're going to lose Mr. Stone. You've got sense enough to know any man would pick her over you if he had the chance."

"How dare you," the widow gasped.

"You are simply making matters worse," Wesley told the boy. "Your sister's own actions have condemned her."

"Maggie's done nothing wrong," Micah said.

"Look at her," Eunice said. "She looks well used."

Maggie could just imagine how she looked, her hair a mass of tangles, her dress rumpled and grass-stained. She stepped forward, her topaz eyes afire, the blood pounding through her veins as she realized the truth. "You are jealous. You think I've had what you so obviously want."

Eunice Arnold, in a very undignified manner, reached out and slapped Maggie squarely across the face. "You whore!"

Without thought, acting simply on instinct, Maggie returned the slap full force, practically knocking her opponent to the floor.

Staggering from the force of the stronger woman's blow, Eunice screamed, "He only wanted to bed you as he would any whore. You mean nothing to him. Less than nothing. Aaron will marry me. He wants a lady for a wife, not some dirty farm girl who runs around in rags and spreads her legs for any man who wants her."

Maggie moved so quickly that she knocked Eunice to the floor and was on top of her before anyone realized what had happened. Unaccustomed to fighting, the elegant Mrs. Arnold found herself at a great disadvantage as her attacker began an onslaught of clawing, scratching, hair pulling and repeated slaps.

"Dear Lord." Mathilda swooned in a near faint, her son catching her swaying body. "Do something, Wesley, before Maggie kills her."

But Wesley did nothing except hold his mother, his silver eyes alive with some inner demon as he watched the two women struggling, a strange smile curling his lips when he saw a trickle of blood on Eunice's lip.

Micah grabbed his sister from behind and hauled her battling body off of her nearly unconscious rival. "Maggie. Maggie!"

Gradually Maggie calmed, but trembled with anger and frustration and fear. It frightened her to think that she was capable of such hatred, that she could brutalize another human being. She hated Eunice Arnold, and, for a split second, had wished her dead.

Wesley released his mother long enough to help a badly disheveled Eunice. Standing shakily, she glared at Maggie. "You'll pay for this," she warned as Wesley assisted her.

"You pack your bags, girl," Mathilda bellowed, her fat face splotched an unseemly pink and white. "I want you out of this house tonight!"

"I'll go," Maggie said. "I'll be glad to go."

"If Maggie goes, we go too." Judith stood in the kitchen doorway, tears streaming down her face.

"No," Maggie cried. "You and Micah must stay. Aunt Tilly wouldn't punish you for what I've done."

"The children can stay. They're far better off under my care and away from your sinful influence," Tilly informed them.

Eunice turned and walked down the hall to the front door, stopping after she stepped onto the porch. "I can promise you that no decent person in this town will have anything to do with you after today."

"You go to hell!" The condemnation rumbled from Micah's mouth.

"If you leave, I'm going with you," Jude whined, running into her sister's arms.

Maggie held Judith tightly, trying to soothe the child. "You and Micah have to stay here. Uncle Chester and Cousin Wesley can help Micah get some education and a job. And Aunt Tilly can help you become a lady."

"I won't stay here without you," the little girl cried. "I'll go find Thayer Coleman. He'll help us."

Judith pulled free of her sister's hold and ran into the kitchen. When she heard the back door slam, Maggie issued an order. "Go after her, Micah, before she gets into trouble. I'll go up and pack. We'll talk when you get back."

"I'll get her," he said. "But when we get back, we'll decide what to do as a family."

"All right. But for now, go find Jude."

Maggie walked past her open-mouthed aunt and a haughtily disapproving Wesley, rushing upstairs to her room, slamming the door behind her.

She looked around the small room that she had come to love during the past month, her eyes lingering on the lock-stitch sewing machine sitting near the window, a piece of pink organdy lying on the treadle where it had fallen. One step at a time, Maggie moved about, looking and touching, trying to come to terms with leaving.

Everything that had happened was her own fault. From the moment she looked into Aaron Stone's green eyes, the world had faded away. Although she had been unwillingly attracted to him in Chattanooga, she had had the good sense to fight her feelings, but circumstances and her own lustful weaknesses had led her astray.

She had destroyed all her hopes and dreams by acting impulsively. Micah and Jude would have to stay on with the Gowers even though their chances of having a good future were practically nonexistent, thanks to her stupidity. People would not soon forget that they had an older sister with the morals of an alley cat.

Maggie had no idea where she would go or what she would do. She would be forced to use her meager savings to pay for a place to stay until she could find work. She wondered if Mrs. Mobley would be willing to help her find a position somewhere, but doubted if any lady would want to associate with her once the word of her downfall had spread through town. No doubt, the Widow Arnold would see to that.

Just when she had begun to believe that she would be able to keep her promise to Pa, her whole world fell apart, leaving her with nothing, and with no one to turn to.

Aaron tried his best to keep up his side of the conversation with Eunice as Phineas drove them to the opera house for a performance by a traveling minstrel group, but his mind was on another woman, a woman whose tear-stained face was forever etched on his heart. He felt like a cad for the way he had treated her, although he had had no intention of seducing Maggie. He had wanted them to be friends, had hoped they could work together to overcome the unwanted attraction they had for one another. An experienced man like he was should have known how dangerous it could be to share a day alone together.

Maggie Campbell's red-haired beauty allured him to the point of madness. Just being near her made his body grow hard with need. If only he could react to Eunice like that. But the widow's serene, blond loveliness left him cold. Surely, once they were married, and she allowed him a husband's privileges, he would want her as passionately as he did his fiery farm girl.

Phineas stopped the carriage directly in front of the two-story red-brick building that housed the local opera house on the upper level and the post office on the first floor. Light poured from the small-paned windows upstairs, and a group of young dandies had congregated on the white columned porch.

Eunice, her slender hand reaching for Aaron's, smiled down at the handsome man whose big body strained against the confinement of his dark blue suit as he helped her from the cabriolet, her peach satin dress shimmering in the soft lamplight. No sooner had Aaron assisted his date from the carriage than Thayer Coleman, dressed dapperly in a charcoal-gray frock coat and breeches, approached him.

"Aaron." His friend placed a hand on his shoulder.

Eunice eyed the man suspiciously, her slender fingers tightened their grip on Aaron's arm.

"Well, good evening, Thayer," Aaron greeted the other man. "I didn't expect to see you here tonight. I thought you had other plans."

Aaron knew good and well that Thayer had intended to have a high old time at Loretta's tonight, drinking, playing poker, and bedding one of the establishment's soiled doves. He couldn't imagine why the man was here unless he was deliberately trying to ruin the evening Aaron had planned with Eunice.

"My plans were changed when little Miss Judith Campbell came strolling into Loretta's with her big brother chasing after her," Thayer said without a trace of humor.

Aaron laughed. "My God, man, you're irresistible even to babies."

"Aaron, dear, we're going to miss the opening if we don't hurry," Eunice said. "I'm weary of hearing about that bunch of Tennessee trash Mathilda Gower took into her home."

"Eunice!" Aaron said. "What's wrong with you? I've never heard you speak so unkindly about anyone."

"We need to talk. Now," Thayer told the other man.

"I will not stay and listen to this." Eunice's voice had become shrill with bitterness. "I see Cousin Edmond and his wife. I shall be with them when you care to join me."

With that said, Eunice walked away, the rustle of satin echoing in Aaron's ears. "Eunice . . ."

"Let her go for now," Thayer said, nodding and smiling courteously in greeting to several friends as they passed the two men on the street corner. "We, my friend, have a problem."

"What the devil are you talking about?" Aaron was totally bewildered by Thayer's unexpected presence as well as Eunice's uncharacteristic behavior.

"Jude and Micah are in my carriage across the street," Thayer told his friend. "I'm taking them home with me for the night, but I thought you might want to know that your little excursion today is fast becoming public knowledge."

"What the hell do you mean by that?" Aaron asked, attracting the attention of a few bystanders.

"Lower your voice, man," Thayer said. "It seems that one of the Waites' servants saw you and Maggie leaving town together this morning and rushed home to share the news with the other coloreds. Unfortunately, Eunice overheard the conversation and put two and two together."

"How could she know I spent the entire day with Maggie?"

"It also seems that she stationed one of her papa's men to watch the house for your return. She stayed at the Gower house where they all waited for word on your arrival," Thayer said.

"Eunice was at the Gowers' when Maggie got home?" Aaron cringed at the thought of a confrontation between the two women.

"It seems that Maggie was met by Eunice, her aunt Tilly, and the good reverend, and was given a sound tongue lashing."

"My God!" Aaron bellowed, again attracting attention. "Eunice never said a word to me about it."

"Then you are the only one. Half the good ladies in this town know that Maggie Campbell used her wicked body to seduce you, against your will. And then she proceeded to attack the Widow Arnold, both physically and verbally."

"The hell you say!"

"You need to find Maggie and help her. Bring her back to my house."

"Find Maggie? Where is she?"

"Her aunt sent her packing," Thayer said, leading his friend across the street and away from any curious eyes. "Jude and Micah left home to find me and finally tracked me down at Loretta's. When we went by the Gower place to get Maggie, her uncle said that she had taken her things and gone looking for her brother and sister, worried because they hadn't come home."

"Didn't Gower try to stop her?"

"He wasn't at home when she left. He was worried about his niece, but he admitted to me that he won't be able to live with his wife if he lets Maggie stay on there."

"You take those children home with you," Aaron instructed. "I'll find Maggie."

Maggie was trying to hold back the tears that were slowly choking her. Tired, alone, and frightened for Jude and Micah's safety, she had walked the dim streets of Tuscumbia at twilight. She had stopped at the Coleman house only to be told that her siblings had been by and had gone. Less than half an hour ago, she had checked her uncle's store, hoping to find them there. She had walked up Main Street, past the opera house, remembering that Aaron would be there tonight with Eunice.

Eunice Arnold had won. Maggie Campbell had lost. *No! Not by all that was holy,* Maggie decided. She would not give in to self-pity. Somehow, someway, she would get through this horrible night. Everything would be all right, if only she could find Micah and Judith. Where could they be?

She paused in front of the three-story county courthouse and leaned against the fence enclosing the grounds. Finally allowing herself to cry, she prayed for help. Her sister and brother were innocent of any wrong. She and she alone was guilty of lusting after a man to the point that she had shamed herself and her family.

"Maggie," a male voice called out.

Wiping the tears from her eyes, Maggie turned to face Wesley Peterson, who stood a few feet away.

"What do you want, Wesley?" How had he found her? Had he been following her since she left his mother's house hours ago? Why wasn't he at the Brush Arbor meeting?

"I've come to save your soul," the good reverend said, walking slowly toward her.

"Please, just leave me alone," Maggie pleaded, turning away from her cousin.

"You must come with me this very night to the meeting and confess your great sin publicly." Wesley grabbed her by the shoulders, shaking her soundly, his eyes frenzied, his voice quivering with saintly conviction.

"No!" Maggie screamed. "Go away. Leave me be."

"You've given your virgin body in an act of sin," Wesley railed, shaking Maggie repeatedly. "You must tell me, tell us all, how you allowed the devil to enter your body."

She pulled free, dumbstruck by the wild look in his silver eyes. When he reached for her again, she started running, Wesley following at a fast pace for a man so fat.

Dear Lord in heaven, is he insane? She could not let him catch her. She refused to be hauled in front of this congregation to be forced to repent of a wrong she hadn't committed. She had allowed a man to kiss her, to fondle her, to look upon her naked breasts. Yes, she knew that she had sinned, but, for the life of her, she could not stop loving Aaron Stone, and perhaps that was the biggest sin of all, the one for which God would punish her.

She continued running faster and faster, trying to get away from the tormenting sound of Wesley's heavy footsteps and his loud ravings of sin and damnation. The worn leather of her shoes offered little protection from the hard ground, scattered with small rocks and rutted from wagon and carriage travel.

After having put a distance of two blocks between them, Maggie crossed the street to the east side of town and stopped in front of the Deshler Female Institute. The light from the cloud-covered full moon made the square building visible, a dome-shaped bell tower dominating the brick structure.

"Sinner!" Wesley preached. "I, the servant of the Lord Almighty, will purge you of evil."

Maggie shuddered at the sound of the man's voice, fear enveloping her. A silent scream issued from her mouth just as she heard horses' hooves and the cling-clang of an approaching carriage.

"Maggie!" Aaron shouted, stopping the cabriolet.

Wesley was almost upon her, his fleshy hands reaching out.

She saw Aaron running toward her, his arms open. Without a thought, except to reach the safety of his strong arms, Maggie turned from Wesley and ran into Aaron's comforting embrace.

The two men exchanged glances as Aaron held a trembling, sobbing Maggie. His jade eyes issued a warning to the good reverend whose own cold eyes prophesied doom.

"I'm here, Maggie," Aaron said, picking her up in his big arms and carrying her to the carriage. "I'm here, love. I'm going to take care of you. Don't cry."

"Oh, Aaron," she said, weeping uncontrollably. "I . . . I've ruined . . . everything . . . all our lives."

"Hush, hush." He kissed her forehead lightly. "It's all my fault. You've done nothing wrong."

"I love you," she said. "And that is wrong."

"Oh, Maggie." Aaron held her close, realizing that he loved her, too.

Chapter 9

In the white cedar-floored entrance hall of the Coleman town house, Maggie Campbell held out her arms to a teary-eyed Judith.

Propelling her petite body into her sister's, Judith cried out, "Oh, Maggie. We were so worried about you."

Maggie hugged the child tightly, stroking the back of her tiny head. "You shouldn't have run off, Jude. When you and Micah didn't come back I got scared something had to happened to you all, so I went looking everywhere trying to find you."

Clinging to her sister, Judith rationalized her actions. "I had to find Thayer. I knew he'd help us. But he wasn't home, so we had to go all the way over to the place to get him."

"What place?" Maggie asked, looking over the top of the child's head to where Thayer Coleman stood in the parlor doorway, Micah at his side.

"It was a fancy place," Jude said. "With a long bar, and huge mirrors, and lots and lots of painted ladies. Micah said they were fallen angels, but they didn't look like angels to me."

Aaron, standing behind Maggie, could not suppress a chuckle. Looking across the foyer at his friend he saw a slight flush on Thayer's smiling face.

"Micah, you don't meant to tell me that you allowed Judith to go into a . . . a . . . a house of ill repute?" Maggie glared at her brother.

"I couldn't stop her, short of killing her," the boy said. "Anyhow, we had no choice. We had to find Thayer."

"Thayer?" Maggie asked. "Haven't you two forgotten your manners using Mr. Coleman's Christian name so freely? Just because I'm the talk of the town doesn't mean you two can turn into heathens."

"It's all right, Miss Maggie," Thayer told her. "They've been given permission. The three of us have become quite good friends tonight."

"Come on in," Aaron said, lifting Judith onto his hip before taking Maggie's hand. "Let's go into the parlor and sit down. We have some things to talk about."

"Indeed we do," Thayer said. "Come on. I can ring for Ludie if anyone would like something to eat or drink."

Everyone gave negative answers as they entered the front parlor, a room of understated elegance with flowered silk-papered walls and velvet-carpeted floors. Two brocade sofas flanked the fireplace, a brown marble-topped table between them.

"Please sit down, everyone," Thayer invited.

Aaron placed Judith at her sister's side on the sofa and went to stand by an open window, the night breeze blowing softly against the lace curtains. It had been years since he had felt such a sense of confusion and desperation. The realization that he was in love with Maggie had startled him. He had never expected to know this all-consuming emotion.

"I've told Micah and Jude that I want the three of you to stay here," Thayer said, leaning against the brown marble mantel behind him.

"We couldn't," Maggie said. "What would people say?"

"Miss Maggie, at this point other people's opinions should be your least concern," Thayer reminded her.

"I'm not thinking about myself," Maggie replied. "I know my reputation is lost. But what of Jude and Micah? They shouldn't even be with me. They should have stayed at Uncle Chester's. They have to go back. That's their only hope."

"I won't go back. I won't!" Judith declared loudly, grabbing her sister around the waist and holding tightly.

"Neither will I," Micah said. "We're a family and we'll stay together."

"I'm afraid, for tonight, we will all be under the same roof," Thayer admitted. "But tomorrow I'm leaving for Silver Hill to spend the summer. I'm expecting my mother as well as my sister and her family to join me next week. Aaron is moving to White Orchard to oversee the completion of its renovation."

"So no one could say there is anything improper going on here when Thayer and Mr. Stone are gone," Micah told her.

"We can't accept charity," Maggie said.

"You are going to need assistance, Miss Maggie," Thayer said. "I want to help. As a friend, allow me to offer my home. It will be unused the whole summer."

Maggie's uncertainty weighed on her heart. She had to think of the children. What was best for them? "If we stay, we'll earn our keep."

"My God, woman," Aaron said, wanting to shake the stubborn redhead one minute and longing to hold her in his arms the next. "Can't you just accept our help? It's my fault that your family is in this situation."

"I'm to blame," Maggie said, too tired to cry anymore. "Aunt Tilly warned me that we had to keep spotless reputations."

"To hell with your Aunt Tilly," Aaron told her. "You'll regain your reputation. I'll see to it that everyone knows of your innocence. Any fault in this matter is mine alone."

"Folks aren't going to forget that Maggie beat the daylights out of Mrs. Arnold," Micah said, grinning at his sister.

"I'm not sorry I hit her back," Maggie said. "She had no right to call me a whore."

"Eunice called you a . . . a whore?" Aaron asked, astounded at the news. "I've never known her to behave like this."

"What if I bring in a sewing machine for you?" Thayer tactfully changed the subject. "You can earn a living sewing. As for Micah, we will find him a job so he can earn enough for school."

Aaron eyed his friend, knowing the other man was right to drop the matter of Eunice Arnold. There would be time enough to deal with that situation later. For now, Maggie had to be his main concern. He could probably think more reasonably if his feelings didn't keep getting in the way. He had never intended to fall in love, most definitely not with a girl who could never make his dream of respectability come true.

"I want to help too," Jude said, sulking. "Maggie's going to take in sewing again, and Micah is going to get a new job. What can I do?"

Kneeling before her, Thayer took the child's hands into his. "Your job will be to help Maggie until school starts, and then your job will be to work hard and learn all the things a proper young lady should know."

"I guess I'll have to become a lady," Jude groaned, her freckled face marred by a frown. "You want me to be a lady. Maggie wants me to be a lady."

"We all want that," Micah said.

"Then, it's settled." Thayer stood, lifting Jude to her feet. "There will be no charity. The Campbells will earn their keep."

"And I'll learn how to be a lady," Judith said, yawning.

"Bedtime for you, young lady," Thayer said, laughing. "I'll ring for Ludie. She can show you all upstairs to your rooms."

"Don't disturb her," Maggie said. "Tell us and we can find the way."

Aaron put a hand on Maggie's arm, stopping her departure. "Thayer, why don't you show Jude and Micah upstairs. I need a moment with Maggie."

Agreeing, Thayer and the younger Campbells left the parlor.

"I intend to do everything I can to help you," Aaron told her once they were alone.

"Thank you."

"I know it may be impossible to undo the damage, but I will try. After all, we didn't . . . I mean, you're still a . . ."

"I should go see about Daisy. I've been so concerned with my problems, I'd almost forgotten about her," Maggie said, ignoring his pitiful attempt at consolation.

"Don't change the subject, damn it!"

"I see no point in discussing the matter further."

"Maggie . . ." Sensing her determination to end their brief conversation and seeing the wariness in her sweet, sad face, he agreed. "Very well."

"Thank you. Now, if you'll excuse me, I think I'll go check on Daisy."

"There's no need. Phineas gave her more pain medication before he drove me to the opera house. He expects her to sleep until morning."

"In that case, I think I'll retire for the night." Thus said, Maggie walked out, leaving Aaron staring after her.

At the top of the stairway, she found Thayer on his way down. He smiled at her.

"I've put you and Jude in the first room on the right."

"Thank you, Mr. Coleman."

"Thayer. Remember, we're all friends now."

Maggie tried to smile as she nodded yes.

Judith squirmed restlessly in the bed. Maggie, lying beside her, longed for sleep that would obliterate the day's happenings.

"Thayer said that we were all invited," Jude said, laughing.

"What?" Maggie had been only half-listening to the child's endless chatter.

"The party. The party."

"What party?"

"You haven't been listening," Jude said. "I've been telling you about the big party that Thayer is going to have at Silver Hill. I'll have to stay and watch from upstairs with his niece, Rachel, because I'm not old enough to go to a formal party yet. But he expects you and Micah to be there."

"Oh, Jude. We can't..." Maggie stopped midsentence as she looked at her young sister, whose pretty little face was filled with youthful hopes and dreams. "Honey, it'll be wonderful. We'll all have such a good time."

"You'll have to make yourself a new dress. Something so beautiful that every woman there will envy you."

Maggie listened as her sister talked on and on about the big party, about Thayer's family, and about Silver Hill. Finally, after nearly an hour of nonstop talking, Judith succumbed to sleep, but Maggie remained wide awake.

She could hear sounds from outside, insects and night birds, the distant rumble of a train, and the gradually increasing roar of the wind. Going to the window, she tiptoed quietly so that she wouldn't disturb her sleeping sister. Outside the world was total darkness, huge rain clouds obscuring the moon and stars. A sudden flash of lightning illuminated the Colemans' yard, the lawn green and well kept, rows of petunias lining the walkway.

Maggie longed for rain. Perhaps it would lull her to sleep and wash away all her worries. She wondered if Aaron was asleep. It was dangerous to think about how close he was, how easy it would be to go to him, how good it would feel to be in his arms. She had to stop thinking about what could never be.

Thunder shook the house and lightning filled the world with its brilliant flash as the wind howled, and tree branches swayed, scraping across the window panes. Then the rain came. Fast and hard and loud.

Maggie's restlessness increased as the rain poured down. She had tossed and turned until her body ached. If only she could stop thinking about Aaron, she might be able to sleep.

Deciding that movement might help her pass the hours till morning, she opened the bedroom door and walked down the hall. She tried to be quiet, not wanting to awaken anyone fortunate enough to be sleeping. Maybe she could light a lamp downstairs and find something to read. A man like Thayer was sure to have newspapers, even books, somewhere in the house. She had enjoyed reading the *Atlanta Constitution* that Uncle Chester received by mail. She especially liked the Woman's Kingdom section.

The hallway was so dark that she had to feel her way along the wall, stepping carefully down the stairs, clinging to the railing. Flashes of lightning, visible through the parlor windows, allowed her a brief glimpse of the entrance hall. An open door behind the stairs revealed a dim light. Beckoned by the pale glimmer, Maggie entered the room and found herself in the kitchen, a kerosene lamp glowing faintly in the center of the eating table. Its fuel was almost gone. No doubt one of the servants had forgotten to extinguish it before retiring.

Again thunder boomed and the house trembled. Maggie rushed to the outside door, flinging it open so she could watch the lightning streak across the black sky.

She loved the rain. Pa had always said it was a farmer's friend. Tonight it was her friend, the sound of the steady downpour crooning to her like a mother to her babe. She watched and listened from the doorway, the strong wind blowing moisture onto her face and body.

Although the night was summer-warm, the rain was cool, refreshing her with its touch.

She wondered if Aaron liked the rain. Would he enjoy standing here with her, watching the lightning and savoring the taste of fresh rain on his lips? Was he lying awake upstairs listening to this sweet music? Was he thinking about her? She had told him that she loved him, but he had not responded. Did he love her? He had come to her when she needed him, when her whole world was falling apart. Would the events of this terrible day change things for him with Eunice Arnold?

Aaron Stone stood in the hallway, gazing through the open kitchen door. He could see Maggie at the back door, the pale lamplight silhouetting the shape of her womanly body beneath her sheer muslin nightgown. He had been watching her since she came down the stairs, feeling her presence even before he heard her light footsteps. Unable to sleep, he had been sitting in the back parlor, dulling his senses with a bottle of Thayer's best whiskey.

His body was hard with need, the sight of Maggie, the memory of her naked flesh, making him sick with longing. Burning desire, coupled with the liquor's influence, had brought forth the primeval forces within him. He was a male animal driven to mate with the female who had aroused him.

He stepped into the kitchen, his eyes never leaving Maggie's enticing form.

She knew Aaron was behind her there in the kitchen. She didn't need to turn around to be certain of his presence. She could feel him.

Hesitating because of some innate knowledge that seeing him would destroy her defenses, she continued to watch the storm, her heartbeat so loud in her ears that it blocked out even the thunder. She was on fire. If she faced him, she would be lost.

Unable to fight the need to see him, she turned slowly, aware that he had moved to within a few feet of her. Just as she looked up, their eyes meeting, the lamplight flickered several times and then died, throwing the room into darkness. She had seen raw hunger on his face, the expression so primitive that it had frightened her.

"Maggie." His voice was a hoarse groan.

"No," she whispered.

A clap of thunder echoed through the stillness. Maggie tensed. She felt like a trapped animal. She had to escape. Lightning ripped through the black sky, momentarily lighting the room. Aaron's jade eyes were wild. She could feel how desperately he wanted her.

Without a thought, Maggie ran out into the stormy night, rain pelting her body as she fled across the yard. Like a hunter after his prey, Aaron followed her, his long legs taking two steps for her every one.

He caught her, there in the rain, clutching her shoulders with his big hands, turning her to face him. Her gown was drenched and clung to her body like a second skin, almost transparent in the stabbing flashes of light.

She trembled with fear and desire as she gazed at Aaron, his golden hair curled with moisture, his shirt clinging damply to his broad shoulders, his face wet and fierce. She felt exhilarated by his savage presence, he and the storm seeming to have blended into one entity, brutal and compelling.

His mouth claimed hers with barbaric force, prizing her lips apart, his tongue plunging into her, taking his pleasure. She groaned, clinging to him as he pressed his big body against her. She could feel his arousal stirring against her stomach, and her blood ran hot with need. As the kiss went on, becoming deeper and wilder, she could taste whiskey and then blood, her own blood from her brutalized lips.

He lowered her to the soaked earth beneath them, jerking her gown above her hips and unbuttoning his breeches, freeing his desire. With one traumatic thrust, he entered her, piercing the veil of her innocence as she cried out in agony.

Maggie was stunned by the pain that shot through her body. He was so big and hard that she felt as if he had ripped her apart.

"Oh, Maggie, Maggie," he cried out, ramming into her over and over again as the storm raged on about them, the rain covering their undulating bodies like spring blossoms covering a green field.

Tears filled her eyes as she clung to him, her hips moving instinctively against him, the pain easing slightly as he moved within her. As suddenly as he had taken her, he plunged into her one last time, shaking with release, a cry of triumph falling from his lips.

As if only then realizing that he had taken this woman wildly in the pouring rain, Aaron rose up enough to lift her into his arms and run to the carriage house.

Grabbing a woolen blanket from a nearby hook, he threw it on the dirt floor, easing Maggie down to lie on it as he leaned over her, removing his soaked shirt. She could barely see him in the darkness, but she could feel him, feel his strength. After what had just happened, she should fear him, but she didn't.

"Forgive me, Maggie," he pleaded, bestowing sweet kisses all over her damp face. "I didn't mean for it to be like that. I know I hurt you, and I'm so sorry, so very sorry, my love."

"It's all right," she whispered. And it was. He had taken her hard and fast, with no thought of her pain or pleasure, but she knew that this first time for them could have been no other way.

"Oh, Maggie. Let me love you again. This time, I'll make it right for you." His big hand caressed the creamy smoothness of her neck.

"Aaron?" Could he possibly want her again so soon? Did he intend to make love to her now?

"Let me remove your wet gown, love," he said as he tugged the sodden cloth over her head.

She gasped at the feel of total nakedness. Her body, chilled from the rain, shivered and lifted up, seeking his warmth.

"I wish I could see you," he moaned, removing his breeches, then lowering himself to lie beside her on the blanket.

His lips sought hers in a kiss so tenderly sweet that Maggie thought she would cry. His hand cupped her face as he kissed her again, feathery light kisses.

"Aaron. Oh, Aaron."

At that moment, she was everything to him, the very air he breathed. He could not imagine his world without her in it. Nothing in his life had prepared him for loving Maggie Campbell.

He kissed her forehead, each eyelid, each cheek, her nose, her chin. She quivered from the sensations he was creating with his gentleness. His lips moved upward to her throat, seeking and finding her tiny earlobe. He bit down, nibbling tenderly, his tongue circling the crevice before going inside, moving in and out rapidly.

Maggie cried out, her body thrusting forward into his. He was as naked as she, and the feel of his manliness stirred her desires. She reached out and touched him. Her fingers embedded themselves in the thickness of his chest hair, clinging to him, then gradually exploring. Aaron jerked, his body wild for her again. But he refused to let his passion rob them of a long, sweet loving. He intended to give her pleasure beyond bearing. He loved this woman, and she was his, his and his alone. She had never belonged to another man, and she never would.

She wet her lips, staring up at him, unable to see his face clearly in the darkness. Taking the initiative, she kissed him, her tongue outlining his lips.

"Kiss me properly," Aaron laughed, one arm going under her shoulder while the other lifted her closer to his naked body.

She dipped her tongue into his mouth, then quickly removed it. He laughed again.

"Open your mouth and let me show you how to do it again."

And she did. And he did.

The chilliness of the moist, night air was soon replaced by the scorching heat of his masculine body lying so intimately against hers. Her soft cries of pleasure filled the carriage house when his mouth closed over the throbbing peak of her breast. The sucking motions of his mouth drove her wild. She wanted more, so much more. She could feel the wiry softness of his chest hair as it rubbed across her belly, thrilling her with new sensations.

"Aaron . . . I . . . what?" What was happening to her? She was afraid she might soon burst into a thousand pieces if he didn't stop feasting at her breast, but she didn't want him to cease his loving. It felt so right.

"I love you, Maggie." His hands and mouth were everywhere, all over her body, all at once. And then he was kissing her, urgent, savage kisses, as his big hand went beneath her, lifting her up against him. He rubbed their lower bodies together, his masculinity seeking a place between her closed thighs.

She wanted him to be inside of her again. She wanted the plunging movements of his huge shaft as it impelled her body.

She could feel the rough hairiness of his legs as one knee nudged her legs apart, his body as hot and damp as her own. She writhed against him, loving the feel of his huge body pressing down on hers.

Her fingers ran down the length of his back and up again to thread through the silky thickness of his hair while he seared her neck with fiery kisses. His hand, between their bodies, stroked her, squeezing her breast, gliding over her smooth stomach, and then lower, touching the downy thatch of red hair.

"Dear God, sweet Maggie, I want you so."

Aaron's hand cupped her femininity, sending flames of hunger shooting through her. His fingers moved down, across, and in, finding every pleasure-giving spot, eliciting cries of love and desire from her well-kissed mouth. His fingers worked an ancient magic, learning with each delicate stroke how to pleasure her, knowing from every soft sob of joy how close she was to blissful release. Suddenly his fingers were gone, and in their place was a hot, swollen spear pushing in her, slowly, gently giving her body time to adjust, time to accept this throbbing, demanding part of him. Then with one sure plunge their bodies joined in a frenzied need, moving together in an age-old rhythm of mutual passion.

Maggie gasped, her nails raking his back as ecstasy claimed her, spiraling her through a maelstrom of pleasure so pure and sweet that she thought she must be dying.

He cried out his release, the cry of a healthy male animal in the throes of rapture.

"Aaron," she breathed against his shoulder, her body trembling in the aftermath of such an intense loving. "I love you."

"And I love you, my Maggie, with all of my heart."

Chapter 10

Maggie lifted the cup to her lips and drank, savoring the taste of the creamy, sweet coffee before swallowing. Looking across the room to the lacy dress lying on the bed, she wondered if she were doing the right thing preparing her family to attend Thayer Coleman's party. Jude and Micah had pleaded, and Thayer had been adamant, insisting on sending his carriage for them.

She set the china cup aside on the small cherry table to her left as she rested her head against the back of the Hepplewhite wing chair. Her slender fingers ran across the brocade-covered arm. It was amazing how easily she had adjusted to the luxurious surroundings found at the Colemans' town house during the two weeks they had been in residence.

Even though she tried not to think about the night they had arrived, she had been able to think of little else. In her mind, she had relived the night of the thunderstorm again and again. She had given her precious virginity and all her love to Aaron Stone, and he had taken them greedily, giving her pleasure beyond bearing and promises of love. But when she had awakened the morning after, Thayer had told her that Aaron had left town on urgent business. He had handed her a large white envelope with her name scrawled boldly across the front. She had read the letter, hastily crumpled it into a wad, and thrown it across the room, cursing its writer while hot, salty tears filled her eyes. He had taken full blame for everything. Extolling her innocence, begging her to forgive him. He admitted that he loved her, assured her that he would never forget her, and promised to help her in every way he could. But, he was confused and uncertain about his life. He was going away for a few weeks to try to come to terms with his inner feelings and his life-long dreams. He suggested that they would both be better off to forget one another and move ahead with their lives.

Later that same day, she had found the crumpled letter in her room, smoothed out and resting against her pillow. Thayer admitted that he had found it, read it, and returned it to her. He had held her in his arms while she cried, and raved, and cursed.

She had never known anyone like Thayer Coleman, who, by his own admission, was a wealthy, young rake, but who possessed so much kindness and compassion. He had secured Micah a position at the First National Bank in Sheffield, and had purchased a sewing machine for her. Since his departure to Silver Hill, he had returned to town several times. Even though Maggie was certain that the purpose of his trips was for a night at Loretta's, she and Jude looked forward to his visits. He always ended his stay by taking Jude to the ice cream parlor thus ensuring her continued adoration.

And Thayer's family had been as friendly and kind as he. Only three days ago, he had brought his mother and sister into town to meet the Campbells. Neither had mentioned the circumstances forcing Maggie to accept Thayer's hospitality, but she was certain that they knew. His sister, Reba Quennel, had even arranged to have Maggie design several new dresses for her to accommodate her expanding waistline.

"Excuse me, Miss Maggie." Daisy stood in the doorway holding a small box.

"Come in, Daisy."

"Mrs. Mobley done sent this over for you." The Negress entered, placing the box in her mistress's lap.

Maggie opened the lid and gasped. There inside was a pair of kidskin pumps with satin ankle ties and small turquoise velvet bows.

"They match your dress, Miss Maggie," Daisy said, reaching out to touch the shoes. "Look, there's a note."

Maggie picked up the note and read Mrs. Mobley's best wishes for tonight.

"Mrs. Mobley is the dearest person." Maggie's eyes misted with tears. "She's the only lady in Tuscumbia who isn't shunning me.

She's allowing me to keep on sewing for her and the twins. And then, there's my party dress."

"Yes'am, she's one fine lady."

"When Jude told her about the party, she insisted on giving me the material for a new dress." Maggie remembered the day Alice Mobley had handed her the package and smiled happily while Maggie opened it to reveal the most beautiful silk grenadine material and endless yards of Mechlin lace.

"Oh, Daisy, I wish I knew if I were doing the right thing by going to this party tonight." Maggie knew that her presence there was bound to cause a stir. Not one decent lady in town, except Mrs. Mobley, would even speak to her, and when the Campbells had attended church this past Sunday, the good citizens had treated them as if they had the plague. Uncle Chester had watched them from afar, a sad plea for understanding in his eyes. And Cousin Wesley's sermon had been, appropriately, on the sins of the flesh.

"You got to go. Miss Jude'll lay down and die if you don't." Daisy lifted the box from Maggie's lap, took out the shoes, and placed them on the bed beside the evening gown. "And you don't want to disappoint Mr. Thayer. You going to be his lady for tonight."

"Oh, yes. I'm well aware of her plans. But they could work to her advantage. She knows that she will have to become a lady if she wants to marry a man like Thayer."

"When I told her that Mr. Thayer seemed interested in you, she clean bit my head off. She said you done had Mr. Aaron and that you couldn't have Mr. Thayer too."

Maggie sighed. "Oh, Daisy, I don't have Mr. Aaron."

"Yes'am, I know. But you just wait. Sooner or later, that man's bound to come to his senses."

"I'm not so sure."

"Phineas said he was sure hoping Mr. Aaron don't marry that awful Widow Arnold." Daisy could not suppress a shy smile.

"How is Phineas today?" Maggie knew that Daisy had been living with Phineas ever since he had nursed her back to health after the mysterious beating that Daisy still refused to discuss with anyone. Maggie approved of the love match between the two servants and, ironically, envied them the freedom to live together so openly. None of the fine white folks concerned themselves with the personal lives of the Negroes.

"You rather I didn't say nothing about that woman?"

"She'll be there tonight. First at dinner, with her parents there too, and then at the party. Aaron's going to be there with her." Maggie's heart ached with the knowledge. Reba Quennel had told her that attending tonight's affair could be sweet revenge and an opportunity to let the locals know that she was ashamed of nothing she had done.

"You going and you best hold your head high. You going to be on the arm of Mr. Thayer Coleman and ain't nobody going to dare say a word against you."

"I hope you're right."

"I'll just bet Mr. Aaron'll be jealous as all get out."

"Good!" Maggie hissed, determined to see to it that he was.

Three hours later, Maggie and Jude, dressed in their Sunday best tan muslins, sat in Thayer's carriage while Micah helped Phineas load their belongings. Micah, boyishly handsome in his white cotton shirt and brown broadcloth trousers, grinned excitedly as he jumped up into the carriage.

"The big night is almost here," he announced.

"You have yourself a good time, Miss Maggie," Daisy called out as the carriage moved away from the Coleman town house.

Maggie relaxed as they rode through town and onto Memphis Pike. She noticed that the summertime green of the scenery had changed a little in the weeks since her visit to White Orchard. Thayer had told her that Silver Hill was farther west, almost on the Mississippi-Alabama state line, and that the acreage lay almost equally in both states.

She was very fond of Thayer and knew he cared for her as well. He had made it perfectly clear that, if he were Aaron Stone, he would marry her in a minute, with no doubts or delays. He didn't give a damn about local society and respectability. Maggie had pointed out that being a Coleman had made him a bit arrogant. In his customary good-natured way, he had agreed.

"I wish I didn't have to eat with the babies," Jude said. "It's not fair that Micah gets to eat with the grown-ups."

"Micah will be seventeen in another month," Maggie said.

"Don't worry, heathen. I'm sure you'll attend more than your share of fancy dinners and big parties one of these days." Micah reached out and mussed his little sister's hair.

Maggie was sure Micah was right. One day, Judith Campbell would be a lady, with all doors open wide to admit her.

All doors, except the Colemans' and Mobleys', were closed to Maggie and could very well stay closed forever. She had risked a great deal to be with Aaron that Saturday at White Orchard, and she had lost. Her reputation was ruined, and only through Mrs. Mobley's continued friendship and patronage of Miss Loretta and several of her "girls" was Maggie able to earn a living sewing. She had no doubt that Thayer had arranged for the local madam's business. Maggie was not too proud to sew for the woman and her friends. She knew their money was tainted with sin but tainted money spent as well as any other kind, and it would buy Micah and Jude proper educations.

Maggie clutched her small cloth handbag lying in her lap. Inside, in a tiny black case, was a pair of diamond and aquamarine earrings. Phineas had delivered them to her the day before, saying the box had been left without a note. She was almost certain that they were a gift from Thayer, and she had every intention of returning them. But what if he had not sent them? What if they had come from Aaron?

The thought of seeing Aaron again excited her as much as it frightened her. He had neither come to see her nor sent a message in the two days since his return to Colbert County. It seemed obvious, considering the fact that he would be Eunice's escort tonight, that he had decided to pursue his life-long dreams, thus rejecting Maggie and their love for one another.

She had no intention of making things easy for him. If he wanted to turn his back on her and the kind of happiness they could have together, she was not going to help him. She might not be the genteel wife he had dreamed of having, but she loved him more than Eunice or any other woman ever could. With her reputation ruined and her heart already lost, she was willing to try anything and everything to win her man.

*   *   *

Maggie loved the view from the carriage as it moved along the road leading to the Coleman mansion, rows of huge silver maples lining the upwardly inclined entrance and hundreds of azalea and camellia bushes clustering around the great semicircle drive. It was obvious that this plantation had been well and lovingly cared for over the years, and that, by the grace of God, it had escaped the ravages of the war.

Seven enormous Doric columns graced the front portico and nine more adorned one side where the veranda extended the full length of the rectangular structure in a sumptuous manner. The corner brackets were so elaborate that the larger ones almost bordered onto consoles. A partial balcony, centered over the elegant front entrance, and the huge veranda boasted iron-lace banisters.

Thayer stood on the portico, smiling and waving. When the carriage came to a full stop, he rushed down the twelve wide steps leading from the veranda. He looked dashingly handsome in his tan trousers and cream linen shirt, every bit the young country gentleman at home.

"I thought you all would never get here," he said, laughing as he helped Maggie from the carriage. "Mama and Reba are in the children's parlor having tea with our little Rachel."

Micah stepped down and turned to assist Jude, who refused his aid, standing firmly in the carriage eyeing Thayer and Maggie.

"Silver Hill is unbelievably beautiful," Maggie told him. "Now I know where it got its name."

Thayer drew her hand to his lips, bestowing a gentlemanly kiss. "Grandmother Coleman said that a hillside covered with so many silver maples was a miracle."

"Your grandmother was right." Maggie pulled her hand free. She liked Thayer, but she did not want to encourage any romantic attention.

"Could somebody help me down?" Jude demanded, her tiny arms reaching out toward Thayer.

Micah groaned and rolled his eyes heavenward. Thayer winked at Maggie before turning to place his hands at Judith's waist. The moment he lifted her she threw her arms around his neck, holding tightly.

"Judith, why don't you and Maggie go inside and join the other ladies while I give Micah a hand with your things," Thayer suggested, lowering her to the ground.

"Let Micah get our things," Jude said. "You promised to show me your house."

"Judith Campbell!" Maggie scolded.

"Micah, get Toe Joe to help you," Thayer said. "I'm afraid I do have a prior obligation. I did promise Miss Judith a tour of Silver Hill. Of course, you'll join us, Miss Maggie."

Maggie ignored her younger sister's heated glare. "Of course. I would love to see your home."

"My grandfather built Silver Hill in 1835 when my father was just a boy." Thayer guided the Campbell girls up to the veranda and into the forty-six-foot-long entrance hall that divided two rooms on either side.

Standing to the right, in the front parlor doorway, was Martha Coleman, a squirming toddler on her hip. Maggie thought that Thayer's mother was the most distinguished woman she had ever met. Even with a disgruntled child in her arms, she appeared queenly in her black taffeta dress, the robin's egg blue silk of the underskirt and sleeves a perfect match for her pale eyes.

"We're so glad you all have arrived," Mrs. Coleman said, moving out into the hallway. "I'm afraid you must excuse me. I need to find Ludie and have her put our little Martin down for his nap."

"We're pleased to be here, Mrs. Coleman. Thank you for inviting us." Maggie could not imagine anyone in the entire state of Alabama daring to criticize a woman of Martha Coleman's standing. Daisy had told Maggie that Phineas said that not only had the woman married one of the richest and most sought-after bachelors in the South, but that she had inherited a fortune from her father, a man whose wealth and power extended all the way to the nation's capital.

As Mrs. Coleman disappeared down the hall, an awestruck Judith stood gazing upward at the stately staircase, unsupported and extending in a straight line twenty-four feet to the second floor. The hand-carved mahogany banister swerved about face and ran halfway down the upstairs hall and there made an exquisite climb to the attic.

"It's forty-eight feet to the top," Thayer told them. "It's one of the best features of this old house."

"I've never seen anything like it," Maggie said, walking over to touch the banisters as she looked straight up, the sight impossibly impressive.

"My mother, my aunt, and my sister came down these stairs on their wedding days and were married in the front parlor." Thayer walked to Maggie's side. "Someday, when I marry, I want my bride to walk down this staircase to me."

"Is there a back stairway for the servants like at the town house?" Judith inquired, nudging her petite body between Maggie and Thayer.

"Jude, you ask too many questions," Maggie laughed. "At this rate, you should know everything by the time you're fifteen."

"The servants' stairway leads up from the side portico. It makes it easier for them to carry up wood for the fires and water for bathing." Thayer smiled down at Judith.

"That's what I want right now," Jude said. "I want a bath upstairs."

"I think a bath before dinner can be arranged for both of you ladies." Thayer took Maggie's arm in his and clasped Judith's hand. "Shall I show you to your rooms? We can continue the tour later, perhaps even tomorrow before you all return to town."

Maggie stood at the edge of the bed looking down at the two dresses lying there. Neatly arranged in the center was the lovely lace and grenadine dress for tonight's party. She had spent endless hours on its design and production. She desperately wanted to be beautiful for Aaron.

Trying to erase him from her thoughts, she lifted the other dress, the tan Sunday dress she had worn to Silver Hill today. She had taken great pains to make this dress, and Jude's matching one, to suit Aunt Tilly. The bodice was simple with a high, round neck and small, stand-up collar. It was the kind of dress a preacher's wife might wear. She did not want to think about Wesley. She had thought he loved her, but if he did, he had not been strong enough to withstand public opinion. Not once since the night he had followed her down Main Street demanding her repentance had he attempted to see her.

"Can I stay in here a little longer?" Judith asked, as she splashed around in the brass bathtub sitting in the middle of the huge bedroom.

"No. Get out now and get dressed."

"Oh, all right."

Maggie laid the tan muslin in a nearby chair and turned to pick up the evening gown. Lifting it over her head, she quickly slipped it down her body, clad in corset, chemise, drawers, and petticoat. Her undergarments were plain with very little decoration, but the dress was a dream creation.

"Your hair looks so pretty," Jude said, as she slipped into her cotton drawers. "Wasn't it nice of Miss Reba to curl it for you? Oh, don't forget to tie that velvet ribbon in it."

"I've got it right here." Maggie held up the yard of dark turquoise velvet. "And Ludie brought me a white rose to go in my hair just like I asked her to."

"I should have known that you'd stick a rose on you somewhere."

"I love roses. Someday, when I have my own home, I'm going to have a garden full." Maggie knew she might never have a home of her own. What if Aaron never came to his senses? What if he married Eunice? She had less than three months to win him away from the other woman. By September, he would be free from his bet with Thayer and could propose to the widow. Thayer had assured her that Aaron was a man of his word and would pay off his wager.

The door opened quickly and a small, dark-haired girl wearing a daffodil yellow dress came running inside, laughing and out of breath. Martha Coleman appeared in the doorway elegantly attired in crimson silk, a white lace fichu knotted over the basque of her dress.

"Good evening, my dear. Rachel has come to get Judith, and I've come to bring you something, Maggie."

She had been in awe of Thayer's mother from the moment they had met, but the woman's kindness and understanding had put her somewhat at ease. If a lady, who was obviously the grande dame of local society, could accept her, then there was still hope that she could redeem herself. She couldn't bear to think that her bad reputation might hinder Micah's and Jude's chances for a happy future.

"Come on, Judith." Little Rachel took the older child by the hand, leading her out of the room. "Ludie has set up a party in the nursery for us and my dollies. We're having milk and cookies and a bowl of berries."

When the children exited, Martha closed the door. "Where are your earrings?"

"What?"

"The diamond and aquamarine earrings?"

"How did you know . . . I mean . . . I thought . . ."

"Did you think that Aaron or Thayer had sent them?" Martha walked over to Maggie and handed her a long black jewel case.

Taking the offered case, Maggie opened the lid. Inside, on a black velvet bed, lay a diamond necklace, five square-cut aquamarines attached at equal intervals. "Mrs. Coleman!"

"I sent the earrings as a gift. I want you to have them. The necklace is on loan for tonight." The older woman took the necklace from the case and instructed Maggie to turn around and allow her to put it on her.

"There," Martha said, pleased at the way the jewels matched Maggie's dress. "Put the earrings on before Thayer comes to escort you down for dinner."

"But Mrs. Coleman, why?" Why would Thayer's mother give her expensive earrings and loan her the matching necklace? Had Thayer asked her to do it? Did this mean that Thayer cared for her and his mother approved?

"Now, Maggie, I know you're not in love with my son." Martha Coleman placed an arm around the girl's shoulder.

When Maggie started to speak, the other woman hushed her. "No, no. Have no fear. Thayer is not in love with you. He is extremely fond of you and wants to help your family."

Relief rushed over Maggie like a giant wave. She never wanted to hurt Thayer. He had been so good to her, to all of them. "We're very fond of Thayer."

"My son isn't ready for marriage yet. He has a notorious reputation with the ladies as does my brother. He's the man I think would be perfect for you."

"Your brother?"

"These jewels belonged to my father's mother. They've been handed down from father to son for four generations to give to the son's bride."

"Then why?" Maggie had never been so confused in her life. She had never heard Thayer speak of an uncle. She had never heard one word of gossip about Mrs. Coleman's brother.

"I'll explain later, my dear. Just enjoy wearing the jewelry tonight. And keep the earrings. If you don't marry my brother, you can return them. If you do marry him, I'll give you the necklace."

Speechless, Maggie simply nodded.

"Good." Martha gave Maggie an affectionate hug before leaving.

Would Mrs. Coleman's brother be at the private dinner tonight or the big party afterward? Why had no one ever mentioned this man? Perhaps there was something mysterious about him, something the Colemans were trying to hide.

If there was one thing she didn't need right now, it was another man in her life. She was glad that Thayer wasn't in love with her. That was one complication she wasn't sure she could handle.

She loved Aaron Stone. There would never be another man for her. Somehow, someway, she had to come to terms with reality. The man loved her, but, for some reason, marriage to Eunice Arnold represented a life-long goal he was not willing to abandon. If only she knew more about him, about his past, maybe she could understand. Loving him had jeopardized all of her own plans. If only there were a way she could keep her promise to Pa and have the man she loved, too. Even if Aaron were to marry her, she doubted anyone would ever be able to be accepted as a lady with a sister like her.

Why did life have to be so complicated? Back home on the farm, things had been a lot simpler. They had lived life by the seasons, planting time and harvest time. Neighbors were plain folks, most sharecroppers like themselves. If Pa hadn't died, if they had never come to Tuscumbia to live with Aunt Tilly and Uncle Chester, she would never have met Aaron. She would probably be marrying Benny and looking forward to her life. Of course, Micah would've run off somewhere looking for adventure and never gotten a good education. And Jude would never have become a lady. She'd have married a local boy and spent her days as a farmer's wife.

Maggie picked up her small cloth bag and pulled out the black case containing the earrings. Before putting them on, she ran her fingers across the exquisite necklace adorning her neck and wondered why Martha Coleman had been in possession of the set if it were always passed down from father to son. Why didn't her brother have it?

A light knock on the door interrupted her thoughts.

"Yes?"

"It's Thayer. Are you ready?"

Maggie opened the door, smiling.

Thayer gazed at her, stunned and almost speechless. "Well, well, well."

"Does that mean you approve?" She turned around slowly, giving him a complete view of her dress.

"You are beautiful."

"Isn't the dress magnificent?"

"You're magnificent."

Blushing, Maggie smiled up at her escort. "Thayer, you do talk so pretty."

"Pretty talk for a pretty lady."

"Oh, wait just a minute," she said, turning to walk back to the bed, picking up the white rose and placing it in her hair, the stem beneath the velvet ribbon.

"The necklace and earrings are perfect on you." Thayer offered his arm.

As they walked out of the room, Maggie hesitated. "Was it your idea that I should wear them?"

"Oh, no. It was entirely Mama's."

"Why have you never said anything about your uncle?"

"My what?" Thayer's dark eyes searched Maggie's face for an answer.

"Your mother said that this jewelry will go to your uncle's wife, and she thinks he's the perfect match for me."

"My God! My mother is one devious lady." Suddenly Thayer began to laugh as he led Maggie down the hall.

"You aren't going to tell me any more?"

"I wouldn't dare. This seems to be Mama's little game. I'll let her play it out to the finish."

"Thayer, do you or do you not have an uncle?"

"Yes and no."

"What does that mean?"

"It means that my mother was the only child born to her parents within the bonds of holy matrimony."

"Her brother. Is he . . . ?"

"Yes, sweet Maggie. My mother's brother is a bastard."

"Oh."

She let the matter drop. No doubt it was an embarrassment to the Coleman family. And perhaps that was why they were more understanding of her situation than the other local citizens.

Just before they reached the dining room, Maggie's steps faltered, fear gnawing at her insides.

"It will be all right," he assured her.

"But Eunice is in there with her parents." Maggie could imagine what the distinguished Mr. Waite would have to say about her appearance.

"Once you've dined with the Colemans and the Waites, your reputation will be on the mend."

"They'll never allow it. They'll leave."

"Oh, dear girl, never underestimate the power of Martha Leander Coleman. No one would dare leave her dinner table without her permission."

"She's doing this for me."

"And for her brother." Thayer laughed as he led her through the open doorway and into the enormous dining room.

A long, oak banquet table sat in the center of the huge, brightly lit room, kerosene lamps glowed brightly on each end of the buffet, and a French imported bronze chandelier hung from the high ceiling. Eight chairs lined the side of the table, and at each end were Jacobean velvet upholstered armchairs. Martha Coleman sat at the head of the table like an empress holding court.

Maggie had tried very hard not to look at anyone seated except Mrs. Coleman, but the sound of a loud gasp caught her attention. Eunice Arnold, half-raised in her chair, glared hostilely at the couple entering. Beside her, Aaron Stone sat, immobilized, his green eyes devouring the woman he had spent weeks trying to forget.

Chapter 11

Aaron stood in the corner of the parlor watching Thayer, who held Maggie in his arms as they danced around the room, dozens of the county's best citizens enjoying the same waltz.

From the gleaming, wide-planked cherry floors to the radiant bronze chandeliers, the twin parlors provided ample space and elegant accommodations for the many guests. Servants had rolled back the velvet carpets, and the small string band was producing lilting dance music. Dark-suited black servants poured expensive wines and aged whiskey into crystal containers, and white-aproned Negresses constantly refurbished silver trays with a variety of edible delights. Two porcelain vases, filled with summer flowers, adorned each end of the magnificent Carrara marble mantel in the large room.

Aaron had been totally shocked to see Maggie and Micah as guests at Martha Coleman's private party, and only at Martha's decree had Eunice and her parents endured the ordeal. Even though it was obvious that the Campbells had been aware of the guest list in advance and had chosen to attend anyway, the only two people who seemed to enjoy themselves were Thayer and his mother.

Maggie was the most beautiful woman in the world, and every man there tonight seemed to be aware of the fact. But Thayer had monopolized her for nearly every dance, smiling at her, laughing with her, and holding her hand to his for stolen kisses.

Aaron boldly raked her body with his gaze, hypnotized by the sway of her womanly shape attired in a gown whose fine turquoise silk grenadine bodice extended to the hipline where yards of exquisite white Mechlin lace hung in tiny, slightly flared rows to the floor. The same delicate lace graced the deep-cut, square neckline and created cap sleeves. An enormous dark turquoise taffeta bow accented the beginning of a short lace train that extended from the base of her spine to several inches beyond the hemline of her dress.

He was damned curious about the jewelry she was wearing. Knowing it could not be hers, he had come to the conclusion that Thayer had to be her benefactor, which led to questions that were tormenting him. Exactly what was going on between Maggie and Thayer? Was Thayer in love with her? Had he bedded her yet? The thought of Maggie, naked and aroused, in his friend's arms ripped his insides like the blade of a sharp knife.

For two weeks, he had unsuccessfully tried to forget the passionate redhead who had given him her virginity. Of all the women he had bedded, none had been as sweetly loving as Maggie. In her innocence, she had given him pleasure that not even the most skilled New Orleans whore could have. She haunted his thoughts day and night. She was as addictive as morphine, her full, round breasts a lure and the treasure between her thighs an entrapment.

He knew he was hard with desire, and there was nothing he could do except hope to control his thoughts. At that very moment, the music stopped, and Maggie looked across the room toward him. Their eyes met, each of them unable to look away. He saw love and longing in her golden eyes. A plea to come to her in her gaze.

"My goodness," Eunice said, fussing as she walked up to Aaron, her diamond and garnet necklace catching the light from a nearby candelabra. "I despise dancing with that Tobin Smythe. He stepped all over my feet."

She raised the Argentan lace hem of her pale pink, silk mull dress to inspect her rose slippers.

"What?"

"I think my slippers may be ruined. I know my night is. The very idea that Martha Coleman would invite that woman here tonight and force my family and me to have dinner with her!"

"Eunice, I've told you that the girl is innocent of any wrongdoing, and I refuse to discuss her with you."

"She's set her cap for you, and I think—"

"Be quiet!" Aaron warned in a softly stern voice, then took Eunice into his arms as the music began.

Maggie partnered again with an attentive Thayer, watched as Aaron and Eunice danced around and around, slowly moving in her direction. Maggie, who seldom even disliked anyone, decided that she hated Eunice Arnold, even though she was honest enough to admit that Aaron's pride and unrelenting need for respectability was what was keeping them apart and not the widow. Simply because she had had the good fortune to be born into a prominent family, she was in Aaron's arms, and she was the woman most likely to become his wife. Why was the man so driven to overcome his mysterious past?

"I think Aaron would like to kill me," Thayer whispered in her ear. "He keeps glaring at me and drooling over you."

"Thayer. What a thing to say."

"It's true. The man can't keep his eyes off of you. I think a little jealousy will do him some good."

"I'm afraid I am as jealous as he is."

"Are you? Well, try not to be. I've been telling him for months that Eunice is the wrong woman for him. But the damn fool is obsessed with the idea of overcoming his birth and acquiring what he thinks is his rightful place in society by making a proper marriage."

"We love each other," Maggie admitted, her eyes filled with tears.

"I know. Damn, Maggie, if I loved a woman like you, I'd move heaven and earth to make her mine."

"Oh, Thayer."

"I'm on your side and on the side of that foolish friend of mine. I only hope he comes to his senses before it's too late."

Maggie wanted to walk right up to the other couple and pull Aaron out of Eunice's arms. She wanted to demand that he stop destroying all their lives and choose between them immediately. He had to know that a marriage to Eunice would be doomed to failure as long as he loved and desired another woman. He might be fighting it with all his might, but she could tell that he still wanted her as desperately as she did him. And he still loved her too. It was there, in his eyes.

For the past two weeks, she had relived their night of lovemaking, the night she had lost her innocence while the heavens split apart and filled the world with the roar of thunder and crackling flashes of lightning. She could almost feel the rain that had soaked her body while the storm about them raged as furiously as the storm of their passion. She tingled from head to toe at the memory of his big, hard body joining hers. It had been fast and powerful, creating a pain that had given way to surprise. Even without fulfillment, that first time had been so right. A slower, more gentle mating, like the one that came later, would have been impossible because their needs had been building steadily since the day they had met in Chattanooga.

Maggie knew before even looking his way that he was watching her again. They stared at one another, neither willing to look away, both willing to gaze longer, unaware that others might notice.

She thought he looked gloriously handsome in his black suit, the frock coat fitting his broad body perfectly. She wondered if Eunice would run her fingers up and down the ruffles of his white silk shirt before unbuttoning it to explore his hairy chest. No! She would not let herself imagine the other woman enjoying the pleasures of his lovemaking.

"Maggie," Thayer called.

"Hmm?" She was still looking at Aaron and feeling oddly warm.

"Would you like to take a stroll on the veranda?"

"What?" No, she did not want to go anywhere. She wanted to stay right here and continue feasting her eyes on the glorious sight of Aaron Stone, his dark gold hair glistening in the chandelier light.

"I think you and I should go outside and see what develops."

"Thayer, what are you talking about?"

"I'll bet that if we stroll out to the veranda that my big friend will follow us."

"You make too many bets."

"Ah, but I usually win. If I lose you don't have to pay me back for the sewing machine I bought you. If I win, you give me a kiss."

"A kiss?"

"If Aaron sees us kissing, he'll be so jealous, he'll be up all night getting drunk."

"Well . . . I do believe I'd enjoy a stroll on the veranda. It is a bit warm in here."

Thayer laughed, took her by the arm, and led her out of the parlor, down the hallway, and onto the wide veranda. The night air was warm and filled with the after-dark sounds of insects and owls and soft summertime wind. A million stars illuminated the sky, while a pale yellow moon covered the world with its diaphanous glow. The fragrant smell of flowers and freshly cut grass blended with the residue of smoke that had come from the basement kitchen.

Aaron watched, filled with raging jealousy, as Thayer escorted Maggie from the room. He had to follow. He had to know where they were going and what they were doing.

As soon as the dance ended, he excused himself, telling Eunice that he wanted to step outside for a smoke. Giving her no time to object, he rushed from the parlor. There were several couples in the hallway, but none of them was the couple he sought. His gaze lingered on the staircase, doubts filling his mind. Surely they had not gone upstairs. If Thayer made love to Maggie, he'd kill him. She would belong to no other man. Dismissing the thought of dashing upstairs, he made his way to the veranda and lit a cigar the minute he stepped outside.

Soft gray smoke curled upward as Aaron leaned against the iron-lace banisters, his eyes searching for the missing couple. When he heard the muffled sound of voices, he moved to the end of the front portico. There at the far end of the side veranda stood Thayer, with Maggie in his arms. While he watched in silent anger, he saw Thayer take the beautiful redhead and kiss her passionately. And she responded, damn her. She responded. It was all he could do to keep himself from storming down the veranda, ripping Maggie out of the other man's arms, and beating the hell out of him.

Unconsciously, his left hand reached inside his vest to stroke the gold watch in the pocket. He watched as Maggie laid her head on Thayer's chest while he stroked the flaming red curls cascading down her neck.

Aaron took one last draw on the cigar, then crushed it in his hand.

Throwing the crumpled flakes of tobacco to the floor, he turned and stomped away.

Maggie had enjoyed Thayer's kiss. It had been very pleasant for both of them, but the knowledge that Aaron had witnessed the loving exchange and had reacted appropriately was far more wonderful.

"And now for Act Two of tonight's skit," Thayer said, taking Maggie's hand. "Back inside."

"Oh no," Maggie told him. "I'm not going anywhere until I know what you have planned in that devious mind."

"Don't you trust me?"

"Only partly. We're dealing with my life here, with my future, and Jude's and Micah's. As much as I want Aaron, I can't forget my obligations. I did once, and look what trouble that caused for all of us."

"If Aaron marries you, the gossip will eventually die down. Besides, I can see to it that Micah has a secure future. He's a bright boy with a great deal of ambition of his own."

"And what about Jude? Will people ever accept her as a lady when she has a sister like me?"

"Maggie Campbell, you are a lady, in the truest sense of the word. Jude loves you, and she's proud of you. Anyway, Judith may become a lady outwardly, but not all the schooling and proper training in the world will tame that curious hellion living inside her."

"Oh Lord, I had so hoped."

"You're a strong, hot-blooded woman, Maggie, but you're gentle and giving. Judith was born to be a taker, and nothing you do can change that."

"All right. For tonight, I'll forget about tomorrow. What's your plan?"

"Now, that's more like it. Let's go inside for another dance. I feel an overwhelming desire to change partners in mid-dance."

And exchange partners was exactly what he did. In the middle of a romantic waltz, Thayer tapped Aaron on the shoulder, pulled Eunice into his arms, and danced away with her. Realizing that people were beginning to stare at the two of them standing awkwardly in the middle of the other dancing couples, Aaron pulled Maggie into his arms. Nothing had ever felt so right. As the music continued and their bodies moved across the dance floor, Aaron gradually held her closer and closer. He wanted to crush her to him, to take her lips in a demanding kiss. But more than anything, he wanted to sweep her up into his arms, stride up the staircase to a bedroom, and make love to her all night.

"You've certainly become good friends with Thayer."

"He's been exceptionally kind to us. So have his mother and sister."

Aaron felt a great sense of curiosity about Martha Coleman's interest in Maggie. Why had the highly respected woman chosen to champion this girl? "Martha seems determined to make the locals accept you. She's not preparing you to become her daughter-in-law, is she?"

Maggie smiled, thrilled by Aaron's jealousy. "I'm not sure what Thayer's plans are, but his mother seems more interested in me as a sister-in-law."

"A what?" Aaron roared, attracting the attention of the couples around them.

"I think Mrs. Coleman is making plans for me to marry her brother."

"The devil you say!" Aaron said, wondering just what dear Martha had in mind. Did she think that a girl with Maggie's ill-bred background would be a suitable mate for her bastard brother? He decided right then and there that he would have a long talk with Thayer's mother.

"It's strange, isn't it? I wasn't even aware before tonight that Thayer had an uncle."

"And you, Maggie, how would you feel about marrying a bastard?"

She held his hand tightly and gazed boldly up into his eyes. "If I loved him, I would not care."

Oh God, why did she say that? Eunice would never say such a thing. If she knew the truth about his parentage, she would probably refuse his proposal. But Maggie? He could not allow himself to think about it.

The music had ended several minutes before either of them realized. Slowly, reluctantly, he released her, his arms feeling empty without her. Just as she turned to walk away, he placed a big hand around her wrist. She hesitated, then looked up at him. His other hand moved toward her fiery hair, then gently grasped the white rose tucked in the velvet ribbon, and held it within his fingers.

"To remember how beautiful you are tonight." He placed the rose in his pocket.

"Oh, Aaron."

"If I send for you later, will you come to me?"

"I . . . Aaron . . . I . . ."

"Will you?"

"Yes."

Maggie held the note in her trembling hands as she stood outside the closed library doors. Phineas had brought her the briefly worded message less than ten minutes ago. Without any debate, she had dressed quickly and rushed downstairs at this after-midnight hour, all the guests having gone home long ago. Undoubtedly, Aaron had made some excuse not to leave with Eunice and her parents.

Slowly she pushed back the doors and stepped into the shadowy room, one small lamp burning dimly on the oak trestle table, the brass hardware glowing in the mellow light. Aaron sat on the dark leather sofa near the corner fireplace, his head resting against the back, his eyes closed, a snifter of brandy in one hand and a cigar in the other.

"Come closer, Maggie." The sound of his deep voice startled her. She had not known that he was aware of her presence.

A sparkling glow reflected off the polished tiles surrounding the fireplace, and a stream of milky-white moonlight poured through the two long, lace-curtained side windows. Maggie moved closer to the big man who sat sipping brandy. She walked around the sofa to stand in front of him, noticing the weariness in the emerald eyes that gazed up at her.

Setting the snifter on the floor and dropping the cigar into the remaining liquor, he reached out and took both of her hands. "Sit with me, Maggie." He pulled her gently down onto the sofa.

"I owe you an explanation for my behavior." He brought both of her hands to his lips, kissing them several times before releasing them.

"Why did you—"

He placed an index finger across her lips. "I love you, Maggie Campbell."

"Oh, Aaron, I love you." She moved to embrace him, but he stopped her by grabbing her shoulders.

"Before the end of the year, I plan to ask Eunice to marry me. I want you to know why I've made this decision."

Maggie sat silently, staring in disbelief. How could he tell her that he loved her, and, practically in the same breath, tell her he planned to propose to Eunice?

"Will you let me explain?" He searched her blank face for an answer.

"Yes. Oh, yes. I want to hear your explanation."

"What I'm going to tell you would destroy me socially if it became public knowledge." He didn't add that Eunice Arnold would probably reject his proposal if she knew.

"I'd never do anything to hurt you." Maggie's fingers reached out to touch his face, slightly rough with stubble.

"I know," he whispered, savoring the feel of her fingers caressing his face.

"Tell me."

"It's a pitiful, boring tale."

"I want to know."

"My mother was a beautiful New Orleans girl from a good family, but her mother was a widow and they weren't wealthy."

"You loved your mother a great deal, didn't you?" She could tell from the tenderness in his voice and the faraway look in his eyes.

"Yes. And I hated her a great deal. I didn't find out the whole truth until after her death. All I remember is the two of us living alone in a big house, with servants, and a carriage, and—"

"What about your father?"

"I had no father. I learned from the early age of six to hate the word *bastard*."

"People called you—"

"Oh, yes. I was called a bastard frequently, and my mother was called a whore. But she wasn't. In all the years of my childhood there was only one man."

Aaron placed his hand over hers as it rested against his cheek.

"He was a wealthy man twice her age. He was very good to me. I can remember sitting in his lap while he read to me."

"What about your real father?"

"My mother never discussed the events surrounding my birth. When I grew older, I assumed she had simply sold herself to the highest bidder after losing her reputation by having an illegitimate child. I was only partly right."

"What happened to your mother?"

"My mother and her lover were killed when there was an explosion on their steamer. They had gone away for a holiday together at Point Clear on the gulf." An almost invisible mist clouded his vision.

"How old were you?"

"I was sixteen and away at school. Oh, that's right. I didn't tell you that my mother's lover provided me with the best of everything, even a private education."

"What did you do after her death?"

"I ran away from school. I thought I had nothing left and that there was no one to pay the bills."

"What did you do?"

"I did everything. I did anything. I'm not proud of some of the things I did in my eagerness to make a lot of money fast. My youthful greed nearly got me killed on more than one occasion."

"Oh Aaron, no." She wanted to hold him in her arms and make all the painful memories go away. She imagined how devastating it must have been to find himself alone and penniless at sixteen. The same age as Micah.

"That's how I met Phineas. He saved my life one night in a New Orleans barroom. We've been together ever since. He's a man I respect."

"Aaron, no one in this state knows anything about your past. Why is it so important to marry Eunice? You're respected and accepted by people here."

"There's a good chance that the truth will come out someday."

"How would Eunice feel if it did?"

"She would already be my wife by then. I think she'd remain loyal to me. Especially with Martha Coleman defending me."

"Mrs. Coleman is a remarkable woman."

"I owe her so much." Aaron pulled Maggie into his arms, loosening the ribbon holding her long, red hair in place.

"There's more, isn't there? For some reason, you think you have to have a place in society."

Stroking the back of her head, his fingers threading through the strands of fiery silk, he sighed. "The lover with whom my mother died, her only lover, was my father."

"Why didn't they ever marry? Why didn't they ever tell you the truth?"

"He was married to a woman who had been an invalid since the birth of their only child. He was duty bound to stay with a woman he didn't love."

"How horrible for all of them."

"His wife never knew."

"How do you know that?"

"Because five years ago, I went to Point Clear wanting revenge against the family of my mother's lover. They were vacationing at the place where my mother had died."

"You met your father's wife?"

"No, she had been dead for several years by then." Aaron tightened his hold on Maggie. "My father's daughter was there with her husband and son. You can't imagine how I hated her."

"You met her?"

"Yes."

"Did you tell her who you were?"

"She knew. Actually she knew more than I did. She knew the whole truth. The minute I approached her, she knew the whole truth. Right away, she called me by my name. She said she had been searching for me since her father's death. I didn't understand."

"She already knew of your existence."

"Yes. She had known about me and my mother since I was a child. She had had detectives looking for me to tell me about my inheritance."

Maggie pulled back just enough to look into his face. "Your inheritance?"

"I ran away as soon as I was told of my mother's death." Moisture filled Aaron's eyes. "I didn't know he was my father. I had no idea he would leave half his estate to me. She was a stranger to me, even though she was my half-sister, but she was the one to tell me who my father was. He should have told me. He and my mother."

Maggie saw such raw pain on his face that she could barely look at him any longer. "Oh, Aaron."

"I told her that I didn't want his damn money. I was already rich." He reached inside his vest and pulled out his gold pocket watch. "That's when she gave me this. It's his. She said that my half of his estate would be waiting for me when the day came that I could forgive him. She said that it would take time, but that eventually, I would—that she had."

"And that day hasn't come, has it?"

Aaron pulled her up from the sofa with him as he stood, leading her to the fireplace and pointing to the portrait hanging over it. "That's my father, Richard Aaron Leander."

Maggie stared at the gilt-framed portrait of a handsome blond man in the prime of life, his pale robin's-egg blue eyes alight with devilment. Except for the eyes, it was like looking at a portrait of Aaron.

"Leander." Maggie remembered that name. "Martha Coleman is your sister?"

"Yes." Tears flooded his eyes, threatening to overflow. "Don't you understand? I'm the son of a man who was one of the wealthiest and most powerful in the South, and I can never claim him or my birthright because I'm a bastard."

"But he wanted you to have it, to have half his fortune."

"All the wealth in the world can never buy me legitimacy, can never give me respectability." He gazed up at the portrait, transparent streaks of tears dampening his manly face.

But Eunice Arnold can, Maggie thought, finally understanding why he was so obsessed with a proper marriage. She also understood that Martha Coleman knew what Aaron would not believe—that his father would tell him love was far more important than all the respectability this life had to offer. Somehow, she had to help Aaron. She had to make him see the truth. The only way either of them could ever be truly happy was together. The only way they could ever be to-gether would be for them both to give up their dreams. Could she? Would he?

"I never want to hurt you, Maggie." He took her in his arms, hold-ing her tenderly. "I had no right to make love to you when I can't offer you marriage."

"Will tonight be good-bye? Is this the end for us?" She pulled away, waiting for his reply.

"I want you, but I won't lie to you. I plan to marry Eunice." He turned from her, ashamed of wanting her passionately and loving her so completely when he had no right.

"I want you," she whispered as she walked to stand in front of the tall windows, moonlight setting her hair aflame. "One . . . last . . . time."

When he turned around, he stood motionless, devouring the sight of her as she unbuttoned her tan muslin dress, slipped her arms out of the sleeves, and pushed it down her hips, letting it fall silently to the floor. Her cotton petticoats followed, and then the chemise, leaving her standing in the moonlight wearing only a corset and drawers. She breathed deeply, her large breasts rising and falling enticingly.

"Maggie—"

"No. Don't say anything. Not yet."

Ever so slowly, she unlaced her corset, easing it away from her body. Her full breasts glistened like ivory globes, the lamplight's glow turning her jutting pink nipples to a dusty rose.

Aaron groaned. He wanted to touch her, but he waited. Her slen-der fingers loosened the string on her drawers, and then, with slow tantalizing grace, she stepped out of them, throwing them aside on top of her other clothing. Unashamed, she stood before him in all her naked glory, like a goddess offering herself to a mortal man.

Aaron removed his coat and vest, dropping them to the floor as he walked to Maggie, his big body trembling with desire.

He touched her face, gently running his fingers from temple to jawline, detouring once to circle her lips. He took her face in both hands and covered her lips with his. The kiss began like a gentle rain, but soon turned into a maelstrom of raging passion. His tongue parted her lips, plunging inside, delving into her honeyed sweetness.

She responded, her own tongue wildly searching his mouth, mating with his.

An agonizing groan erupted from him when he prized his lips from hers and fell to his knees, circling her hips with his arms as he laid his head against her stomach and clutched her buttocks in his big hands. When his lips spread hot, wet kisses across her abdomen, Maggie's knees buckled, and she cried out his name.

His hands moved in seductive strokes up and down the backs of her thighs while his tongue drew a loving path from her waist to the thatch of red curls covering her femininity.

"I want to taste you," Aaron moaned as his fingers moved between her thighs, gently parting them to give him access to the secret part of her. His fingers delved gently into her waiting warmth.

"Aaron!" she gasped.

He placed his fingers to his lips, sampling her essence. "You taste so sweet."

He lowered her gently to the floor and parted her thighs as his mouth and tongue replaced his fingers and drank his fill of her precious sweetness.

Maggie felt as if she were on fire, as if her body were ready to explode while Aaron continued loving her so intimately. She wanted him to stop, but she wanted him to go on forever. A spiral of pleasure began building deep within her, and with every stroke of his tongue she drew closer and closer to fulfillment. Then, her body burst into a flame that consumed her, red-hot sensations racing from her womanly center.

"Oh Aaron, Aaron," she cried, trembling with completion.

He raised his head and smiled down at the angel lying so wantonly before him. He tugged off his shirt and threw it aside. He pulled her to him, lifting her into his arms and walking across the room to the sofa. He gently placed her on the soft, dark leather.

Watching him as he stripped out of his trousers and drawers, she rested against the sofa's warmth. In the shimmering glow of lamplight, he stood naked, his manhood boldly erect. The pale light had turned his hair to silvery-gold and his flesh to solid bronze. His eyes gleamed like polished jade.

He lowered himself to her, his mouth taking hers in a kiss of total possession. He tasted faintly of cigar and strongly of good brandy, and nothing had ever tasted half so wonderful.

His naked flesh touched hers, one big long leg curling against hers as the other nestled between her thighs. His muscular legs were hard and hairy as they rubbed her delicate skin.

Maggie's hands clutched him to her, massaging the bulging muscles in his big arms as he held himself above her, looking into her eyes. She put her mouth on his neck, her tongue gliding along the pulse beating wildly there, continuing the journey until her mouth encountered the springy fullness of his abundant chest hair. Spreading light, teasing kisses across his chest, she stopped at one tiny, male nipple hidden beneath the golden curls. Her tongue circled, stroked, and circled again.

"Oh Maggie."

Her hands moved onto his chest, threading their way through the hair, savoring its silky feel against her fingertips. When one hand inched downward, fondling his stomach as her face nuzzled against his chest, Aaron stiffened, taking her hand and leading it below his waist.

"Touch me," he pleaded. "I want to feel your hand around me."

Obeying, Maggie enclosed his manhood within her hand. "Like this?"

Covering her hand with his own, he squeezed, then taught her the movements to please him.

Her touch drove him wild. He groaned and sighed and whispered outrageous love words into her ears. When he could bear no more, he pulled away from her, his own big hand lifting her breasts. He savored the sight of her perfection, his mouth hungry to suckle her beauty. Maggie jerked once, twice, when his mouth covered one begging nipple and his fingers toyed with the other.

"I want to love you." He spread her legs apart with his knee as he pushed his manhood against her feminine mound. "Feel how badly I need you."

"Make love to me, Aaron. Make this night one we'll always remember."

With one earth-shattering lunge, he joined their bodies in sweet ecstasy. For only moments, he lay unmoving inside of her, simply enjoying the feel of perfect union. Gradually he moved, encouraging her body's undulating responses. His mouth continued feasting at her breasts while her hands rubbed his chest, glorying in the sensations created by feminine flesh against manly hair.

Harder and faster he plunged, his breath ragged with passion. Her hips moved up and down, reaching for the pinnacle of bliss.

"Oh my God, woman, it's never been so good."

"Love me. Love me."

In a blinding flash of completion, they reached fulfillment together, their bodies throbbing with a pleasure so intense it was almost unbearable.

"I love you," he cried, his body trembling with release.

"I love you," she sighed, satiation covering her like a downy, warm quilt.

They lay, naked and replete, touching, kissing, and whispering the sweet nothings of lovers. Much later, Aaron eased away from her. She watched him go to the desk, retrieve a bottle of pale brandy, and pour a liberal amount into two large, tapering glasses.

He returned, handling her one of the snifters. Maggie looked at the yellowish liquor, sniffing its distinct aroma. "What is it?"

"Pale brandy. Try it. It was my father's favorite."

Maggie raised the snifter to her lips and tasted sparingly. She was not accustomed to the taste of liquor, and she did not like it. "Phew . . ."

He laughed, and then sipped from his glass. "It's an acquired taste."

"It looks yellow," Maggie said, gazing into the snifter.

"That's because it was stored in oak casks. It reminds me of your eyes. I'll never drink it again without thinking of you."

Completely, unashamedly naked, they sat on the dark leather sofa in Martha Coleman's house, and looked at each other, fresh longing awakening within them.

"I want to love you again, but I know it must be nearly dawn. You need to return to your room." He stroked her cheek with his fingertips.

"I don't want to leave you. Not now, not ever."

"Parting from you is like being damned to hell."

"I know." She pulled his hand to her lips, pressing a kiss into his open palm.

"Forgive me?"

"I can't. You'll be ruining three lives if you marry Eunice."

"I . . . I'll do what I must."

Maggie stood. Her hair, tumbling in soft, wild curls to her waist, fell across her breasts as she bent to retrieve her clothing. Moonlight and lamplight combined to illuminate her perfect, young body, covering it with a gauzy cream blush.

"Then heaven help you, Aaron, because you've doomed us all to torment."

Chapter 12

Maggie sat at the square wooden table, a large blue bowl in her arm and a long spoon in her hand. The hot August sun filled the spacious kitchen of the Coleman town house, making the already warm room sweltering. She could feel the rivulets of perspiration trickling down between her breasts as she steadily continued beating the cake batter. Sitting beside her, Daisy wiped the sweat from her face with the edge of the soiled gingham apron, and then continued shelling the pile of purple hull peas lying on the table.

A slight breeze came through the open back door, but its humid warmth gave no relief. Heat from the nearby stove added discomfort to this prenoon summertime day.

"I hope Mr. Micah appreciates you baking him a pound cake on a day this hot," Daisy said, popping open another shell.

"Well, it's not every day a boy turns seventeen."

"He's sure enough going to think he's a man now."

"I wish Thayer hadn't offered him that job on Aaron's riverboat. That's all he's talked about for two weeks now." Maggie was afraid her brother would accept the offer and spend the next few years seeking adventures on the river instead of going off and getting himself an education.

"Well, if your plans for Mr. Micah don't work out, there's always Miss Jude," Daisy laughed as she dropped a handful of pea pods into her lap. "Her spending time with Mrs. Mobley's twins is bound to be good for her. Could be some of their highfalutin ways will rub off on her."

"I sure hope so."

"She's mighty worked up about Mr. Thayer taking you all to the opera house tonight for Mr. Micah's birthday. I ain't never seen a child so love-sick over a grown man."

"I worry about it sometimes, but I figure she'll grow out of it. It seems you're the only one in the family who's going to get the man she wants."

Daisy blushed but smiled shyly as she lowered her head, concentrating on her task. "He's a fine man, Miss Maggie."

Maggie could hear Aaron's voice saying, "That's how I met Phineas. He saved my life one night in a New Orleans barroom. He's a man I respect."

So much had happened in the four weeks since Thayer's party. The dry, blazing hot month of July had faded into the first days of humid, overcast August, and she had seen nothing of Aaron. She had become convinced that the night they had shared at Silver Hill would be their last. No doubt, he was working hard at finishing the restoration at White Orchard and biding his time until he could ask Eunice to marry him. She was trying to put the pieces of her own life back together, but keeping her promise to Pa seemed less likely every day.

The atmosphere in town had changed some. Since word had spread that Martha Coleman had wined and dined the Campbells at her private dinner party, a few ladies deemed it acceptable to speak to her now, and she had actually acquired two more customers.

She did not like to think about the creature who had called on her a week ago inquiring about her services. It seemed that Miss Verda, a new girl at Loretta's, was far more interested in getting a look at Thayer's new lady friend than having any dresses made. Maggie had told that painted trollop a thing or two and shown her the door. The very idea that anyone would think that she, Margaret Mary Campbell, was Thayer's latest mistress!

Unfortunately, Jude had witnessed the scene and asked Maggie countless questions. It had taken her quite some time to convince the child that there was nothing going on between Thayer and her. Right now, she could still manage to handle Judith, but Micah was something else altogether.

If Micah took the steamboat job, he would never finish school.

She had long since given up her plans for him to join the ministry, but had continued hoping that he'd want to make something of himself. Lord only knew what kind of trouble he'd get in traveling the river. In no time, he'd be smoking and drinking and bedding whores. Maggie shuddered at the thought. She figured Pa would be disappointed that she hadn't been able to steer the boy in the right direction. But how could she make endless years of schooling compare favorably to unknown adventures on the riverboat routes?

"May I come in, Cousin Margaret?" a quiet voice called from the back porch.

Startled, Maggie jumped, then turned around to see Wesley Peterson, hat in hand, standing outside the kitchen door. Daisy stopped shelling peas, her hands trembling as she clutched the pan in her lap.

"I couldn't get any answer at the front door, so I assumed you were around here at the back. I had the devil's own time finding a path back here." Wesley, his pudgy face red and sweaty, stepped inside the kitchen. Grunting, he said, "Mighty hot day we're having."

Maggie set her spoon and bowl on the table and stood to face the uninvited guest. "What are you doing here, Wesley?"

Daisy moved to stand, but dropped the pan of peas and an apron full of empty hulls onto the floor. She quickly fell to her knees, trying to retrieve the spillage. Her hands were shaking so badly that she stopped and clutched them together in an effort to calm herself.

Noticing the other woman's agitated state, Maggie eyed Wesley briefly, and then turned to help Daisy as she stood behind Maggie, her head bowed.

"I'd like to speak to you alone, Cousin Margaret."

"No, Miss Maggie," Daisy whispered, grabbing her mistress by the arm. "Don't you see that man alone."

Puzzled by Daisy's actions, Maggie turned to the woman. "What's the matter with you?"

"Nothing, Miss Maggie. I just think I should stay." Daisy's pale blue eyes glowed with some inner knowledge that frightened Maggie.

"I'll be all right. You go on and get some chores done upstairs. Cousin Wesley won't be staying long."

Pleading silently with her mistress, Daisy hesitated a few minutes, but left the room quietly when she realized her warning was going unheeded.

"You give that gal too much freedom," Wesley said, walking toward Maggie.

"Daisy is free. Her people have been free for over twenty years now."

"They need to be kept in their place and not allowed to get any big notions about bettering themselves."

"Wesley, why are you here?" Maggie could not imagine why her cousin-by-marriage had finally made his way to see her after six weeks of totally ignoring her existence.

"My mission is twofold, dear Margaret." He stood directly in front of her, a broad smile softening his already flaccid features. "May I sit down?"

She did not want him here. She was not interested in anything he had to say, but common courtesy obliged her to invite him to join her. "By all means, please sit down."

He helped seat Maggie before seating himself and rushing into conversation. "I want you to know that I regret everything that has happened. If I had not been so shocked, I would have been able to have seen things more clearly from the beginning and perhaps have helped you sooner."

"I'm afraid I don't understand. Are you saying that you want to help me? Don't you think you're a little late?"

"Oh, my dear, I think not." He reached across the table to take her hand. "I'm here to offer you a chance for forgiveness and a redeeming life."

Maggie snatched her hand away, glaring into his gentle gray eyes, seeing a glimpse of the kind and caring man she had known and liked those first few weeks in her uncle's home. "Please just go away and leave me alone."

"But you don't understand. I'm not here to condemn you. You're a young girl who has made a mistake and needs forgiveness. I have forgiven you, dear Margaret, as has God." Wesley reached for her hand again.

Maggie jumped away from him, pushing back her chair and quickly standing. "If that's all you've come to say, then you've said it, and now you can go."

Looking up at the beautiful redhead, he sighed. "Oh, dear girl. I'm here to offer you the chance to redeem yourself in the eyes of this community. Once the good people see you working so devoutly at my side, they will know that you've turned from the evil ways of sin."

"Wesley!"

"We will never speak of what has transpired between you and Aaron Stone or young Coleman. I feel inspired by God to give you the chance for salvation. I think God has ordained our marriage."

"Our marriage?"

"Yes, dear Cousin Margaret, I'm asking you to be my wife."

At first, she was sure she had misunderstood, but when she realized that the good reverend had actually proposed marriage to her, she felt giddy and was unable to keep from laughing.

"I find nothing amusing in this."

"Oh, Wesley, whatever would Aunt Tilly say?"

"I've spoken to Mama," he admitted. "She has not given us her blessings yet, but I'm sure she will. After all, you are friends with Mrs. Coleman now, and Mama was greatly impressed that the dear lady has publicly accepted you."

"I see. And what about us? We aren't in love with each other." Maggie wasn't sure she even liked Wesley anymore.

"Oh, but Margaret, I do love you. And, I thought . . . that is to say . . . considering the fact that you'll not be coming to our marriage bed a virgin, your gratitude should eventually grow into love."

She didn't know whether to laugh or cry, or tell Wesley Peterson to go to hell. The very thought of making love with this self-righteous idiot made her physically ill. "I can't accept your offer."

"Don't be hasty. Take time and think about it. I won't rush you, but I will be back when you've had time to consider the matter."

"Wesley, I don't need time."

"Oh, but you do, my dear. When you've thought it through, you'll realize that I'm your only hope."

She stood and watched him leave, amazed that she had never realized the truth about Wesley before now. It seemed as if two different people possessed that large, round body: one, gentle and giving, the other, vindictive and quite insane.

Daisy walked into the kitchen, her blue eyes searching Maggie's face for understanding. For long moments the two women stared at each other, an unspoken question and reply being exchanged.

Maggie was glad to finally be outside. Even with every window open and an abundance of hand fans, the opera house had been steamy with a midsummer, Southern-night heat. She felt wilted, and wondered how the serene Widow Arnold could appear so cool, standing there on the white-columned porch, her ivory cambric dress unstained by perspiration, every pastel bow still neatly tied as they adorned the entire length and width of her skirt.

The last two hours had been sheer torment. Between the smoldering discomfort of the humid night and the presence of Aaron and Eunice sitting directly across the aisle, the entire evening's festivities had been ruined. She had barely noticed any of the play performed by local would-be thespians. From the moment she had caught sight of Aaron's broad back as he turned to allow Eunice to precede him to their seats, Maggie had seen nothing but the golden couple, had heard nothing but the thud of her own angry heart beating in her ears, and had felt nothing but a soul-searing jealousy.

Aaron looked so handsome in his tan breeches and nut-brown coat, his gold silk tie, a shade darker than his mane of thick, blond hair. He had spoken to Eunice, and Maggie hated her. He had smiled at Eunice, and Maggie's heart broke. He had held Eunice's hand, and Maggie gasped, barely able to hold back the tears.

Once or twice, Thayer had patted her hand gently, and she had smiled at him in thanks. The last time, after patting, he raised her hand to his lips and looked past her across the aisle. Maggie's eyes followed and immediately clashed with Aaron's deadly jade glare. His lips had thinned to a hard, straight line, his jaw clenched tightly. She had looked away then, and prayed for the performance to end soon.

A gentle, warm breeze touched Maggie's face and brushed stray curls forward about her bright pink cheeks. Aaron looked across the few yards that separated them there in front of the opera house. He longed to go to her. Why the hell hadn't Thayer told him that he was bringing the Campbells here tonight? He had stayed far away from Maggie these last four weeks, as much for her sake as for his. He could offer her nothing except heartbreak and shame, and she deserved so much more.

It was obvious that she had a hard time controlling her thick, red hair. The bun atop her head was loose and tiny strands framed her face and curled down her neck. He remembered the feel of that silky mass, could, even now, smell the rainwater sweet aroma. He could also remember the feel and smell and taste of other fiery curls.

He cursed himself for being all kinds of a fool. During these past weeks, he had secluded himself at White Orchard, working day and night, driving the workers to the breaking point, trying to prepare the mansion for his bride. But it was not Eunice Arnold's face he saw reflected in the ornate gold mirror in the master bedroom, nor was it Eunice's happy laughter he heard in the long hallways. Maggie haunted every room in the old house, every acre of land over which he rode. And her presence was so alive in the pear orchard that he often thought he could see her lying there in the green grass, her arms reaching up to pull him onto her naked body.

He heard her laugh at something Thayer said, and white-hot jealousy shot through his body like fire. He had no right to be jealous of any man Maggie chose to be with, but the thought of her giving herself to anyone else was agonizingly painful. Had she slept with Thayer? Did he love her? Would he marry her? Damn, he had to stop tormenting himself over a woman he couldn't have. He had made his choice. He had to stay true to his dreams. He owed it to himself. He owed it to his mother.

Taking Eunice by the arm he led her away past the crowd, trying to avoid Thayer and Maggie on their way to where Phineas was waiting with the carriage. He thought he had made it safely away, but he felt a hand on his shoulder and heard Thayer's voice. "You seem in a hurry tonight, Aaron. I wanted to talk to you."

Dreading to turn around, he hesitated. Then he and Eunice turned together to the other couple.

"Hello, Thayer," Aaron said.

Eunice merely smiled and nodded, completely ignoring Maggie, who was busy inspecting the ground.

"My, Eunice, don't you look lovely tonight." Thayer's lazy gaze moved over the willowy blonde.

"Thank you."

"Oh, you both remember Miss Maggie, don't you? Tonight's her brother Micah's seventeenth birthday, and we're enjoying a little family celebration."

"I didn't know you were part of the Campbell family," Aaron said.

The people near the two couples were all watching, whispering, and pointing. Maggie felt very uncomfortable being the center of so much attention. She could well imagine what everyone was saying. How many of these good people thought that she was now Thayer Coleman's mistress?

"You might say that I'm an honorary member," Thayer said. "Isn't that right, Maggie?"

Thayer had called her name, but she wasn't sure what he had said. She was too busy trying not to look at Aaron, and wishing that she had gone on the buggy with Micah and Jude.

"Aaron, I do need a private word with you," Thayer requested. "I promise to only keep him a few minutes, Eunice."

Suddenly Maggie found herself alone beside the Widow Arnold, the two men moving toward a less crowded area. She uttered up a prayer, asking God to keep her from clawing out the other woman's eyes.

"It's rather warm tonight, isn't it?" Eunice said, looking around her, avoiding facing Maggie directly.

"Yes."

"I understand your family is still living in Thayer's house."

"Yes."

"Are you taking in sewing?" Eunice's brown eyes traveled the length of Maggie's dress, from the simple high-necked bodice to the long, slightly tapered skirt.

Self-consciously, Maggie straightened the green gingham bow centered at her waist where her polonaise of the same tiny checks met in soft gathers. "Yes, I am."

Why was the woman trying so hard to carry on a polite conversation when it was apparent that she hated Maggie as much as Maggie hated her? Obviously, genteel ladies were taught that social graces had to be observed in public under any and all conditions.

"Did you enjoy the play?" Eunice asked, a tight smile on her pale face. "Aaron found it quite amusing. I'm sure that once we're married, we will continue to come here often."

"It'll be a long drive from White Orchard."

"Oh, dear, you can't mean you actually think Aaron will want to live on the God-forsaken plantation once he marries me? He knows I love living in town."

"Does he?"

"Of course he does. White Orchard might be suitable for a summer place, but I have plans for us to build a new house in town."

"I see." Oh, yes, Maggie could see. She could see how completely miserable Aaron would be married to the good widow.

"You heard about Rube Whitcomb escaping from jail, didn't you?" Thayer asked.

"Is that why you dragged me all the way over here, to tell me something I knew before noon today?" Aaron growled, taking a cigar from his coat pocket.

"I guess you're not worried since I'm the one he was shooting at."

"We both testified against him, and I'm the one who pressed charges. But I figured he's long gone from these parts by now." Aaron lit the cigar, the silver smoke spiraling out into the darkness.

"Yeah, that's what I think."

"Then what's this all about?"

"I thought you might want to join me tonight. I'm taking young Micah Campbell out on the town to celebrate his birthday the way gentlemen should."

"You're taking him to Loretta's?" Aaron laughed, then took a puff on his cigar.

"Damn right. What better way to celebrate? I think it's the perfect birthday present for the boy."

"Have you asked Maggie?" Aaron could imagine her reaction. She felt very maternal about her younger siblings.

"She'd only worry if she knew."

"Worry? She'd flay the daylights out of you, and him, too."

"Micah wants to go. He's eager to drink hard liquor and have his first woman. Come with us. Verda's back in town, and she's working at Loretta's now. You'd enjoy a tumble with her. She's one sweet—"

"I have to take Eunice home."

"So take her home. Meet me at the town house. We'll wait for you."

"I don't think so."

"What happened, did Maggie castrate you?"

Aaron felt heat suffuse his face. Damn Thayer! The man knew him too well. He hadn't had another woman since the day he'd met Maggie Campbell in May. Here it was August, and he still had no desire to bed anyone but the flame-haired witch who went wild in his arms.

"Wait for me." Aaron threw his half-smoked cigar to the ground, crushing it with his foot. "I'll meet you as soon as I escort Eunice home. I'm looking forward to seeing Verda again."

Maggie planted both small fists on her hips and glared up at Aaron Stone. There was nothing she would like better than to slap his face. He had arrived only minutes earlier, standing in the doorway, refusing to come in. Thayer and Micah were standing directly behind her in the foyer.

"I said, where are you planning on taking Micah for this all-male party?" she demanded.

"Ah, Maggie, quit making such a fuss and just let us leave," Micah said.

"I promise I'll look after him," Thayer added, placing a brotherly arm about the young man's shoulders.

"I can well imagine what you two have in mind for him," Maggie said. "You'll have him smoking and drinking and gambling and worse."

"And worse, Maggie?" Aaron asked, looking past her at the two young men shaking their heads and waving their arms, warning him against pushing this mothering female too far.

"You know very well that I'm talking about whores," Maggie said. "Just because you and Thayer have bedded every whore in the South doesn't mean my brother should."

"Ah, Maggie, it's my birthday." Micah moved closer to his sister and placed a hand on her tense arm.

"You want to go, don't you?" she asked, her yellow eyes flashing golden sparks.

"Look, Maggie," Thayer intervened. "I'll admit we're planning on going to Loretta's, but I promise that we'll take care of Micah and bring him home all in one piece come morning."

While she stood with her back to them, her shoulders shaking from rage and unshed tears, Thayer pulled a reluctant Micah toward the waiting carriage.

Aaron hated to see her so upset, but sooner or later she'd have to let go of Micah and allow him to live his own life. She had been a mother to him far too long.

"Maggie."

"What are you still doing here?" she screeched as she twirled around to face him.

"Micah is a young man with needs. It's only normal he'd want a woman." Aaron was so close to her that he could feel the warmth of her body.

"Damn you!"

"Quit thinking like a mother. You can't keep him away from what he wants. He should have already had his first woman before now."

"And of course, who should know better than you. You probably had your first woman when you were twelve."

Aaron laughed, realizing that all of her spitting and scratching was as much over the fact that he was going to Loretta's as over anything else. "Hardly, I was sixteen."

"I don't want to know."

"Yes, you do."

"No, I don't!"

"Maggie, you're jealous."

"What?"

"You don't like the idea that I might enjoy the pleasure of another woman in my bed." He grabbed her by the shoulders, shaking her gently. "Will you calm yourself if I promise to stay away from all of Loretta's girls?"

"I don't care what you do. You're not my husband. You're not my fiancé. You're not my anything!"

"Oh, but Maggie, I am. I'm your lover."

She looked up into his smiling face. He was so cocksure. She longed to strike him. She'd show him! But when she raised her hand to slap him, he grabbed her wrist seconds before her palm made contact with his cheek.

"Temper, temper, Maggie." He pulled her into his arms, holding her close as she struggled to free herself.

"Let me go!"

"Not until you calm down."

She stopped struggling and stood perfectly still, her eyes fixed on the silky sheen of his tie. "They're waiting on you. Go on!"

"I'd rather stay here with you, but we both know that I can't."

"Don't do this to me," she cried. "Don't do this to us."

His lips moved over hers, savoring the taste.

"No, don't," she sighed.

"Oh, sweet Maggie, I have to."

Their mouths joined, open and waiting, their tongues mating in a frenzy of need. He stroked her back with his big hand as her arms reached up to circle his neck. In one deft movement, he pulled her hair free from the loose bun confining it.

She could not resist this. Maybe she didn't really want to. Did he own her, body and soul? Perhaps. And it was just possible that she wielded the same power over him.

"I want you," Aaron groaned, burying his face in the rainwater sweetness of her hair as his lips nibbled on her ear.

Her feet dangled in the air as he held her tightly. His mouth covered hers again.

"Aaron!" Thayer's voice called loudly from the carriage where he and Micah waited, Phineas standing vigil by the horses.

Aaron lowered Maggie's feet to the porch, his head descending as he continued kissing her.

"Let's go," Thayer called out again. "We want to get there before midnight."

"I have to go," Aaron said, still holding her in his arms.

"I am jealous." She pulled back, looking up into his emerald eyes so full of desire.

The moonlight shimmered dark and then light as a cloud passed across the yellow globe. Far in the distance a dog barked, and close by the carriage horses whinnied. Reality and unreality blended.

"I haven't bedded another woman since the day we met."

"Aaron?"

"Maybe I should. Maybe it would free us both."

"No. Please, no."

He kept walking toward the waiting carriage. "Let's get going," he called out to Thayer. "I want to get to Loretta's and have a celebration drink with Verda."

Maggie stood on the herringbone brick walkway watching the cabriolet drive away. She choked back the tears as pain gripped her chest. Damn Aaron Stone! Damn men!

She turned and walked toward the porch, stopping to pick a bud from the pink rosebush growing near the steps. She held it to her nose, breathing in its uniquely sweet fragrance.

Would Aaron make love to this Verda creature? The thought was more than she could bear. Hot, salty tears ran from her topaz eyes and covered the tender petals of the rosebud she held tightly in her hand.

Chapter 13

Maggie rested her head in her hands as she sat curled up in a brown leather wing chair in the town house library, the wrinkled edge of her green muslin dress wrapped over her bare feet. Moonlight cast shadowy images against the paneled walls and numerous bookshelves while she sat alone staring out the long, narrow windows into the backyard. She had not made any attempt to go to bed because she knew sleep would be impossible. After checking on a peacefully sleeping Jude for the third time, she had finally retreated to the library where she had been sitting and thinking for hours.

It was useless worrying about Micah. No doubt, he was having the time of his life. He would never have made a minister anyway. He enjoyed worldly pleasures far too much. Maybe all of the Campbells were doomed to sins of the flesh.

Ever since Ma had died when Jude was born, Maggie had taken over. Mothering had come naturally to her. But Micah didn't need that anymore. She had to let go. Aaron and Thayer had forced her to accept the fact that her little brother was a man, and men made their own decisions and lived their own lives.

She couldn't help but wonder what decisions Aaron had made once he got to Loretta's. Was he, at this very minute, in bed with the bosomy Verda? Had he been with her all night?

Maggie hurt. The pain was everywhere. It was inside her body, tormenting her mind, ripping her heart to shreds. It was all around her, crushing down on her, suffocating her. Moment by moment, the anguish of jealousy steadily grew until she was afraid that she was going insane. She was tempted to go to Loretta's, to find Aaron, to see what he was doing, and with whom. The reality could be no worse than the images in her mind.

She reached into her dress pocket and pulled out the tiny pink rosebud she had plucked so many hours ago. It was already dying, darkness edging the petals. Like dreams, so beautiful when fresh but destined to an early end, the flower lay in Maggie's palm, a symbol of all she had hoped, a reminder of all she had lost. Had it been only ten weeks ago that she had left Grovesdale with a heart full of wishes and a head full of plans? Micah would probably take that job on Aaron's steamboat and spend his life roaming the river. That was a far cry from the respectable profession Pa had wanted for him. And what about Jude? Was it foolish to expect that dream to come true? Maggie's own reputation might prove to be the major reason this town would never accept Judith as a lady. Had her love for Aaron destroyed everything?

She didn't want to love him. She wanted to hate him, and a part of her did. That aching part of her heart, that tortured part of her brain that could so vividly see his big, gloriously naked body twined around that brunette whore. Oh, God! The pain. He didn't really love her. If he did, he couldn't do this.

Placing the rosebud back in her pocket, she jumped up and ran to Thayer's desk, rummaging through the drawers, feeling over the contents there in the darkness. She found a cigar, pulled it out of the box, and held it in her trembling fingers. Holding it to her nose, she breathed deeply, inhaling the aroma of tobacco as she crushed it in her hand. One by one, she took them from the box, crumpling them to pieces, letting the fragments fall across the desktop.

When the tears began again, she brushed them aside with tobacco-stained fingers. She moved to the window, standing solemnly as silent cries of suffering filled the room. Staring out the window, she caught sight of Daisy moving across the backyard from the cabin toward the house. Wondering why the servant girl was up and entering the house at this time of night, she decided to find out.

When Maggie entered the kitchen, she quickly blew out the candle she held since Daisy had apparently lit the kerosene lamp that was burning brightly on the square, wooden table. The servant was just starting a fire in the cook-stove.

"Daisy, what are you doing?"

Daisy gasped and jumped. "Lordy, Miss Maggie, you scared me."

"It's not daybreak yet. What are you doing heating up the stove?"

"I wasn't feeling none too good, Miss Maggie. I figured I'd make myself some coffee and get me an early start."

Maggie stared at the woman, suddenly noticing how pale her golden skin appeared. There were dark circles under her eyes and her hands were shaking.

"Daisy, what's wrong?"

"Sit down and let me fix that coffee. You ain't been to bed all night, have you?" Daisy quickly placed coffee beans into the grinder, turning the crank. "Don't worry yourself so about Mr. Micah."

"You know where he is?"

"Yes'am. My Phineas was driving them there." The girl poured the freshly ground coffee into the metal pot, added water from a nearby bucket, and placed it on the stove.

Maggie pulled out a high-backed chair and sat down at the table. "Aaron went with them."

"Yes'am."

"I think he's with that horrible Verda. You know, that woman who came by here the other day."

"Does that bother you more than knowing, if he marries Miz Arnold, he'll be in her bed every night?"

"Oh, Daisy," Maggie cried.

Daisy held her seated mistress against her, stroking her hair, patting her back. "Hush now, Miss Maggie. You going to make yourself sick. Things is the way they is. Ain't no need to fret so."

Pulling back, Maggie looked up at Daisy. "Nothing's gone right since we came here. All my plans have been ruined. Micah's out getting drunk and . . . and half the town thinks Aaron and Thayer are passing me back and forth like a bottle of whiskey. And you, Daisy . . . look what happened to you."

"Don't you worry about me. Things is working out. Phineas done ask me to marry him."

"Oh, that's wonderful." Maggie jumped up, swinging the girl around and around.

Daisy laughed, but jerked away, holding on to the table. "I'm sorry. I'm afraid I'm getting sick again."

"What is it?"

"It ain't nothing catching. It's just a sickness a woman sometimes get when she's going to have a baby."

"Daisy?"

"Phineas knows. That's why we want to get married next week."

"A baby. Oh, Daisy, are you happy?"

"Oh, Miss Maggie, I wish I was."

"But why aren't you? You and Phineas love one another, and you're going to be married."

"Sit down, Miss Maggie. I'll see about the coffee."

Daisy took two stoneware cups and saucers from the small corner cabinet and placed them on the table, then poured them full of fresh, hot coffee. Seating herself, she turned to her mistress. "We want to marry next week and move to White Orchard. Phineas don't want nobody to know about the baby till after we're married."

Maggie smiled, thinking how kind Daisy's future husband must be to want to protect her. Under the same circumstances, would Aaron do the same? "He's trying to be gentlemanly."

"He's trying to protect me from this baby's father."

"What?"

"This ain't Phineas's child. We never been together yet. After what happened, I didn't want nobody touching me."

"Are you saying that this child belongs to the man who beat and raped you?"

"Yes'am."

"Oh, dear Lord!"

"You won't never tell nobody, will you, Miss Maggie?"

"Oh, Daisy," Maggie cried, her hands covering the other woman's as they lay on the table. "It's my fault. It's all my fault. Everything. I should never have brought us here."

"You hush up. It ain't your fault. You did what you had to do."

"He asked me to marry him." Maggie looked Daisy squarely in the eyes.

"You know, don't you? You knew today when he left here."

"Yes, I know. I finally realized that Wesley is insane. Oh, not the good Reverend Peterson part of him that he shows to the world. That side of him had me fooled. He was so good to me. To all of us."

"That's why I couldn't tell you. You was counting on him and his ma to help you with Mr. Micah and Miss Jude."

"Oh, Daisy, when I think about what he did to you."

"Don't. I try not to. You just stay away from him. He said I'd been sleeping with Phineas. He had been watching us. He was standing in the shadows, watching Phineas kiss me good night. He said I was the devil's seed, put on this earth to tempt men to sin."

"Does Phineas know that it was Wesley?"

"Oh, no! He must never know. He'd kill that man if he knew."

Daisy laid her head on the table and cried as Maggie comforted her, the two women sharing a secret they could tell no one.

Maggie wondered if Aaron Stone was half the man his black friend was. Phineas loved Daisy enough to marry her knowing that she carried the child of the madman who had raped her. Would Aaron be unselfish enough to give up his obsession for respectability to marry the mother of his unborn child?

She wasn't positive, but she had suspected that she had conceived Aaron's child the first time they had made love. She had missed her monthly flow for the first time since it had started when she'd been eleven.

Should she tell Aaron? Would he marry her? Would he even believe the child was his with half the town thinking she was Thayer's mistress? Perhaps she should tell Thayer. Maybe he could help her. He was Aaron's best friend. He knew him better than anyone else.

Without a husband, she would be branded a whore and her child a bastard. If that happened, there would be no hope for them anywhere, and the fate that had befallen Aaron would haunt his own child. And Jude, poor little Jude. Any hope for her future would end.

"Please, dear God, help us," Maggie prayed.

Aaron had seen the light in the kitchen before he helped Phineas drag the two drunken men onto the back porch. Micah had passed out on the carriage ride home, and Phineas had the boy thrown over his shoulder while Aaron supported a staggering Thayer.

Aaron wasn't surprised to see the two women sitting at the kitchen table. He had suspected that Maggie would be waiting up for them.

"Oh, Lord!" Maggie screamed, running to Phineas, touching her brother's tousled auburn hair. "What happened? Is he hurt?"

"No, ma'am," the big black man said smiling.

"Calm down, Maggie. He's fine," Aaron assured her, his arm under Thayer's arm as he pulled him through the room. "He's drunk. He passed out."

"Damn your rotten hide, Aaron Stone," the redhead yelled.

"Oh, Maggie, sweet Maggie," Thayer blubbered, reaching out to her.

"We'll get these two to bed, Miss Maggie," Phineas said as he looked at Daisy, his dark eyes warm with love.

"Sit back down, Miss Maggie," Daisy said. "Phineas will take good care of Mr. Micah."

"Go on, Phineas," Maggie said. "And you help Thayer. But I want to have a word with you, Aaron Stone, unless you're about to pass out drunk yourself."

"Leave it be, woman," Aaron said, leading his friend out of the kitchen.

Angry and determined, Maggie followed the men to the back stairway. "Don't you order me around. I'm not through with you."

"Then shut up yakking, and we'll have ourselves a real showdown as soon as I put Thayer to bed. Just wait right here." Aaron moved slowly up the steps, a tipsy Thayer humming happily, and Phineas following, Micah still out cold across his big shoulder.

Maggie paced back and forth in the dark hallway. Men! They had to be the dumbest creatures God ever made. How could getting so drunk you couldn't even stand on your own two feet be fun? She had a few things she wanted to say to Mr. Stone if he could find his way back downstairs. Well, if he couldn't she'd just go upstairs after him. She intended to find out just what had happened to Micah tonight, and she would ask Aaron, point blank, if he had bedded another woman. She had tried to convince herself that, no matter what he said, he would never marry Eunice Arnold because he didn't love the woman. But if he had made love to one of Loretta's whores, it would mean he didn't really love Maggie either.

She stomped her foot and whirled around, going back into the kitchen. She was tired of waiting in the dark hallway. She'd just pour herself another cup of coffee and bide her time. If Aaron didn't have enough nerve to face her, she'd know the truth.

Aaron opened the kitchen door quietly and looked inside. Maggie stood, coffee cup in hand, looking out the back door. Her green dress was terribly wrinkled. Her long, cinnamon hair hung in loosely tangled curls to her tiny waist. He wanted to go over and take her in his arms, but he knew she would turn on him like a spitting kitten if he touched her. She was primed and ready for a fight, so he decided it was best to get it over with. Then, maybe . . .

"Micah's in bed, safe and sound," Aaron said.

She kept her back to him. "I want to know exactly what happened."

"Every detail?"

"The main details."

"We drank, played cards, told jokes, and were entertained by Loretta's ladies."

"Micah didn't have much money."

"It was our birthday present. I think he enjoyed it."

"How would he know? He passed out. He probably won't even remember."

"He didn't pass out until we were on our way home. And believe me, he'll remember. This was a night he'll never forget."

Maggie turned to face her tormentor. "Did he . . . was he with . . ."

"We introduced him to Verda. You'll have to ask Micah if you want the details on what they did alone together in her room." Aaron walked into the kitchen, a smile on his handsome face.

"You didn't mind sharing Verda with my brother?" Maggie's eyes flashed amber fire. "Did you have her first, or did you have to wait?"

"My dear Miss Campbell, that's a very personal question."

"Damn you," Maggie screeched, hurling the empty coffee cup at Aaron's head. With a resounding thud, it clipped him directly above his right eye, then fell, crashing onto the floor.

"Good God, woman. Are you trying to kill me?" He reached up, running his fingers across the small bump swelling at his brow.

"Yes. Maybe Rube Whitcomb will shoot you again now that he's escaped. He'd do the world a favor by killing you this time."

"So, you'd rather see me dead than in the arms of another woman?"

"You can bed as many whores as you want to. I don't care. I just want you to stay out of my life and out of Micah's."

"I can't do that," Aaron said, looking down at the stain on his fingertips. That darn fool woman had actually drawn blood. "Micah's leaving in a few days to start work on the *Chattanooga Belle*."

"Why couldn't you and Thayer mind your own business?"

"Micah's a man, old enough to make his own decisions."

"With a little help from his new friends. Are you proud of yourself? Proud that you introduced a boy to . . . to . . ."

Aaron moved toward Maggie, who backed up against the door. "Why don't you say what you really mean? Why don't you admit what's bothering you?"

She glared at him, damning him to everlasting torment. "How could you make love to that . . . that . . . woman . . . to any woman, if you really love me?"

He reached out for her hand, but she jerked it away, bracing herself against the door, her tense stance daring him to touch her.

"I really love you."

"Then how could you . . . I closed my eyes and all I could see was the two of you."

"Don't, Maggie." He grabbed her trembling hands.

"Don't touch me. I hate you!" She pulled out of his grasp, rushing past him through the kitchen.

"Maggie, wait. Please listen." He followed her out into the dark hallway.

"I won't listen. I don't want to know."

"I didn't make love to Verda."

"I . . . don't . . . believe . . . you," she cried, stopping at the foot of the back stairway, her uneven breathing punctuating every tortured word.

Please God, make her believe me. Aaron felt helpless against the lie he had presented earlier and had tried to perpetuate. He had wanted Maggie to think he was going to bed with the luscious Verda.

It had been a mistake. The only woman he wanted to bed was Maggie. Going to Loretta's had only confirmed his suspicion that he had no desire for other women, no matter how seductive their charms.

"I haven't had another woman. Not tonight. Not since the day I met you."

Maggie held her breath. Could she believe him? Would he lie? If he were telling the truth . . . if he really loved her.

"I swear, Maggie. I swear it's the truth."

"Aaron?"

He wanted to touch her, but he was afraid. He couldn't bear it if she rejected him. "I want only you."

"But it doesn't matter. Can't you see? If you're going to marry Eunice—"

"It does matter. It matters that you believe me."

"Go away, Aaron. Go away and leave me alone. I can't stand any more of this. I hurt . . . I hurt so badly."

He felt as if his heart had been ripped from his body. He could feel her pain, was actually experiencing the anguish she suffered. He had never known it was possible to become so much a part of another human being that her joys and sorrows were his own. What had he done to this woman? She had loved him and forgiven him of so much already, would her generous heart pardon his selfishness one more time?

"Let me take away the hurt," he pleaded. "Let me show you how much I love you."

Not waiting for a response, Aaron swooped her up into his arms, her soft body instinctively cuddling against his massive chest as her hands closed about his neck.

"I hate you for doing this to me," she said, listening to the hammering of his heartbeat as her head lay against him. "Loving you is destroying me."

Part of her wanted to resist him, knowing that she would never be more to him than a mistress, but the ancient female animal within her demanded satisfaction. Held securely in his arms as he took the back steps upward to her bedroom, Maggie longed to know again the passion she had shared with this man. It didn't matter that he smelled of whiskey and stale smoke, or that his coat reeked of cheap whore's perfume. Deep within her heart of hearts, she knew there had been no other woman for him.

He wanted to be inside of her now, finding the sweet oblivion that could be found only in her. He was obsessed with this temptress whose innocent love had captured his rogue's heart and possessed his very soul. Had his father felt this way? Had his insides burned with desire every time he looked at the woman he loved? Was that why Richard Leander had bedded a girl his daughter's age, impregnated her with his bastard child, and had never been able to give her up? Was that how it would be for him? Would he be able to stay away from Maggie once he was married to Eunice?

Pushing the door to Maggie's bedroom open with his booted foot, he moved to the oak tester bed, laying her tenderly upon it. Huge, sculptured posts and an intricately carved headboard supported the gossamer lace canopy. The summer light covers were turned back, revealing the pristine whiteness of the soft cotton sheets and delicate, hand-embroidered pillowcases.

Maggie's long, red hair spread across the pillow like a fire blazing in the snow, and her topaz eyes gazed up into his, shining with a hunger that was ravaging her woman's body.

The soft, hazy light of dawn shone through the windows as the heavens gave birth to a new day, the first filtered rays of sunlight permeating the room. Aaron could see her clearly, warm and waiting, and his. She was so beautiful.

His big hands, trembling with desire, slowly, methodically began to undress her as she lay pliant and willing. He threw her dress to the floor, and then stroked the creamy softness of her naked shoulders and arms. He watched fascinated by the way her body quivered with longing as he continued to stroke her, his fingers caressing her slender neck, brushing across the upper swell of her breasts still hidden beneath the thin chemise.

"I want to look at you," he whispered, his lips almost touching her ear as he eased her chemise off, tossing it aside. "I want to see your breasts fill my hands. I want your nipples to grow hard beneath my fingers."

She arched her back, lifting herself to help him discard her corset. When he covered her breasts with his palms and squeezed gently,

Maggie whimpered, ripples of promised pleasure dancing across each nerve ending.

"I dream of your breasts." His mouth lowered, his tongue flickering over one erect tip and then the other.

With her body still shivering, he kissed each breast, his mouth moving to caress her waist and then her belly as he pulled her drawers downward over her hips, her shapely legs, and her dainty feet. She lay before him completely naked, the pink glow of dawn bathing her in its iridescent light.

Maggie looked up at the big blond hovering above her, the eagerness in his emerald eyes at war with his patiently progressive actions that were fueling the fire of their passions. Even fully clothed, he was huge and hard and manly. The very fact that she was vulnerably naked while he remained dressed created erotic sensations within her.

He lay beside her on the soft feather bed, his hands soothing her feverish flesh as his lips took hers in a series of quick, intense kisses. He explored her face with his mouth, worshipping her forehead, her eyes, her cheeks, her nose, her chin, finally closing over her open mouth, their tongues joining in a frenzy of inducement. They begged silently, pleading for pleasure only they could give each other.

"I want you," she moaned, reaching for him.

He grabbed her hand, halting her. "And you are going to want me even more." He brought her hand to his mouth, his tongue drawing circles around and around, inside her palm. "You'll want me more than you want air to breathe. And then, when I make you wait just a little longer, I'll take you and give you a pleasure beyond bearing."

Maggie cried out, her body fighting his rejection, demanding his penetration. "Don't make me wait. Love me now!"

How could he do this to her? Did he realize that she was already half mad with desire? Her body ached with need. Her breasts were swollen and sore and overly sensitive. Her flesh tingled from his constant administrations, and the secret place between her thighs throbbed almost painfully.

His tongue slid up and down each finger of her hand, slowly, tantalizingly sucking each tip. Her hand trembled.

"I love the taste of you," he groaned against her wrist as he began kissing the inside of her arm.

"Aaron, love me. Please love me."

"All in good time, sweet Maggie," he promised, standing up beside the bed, shrugging out of his coat and shirt.

Ivory sunlight fell across his massive, hairy chest, turning his bronze skin and tawny curls to pale gold. His big, muscular arms pulled her against him, the feel of her fully aroused nipples brushing his flesh, almost sending him over the edge, making him forget his deep need to pleasure her thoroughly.

She reached between them, stroking him, her fingers running through his chest hair. He grabbed her hand, pulling it away from his body.

"You mustn't touch me. Not yet," he said, holding both of her hands behind her back.

"But I want to touch you. I need to touch you. It would please me if I could touch you." She squirmed against him, trying to free her hands, but simply creating more flesh-against-hairy-flesh stimulation.

"It will please you even more if you wait."

"Damn you, Aaron Stone. I can't bear any more of this. Let go of my hands."

Immediately he released her, a wide, sly grin curling his lips. She touched him, his face, his neck, and his shoulders. She buried her face in his silky chest curls, her eager mouth planting kisses everywhere.

But as quickly as he had freed her, he flipped her over on her stomach, pinning her to the bed when his big body covered hers, his hands bracing him above her.

"Aaron!"

"Hush, my love."

She shuddered from head to toe when his mouth made loving contact with the heated flesh of her back as he anointed every inch of her from neck to heels with hot, provocative kisses.

"Aaron, please."

"Please what, my Maggie?"

"Please make love to me."

"I am making love to you."

"I want more."

"Do you want me inside you? Do you?"

"Yes."

"Then tell me."

"Oh Aaron. I want you inside me now!"

He stood up, allowing her to turn over and watch while he stripped off his breeches and tossed them to the foot of the bed.

He hovered above her, naked and manly proud, his golden shoulders heaving from the force of his labored breathing, beads of sweat dotting his brow.

"I've never wanted anything as much as I want you," Aaron said, gazing at her beauty, loving her more than he had ever thought possible.

Her legs opened instinctively to receive him, urging him inside her. At long last, he thrust himself into her hot, wet warmth, groaning, trembling as he plunged again and again. Maggie's hips moved in frantic rhythm, encouraging each stab of his swollen manhood. Taking, giving, taking, they drove themselves to the very brink of fulfillment. As she shook with release, the sensations of pleasure rippling through her body, she heard his harsh cry and felt his seed spilling into her, filling her with his love.

Satiated and exhausted, they slept in one another's arms, waking later to make love again. Before the sun blazed high in the sky and the reality outside intruded on the lovers' fantasy world, Aaron took her yet again, knowing this would have to be their last time together.

Chapter 14

"It's hotter than blue blazes," Judith said as she sat by the open window, fanning herself with the silk fan Thayer had given her, a reward for her good behavior the last few weeks.

"I hope the rain holds off until Daisy and Phineas can get to White Orchard." Maggie looked out the window at the cloudy sky, a heavy gray haze obscuring the sunshine.

"I'm not going to get married in August," Jude declared, laying her fan on the kitchen table. Taking the dipper from the water bucket, she put it to her lips and drank greedily. "I think I'll marry Thayer in the spring before it gets so blooming hot."

Maggie laughed. "You do that. But, for now, run into the parlor and see if Daisy's about ready to get this wedding started."

"I don't want a little-bitty wedding like this, with just the preacher and three guests."

"No, I'm sure you don't. You'll want hundreds of people there and a brass band playing."

Judith giggled. "Maybe not a brass band, but an organ playing, and afterward a grand reception with lots of wine and music."

"Go on." Maggie swatted the child on the bottom. "Get in there and ask Daisy if she's ready."

Maggie busied herself, setting a small cake on the table, arranging six crystal glasses by the china plates, and placing the bottle of wine Aaron had brought.

Perspiration trickled down between her breasts, her drawers stuck to her skin with moisture, and damp tendrils of fiery hair curled about her flushed face. She hated that the day was so unbearably hot, making any movement more strenuous than breathing a discomfort. She wanted everything to be perfect for Daisy.

She had grown to love Daisy over the years since Pa had first brought the battered, half-starved fourteen-year-old home. Ma had been dead two months and Maggie, at eight, had been struggling to take over her duties. She and Daisy had worked side by side, cooking, cleaning, canning, gardening, and mothering Micah and Jude. Maggie had always known that Daisy was a servant, but somehow, on their poverty-stricken Tennessee farm, it hadn't mattered all that much. The young Negress had known her place and kept it, but with the Campbells she had been one of the family.

And now the family was going off in different directions. After today, Daisy would be Phineas's wife, and they'd have their own family, living and growing up at White Orchard. Micah was already gone, gone up the river to a new job and a life far removed from the one Maggie had planned for him. He had promised to write, but she wondered if he would. He was half man and half boy, on the verge of maturity, longing for adventures that could satisfy the wildness in him.

Jude had a different kind of wildness in her, an all-consuming rage for life. That child was born wanting and taking, and Maggie was afraid she might never get enough. Was there any hope of turning that little hellion into a proper lady?

Maggie lifted a red rose out of the cup of water sitting in the window and pinned it on the bodice of her tan muslin dress. During blooming season, Ma had always pinned a rose on herself and on Maggie before heading off to church the Sundays the circuit preacher came to Grovesdale. Roses would always mean happiness to Maggie. They'd always remind her of her ma.

She'd been thinking a lot about her mother lately. Maybe it was because she was carrying a child of her own and wondering what was to become of them both. Even as a last resort, she could never marry Wesley now that she knew what kind of man he really was. She wanted to tell Aaron about the baby, but her stubborn Scottish pride kept her from it.

Jude stuck her head in the kitchen doorway and motioned for Maggie. "Come on. They're ready. And Daisy wants me to sing."

"Oh Jude!"

"I'm going to sing 'Beautiful Dreamer.' Hurry up."

When Maggie entered the elegant parlor of the Coleman town house, she could actually feel the love and happiness radiating from the black couple standing, in their Sunday best, before the minister, an open Bible in his ebony hands. The room was quiet with the hushed stillness of a lazy summertime day. Jude cleared her throat once, and then began to sing, high and sweet in her clear soprano voice.

When the song ended and the minister began the ceremony, Maggie turned her head slightly to catch a stolen glance at Aaron, who stood a few feet to her left, idly stroking his gold pocket watch. She hadn't seen him since he had kissed her good-bye in her bedroom upstairs ten days ago. She was a fool when it came to that man. All he had to do was call, and she went to him. What would happen if he married Eunice? Would he want her to be his mistress? Did she have the strength to resist him?

Undoubtedly, he had been working outside because his hair was sun-bleached to a yellow white, and his dark complexion was a deeper bronze. He had never looked more handsome than he did today in his ivory coat and dark blue trousers.

She could feel his eyes on her and wondered if he was remembering as she was the last time they had made love. Without speaking, they both knew that they had to end their affair. They were destroying themselves and everyone they held dear. If Aaron could never forgive his father and accept himself for who and what he was, there was not hope for them. Could she tell him about his unborn child? Did she have the right to burden him with a knowledge that could only lead to more heartbreak? He was already torn between his love for Maggie and his determination to claim a birthright denied him.

Aaron had missed her terribly, had longed to come to her and love her again and again. He had admitted to himself that he was obsessed with this flame-haired witch whose luscious body and tempestuous lovemaking tormented his every thought. He had worked like a madman at White Orchard, spending every daylight hour from dawn to dusk outside in the fields or on horseback. No matter how weary and exhausted, he had been unable to erase the sight of her sleek, naked body from his mind. He had lain alone in bed every night remembering the taste, the feel, the scent of her body, hot and aroused, begging him to take her.

She looked so beautiful today in her plain tan dress, the big red rose adding a touch of color to the muslin's drabness. The humidity had curled her wavy hair, moist strands framing her creamy face. Her full, pink lips parted slightly, tempting him to partake of their sweetness.

He had never been so confused and uncertain. For five years, he had planned and dreamed and worked. His one goal was to gain his rightful place in society by finding and marrying a woman whose social prestige was unquestionable. He had hated Richard Leander, had even despised his own mother. Having consummated their love without a marriage license, they had denied their only son his heritage.

Phineas held Daisy in his arms while tears filled Maggie's eyes and Jude rushed to grab the black woman.

"I'm Miz Phineas Moulton," Daisy said, holding up her left hand where a plain gold band glistened brightly.

"And I'm a happy man." Phineas beamed with pride.

"And a lucky man." Aaron patted his friend on the back. "You've married the woman you love."

So could you, Maggie thought. *If you'd be willing to let go of your dreams, forgive your parents for loving each other, and accept what no power on earth can ever change.*

"I'll get the cake. Jude, you help me bring in the refreshments," Maggie ordered.

"Do I get a glass of wine too?" Jude asked, smiling demurely up at Aaron.

"You most certainly do not, young lady," Aaron told her.

Maggie looked at Aaron and smiled. Looking at her and not being able to touch her was breaking his heart. After today, he'd have to make a point of staying away from her.

"It's not fair," Jude said. "Grown-ups won't let you do anything fun when you're ten years old. All I hear is 'no you can't' and 'don't do that.' I wish I were seventeen like Micah. You just wait. I'm going to do everything then. I might even run off on a steamboat."

"Come on, little adventuress, you can help me pour the wine," Aaron said.

* * *

Maggie sat on one brocade sofa sipping wine from a crystal glass as Phineas and Daisy sat across from her on the twin sofa, gazing into each other's eyes. Jude sat on the floor between them, her lemonade glass resting on the brown marble-topped table where a bouquet of red roses filled a round, silver vase, their flowery scent saturating the air. Aaron stood by the windows, an empty wineglass in his hand, watching the preacher disappear down the front brick walkway.

"I guess we need to get started," Phineas said. "We want to get home to White Orchard before the rain sets in."

"Your house is all ready," Aaron told the happy couple. "Thayer sent Ludie over with a week's worth of food."

"Thank Mr. Thayer for us," Daisy said.

The moment she heard the door chimes, Maggie rushed to the foyer, wondering who would be calling. All their acquaintances were aware that the black couple was getting married today. Perhaps some of Phineas's friends were stopping by to wish the newlyweds happiness.

When she opened the front door, she gasped in surprise. There stood a neatly groomed Wesley Peterson, a book under his arm.

"Wesley!"

"Good afternoon, Cousin Margaret. May I come in?"

"I . . . we've just had a wedding here and—"

"Yes, yes. Of course. That's one of the reasons I stopped by. I have a gift for the couple."

"You . . . you . . ." Maggie stood staring at the reverend, unable to believe he was actually standing there saying he had a wedding gift for the woman he had beaten and raped.

While Maggie watched, open-mouthed and speechless, Wesley walked into the foyer. "It's a Bible. Every home, white or colored, should have one. May I give it to them?"

"No!"

"Why, Cousin Margaret, whatever is the matter with you?"

"Daisy and Phineas were just fixing to leave. They've a long ride ahead of them to White Orchard." Maggie moved quickly alongside Wesley as he walked toward the parlor.

"I'll just give them the Bible and wish them well." He was at the open parlor doors, Maggie beside him. "Then perhaps you'll spare me a few minutes of your time. We have some important plans to make, dear Margaret."

Oh Lord, what could she do? Maggie grasped his arm, but he continued walking. "Wait."

But Daisy saw him, her blue eyes widening with fear. Wesley walked over to the sofa, Maggie unable to slow his stride.

"Congratulations, Daisy. I have a present for you and Phineas." Wesley held out the Bible to the young woman. "It's the Good Book."

Daisy's slender body tightened, her huge eyes darting from the small book in Wesley's hand to the man's smiling face, then to Maggie's concerned amber eyes. "No. No. I don't want it."

"I'll take it," Maggie said, grabbing the Bible out of the minister's fleshy hand. "Thank you, Cousin Wesley."

"You all seem to be celebrating," Wesley said. "The Lord is always with us on these happy occasions. Perhaps you'd like me to pray for these two people on their wedding day?"

Daisy trembled, her nervous hands clutched together in her lap. "No, please. We . . . we have to go."

Phineas turned to his bride, his big hand covering hers. "What's wrong, Daisy, you shaking all over."

"Miss Maggie," the servant girl pleaded.

"Phineas, you take Daisy on out to the buggy. You two go on now," Maggie said, placing her hand on Wesley's arm. "Wesley's come to see me. We—"

"You don't want to see this man, Miss Maggie." Phineas stood, his gigantic body rigid. "And neither does Daisy. You both afraid of him."

"No," Daisy cried. "We ain't. Please, Phineas, let's go, I want to leave now."

"Not till you tell me why you and Miss Maggie behaving like this." Phineas stepped right up to Wesley. "Maybe you can tell me, Revered Peterson."

"See here, Phineas, you forget yourself," Wesley said.

Aaron walked between Wesley and Phineas, his hand reaching out to grab his servant's arm, his stern look reminding the man of the danger he was evoking. "Take your wife and go home, my friend. There'll be another time and another place."

"Please, Phineas." Daisy placed her trembling hand on her husband's shoulder as she stood behind him.

"My goodness," Wesley said. "This is quite a to-do over nothing. I merely sought to be Christianly. But you need to remind your coloreds how they should and shouldn't conduct themselves, Mr. Stone."

Maggie tugged on the reverend's sleeve. "I think now is a good time for us to talk. Let me pour you some lemonade out in the kitchen." She had no desire to be alone with this man, but, in order to spare Daisy another moment of this insanity, she had no choice.

"That would be delightful, dear Margaret." Wesley offered her his arm, escorting her out of the parlor when she accepted.

"Delicious lemonade," Wesley said after finishing his second glass while sitting at the kitchen table. "Most refreshing on such a hot day."

Maggie had listened with great relief to the sound of the buggy leaving. If Phineas and Daisy were finally on their way, tragedy could be avoided, at least for the time being. No doubt, Phineas and Aaron both suspected the truth about Wesley, and she wondered just what Daisy's new husband might do.

"How could you have come here, today of all days?" Maggie demanded, standing beside the seated man, her cat-eyes afire with hatred.

"I'm sorry, Margaret. I simply wanted to give Daisy the Bible before speaking with you about our own marriage." He reached for the large pitcher, pouring himself a third glass of lemonade.

"Our marriage?"

"Mama isn't pleased, but, if you will agree for us to live with her and Chester, she'll give us her blessings. She thinks that, under her guidance, you and Judith have a chance."

"Wesley, I have no intention of marrying you."

"Now, my dear, I know you must feel yourself unworthy, but I'm a forgiving man."

"A forgiving man? I thought I knew you, but I was so wrong. I had no idea what you were really like."

He sipped the cool liquid, removed a linen handkerchief from his coat pocket, and wiped the perspiration from his florid face. "Surely you've always known of my fondness for you? I will admit that your indiscretion with Mr. Stone hurt me deeply. And that it became public knowledge made me heartsick."

"You were heartsick?" Maggie hissed, glaring down at him. "If you were, it was because this whole town knew you wanted to marry me. You had even told Brother Osborne. Then I did the unforgivable. I offended Eunice Arnold by spending the day alone with a man she considers her private domain."

"Margaret, Margaret. You can redeem yourself."

"Can you redeem yourself, Wesley?"

"What?" His silver eyes hardened as he reached out to grasp Maggie's wrist. "You must explain yourself."

"There's no need for you to deny it. I know. I know what you did."

The good reverend released her wrist, raking her from head to toe with his cold, gray stare. "And of what are you accusing me?"

"Daisy told me. You beat her. You . . . you . . ." Maggie could not bring herself to say the word. The thoughts it conjured up in her mind were too painful.

"She has lied to you!" Wesley bellowed, easing his bulky frame from the chair.

"No. No, she didn't lie. Why, Wesley? Why? What kind of a monster are you?" She stepped away from the wide-eyed man reaching for her.

"She's evil," he shouted. "The devil's child. I saw her there by Auntie Gem's cabin, letting her lover paw her. When he left, I went to her to try to save her soul. I told her to repent and pray. She refused."

"Oh, dear Lord." Maggie had no doubt that this man was insane. She suddenly felt alone and frightened. Where was Jude? And where was Aaron?

"I had to beat the evil out of her. I had to cleanse her soul so she could repent. But the devil was strong in her. She forced me to do the unspeakable."

Maggie gradually backed away, but he followed and pinned her against the wall, his meaty hands grabbing her shoulders. "No, Wesley."

"There is evil in you. I and I alone can save you. You must repent."

Maggie's scream echoed through the stillness of the town house as she watched, horrified, when he drew back his hand to strike her. Her eyes closed tightly, she struggled against her attacker, and screamed again.

The expected blow never came. She swayed and opened her eyes when she was abruptly released. Aaron Stone had jerked Wesley away, his big fists landing blow after blow to the other man's jowled face and flabby body. Wesley staggered, and then fell, his rotund form sprawling across the floor.

Aaron stepped over his defeated opponent to pull a trembling Maggie into his arms. She went willingly, clinging to him, tears streaming down her face.

"Hush, Maggie mine. It's all right. I'm here now."

He held her securely within the safe haven of his strong arms. He would have liked nothing better than to have killed Wesley Peterson. It would have been easy to have snapped the fat swine's neck, but that would have terrified Maggie even more.

"He . . . he's the . . . one . . ."

"Hush, sweet love, hush. I know." His big hand stroked her, yearning to soothe away all the pain and fear.

Wesley struggled to his feet, standing unsteadily as he glared at the couple holding one another. "You're no better than your nigger. Whores, both of you. Seeds of the devil."

Aaron pulled away from her, longing to strike the reverend's already bruised face.

"No, please, Aaron." Maggie held on to him slightly. "Get out of here, Wesley, and don't you ever come back."

"I shall go, but His vengeance will fall upon you both, like fire from heaven," the madman roared. "There are those of us who do our Lord's bidding. We know how to rid the world of evildoers and troublemakers. Be on watch, Aaron Stone, and warn your nigger. You won't know the hour when we shall strike."

Maggie clung to Aaron while the two of them watched Reverend Peterson stagger through the kitchen door.

"Jude?" Maggie cried.

"It's all right. I sent her upstairs when we heard you scream."

"Thank God Phineas and Daisy left when they did."

"I want you to wait here," Aaron said, pulling away from her to follow the other man.

"No, Aaron, please." She ran after him as he hurried through the hallway and foyer to the open front door where Wesley stood, bracing himself against the door frame.

"Stay here," Aaron told her.

She threw her arms around him, slowing his stride. He could move no farther without dragging her. "Don't. Not now, not like this."

"He's dangerous, Maggie. He's like a mad dog. He needs to be destroyed."

"No. No. What are you saying? Daisy isn't the first woman he's . . . ?"

Aaron stopped and held her, not wanting to answer her unfinished question. For long moments, they stood there while the reverend made his way outside to his buggy.

"I've heard talk at Loretta's," Aaron admitted. "I never paid much attention."

"What did you hear?"

"That the saintly preacher occasionally arranged for Loretta to send him a woman over to the church building at night."

"No, not the church."

"Rumor was that he beat the girls so badly that none of them would agree to go back."

"Oh, Aaron. Please hold me."

She rested her head on his chest and cried while he held and comforted her. Where would it all end? Her life had become a nightmare, her hopes and dreams destroyed, her plans all gone awry.

What kind of man was Wesley? He had been gentle and kind, taking time to help Jude with her schoolwork, insisting on paying for Micah's tuition. He had stood against his mother to help the Campbells time and again. But then he had chased her down Main Street that night, spouting sin and salvation and repentance. And today he would have struck her, perhaps beaten her as he had Daisy. As he had those other women.

"Try not to think about it," Aaron said, kissing the top of her head.

"Daisy's carrying his child." Maggie wondered how the woman could endure having a baby by a man so demented.

"I know. Phineas told me that the child belonged to the man who had forced himself on her. He loves her enough to accept the child. He'll raise it as if it were his own."

"Phineas is a rare man indeed."

"Yes, he is."

Aaron wondered if he were in his friend's position would he be able to watch the woman he loved grow bigger each day with the child of a man who had raped her. There was no doubt in his mind. He would kill Wesley Peterson. So, was it only a matter of time?

"Don't let Phineas do anything crazy," Maggie said as Aaron led her over to the table where he sat down, pulling her onto his lap.

"He's not stupid. He knows how to handle himself."

"Promise me you won't do anything."

"All I want to do is help you. I've already caused you so much pain."

He could not resist the sweet temptation of her lips. They exchanged a kiss as gently loving and gossamer light as a kiss could be. He rubbed the back of his hand across her smooth cheek. "Let me help you, Maggie. Let me pay for Jude's school. Let me buy you a house and give you enough money to get by until you can earn a living as a seamstress."

She gazed into his dark green eyes. "Has anything changed? Have you decided not to ask Eunice to marry you?"

Taking her face in his hands, he looked directly into her golden eyes. "Nothing has changed. Next month, I'll propose to Eunice."

Her breathing quickened as she glared at him, placing an arm around his thick neck. "Are you asking me to be your mistress?"

"No, Maggie. I wasn't asking that kind of sacrifice from you."

"Will you be able to give me up?"

"I don't know." The very thought of giving her up was unbearable. But what kind of life could he hope to have with Eunice if he started their marriage being unfaithful to her?

"Thayer has offered me his assistance."

"He's done what?"

"If you don't want me as your mistress, perhaps Thayer does," she lied. She hated being dishonest with him, but desperation could make a woman do strange things.

"The hell he does!"

Maggie could feel the big man's body stiffen, his hands grabbing her waist.

She removed her arms from around his neck, twisting to free herself. "Thayer isn't ashamed of me. Who knows, he might offer me marriage."

"Thayer's not in love with you. Bewitched maybe, but not in love. He's not ready for marriage." He held her firmly as she struggled to get out of his lap.

"If that's true, then maybe I'll settle for being his mistress. At least he won't have a wife to betray."

"Stay out of Thayer's bed. You belong to me."

"How do you know I haven't already been in his bed?" she taunted, her gleaming eyes filled with defiance.

"I know. I know because you are mine." His mouth took hers in a kiss of pure possession, verifying his claim.

She tried not to respond, but her lips betrayed her, parting to accept the thrust of his ravaging tongue. He kissed her long and hard, the very savagery of it arousing her passion.

And then the kiss was over, and Aaron pushed her from his lips as he stood. "If you want to be a mistress, then you'll be mine. Think about it. When you decide, send me word."

He walked to the door, hesitating briefly. "If you need anything, I'll provide it. Don't involve Thayer in what's going on between the two of us."

He turned and walked away. Maggie stood staring at the closed door for quite a while. Had he meant what he'd said? Was he the kind of man who could marry Eunice and keep a mistress? She hadn't thought so. But then she had never suspected the kindly minister who had befriended her family was capable of inhuman brutality.

Covering her face with her hands, she began to cry. Things could not go on this way. She had to make some decisions, decisions that would affect the rest of her life and Jude's. Micah had taken control of his own life so she no longer had any responsibility for his destiny, but she still had her sister to think about and, now, her unborn child.

She could not stay on here indefinitely accepting Thayer's charity. In a few months her condition would begin to show, and she would be forced to either tell Aaron the truth or leave town. What would Aaron do if she told him? Would he give up his dream, marry her for the child's sake, and spend the rest of his life hating her? And if she told Thayer, what would he do? Could she risk telling either man?

Perhaps she should pack up and move away from Tuscumbia to someplace where nobody knew her. Maybe she could pass herself off as a widow and try to make a new life, find new dreams to replace the old. But how would she be able to take care of herself and Jude and a baby? She was a woman alone, with no money and no man of her own.

Where can I go? What can I do?

Chapter 15

Maggie pulled her shawl tightly about her shoulders as she stepped down from the buggy, the cool autumn breeze blowing her already disheveled hair about her face. It had turned cold sometime during the night, and everything was blanketed with an unseasonable wintry frost on this late September morning. As soon as Judith jumped down, handing Auntie Gem her small valise, the black manservant drove Aaron Stone's cabriolet away.

"How is she?" Maggie asked, taking hold of the woman's trembling hands.

"She ain't none too good. I'm mighty worried about her." Tears filled Auntie Gem's tired, dark eyes.

"The baby?"

"She done lost it, about an hour ago. I'd say it was a blessing, except for what it's done to her. I ain't never seen a gal lose so much blood." Auntie Gem looked at Judith as if just remembering the child's presence. "Maybe I shouldn't have said so much."

"It's all right," Maggie assured her. "Has anyone sent for a doctor?"

"Mr. Aaron did, but we ain't heard nothing. I don't figure there's much a doctor can do. Things like this, a woman just heals up right or she don't."

"Is she asleep?"

"She's been sleeping on and off. Phineas done give her some laudanum, but she's been calling for you. Mr. Aaron sent Moses for you as soon as Daisy took sick before daybreak this morning."

Auntie Gem led the Campbell sisters into Daisy and Phineas's neat, one-story frame house, the frost-covered tin roof almost as white as the building itself.

When Maggie walked through the warm kitchen, she could smell the spicy aroma of cinnamon and overripe apples. A pot of fresh coffee sat on the cook-stove, a plate of day-old fried pies on the nearby wooden table. Crystal bright sunshine filled the room with a soft pink glow as it streamed through the red-gingham-curtained window.

"Jude, you stay in here," Maggie said. "Maybe Auntie Gem will fix you something to eat. I know you must be hungry after our long ride."

The old woman nodded, putting the valise on a corner table, and urging the sleepy-eyed child to sit down. "You go on, Miss Maggie. I'll scramble some eggs and cook up some biscuits. You see if you can get Phineas and Mr. Aaron to come out here and eat."

Maggie opened the bedroom door, stood on the threshold, and peeked into the shadowy room. The bleached muslin curtains had been pulled, filtering the morning sunlight. Daisy lay on an iron bed, her still body covered with several quilts. Maggie moved slowly into the room. She immediately noticed Phineas sitting in a cane-bottomed chair on the far side of the bed, his dark eyes staring down at the sleeping woman. A few feet away, in the corner, Aaron Stone stood leaning against the wall, one big booted foot propped behind him.

"Phineas," Maggie whispered.

Looking up, his eyes red, tears wetting his long, dark lashes, the man stood. "Miss Maggie. She been asking for you. She's been so sick and half out of her mind."

"She is going to be all right." Maggie moved to the bed, wanting to see Daisy and hoping she could comfort the woman's husband. "She's young and strong, and the Lord will take care of her."

"She wants me to bury the baby, Miss Maggie, and there ain't no baby. There ain't nothing but . . . a tiny lump of . . . How can I bury her baby when there ain't no baby?"

Maggie walked around the foot of the bed and placed her small hand on Phineas's arm. "You get Auntie Gem to find a box, and you put that tiny lump in it. And you dig a hole and bury it. When Daisy's better, you can show her the little mound where the baby is buried."

202 • *Beverly Barton*

"But Miss Maggie." Tears cascaded down his dark cheeks as he stared at his wife's sleeping form.

"It's what she wants," Maggie told him. "Go on and do it now. I'll sit here with her in case she wakes up or needs anything."

Aaron removed his foot from the wall. Standing big and tall, he walked forward. Maggie looked up into his face. Even with a day's growth of beard and weary eyes, his coat wrinkled and his shirt half unbuttoned, he looked wonderful. She had missed him unbearably in the weeks since he'd stormed out of the town house kitchen. "She's right, Phineas. It's what Daisy wants. Come on. I'll go with you."

Phineas turned to his friend, nodding agreement.

"Maggie's here now. She'll take care of Daisy."

When the two men left the room, Maggie paced back and forth at the foot of the bed, and prayed that the Lord would see fit to spare Daisy's life. She had already suffered so much in her short twenty-four years. It wasn't fair if death claimed her now.

Maggie felt betrayed, betrayed by life that promised and gave so much to others. Betrayed by a God who would allow the innocent to pay for the sins of the guilty.

The days were going so quickly, and she had solved none of her own problems. It was almost October, she was three months along, and nobody knew, save her and the Lord. She would have to do something soon, make some important decisions. If only Aaron had made some move to contact her, but he hadn't. Obviously he could live without her. She hoped he was as miserable as she was.

On several occasions she had almost told Thayer and asked for his help. He stopped by the town house often, always assuring her that she and Jude were welcome to stay on there as long as they wanted. Since his family had left Silver Hill the first of the month, he came to town at least twice a week. Maggie was sure he missed living in town, being close to all the things a young bachelor enjoys.

Martha Coleman had paid her a visit a few days before returning to Franklin, Tennessee, with her daughter's family. She wanted Maggie to know that she prayed for Aaron to come to his senses and marry Maggie before he destroyed himself. Then she offered Maggie and Judith a home with her if Aaron were stupid enough to actually marry Eunice Arnold. Should she go ahead and accept the offer and leave Tuscumbia? No, she couldn't. Not yet. There was still hope. Aaron hadn't proposed to Eunice.

Even if he hadn't proposed to the widow, it didn't mean he was having second thoughts. By now, he probably assumed Maggie had made the decision to become Thayer's mistress. The whole town believed she was. If she told him about the baby, would he know that it was his, or would he suspect Thayer of being the father?

She was aware that there was a strain on Aaron and Thayer's friendship, and that she was the cause. Thayer had actually put himself in the middle, actively fueling the fires of Aaron's jealousy. Maggie had tried to make the younger man understand he was playing a dangerous game that could easily create more problems than it solved.

"Phineas." The word was a soft cry on Daisy's lips as she struggled to open her eyes.

Maggie clasped the other woman's small hand in her own as she leaned over the bed. "He's right outside. Do you want me to get him?"

"Miss Maggie?" Daisy's eyes flickered open and then closed.

"Yes. It's me."

"The baby . . ."

"Hush now. You just rest. Everything is going to be fine." Maggie dipped a cloth into the basin on the nearby table, squeezed out the excess moisture, and tenderly washed the young woman's face.

"The baby's . . . gone . . ." Daisy's voice was so weak that Maggie barely heard what she said.

"Rest. Please, rest."

Maggie sat down when she realized that her friend had fallen back into a drugged sleep. Thoughts of Wesley Peterson filled her mind. She had never hated anyone before coming to Tuscumbia. Now she hated two people. The feeling was strange and almost frightening. If Daisy died, she'd want to kill Wesley. Right now she'd like to see him beaten within an inch of his life. What would Phineas do? If the black man were to even lay a finger on Wesley, they'd hang him.

When Uncle Chester had finally come by two weeks ago to see Jude and her, and offer financial help, she had tried to talk to him about his stepson. But she had soon realized what a weak and battered soul her uncle really was. He was a gentle, tenderhearted man trapped in a marriage to a strong, domineering woman whose sharp tongue and hateful manner gave him no peace. How could Maggie inflict any more pain on the poor man by telling him about Wesley? Even if he knew the truth, what could he do?

Maggie and Phineas had been taking turns sitting at Daisy's bedside all day. Dr. Cooper had come and gone, saying pretty much what Auntie Gem had—that the girl's body would heal itself or she'd die. Nature had a way of deciding these things.

She was so absorbed in her private thoughts that she hadn't heard the bedroom door open or the footsteps of the man who walked up to her chair, but she did feel the gentle hand on her shoulder. Hoping and half-expecting to see Aaron at her side, she turned slowly, looking up into Thayer Coleman's handsome face.

Maggie was sure she looked as rumpled and fatigued as she felt, but, knowing Thayer had come for her sake, she smiled and placed her hand on his where it rested on her shoulder.

"Auntie Gem has some supper ready. Phineas has eaten and is ready to sit a while to relieve you." Thayer helped her stand, holding her hand as he led her to the door.

When they stepped into the kitchen, Phineas moved past them into his wife's room, but hesitated briefly to look at Maggie, gratitude in his dark eyes. Aaron was seated at the table, a cup of coffee in his big hand. He glared at the couple as they came into the room. His jade eyes rested on their entwined hands. Maggie tensed and started to pull her hand free, but Thayer held tightly.

"I need to talk to you, Thayer," she whispered as she tried to avoid Aaron's hostile scrutiny.

"We can talk while you eat," Thayer said. "I'll sit with you. You need your rest, my sweet."

Aaron slammed the coffee cup onto the table. The dark liquid sloshed out on his hand. Maggie wanted to scream at Thayer to stop; that in trying to make Aaron jealous, he was making it harder for her to tell him the truth about the baby.

"I can eat later. We need to talk now. Let's go out on the porch." She was sure Aaron had heard every word and was drawing his own erroneous conclusions.

"Whatever you want, Maggie dear." Thayer held her hand securely in his as he led her across the warm, savory-smelling kitchen, and opened the door to the porch.

Outside the sun was setting in a clear, cloudless sky, crimson warmth spreading across the horizon. Softening and blending as they reached the earth, a dozen shades of red and pink streaked wildly into the heavens. The day had begun to cool slightly, the evening breeze rustling gently through the trees.

"Thayer, this has to stop." She faced him, her hands on her hips.

"But it's working, Maggie. Can't you see? He would love to have hit me."

"Oh, Thayer. I know you're trying to help, and I appreciate it. I appreciate everything you've done for me, but I want you to stop making Aaron jealous."

"Why?" He shrugged, sitting down on the white, wooden banister surrounding the porch.

Maggie hesitated before replying. "Because half the town thinks I'm your mistress. After all you've said and done, Aaron probably believes it too."

"We can tell him the truth when he proposes to you."

"He's not going to propose to me."

"He loves you. We both know that."

"Would he love me if he thought I was carrying your child?"

Thayer jumped up, his black eyes wild. "You . . . me . . . what?"

"I'm going to have Aaron's baby." Maggie reached up to touch the overly excited man on his dark, lean cheek. "But if he thinks we've been lovers, he may wonder if the child is yours."

"My God!"

"I don't know what to do."

"Aaron's child? My Lord, woman, you'll have to tell him."

"I can't. I'm afraid," Maggie admitted.

Thayer pulled her into his arms, and she clung to him. She tried to hold back the tears, but all the pain and fear she had been suffering came to the surface. She wept, her body quivering as the tall, dark man soothed her with his tender words and gentle touch.

"Tell him, Maggie. Tell him about the baby. If he's stupid enough to have any doubts, I'll talk to him."

"He's so determined to marry Eunice." She brushed the back of her hand across her eyes, wiping the tears away. "Maybe he won't be able to give up his dreams."

"If he's that big a fool, you're better off without him."

She stood there in his arms, her head resting against his hard chest, and cried until there were no more tears. Her head hurt, her eyes were swollen, and her nose was red, but she felt much better. Whatever decision she made, she knew she had a friend in this man.

"Maggie." He spoke softly as he tilted her head with his hand. "If things don't work out, would you consider marrying me?"

"What?" She wasn't sure she had heard him correctly.

"I said, if Aaron won't marry you, I will."

"Oh, Thayer." At this precise moment, she dearly loved him. What a kind and generous heart he must have to make such an offer.

"No, Maggie, no!" Judith screamed as she bounded up the porch steps. "You can't marry him! You can't!"

"Jude? Where have you been?" Maggie asked. "How much did you hear?"

Judith ran to her sister, her tiny hands pulling, trying to prize Maggie out of Thayer's arms. "I was sitting around by the side of the house playing with Phineas's cat. And I heard everything."

"Judith, you're a child. You don't understand," Thayer said.

"You can't marry Maggie. She loves Aaron. She's going to have his baby," the child cried.

"Listen to me." Thayer knelt down and took Jude's tense little fists into his big, dark hand. "If Aaron won't marry Maggie, she's going to need a husband and a father for her baby. You and Maggie could come and live with me at Silver Hill. We'd be a family."

Jude jerked her hands free, her tiny fists beating repeatedly against his chest. He allowed her to continue striking out at him while she cried and screamed. "No. You can't marry Maggie. You're going to wait for me to grow up and marry me. You're mine and nobody else can have you!"

"Jude." Maggie pulled her little sister away from Thayer, took her by the shoulders, and shook her soundly. "Stop acting like this. Thayer is dear and sweet, and we both love him, but he doesn't belong to either of us."

"He's mine!"

"Judith Campbell, go inside the house and stay there until I finish talking to Thayer."

Her aqua eyes gleamed with turbulence as she stared up at her sister. "I hate you!" Jude yelled, then turned and ran into the house.

"Oh, Thayer, I'm so sorry," Maggie said.

"It's all right. I know Jude fancies herself in love with me. Actually it's rather flattering to have such a fiery little girl claim me as her possession." He smiled and his handsome face became beautiful.

Maggie laughed. Why couldn't she be in love with Thayer Coleman and he with her? "She'll be all right once she understands that I have no intention of marrying you."

"And why not?"

"I love Aaron and probably always will. And someday you'll fall in love. I care too much about you to marry you for all the wrong reasons." Maggie took his hand in hers.

"What about the baby?"

"Do you think your mother's invitation would still be open to me and Jude if she knew I was going to have a child?"

"Mama? Of course, why didn't I think about her? Your child will be her niece or nephew. I'll write and tell her. If we can't get that big, dumb uncle of mine to come to his senses, you and Jude can go to Franklin."

"Are you sure she'll want us?" Maggie could feel his hand squeezing hers reassuringly.

"I guarantee she will."

Maggie reached out to hug him, her heart filled with hope for the first time in weeks. "Thank you. Somewhere out there, there's a very lucky lady waiting for you."

"I hope my lady love is half the woman you are, Maggie Campbell."

Aaron walked out onto the porch, stopping and tensing when he saw Maggie in his friend's arms.

"What the hell did you two do to Judith? She's in there crying her head off. Auntie Gem can't do anything with her!" the blond giant roared.

"I'll go in and see about her," Thayer said, kissing Maggie sweetly on the lips before releasing her.

Aaron refused to even look at his friend when the younger man paused briefly at his side as he entered the house. It had taken every ounce of self-control he possessed not to strike Thayer. The sight of his lips on Maggie's, his arms holding her close, had torn at his insides like jagged glass. Were the rumors true? Eunice had been eager to relay every sordid tidbit of town gossip. Thayer visited Maggie at least twice a week and stayed for hours. Had she done as she had threatened and actually become Thayer's mistress?

"Aaron?" Maggie called from the porch.

He wouldn't look at her. He couldn't. If he did he'd be lost. Lost in the depths of her pale, brandy eyes.

"Aaron, we need to talk," she said. When he made no reply, she moved toward him. "Please?"

Before she reached him, he turned and walked off the porch into the yard, and went straight to where his horse was hitched. "We'll talk in the morning. I'll be back."

He couldn't talk to her now. He was afraid of what he would say to her, of what he would do to her when she told him she was Thayer's mistress. He knew what he had to do, and he knew he had to do it tonight. He had paid off his wager to Thayer Coleman. It was high time he proposed to Eunice.

Maggie hadn't been to bed because Daisy had taken a turn for the worse in the middle of the night. Around dawn a minor miracle had occurred, and Auntie Gem had pronounced the young wife on the road to recovery. After that, Maggie had persuaded Phineas to get some sleep since he hadn't closed his eyes in nearly forty-eight hours. She sat alone by the bed, keeping a silent vigil and offering up personal thanks to a God who had been merciful. She had dozed off in the chair, awakening when Auntie Gem brought her a cup of freshly brewed coffee. Daisy had roused up enough for the old woman to feed her a few bites before she closed her eyes, drifting off into a normal, healthy sleep. It was then that Auntie Gem told Maggie that Aaron was waiting outside on the porch.

She wanted desperately to see him. During the endless night

hours when her friend had come so close to dying, she had done a lot of thinking, a lot of soul searching, and had decided to tell Aaron that she was carrying his child. She owed it to both of them and the baby to tell him the truth. She was beginning to realize that sometimes you had to give up your dreams. Life had a way of never quite working out as you had planned, and sometimes the only way to survive was to change. Four months ago, she had boarded a train in Chattanooga with a valise full of worn clothes, a rebellious young brother, a stubborn sister, a black servant girl, a heart full of dreams, and a head full of plans. One by one the dreams had died. One by one the plans had been altered. But new dreams had been born, dreams of spending her life with Aaron, of having his children. And new plans had formed, plans to send Jude away to school when she was older, far away from Tuscumbia and the scandal associated with her name.

"I done laid out you a clean dress and fetched a bucket of water for you to wash," Auntie Gem said. "I'll stay here with Daisy while you clean up and talk to Mr. Aaron."

"Is Phineas still asleep?"

"Yes'am. That man done wore himself out a-fretting over Daisy."

"We can thank God she's going to be all right." Maggie looked down at her sleeping friend, feelings of love and relief spreading through her.

"Everything's going to be fine for her. But you best get your life in order. You hurry up and get yourself fixed up to see Mr. Aaron. Since I come to White Orchard to work for him, done found out he ain't got no patience. No sir, none at all."

Maggie embraced the old woman whose bony arms circled her with strength. "Thank you."

"Go on now," Auntie Gem said, shooing the girl out of the bedroom.

Maggie hurriedly washed, combed and rearranged her hair, and put on fresh clothes while she rehearsed what she planned to say to Aaron. She prayed that she would choose the right words.

He was sitting on the porch steps, his long legs spanning their length, a cigar in his hand. Although his brown wool trousers and heavy linen shirt were lean, they were wrinkled, looking like he had slept in them. His golden hair appeared windblown and he needed a shave. The moment he heard Maggie's footsteps behind him, he turned to face her, his green eyes heavy lidded and weary.

"Aaron?" A sudden feeling of nausea overwhelmed her. She wasn't sure whether the cause was the baby or her own nervousness.

"Auntie Gem said Daisy's going to be fine. I'm glad. I don't think Phineas could live without her."

"I can understand how he feels." She wanted to reach out and touch him, to go into his arms and never leave.

"Can you?"

"Aaron, I—"

"Let's take a walk, Maggie," he said, putting the cigar in his mouth as he stood up. After taking several draws, he threw it to the ground, crushed it with his foot, and offered her his arm.

He felt warm and alive and wonderful as she allowed him to take her arm and drape it over his. It had been such a long time since she had touched him. She wanted to go on touching him, loving him, belonging to him always.

"I brought the carriage," he told her as they began to walk away from the house. "But I think I'd rather walk if you don't mind. It's not far from here down to the river. Will you be warm enough without a wrap?"

"I'll be fine. It's so much warmer than yesterday morning."

The sun was halfway up in the clear, azure sky, a few tiny, cotton clouds drifted across the vast blueness. The big golden man and the small copper-haired woman walked silently along the path behind Daisy and Phineas's neat frame house. In three directions lay cotton fields, and ahead lay a thicket of trees and bushes through which they could see a glimpse of the Tennessee River.

She wished he would say something, anything to break the unbearable silence between them. He had wanted to talk but he had said nothing.

"How've you been, Maggie?" he asked, not looking down at her or slowing his stride as he led her along the path to the river.

"I've been all right, but I've missed you terribly." She could feel his whole body tense, but still he refused to look at her as they continued walking.

"I wouldn't think you'd have time to miss me with Thayer visiting so much."

"Thayer has been a good friend to me and Jude. He's been there for me when I needed someone."

"Is he a better lover than I am?" Aaron stopped and grabbed her by the shoulders, his fierce green eyes boring into hers. "Are you enjoying being his mistress?"

She trembled, fear and desire claiming her as she saw a fury in his face. "I'm not . . . there hasn't been anyone . . . I still love you."

"Do you?" He gripped her chin in his hand as his mouth curled into a mocking smile. "Would you like to prove it here and now? Are you willing to let me lay you down here by the river and crawl between your legs?"

"Aaron, please, listen to me." She bit her lip trying to hold back the tears. "I love you and if you want me here and now, I'll give myself to you. I have so much to give you, if only you'll let me."

"What can you give me besides that beautiful body?" he sneered.

"Oh, Aaron, don't do this to us. I have something wonderful to tell you." She had to make him listen. If she didn't tell him about the baby soon, she'd lose her nerve. It was far too important to both their futures to keep the truth from him.

"Isn't that a coincidence," he laughed, stepping away from her and facing the calmly rolling water a few yards away. "I have something wonderful to tell you."

"What?" Her heart pounded wildly in her chest as her mind wandered in a hundred different directions trying to imagine what he planned to tell her.

"Last night, I made a trip to Tuscumbia."

Maggie's heartbeat accelerated, the throbbing sound filling her head as her face burned with the terror seizing her soul. *No! No!* she cried inwardly, knowing what he was about to say, knowing he was on the verge of killing all of her new dreams.

"I proposed marriage to Eunice and she accepted."

He wasn't sure exactly what reaction he had expected from Maggie. Perhaps he had hoped to hurt her with his news as much as the knowledge that Thayer was her lover hurt him. Whatever he had expected, it hadn't been the look of raw pain he saw on this woman's face. She turned deathly white, her yellow eyes glazed with shock, her mouth open in a silent scream, her small hands trembling as they reached out for him.

Her lips quivered as she tried to speak. "But . . . but . . . you love . . . me."

Aaron couldn't bear to look at her, the agony etched on her features was suffocating him, but she forced his attention when she grabbed his big arms.

"You made the decision for us when you gave yourself to Thayer." He searched her face for the truth, and what he saw seared his heart like a branding iron.

"I've never given myself to any man but you." There were no tears in her eyes, only the clear undeniable glow of the truth.

"My God!" he cried. "Why did the two of you let me think all the gossip was true?"

"Thayer . . . Thayer thought jealousy would make you come to your senses and give up your plans to marry Eunice." Maggie fell against his hard chest when he pulled her into his arms.

"The fool." Aaron was torn apart inside, not knowing what to say or do. He had to admit that, even though he had been planning to propose to Eunice before he ever met Maggie, the knowledge that this fiery redhead had given herself to his friend had prompted his hasty action last night.

"If you had known the truth, would you have proposed to Eunice?" Maggie was clinging as fiercely to her last hope as she was to the man she loved.

"No, I wouldn't have proposed last night," he admitted. "But, I . . . I'm not sure what I would have done eventually. Lately I've been questioning myself, my values, all the plans I'd made for my life."

"Is it too late? Is there no way you can take back the proposal?"

"Don't you see, Maggie. I'm not sure I'd want to take it back if I could." He was trying to be honest with himself and with the woman he held in his arms. "I can't deny that I still love you, more than ever."

She gasped, her eyes seeking his. They stood there, holding one another, looking into faces filled with love and longing.

If he loved her, there was still hope, wasn't there? He wasn't married to the Widow Arnold yet. She couldn't give up and run away. Not now. There was far more at stake than her own happiness, or even Jude's future. As long as Aaron loved her, he would be miserable married to any other woman, especially a self-centered socialite like Eunice. Somehow she'd have to find a way to save Aaron from himself. But more important than all of them was the child growing inside her body. Aaron's child, a child who deserved to have his father's name.

Chapter 16

Maggie had fed Daisy her supper, coaxing her until she had eaten part of the delicious meal Auntie Gem had prepared. Now she and the old woman worked in silence as they washed and dried the dishes and utensils. They were both bone weary, exhaustion having claimed them. Maggie dried the last plate as Auntie Gem wiped out the cast-iron corn bread skillet and hung it on the wall above the stove.

Maggie wanted the minutes to hurry. Aaron had gone to Tuscumbia to see Eunice and had promised to stop by on his way home.

When he had left her today, he had still been uncertain about his life and the decisions he had to make. She had chosen not to complicate things by telling him about the baby. If he married her, she wanted it to be because he loved her and not because she was carrying his child.

Judith was proving to be a problem. Maggie had serious doubts, as the girl grew older, that she would be able to control her. She had tried to talk to her sister, to explain that she had no intention of marrying Thayer, but the child had run from the room, refusing to listen. It worried her that Jude was so obsessed with Thayer. No good could come of such a thing.

Knowing she could be of little use to Daisy if she had to spend half her time trying to manage her feisty sister, she had asked Aaron to send Moses over with a buggy to take the child to the Mobleys'. She had sent a brief note to Alice saying only what was necessary and asking her to look after Jude for a few days. It would be better for both sisters if they were apart until Maggie could work out her problems with Aaron.

She could still see the bitterness in Jude's eyes, and hear the anger in her voice when she threatened to prevent Maggie from marrying Thayer.

"I'll go see that Verda woman," Judith had threatened. "She'll know what I can do to stop you."

When Maggie had forbidden her sister from going anywhere near that whore, Jude had glared defiantly and said she'd do whatever she had to do.

Maggie couldn't understand why everything had gone so wrong. All she had ever wanted was what was best for her family. She'd promised Pa as he lay on his deathbed that she'd see Micah had a good profession and Jude would become a lady. What would Pa think of her now? He'd be disappointed by how miserably she had failed. Micah was on the river, doing God only knew what. In all the weeks he'd been gone, she hadn't heard a word from him. And Jude! Dear Lord, was there any hope that a child so stubborn and full of temper could ever grow up to be a proper lady?

The dreams for herself and her own future, the ones she'd put in the back of her mind, could never come true. A simple life with a good husband was no longer even a possibility. She was hopelessly in love with Aaron Stone and nothing could ever change that fact. By spring, she would give birth to his child, binding them forever as his own parents had been bound.

She had never imagined it was possible to love someone the way she loved Aaron. He was in her thoughts and in her heart every minute of every day, his handsome features etched eternally in her mind. The sound of his voice touched her very soul, his nearness creating tingling sensations through every nerve in her body. When he was happy, she was happy. When he was sad, she was sad. His joy was her joy, his pain her own. She loved him in every way a woman could love a man, body, heart, and soul. She belonged to Aaron Stone, now and forever.

She knew that giving herself to him without marriage was considered a sin, and she guessed it was, but how could something so wonderful be so wrong?

She would always remember the first time she had looked up into his green eyes there at the railroad depot in Chattanooga. She realized now that no power on earth could have kept the two of them apart. Their love had been meant to be from the beginning. The thought of their first loving sent fissions of pleasure darting through her. She had relived that night over and over in her thoughts, the memory of the thunder and lightning, the hard earth beneath her, the big man above her like a sweet drug enticing her body to yearn for it again.

She slowly licked her lips, recalling the feel of his mouth taking hers in a kiss of urgent longing. Maggie's hands trembled as she placed the last dish in the cupboard. She closed her eyes and leaned her head against the glass-paned cabinet door. She could not bear the thought of Aaron married to another woman.

"Do you hear something, Miss Maggie?" Auntie Gem asked, cocking her scarf-covered head to one side.

"I didn't hear anything. What was it?"

"I ain't sure. Thought it sounded like horses."

"Maybe it was Phineas. He should be through checking on the stock." Maggie dried her hands on the faded cotton apron tied about her waist.

"I don't hear nothing now. Could've been Phineas."

Maggie opened the kitchen door, looking outside into the darkness of late evening, the sky alight with a thousand glowing stars. The nighttime breeze swirled around her, chilling her with its coolness. She could barely make out the tall figure of a man walking toward the porch, but his very size assured her that it was Phineas. He had stopped in the yard several feet away and seemed to be listening. She strained her ears to hear. The world was full of nocturnal sounds, primitive, but soothing. She could hear the soft sigh of the river flowing in the distance. Then she heard it. The sound of horses, horses and riders heading straight toward the house. She searched her mind for a reason. Who was it? Who could possibly be riding hard and fast in their direction? And it was more than one man. From the sound, it was half a dozen or more.

Suddenly they appeared on horseback, eight ghostly apparitions surrounding Phineas, their white robes and hoods glistening like snow against dark, rich soil.

My God! My God! Maggie thought. Who were they and what did they want? Instinctively she knew they meant trouble and that the fear gripping her throat was justified. She had heard tales about a group of men who yielded their own brand of justice to anyone who dared threaten the way of life they longed to perpetuate.

She had to send for help. But Aaron wasn't home. She'd send Auntie Gem to Moses. He could go for help.

With the door wide open, she turned to the old woman at her side. "Go through the bedroom, crawl out the window, and get to White Orchard. Send Moses for Mr. Thayer. And tell him to hurry."

"Yes'am, Miss Maggie. I know what to tell him. Oh Lord, gal, you going to need help. Mr. Wesley, he's one of them. I promise you that."

Not taking time to react to Auntie Gem's information, Maggie hugged her and bid her farewell, then turned toward the porch in time to see three dismount and walk toward Phineas. She didn't know whether to leave the door open or try to close it and chance drawing their attention to her.

"Well, boy, I guess you know what we came for," a dark, coarse voice laughed.

"Y'all go on away from here," Phineas said, his big body standing tall and ready to fight. "I don't want no trouble."

A rotund, robed form stepped toward him. "You forget your place, nigger. You and that blue-eyed slut you married are going to pay. First, you'll pay for your arrogance, and then your woman will pay for her sins. And then," he bellowed, raising a meaty fist into the air, one fat finger pointing to the porch.

Maggie's heart lodged in her throat. That madman was pointing directly at her, and she recognized his voice. It was Wesley Peterson.

"Maggie Campbell is a sinner. She has lain with a man who is not her husband and refused to repent. And now, the evil seed of her shameful deed is growing in her body. But we shall do the Lord's work. Tonight, she too will die."

Reacting strictly from fear, Maggie slammed the door shut, her sweat-soaked body trembling as she slumped to the floor, praying silently for God to send help soon.

Daisy stood in the bedroom doorway. She gazed down at her friend who was hovering on her knees, her face buried in her shaking hands.

"Miss Maggie, what is it? What's going on?"

Maggie raised her terror-filled eyes, seeing the young woman standing there in her cotton nightgown. "Oh, dear Lord."

"Miss Maggie?"

"It's Wesley and a bunch of hooded men. They've got Phineas surrounded. They say they're going to kill us all."

"No . . . no . . ."

Maggie, slow moving, reached out and grabbed the black woman by the shoulders. "Does Phineas have a gun here in the house?"

"No, I don't think so." Daisy's pale blue eyes flickered about the room as if she thought a weapon would miraculously appear.

"Think," Maggie beseeched, holding tightly to the woman's shoulders, shaking her gently. "We've got to do something. We can't stand here and let them kill us."

"There's a rifle." Daisy's face lifted, her eyes brightened with hope. "Oh, no. I think it's still in the barn. Phineas shot some rabbits a few days back, and he skinned them out by the barn. I don't remember him bringing the gun back in the house."

"You check your bedroom. I'll look in the other room. Then we'll go through the kitchen together. We've got to find something. It might be our only hope."

"Where's Auntie Gem? Have they got her?"

"No! I sent her to White Orchard for help. Now stop talking and go look."

Within minutes, the two women had searched the entire house and come up empty-handed except for a broom and a couple of butcher knives.

"I won't let them kill me without a fight," Maggie said, clutching one big knife in her hand.

"You stay here, Miss Maggie," Daisy said. "I'm going out there. If I can't stop them from killing Phineas, then I'll die with him."

"No!" Maggie screeched. "Wait. Let's look out the window first and see what's going on."

There was no way she and Daisy could save Phineas, and unless help arrived in time, they too would die tonight. If they could stay in the house and hold the hooded maniacs off until Thayer came, they might have a chance.

The two women stood at the window looking outside. Suddenly, as if her brain had just begun to function, Maggie turned back quickly and extinguished the lamp.

"Miss Maggie, I've got to go to him. They're tying him to a tree."

Maggie didn't know what to do. Daisy was so weak she could barely stand, but she was determined to go to her husband. If it were Aaron out there, she would do the same.

She looked back out the window, seeing Phineas's huge body strapped to a tree, his shirt ripped apart and his bare back exposed to the night air and to the sting of a whip held securely in one white-robed man's hand. Six of the men were standing nearby, one holding a torch that burned high and bright into the black sky. She realized that it had taken five of them to subdue their captive. She could hear Wesley's voice shouting words of sin and salvation as another hand slashed the corded leather into the large man's back. Phineas jerked once, but made no sound. Maggie felt nauseous and faint.

How could a man profess to be a servant of God, stand before a congregation of devout Christians, preaching a sermon that would bring tears to the eye, and actually be a monster filled with such evil? She had already realized that her uncle's stepson was insane, but never had she imagined the extent of his lunacy. This man, who had claimed to love her, who had proposed marriage together, was going to kill her. Because she had made love with Aaron? Because she carried Aaron's child? But how did he know that she was going to have a child? She had told no one except Thayer, and he would never have told anyone, least of all Wesley Peterson. Jude had known. Surely her sister had not gone to this madman. But Jude didn't know what kind of a man their cousin really was. Had she gone to him and told him about Maggie, hoping that Wesley would marry her? What other explanation could there be?

While Maggie was deep in thought, Daisy opened the door and staggered onto the porch, her slender hands clutching the doorframe. Maggie dropped the knife and reached out for her, but before she could obtain a good hold, the young woman pulled away, walking unsteadily onto the porch. Maggie followed, grabbing her determined friend.

"Please, Daisy, come back inside. I don't think they've seen us."
Just as she spoke, the whip sang its torturous song.

"No!" Daisy screamed, trying to free herself from Maggie's tenacious hold.

The rotund hooded man turned toward the porch, his fat finger pointing in their direction. "Behold the temptations of the devil. Whores put on earth by the evil one to drive men to madness."

Maggie held the other woman's struggling body as she closed her eyes and prayed.

She could hear an approaching carriage. It was too soon to be Thayer. There hadn't been enough time for Moses to get all the way to Silver Hill and return with help. She scanned the small dirt road leading to the house as the vehicle approached, instantly recognizing Aaron's cabriolet. Instinctively, relief rushed through her. Aaron would help them; he'd take care of her. But Aaron had no way of knowing what was happening here. He would ride into this nightmare totally unprepared. Would he have a gun on him or in the carriage? What if Moses had driven him to town and Auntie Gem was still searching for help? Surely by now she had roused some of Aaron's workers.

As she had feared, Maggie saw that the robed assassins had heard and seen Aaron arrive, and two of them were approaching his carriage. Using his buggy whip, Aaron lashed out at his welcome party, but before he could subdue them, Wesley ordered Phineas's beating stopped and commanded that all their attention focus on capturing the big man who was fighting off his attackers. It took three men to drag Aaron from the buggy, the frightened horses galloping away with the cabriolet as soon as Aaron hit the ground.

Maggie flinched when she saw a booted foot thrust into Aaron's midsection. She cried out, her body starting toward the big blond lying in the dirt. She momentarily loosened her hold on Daisy as she stepped forward, but it was long enough for the Negress to pull free and with unbelievable speed, rush down the steps and out into the yard.

"No, Daisy, don't!" Maggie screamed, but her warning fell on deaf ears.

All eyes focused on the blue-eyed quadroon as she walked past the astonished robed men, and went directly to her husband. Her small hand hovered over his lacerated back. When she touched him, he groaned.

While everyone was watching Daisy, Aaron pulled himself to his feet, his eyes searching and finding Maggie. In that one look was a world of promise. Somehow she knew that if there were any way possible, he would save them.

Aaron spit on the ground, trying to cleanse his mouth of the taste of dry dust. "Rube Whitcomb!" he shouted, and the tall man still holding the bloody whip turned to face his accuser. "Your identity is no secret to me, and your appearance here is no surprise. Everyone knows that you're a murdering black-hearted thief with a whore for a daughter."

Whitcomb raised his whip, but the rotund brother's hand came down on his wrist. "Save it for later. You'll have your turn with him. For now we need to finish off this nigger. What say we hang him?"

A massive shout erupted from the hefty man's lips, an echoing roar of consent ringing in the stillness.

"All of you men here tonight aren't cruel or evil men," Aaron rationalized, hoping that one of them would listen. "Do you realize what Wesley Peterson has planned?"

At the mention of the good reverend's name, a hushed silence encompassed the group, and Wesley stood tensely, glaring at his accuser.

"How can you call yourself a man of God?" Aaron moved steadily toward Wesley, no one attempting to stop him. "Do these men know why you brought them here? Do they know that you lusted after Phineas's wife? Do they know that you beat and raped her?"

"Liar!" Wesley screamed, his gray eyes, visible through the slits in his hood, widened in outraged anger. "We have come here to destroy evil. These good men will not listen to your lies."

"One of you must know this man. You must know that beneath his benevolent exterior lies the soul of a lunatic." Aaron stood directly in front of the man of God who was holding a rifle in his hand.

"If he comes nearer, shoot him," Wesley said. "We have no more time to listen to his lies." He turned from Aaron, reached out, and pulled a clinging Daisy away from her husband.

"Your evil ends this night, whore." Wesley raised his huge fist, pounding it into Daisy's face. The battered woman fell to the ground, one shrill cry coming from her lips.

Phineas jerked and pulled, trying to free himself from his bonds, the gashes on his back oozing blood. Aaron moved forward to help Daisy, but stopped dead still when Rube Whitcomb aimed his gun and fired. The bullet grazed Aaron's ankle, a hot sting searing his skin.

Maggie ran from the porch, not knowing what she could do, but unable to stand there watching while Daisy lay unconscious on the ground and Aaron was being held at gunpoint.

"Maggie, no." Aaron moved a fraction of an inch and Whitcomb shot the ground at his feet.

Maggie knelt beside Daisy, taking her head in her lap. Her golden face was discolored and bloody from Wesley's beating, but she was still breathing. *Thank God, she's still alive.*

"Wesley Peterson, may God strike you dead!" Maggie's amber eyes glared up at her cousin who stood above her, jerking the white hood from his round, fat head.

"You will die, Maggie, and your sins with you. I offered you my love and my name and instead of a righteous life, you chose to spread your legs for Aaron Stone. You allowed him the pleasure of your body. And when I offered you forgiveness, you chose to become a rich man's whore."

He was going to strike her. She braced herself for the blow. He jerked her up, letting Daisy's head hit the ground with a thud, his fat hand striking Maggie across the face. She swayed, almost falling.

Aaron reached out, his huge hands grasping the good reverend. Whitcomb turned his rifle around and brought the butt end down across Aaron's head. He repeated the blow twice. Aaron fell, bloody and unconscious.

Maggie screamed, running to him, his big body sprawled in the dirt. She sat down, pulling him into her arms, her finger stroking back the tawny strands of bloody hair that were plastered to his forehead. The dim moonlight shimmered across the yard and illuminated the small round piece of metal lying in the dirt near Aaron's side. She reached out, picking up the gold watch that had belonged to Richard Leander.

This had to be some hideous nightmare. She knew this couldn't really be happening. She could feel the anger and the hatred all around her. It had become a living, breathing thing, blending with ignorance to become a monstrous creature. Even though the night air was cool, her body was drenched in sweat, her mouth dry and parched. Gone were the sweet smells of autumn, the unique aroma of the nearby river, and in their stead was the overpowering odor of blood and battered man-flesh.

"Get on with the beating," Wesley ordered. "I think we'll save the hanging for Stone, if he ever comes to."

"I want the pleasure of filling him full of lead before he hangs," Rube Whitcomb sneered, his long, bony hand stroking the top of Maggie's head.

She jerked away, her eyes filled with terror. "Don't touch me."

"Oh, I'll save that for later, girlie. I fancy getting myself some of what Aaron Stone and Thayer Coleman have been getting for the last few months."

Her stomach was churning so that she thought she was going to vomit. Dear God, she'd rather them go ahead and kill her than have that horrible creature touch her.

The good reverend watched, his florid face beaming with sickening joy as Whitcomb resumed Phineas's whipping. It seemed to go on forever. Maggie sat on the ground, holding Aaron in her arms, praying that he would live, her eyes watching for any movement from Daisy's still body. Her ears were filled with the sounds of Phineas's groans, Whitcomb's singing whip, and Wesley's maniacal laughter. Her nostrils filled with the stench of human suffering and sour male sweat.

She began praying again, praying that somehow Auntie Gem had found help. They couldn't die like this, the victims of a fanatical group of bloodthirsty lunatics. Surely, among eight men, one would step forward and stop this atrocity.

"Please," she cried out. "Please don't do this."

But no one listened. She didn't know if a minute had passed or an hour, but suddenly the eight white-robed men were shouting and running and mounting their horses. Maggie turned her head looking and listening, trying to grasp the meaning of their frantic actions. More horses and riders were coming toward the house. She didn't know who they were and didn't care. All that mattered was that they had scared away the hooded terrors.

A tall, dark man dismounted from a black stallion and ran toward her. It was Thayer. Oh, thank God, it was Thayer. She opened her mouth to cry out his name, but couldn't make a sound. She tried again.

"Thayer." Her voice was so weak that she barely heard herself.

"Maggie." Thayer Coleman stood over her, staring down into her chalky white face. "What's happened here? Moses said there were hooded men here to kill Phineas."

"It was Wesley and that Whitcomb man." The words rushed out of her in one quick torrent.

"Damn them," Thayer said. "What happened to Aaron? Is he still alive?"

"Yes, yes, he's still alive," she cried out, unshed tears finally reaching her eyes, glistening them to a honey yellow. "Do something for him, Thayer. That Whitcomb man hit him over the head with his rifle butt."

"Toe Joe, you ride into Tuscumbia and bring back Doc Cooper," Thayer said. When the black man hurried to obey, his employer called after him. "You ride like the devil, you hear?"

"Yes sir," Toe Joe said as he jumped back on his horse.

"What about the sheriff?" Maggie asked.

"There's nothing the sheriff can do."

"But I know who they were, I saw Wesley's face."

"You don't understand, but we'll worry about righting things later. Isaac, you cut Phineas loose and see to his back."

Thayer knelt down to examine his friend's head. "It looks worse than it is, Maggie. He's got a hard head. It'd take more than a rifle butt to kill this bull."

She held out her bloodstained hands. "He's lost so much blood. And Daisy . . ." She turned to look at Daisy's still form. "She's been through so much already. She may be too weak to live through this."

Maggie sat there in the dirt, Aaron's bloody head in her lap, her hands idly stroking his chest and shoulders while she watched as a badly whipped Phineas fell free from the ropes binding him to the nearby tree. When Thayer's foreman, Isaac, reached out to help him, he shrugged off the older man's hand and crawled on his knees the few feet to reach his wife. He raised himself up, taking Daisy in his arms.

Then Maggie began to cry while she held Aaron and watched the big, black man clutching his wife to his bare chest, keening softly as he rocked her limp body back and forth.

"Is she still alive?" Maggie asked.

Phineas didn't hear, thus he made no reply. Thayer walked over, reached down, and felt for Daisy's pulse. "She's alive, but awfully weak. Maggie, see if you can talk to Phineas. Explain that we need to take Daisy in out of this damp night air."

Before Maggie could speak Phineas lifted his wife into his arms and stood, his own blood dripping from his shredded back. He began to walk one slow, painful step after another, little droplets of blood hitting the ground, sprinkling the earth with crimson moisture. His feet faltered several times, but he finally reached the porch steps. When his foot touched the bottom round, he staggered, falling to his knees, his beloved bundle held securely in his arms. He swayed back and forth, lay Daisy on the bottom step, and fell over into the dirt.

"Help them, Thayer!" Maggie screamed.

Thayer and Isaac were running as Maggie kept screaming for them to help the couple.

She wanted to feel relief. Relief that the horrible hooded men were gone. Relief that Thayer was here and a doctor had been sent for. But she was too afraid to feel any sense of relief. Of the three of them, she was the only one still conscious. Perhaps the others were lucky not to be able to think about the nightmare they had just lived through. But what if she were the only one to survive? Would she want to live without Aaron? She had no choice. She was carrying his child. She had to go on living.

"Maggie." Thayer touched her on the shoulder. "We've put Daisy to bed and sent a man for Auntie Gem. Phineas has come to. Isaac is in the kitchen seeing to his back. We need to take Aaron inside."

She eased his head from her lap when Thayer and several of his men lifted Aaron. She stood there looking after him as they moved across the yard. She didn't follow.

Somewhere out there, eight men were riding free, led by an insane preacher who would stand in the pulpit come Sunday spouting hellfire and damnation to sinners. Thayer had said it would do no good to send for the sheriff. Maybe not, but Wesley Peterson would have to be stopped. But how? And by whom? If Aaron were to die . . .

Chapter 17

Maggie liked the feel of the crisp morning air as it stung her cheeks. It felt so good to be alive, to know that, although death had come so near, it had passed over them, giving her a renewed faith in God. Sunshine fought with the October breeze, and though the sun's warmth brightened the sky, it lost the battle to the chill of autumn.

She knelt down on her knees, reaching out to pick the dark green collards and place them in the lap of her big apron. Auntie Gem said that now was the time to pick them, after a good frost. She suspected that the old woman had known she needed to get out of the house for a while and had sent her to do this chore.

This was the second day after their nightmare experience. A new and lasting fear had been born within her. Not all the assurance in the world, not even Thayer's and several of his men's presence here the past two nights, had lessened that gut-wrenching panic still seizing her. The first night she hadn't slept at all, just sat by Aaron's bedside until he regained consciousness in the morning hours. And last night had been a series of frightening dreams from which she had awakened in a cold sweat.

Aaron had drifted in and out of consciousness all day yesterday and had slept soundly all night. She suspected that when Doc Cooper came back tomorrow, he would pronounce him fully recovered. He had eaten the breakfast she had taken him, and they had talked briefly. He had told her the one thing she hadn't wanted to hear. He was sending Moses to Tuscumbia for Eunice.

Daisy had not survived their ordeal quite so well. The miscarriage, Wesley's beating, topped by the shock of seeing her husband nearly whipped to death, had left the young woman hovering between life and death for the first twenty-four hours. When she finally regained consciousness late last night, she had refused to speak to anyone. She lay in the bed, her pale eyes staring off into space. Not even Phineas's constant attention had roused her from her depression. Doc Cooper had assured them that in time, she should recover.

Phineas, who had endured the most severe punishment of all, seemed to have recovered the quickest. He allowed Auntie Gem to doctor his back, even withstood the torture of wearing a shirt, but he refused to allow anyone to talk about what had happened. When Maggie had tried to discuss it with him, he had told her to put it out of her mind. She would never forget the look in his black eyes when he had said, "There'll be a time and a place." His words echoed the words Aaron had spoken on Phineas and Daisy's wedding day when he had intervened between the black man and Wesley. She would not allow herself to think about what they meant.

Thayer had spent the last two nights helping with Aaron, two of his best men standing guard with rifles in hand. No matter what his reputation as a rich, young rogue, Thayer Coleman was quite a man. His strength and kindness were qualities Maggie deeply admired. Maybe she was beginning to understand why her stubborn little sister was infatuated with him.

When Toe Joe had returned yesterday, bringing supplies from Tuscumbia, he had brought Maggie a letter from Alice Mobley that had confirmed her worst fears. Word of what had happened at White Orchard plantation had spread quickly after Doc Cooper had been summoned. Alice said that Jude had gone into incoherent fits of crying, saying that she was responsible for what had happened and that God would punish her. It seemed that Alice had finally calmed the child enough to get most of the story from her. With the twins' help, Jude had slipped away from the Mobley house and done what she had threatened. She had gone to Loretta's to see Verda, telling the whore that Maggie was pregnant by Aaron who wouldn't marry her, and Thayer had proposed. Verda suggested that Judith go to the good Reverend Peterson. She had told the child that she was sure that he would want to marry his dear cousin and protect her and her innocent child from scandal. Jude had taken the foolish woman's advice, never realizing that Wesley was insane until she saw his reaction to her news. Alice suggested that Maggie come to town as soon as possible to get Jude. The child needed her badly.

She had spoken to Thayer about the situation, and he had promised to return this afternoon and drive her into town. He prayed that she would be gone before Eunice Arnold arrived.

When Thayer had been standing by Aaron's bedside early this morning, saying good-bye, Aaron had asked that he send Moses to town with a message for Eunice. She had remained silent, afraid to ask why he was sending for his fiancée. And as far as Maggie knew the good widow was still his future bride. He had told her nothing different.

She supposed that once she had seen to Jude, she'd ask Thayer to write his mother. Perhaps if Martha Coleman were willing to take them in she could start all over again in Franklin, Tennessee, making a new life for herself and Jude, and Aaron's child. She refused to accept defeat. Even without Aaron, she'd find a way to survive. They were alive. That's all that mattered now.

With her apron full of collards, Maggie walked back to the house. When she neared the porch, she stopped to stare at the big stump of a newly cut tree a few yards away. Closing her eyes, she could see Phineas's raw and bleeding back, could smell the stench of ripped human flesh, and hear leather striking skin. And then she could see Phineas with an axe in his hands, chopping the tree to which he had been bound. She could hear the tree as it crashed to the earth. She had shared his sense of satisfaction, knowing that the symbolic act had been a catharsis for all of them.

Three hours later, the collards had been washed a dozen times, soaked in salt water, thoroughly inspected by Auntie Gem's keen eyes, and put in the big kettle to cook. Maggie sat at the kitchen table peeling potatoes and trying to pretend she didn't hear the buggy stopping outside. Before the door opened, she knew Eunice Arnold had arrived.

The elegant widow pranced in, brushing dust from her myrtle-green woolen dress. The hat adorning her head was black plush with red bird's wing and veil. It amazed Maggie that the woman had ridden over twelve miles in a buggy and looked as if she just stepped out of a Tuscumbia shop.

Flashing her fake smile at Maggie, she said, "I've come to see my dear Aaron. Poor man couldn't wait for me to come on my own. He had to send Moses for me."

Maggie glared at the woman. *I'm not a lady. I don't have to be polite to her.*

"He's in yonder." Auntie Gem pointed toward the back bedroom.

"Thank you. I'll announce myself. You two continue with whatever it is you're doing."

"We're cooking," Maggie said, clutching the paring knife in her tense hand.

"Oh." Eunice turned her back on the women as she made her way to the bedroom.

Aaron had heard the cabriolet arrive. He dreaded talking to Eunice again, but it was something that had to be done. He had been terribly unfair to the woman, but marrying her would only worsen the crime. When he had gone to Tuscumbia three nights ago, rushing off like a fool and asking Eunice to marry him, he had been half crazy with pain and anger at the thought of Maggie's betrayal. Then two nights ago, after learning the truth, he had gone back to town to talk to his fiancée. He hadn't been sure what he wanted to say to her, and had left feeling as uncertain and confused as when he had arrived.

But things were different now. One night of terror had resolved all his uncertainties, allowing him to see clearly for the first time in his life. He had been a total fool, a selfish, unforgiving bastard. His own stupidity had made him more a bastard than an accident of birth. He loved Maggie Campbell. He had nearly lost her. God had been merciful enough to give him a second chance. He had no intention of ruining it. He felt it only fair to speak to Eunice first, to free himself of his commitment to her before he could ask Maggie to be his wife. He had been grossly unfair to both women. He was sure that Eunice would hate him, but it was a small price to pay for everyone's future happiness. Someday the widow would find a man who really loved her and could make her life as complete as Maggie did his.

He had bathed, shaved, and dressed over an hour ago, and now sat on the side of the small wooden bed waiting for the forthcoming confrontation. He had drawn back the heavy yellow cotton curtains so that the bright sunshine could warm the room.

"Aaron?" Eunice called as she entered.

"Come in, Eunice, and please close the door."

Obeying, she shut the door and walked over to him. Leaning down to place a kiss on his cheek, she smiled. "You're certainly looking well for a man who's survived a concussion. I'm pleased you sent Moses for me. Papa had intended to bring me down tomorrow."

He couldn't help but compare Eunice's actions to Maggie's. If Maggie had been in town when she'd heard the news, she'd have found a way to come to him immediately. But then, Maggie loved him. Maggie Campbell would have been asking a dozen questions about the who, why, and what concerning the brutal attack that had occurred. Ladies like Eunice did not ask questions about things so indelicate. But then, Maggie Campbell was not that kind of lady, thank God.

"Sit down, Eunice." Aaron patted the bed, indicating a place for her to sit.

"I hardly think it proper," she said demurely.

"Suit yourself. There's a chair by the window."

She seated herself in the rough-hewn wooden chair that Maggie had occupied so much lately while keeping a vigil as his bedside. "I don't understand why they didn't take you back to White Orchard," Eunice said. "The accommodations there must be better than this crude little place."

He let out a sneering, closed-mouth laugh. "Lady, I was unconscious. The only thought Maggie and Thayer had was for my life, not the nicety of my surroundings. However, I don't find anything wrong with Phineas and Daisy's home. It's warm and clean and filled with love."

"Whatever is the matter with you, Aaron? You're talking so strangely." She crossed her slender ankles, well hidden beneath the fine wool of her dress.

"Am I?" He placed his big hands on the top of his thighs, then rubbed them back and forth. He was stalling for time, dreading this woman's reaction to his news.

"Since Moses is here with the carriage, would you like for me to accompany you back to White Orchard this afternoon?"

Clutching his knees, Aaron looked down at the floor. "Eunice, I owe you an apology. I've made a lot of mistakes in my life, but asking you to marry me was the biggest mistake I ever made. I hope someday you can forgive me for being such a fool."

"What are you saying? It's her, isn't it?" Eunice refused to look at the man sitting on the bed. "Somehow she's convinced you not to marry me."

"I'm sorry. I love Maggie. I've loved her for months."

Eunice clasped her hands together as if in prayer. She rested her chin on her knuckles. "How can you think that she'll make a proper wife? She's nothing but an uneducated farm girl."

"She's everything I want. I don't need a fine lady for a wife. All I need is the woman I love. Try to understand. I would have made your life miserable if we had married. Could you have endured an unfaithful husband?"

"I can't believe that you've actually thought this through." She unclasped her hands, nervously smoothing her skirt. "A man of your social standing surely can't want to marry beneath himself?"

Shocked brown eyes stared at the man who rose from the bed, laughter vibrating his huge chest. "I think there's something you should know about me, something that will make you glad you won't become Mrs. Aaron Stone."

Cocking her platinum head to one side, she cut her eyes in his direction, curiosity brightening their darkness. "Something about your past?"

"I think you should consider this a farewell present. You'll be the one who can inform everybody in the county about my mysterious past."

"I believe you've just called me a gossip," she said, her mouth tightening into a sour pout.

Aaron wondered why he had never noticed what a shrewish-looking female the widow really was. All he had seen was her cool, blond loveliness, her regal bearing, but never the petty glint in her eyes or the haughtiness of her speech.

"I'm a bastard," he told her and waited momentarily while she gasped. "Not just any ordinary bastard, mind you, but Richard Leander's offspring by a woman as young as his own daughter."

"You're . . . you're Martha Coleman's . . ."

"Yes, I'm Martha's brother. A brother that she is more than willing to claim. I'm the fool who's been too ashamed to accept my birthright, too stupid to forgive my parents for loving each other more than they cared about public opinion. I understand now because that's how I feel about Maggie."

"You would have married me with such a secret between us?" she demanded, rising quickly from the chair, her trembling fingers patting the back of her perfectly coiffed head.

"You have been saved from a fate worse than death, my dear Mrs. Arnold. You and I are totally unsuited for one another." He stood up, moving toward her.

An agitated Eunice walked away from him, but stopped when she opened the bedroom door.

"You're quite right. We most definitely are not suitable for one another. And you can rest assured that I will not spread one word of this to a living soul. I should be too embarrassed to admit that I allowed you to pay me court."

In a huff of righteous indignation, Eunice Waite Arnold departed, leaving behind an amused and very relieved ex-fiancé.

"Auntie Gem got her to drink some tea, but she wouldn't eat a bite," Maggie told Phineas. "She's going to be all right. It's just that she's been through so much. It'll take time."

"I know, Miss Maggie, but it's hard for a man to see his wife in such a bad way. I feel like there's something I ought to be doing to help her."

"In the long run, your love is going to pull her through this."

Phineas stood there on the porch watching as Toe Joe disappeared down the road, his horse leaving a trail of dust behind him. "I know you was wanting to get to town to see about Miss Jude, but she'll be all right till you can get there. Mr. Thayer'll be on as soon as he can."

"I know. Toe Joe said he was working as hard as he could to take care of the problem at the mill. But if he can't get away soon, it'll be dark before we get to Tuscumbia."

Eunice Arnold walked out on the porch, her dark eyes glaring at the young woman beside the big, black man.

"Fetch Moses for me," she snapped. "I'm ready to go home."

"You didn't stay long," Maggie said, wondering why the widow's visit had been so brief.

"I didn't want to tire him. That nasty blow on his head has made him not quite himself."

"Has it?"

"Will you get Moses for me?" The Widow Arnold turned her mocha brown eyes on the servant who had not rushed to do her bidding.

"Yes'am," Phineas said, heading for the back of the house.

Eunice eyed the woman who stood on the far side of the porch. Maggie had a bonnet on her head and a heavy shawl draped around her shoulders. "Are you going somewhere?"

Maggie wanted to tell her that it was none of her business, but controlled the urge. "I was expecting Thayer, but he's been delayed."

"Oh?" The tall blonde smiled, moving across the porch in the redhead's direction. "I can't imagine you're leaving Aaron at a time like this."

Now just what did she mean by that? "Aaron seems to be fully recovered. Besides I'd think as his fiancée, you'd have some objections to my staying on here taking care of him."

"As his fi . . . You mean he hasn't . . . Oh, I see."

What was wrong with the widow? She was babbling. "I've got to get to town to see about my sister. She's awfully upset about what happened out here the other night."

"You're going to town?"

"Yes. As soon as Thayer can straighten out a problem at his mill."

"I'd be more than happy to offer you a ride to town," Eunice said, her haughty face softening as she smiled. "There's no longer any reason for us to be enemies."

She did not want to spend hours alone with Eunice Arnold, but she did need to get to town as quickly as possible. She could just imagine what a state Jude was in by now. The entire Mobley household was probably ready to explode.

"All right. I'd appreciate a ride."

"Fine. Fine. Perhaps you can just leave a message for Aaron. He was almost asleep when I left him, and I'm sure you don't want to disturb him."

"I'll just tell Phineas," Maggie said when she saw Daisy's husband coming around the house with Moses following.

"I'll wait in the carriage for you." Eunice walked away, still smiling.

Maggie stopped Phineas as he started into the house. "I'm going to ride into town with Mrs. Arnold."

"Miss Maggie—"

"I know. I know. But she made the offer, and I need to go on before it gets dark. Thayer could be delayed for hours."

"It's a mistake to go off with that woman."

"Thank you for your concern, Phineas, but I'll be all right. She's going to be Aaron's wife. I've got to accept the fact and go on with my life. Tell Daisy that Jude and I'll be back tomorrow and I'll stay on as long as she needs me."

"Yes'am. But you be careful, and don't pay that woman no never mind."

Touched by the man's protective attitude, Maggie patted him gently on the upper arm. Yes, Aaron was right. Phineas Moulton was a good man and a true friend.

Allowing Moses to help her into the carriage, Maggie turned to her companion. "I'm sorry if I kept you waiting."

"It's quite all right," the widow said, turning her head slightly to look directly at the other woman. "We're ready to go now, Moses."

The two women sat silently as the cabriolet rolled along the dirt road leading to Memphis Pike. Maggie was glad that the late September cool spell had come and gone quickly and this first week of October was unseasonably warm. Here in the Southland, the weather was so changeable. It was not uncommon to have a big frost one morning and almost summertime warmth the next day.

"May I ask you a question, Miss Campbell?"

"What would you like to know, Mrs. Arnold?"

"Have you made plans for your future? I mean, are you planning on continuing your relationship with Thayer?"

"Contrary to what you and everyone else thinks, Thayer and I are just friends."

"Is that so?" The widow's eyes widened in amused disbelief.

"You can rest assured that I have no intention of interfering in your marriage. As soon as Daisy is well, my sister and I will be moving."

"Back to Tennessee?"

"As a matter of fact, yes." She didn't have to tell Eunice that they weren't moving home to Grovesdale, but were going to Franklin to live with Martha Coleman. At least, she prayed that the invitation would still be open when Thayer wrote his mother about Maggie's condition.

"Does Aaron know?"

"Not yet. Perhaps you'd like the pleasure of telling him." She had to admit that she still hated Eunice, the selfish, haughty bitch. But if she was what Aaron wanted then more power to him.

Eunice laid her head back against the warm, leather-upholstered seat. She was smiling inwardly and outwardly, a very pleased look on her face.

Maggie wanted the trip to hurry and end. She leaned back and closed her eyes, weariness etched on every feature of her face.

She hoped that when she got to the Mobleys', she'd be able to convince Jude that everything was going to be all right. Her little sister's selfish actions had inadvertently set off a chain reaction that had almost cost four people their lives, but she had acted out of childish hurt, never dreaming what Wesley Peterson was capable of doing. Did she dare tell the child the complete truth? From Alice's letter, Maggie knew that Jude thought Wesley, out of insane jealousy, had told the wrong people about Maggie and Aaron's sin, and that these men had acted on their own.

She had tried not to think about the good reverend. It was only a matter of time until something would have to be done. She doubted seriously if Aaron or Phineas would let the man get away with his deeds. What if they were to take the law into their own hands? She shuddered to think what could happen if they did. Would anybody believe that Wesley was capable of such monstrous behavior? Probably only a handful of the local residents were aware of the man's dual personality. What would it do to Aunt Tilly if she ever found out that her beloved son was insane? As much as she disliked her uncle's wife, she prayed that the poor woman could be spared from learning the truth.

Maggie looked around, recognizing the scenery from previous trips. Thankfully there were still several hours of daylight left because they were just now leaving Pride Station, which meant it was still a good nine miles to town.

Off in the distance she could see another buggy approaching, the driver obviously in a hurry. The horse seemed to be fairly flying, huge clouds of dust billowing up behind him.

As they neared the other vehicle, Maggie's heart lodged in her throat. It was Wesley's carryall. *Oh, dear God, it can't be!* But it was. The reverend slowed his buggy, pulling up alongside the cabriolet.

"Keep going!" Maggie shouted to Moses.

"Nonsense," Eunice said. "Stop this carriage immediately. It's apparent that Reverend Peterson wants to speak with us."

"No!" Maggie screamed.

Moses had slowed the buggy before Maggie could persuade him to keep moving. Wesley raised a rifle from his side and aimed it directly at the black man.

"Merciful heavens, Reverend," Eunice gasped. "Whatever are you doing with that rifle?"

"I don't mean you any harm, Mrs. Arnold," Wesley said in the most gentle of voices. "I was on my way to White Orchard to fetch Margaret. I intend to take her with me, and I don't want any fuss out of this nigger."

"My, my. I should think that would be no problem. I'm sure Miss Campbell would be glad to accompany you."

"Is that right, Cousin Margaret? Will you come with me willingly?"

"No," Maggie groaned, her terror-filled eyes beseeching Eunice.

Moses moved quickly, turning the whip in his hand toward the other vehicle, but before he was able to accomplish his objective, a shot rang out loudly, the sound echoing in Maggie's ear like a cannon blast. She screamed, knotting her hands into tight fists while Eunice swooned in a near faint. The carriage jerked, and then began to move forward, the startled horses whinnying. Suddenly more shots sounded. Both horses made dying cries as their huge bodies slumped to the ground.

"Dear Lord, what happened?" Eunice wailed.

"He's shot Moses and both horses." Maggie looked down at the black man, blood oozing from the bullet wounds in his body. He lay face down on the road, the huge horses beside him, one of them sprawled across his legs.

"But why? I don't understand." Eunice's eyes were glazed with shock.

"Get down, Margaret," Wesley said as calmly as if he were asking her for the next dance. Was he even aware that he had just killed a man? "You get down and come with me and I'll let Mrs. Arnold live."

"No, Maggie." Eunice grabbed the other woman by the arm. "I don't know what is going on, but you mustn't go with him."

"I have no choice. He'll kill us both if I don't," Maggie whispered. "I'll go with him. You walk back to Pride Station and get help."

"I will. I promise, I will." Eunice clutched Maggie's hand just before she stepped down from the cabriolet.

Maggie trembled from head to toe. She had never been so afraid, not even two nights ago. She knew that she was going to die. There was little hope that help could arrive in time.

When Wesley reached out a fleshy hand to help her into his carryall, she refused, pulling herself up into the seat.

"Good day, Mrs. Arnold. Please give my best to your parents," Wesley said as he cracked the whip over his horse.

The Widow Arnold sat there in the cabriolet, her glassy-eyed stare never leaving the other vehicle as it moved rapidly in the direction of Tuscumbia. Maggie kept looking back, praying that Eunice would come out of shock long enough to go for help. It was doubtful rescue would come before Wesley acted upon his insane instincts, but she tried not to give up all hope.

Aaron had never prayed so much in all his life. He was a man who seldom made contact with the Lord, but today every thought in his mind and every feeing in his heart was concentrated in prayer. If a man could make a bargain with the Almighty, then he'd do it. He would do anything, give anything, if he and Thayer could reach Maggie in time.

Young Pete Grimes had come from Pride Station in record time. Breathlessly, he had told them that Mrs. Arnold was at his pa's place, and had said for somebody to take out up Memphis Pike after a gal called Maggie because Wesley had taken her at gunpoint.

He and Thayer had wasted no time discussing a plan of action before they left. All he could think about was what would happen to the woman he loved if they didn't get to her in time.

"Look, there's a buggy stopped up ahead," Thayer said.

"It's them. I recognize Peterson's carryall. Why the hell have they stopped?" Aaron slowed his horse to a trot.

"We can't go riding up and try to overtake them. He's liable to shoot her before we could stop him."

"Let's cut off the road here," Aaron suggested. "We can circle around through the woods and come up behind the buggy."

They left the road and went straight into the woods. When they were directly parallel to Wesley's vehicle, the two men dismounted, leading their horses to the edge of the thicket. They could hear the sound of the good reverend's shouting voice and see the back of his tall, fat body.

"My God," Aaron groaned when he saw Maggie on her knees in the dirt at Peterson's feet. With a few stray tendrils curling about her pale face, Maggie's wildly disheveled hair hung about her shoulders.

"Stay calm," Thayer said, placing a restraining hand on his big friend's arm. "We can't help her if we lose our heads."

Wesley's voice shrilled hysterically. "You have sinned against God and man, harlot. Repent of your sins before you go to meet your Maker."

"He's going to kill her," Aaron said, his green eyes never leaving Maggie's huddled form. "He's holding a rifle in his hand. I'll go out where he can see me and distract him from Maggie while you circle behind him."

"My God, Aaron, be careful," Thayer told his friend as he turned to follow instructions.

The blond giant took several steps out into the clearing, deliberately making as much noise as he possibly could.

"If anyone has sinned and should die, it's me." When Aaron spoke, Maggie jerked her head around, her eyes locking with his, relief and fear combined in her gaze.

"Stone!" Wesley said, turning the rifle toward the intruder.

"Maggie is innocent of any wrong. I'm the one who led her astray. God knows that if anyone should be punished, it should be me."

"No!" The sound of Maggie's frightened voice gained the reverend's attention.

Aaron continued to move forward, inch by inch edging closer to the maniac with the gun. "You're a man of God, Reverend, you can't take a life."

"It is within my rights to do God's will. He speaks to me in all things. I take life only by His instructions." Wesley turned away from the kneeling woman, walking toward the big man. "This woman was to have been my wife, but she gave her innocence to you and then became the paid whore of Thayer Coleman. I offered her forgiveness and a chance for redemption, but she refused me. For these sins, she must die."

"You're wrong." Aaron was almost within touching distance of his objective. "I'm the only man Maggie has ever known. She loves me, and I love her. She could never have been the right wife for you."

"You shouldn't have come after her, Stone. Now, I'll have to kill you, too."

Just as Wesley aimed his rifle at Aaron's chest, Thayer came up from behind him, grabbing him quickly. Unbalanced from the attack, Wesley staggered, and fell forward, managing to land on his knees. Still holding the rifle, he aimed it at Thayer and pulled the trigger. The dark, young man swayed as he grabbed his shoulder, blood seeping between his fingers.

Aaron rushed to Maggie, but was thwarted by the reverend's unexpected action. He grabbed Maggie while they were both on their knees, slowly easing himself and his captive upward, accidentally dropping his weapon in the process.

"Let her go." Aaron held a revolver in his big hand.

"I can break her neck before you can kill me," Wesley warned. "I'll make a deal with you, Stone. Maggie and I will get in my buggy, and then I'll throw her into your arms before I ride away."

Aaron lowered the gun. "Go ahead." Somehow he could manage to catch her. All that mattered was to get her away from that man.

"Throw down the gun," Wesley said.

When Aaron obeyed, the reverend dragged Maggie with him up into the carryall, his rifle still on the ground where he had dropped it when he had made a hasty reach for his cousin.

"Let her go, Peterson." Aaron ran forward, grabbing the side of the buggy. Maggie turned just as Wesley snatched the reins. "Let her go, or you're a dead man!"

Wesley's hideous laughter struck Aaron's nerve endings like a thousand pinpricks. "Jump, Maggie," he yelled when the horse began to move.

He couldn't understand why she was hesitating. Didn't she realize what she had to do to escape? Even if she hit the ground with a few broken bones, it was preferable to dying. He held his arms out to her, hoping he could catch her. Just as the buggy picked up speed, Aaron began running faster. When she jumped, his strong arms went around her, catching her against his chest, but the impact of her body sent them both falling backward, Maggie landing in a sprawl on top of her rescuer.

He ran his hands over her face, her hair, and her shoulders. "Are you all right, love?"

"Yes," she cried, tears clogging her throat. "What about you?"

"I'm fine now that you're safe."

He pushed her up enough where he could sit, pulling her up to her feet when he stood, his arms holding her close.

"Peterson's getting away," Thayer said as he walked over to where his friends were standing, locked in a possessive embrace.

"How bad are you hurt?" Aaron asked, noticing the bloodstains covering the other man's shirtsleeve.

"Damn fool just grazed my shoulder. No telling where the bullet went. I can make it back to White Orchard on horseback. Let's get out of here. We can get the marshal tomorrow. I don't think Peterson's going anywhere. He'll probably go home to his mother, thinking he's safe and sound. He's just that crazy." Thayer placed his hand on Maggie's back just above where one of Aaron's clutched her tightly.

"Yes, please, let's go back to White Orchard," Maggie said.

"Maggie, I want you to go with Thayer. You two take care of each other," Aaron told them. "I'm going after the good reverend. I'll either see him in jail or dead by nightfall."

"No, Aaron. Please don't go," she pleaded, embracing him fiercely.

Pushing her out of his arms, he held her by the shoulders. "You and Thayer get on his horse and go straight back to Phineas's place. I'll be back tonight when I've finished with Peterson."

He shoved her toward his friend. "Get her out of here."

"Are you sure?" Thayer asked.

Aaron didn't answer. He didn't look back as he walked to his horse, mounted, and rode away. Maggie, standing at Thayer's side, called after him begging him to be careful.

She wanted to run after the man she loved, to plead with him not to go, but she knew it would be useless. Aaron had made up his mind to put an end to the nightmare that Wesley Peterson had created for them. She prayed that he could take her uncle's stepson to the sheriff. If Wesley resisted, she knew that Aaron would kill him.

"Maggie?"

"I'll be ready to go in just a minute." She stood there in the middle of Memphis Pike, the soft glow of sunset warming the evening sky. The wind blew chillingly, making her realize that she no longer had her shawl. She undoubtedly had lost it somewhere. Wiping the tears from her eyes, she stared off into the distance watching the last traces of dust from Aaron's departure swirl into the air and disappear.

Chapter 18

Maggie sat at the kitchen window gazing out into the darkness, the faint moonlight spreading across the yard and endless fields. The only sign of life came from the wind's movement and the faraway sounds of woodland creatures. It had turned cooler during the night, so she and Auntie Gem had kept a fire going in the cook-stove, thus warming the house and providing hot coffee for those who could not sleep. She had downed so much of the strong brew that she doubted even some of the laudanum they had given Daisy and Eunice would make her rest.

In less than an hour, it would be daybreak, and Aaron still had not returned. She tried not to think that the worst had happened, but every horror her overactive imagination could conceive replayed itself again and again in her mind. Had Aaron found Wesley and killed him? Or even worse, had the reverend killed Aaron?

And what about Phineas? As soon as she and Thayer had returned, Daisy's husband had saddled his horse, and, without a word, rode away. When Daisy had called for him later, Maggie had been forced to lie to keep her friend from worrying. She was sure that Phineas had gone to help Aaron.

Auntie Gem had taken over like a little general, issuing orders and daring anyone to defy her. She was the one who had made the decision to doctor both Daisy's and Eunice's coffee with medication.

"Ain't no reason for Daisy to fret about Phineas when there ain't nothing she can do," the old woman had said. "And that Miz Arnold is so wrought up, we either going to have to put her to sleep or hogtie her and gag her."

That had been hours ago, and now she and Thayer sat alone in the kitchen while Auntie Gem dozed in a chair by Daisy's bed. She had talked to Thayer for a long time, reliving every detail of her time alone with the mad reverend. Although he shared her concern for Aaron, he assured her that Phineas had joined him, and together they were taking Wesley to the marshal.

"As part of a hooded gang, Peterson might have been exempt from the law, but not as a private citizen. You and Eunice, and Aaron and I can all testify against him."

She dreaded the thought of going to court, of having the whole town exposed to the ugly truth, and having their personal lives become public knowledge. Poor Aunt Tilly. Even she didn't deserve that kind of pain and humiliation.

Maggie closed her eyes for just a moment, but opened them again quickly when visions of Moses's bloody body flashed through her mind. She could see the young, black man clearly, his lifeless body resting in the dirt, a dead horse sprawled across his legs. Her face felt hot and flushed and her pulse raced with remembered fear.

She couldn't stop the gasping sound that came from her mouth or the fresh tears flooding her eyes. She would not allow herself to fall apart. Now when she didn't know if Aaron were alive or dead. She could hold on just a little longer. She knew she could.

"Maggie?" Thayer roused from his sleepy silence. Sensing her frantic state of mind, he pulled his chair closer and put an arm around her quivering shoulders. "He's all right. You can't even begin to understand the kind of man Aaron is. And if Phineas is with him . . ."

"You're trying to tell me that they'll kill Wesley, aren't you?"

"Not necessarily." Thayer tried to avoid looking at this all-too-knowing woman. "It's just that Aaron has been exposed to a side of life that most people haven't. Phineas came from that background. There are places in this world where a man has to kill first and ask questions later."

"Aaron wouldn't kill in cold blood," Maggie argued. "I won't believe he's capable of such a thing."

"Would you love him any less if he were?"

"Would he be any different from Wesley then?" She cried, burying her face in her hands, hot tears soaking her flesh.

"Listen to yourself." He grabbed her shoulders, forcing her to face him. "Aaron will give Wesley a chance, but if he resists, Aaron will not let him go free to harm you or anyone else again. Maggie, I'd do the same. Do you hear me? I'd kill to protect the woman I love."

She stared into the man's ebony eyes, mesmerizing and intense. "Phineas?"

"Phineas will kill Peterson if he finds him first."

She could not sit another minute. She had to get up and move around before she went insane. Maybe another cup of coffee would help.

"You want another cup?" she asked Thayer while she poured herself more, her hands shaking so badly that the cup almost slipped from her fingers.

"None for me."

"Why don't you try to get some sleep? Just because I'm not able to rest doesn't mean you have to stay up with me."

"All right, Maggie," Thayer agreed. "I'll rest my head here on the table for a while. If you need me, I'll be here."

She could see the first faint light of dawn when she gazed out the window again. The dark sky shimmered with the glow of predawn awaiting the birth of another day. Shoving back the curtains, she opened the window slightly. The sounds from the river drifted into the room. The smell of fresh country air blended with aromas of wood smoke and strong coffee.

Because of the darkness, she heard the two riders coming up the lane before she saw them. They were Aaron and Phineas. She pulled down the window, her unsteady fingers clutching at the red gingham curtains.

"Thayer!"

"I hear them. Is it Aaron and Phineas?" he asked, his dark eyes meeting hers when he stood.

"Yes, it's them," she cried, rushing to open the door.

The two men were just dismounting when Maggie and Thayer walked onto the front porch. Aaron looked up, his face haggard and weary. Phineas led both horses toward the barn. He never once looked at the house nor spoke a word to the two people anxiously waiting.

Maggie ran down the steps and threw herself into Aaron's arms. He pulled her close, his big arms binding her to the unyielding strength of his body. "Thank God. Thank God, you're all right," she sobbed, her small hands covering his face, stroking his rough cheeks.

Aaron looked over her head to where his friend still stood on the porch. Had Thayer tried to prepare her for what was about to happen? He hoped beyond hope that she was capable of accepting a half-truth without asking too many questions. He would never tell a loving soul how Wesley Peterson had met his fate. Not even Maggie.

Looking up into Aaron's tired eyes, she asked, "Wesley?"

"He's dead."

"How?" A feeling of relief surged through her, and then guilt settled on her heart.

"Phineas and I found him on the way into town. He was dead when we got to him. We took his body to the marshal," Aaron said, reciting the exact story he had given the lawman.

Maggie watched the expression on the big man's face and noticed the exchange of guarded looks between him and Thayer. "How did he die?" she asked.

"There wasn't a mark on him," Aaron told her, leading her up the steps and onto the porch. "The marshal seems to think his neck was broken. He could have fallen from his buggy."

"Is that what the marshal believes?" Thayer asked.

"Yeah, that's what he believes. What other explanation could there be? The reverend didn't have an enemy in the world. It had to be an accident."

Maggie knew there was a lot more to what had happened than Aaron was telling, than he would ever tell. She doubted that he had killed Wesley himself. Perhaps he had watched while . . . Then again, maybe Wesley had already been dead when Aaron found him. Somehow it really didn't matter anymore.

Aaron held her close, wondering if what had happened would change the way she felt about him. Would she still love him suspecting that he could have prevented her cousin's death? He had known that Phineas would come and find him when he'd sent Thayer and Maggie back to White Orchard. As much as he had hated the good reverend, he knew Phineas had hated him more. He probably could have taken Wesley in to the marshal alive, but so many people would have had to pay for that lunatic's sins. He probably had had no right to play God, but sometimes a man has to do the wrong thing for the right reason.

They were living in a time and place when a man like Wesley Peterson could get away with murder because no one would believe him capable of such a hideous act. But a man like himself was labeled illegitimate from birth and carried that brand for the rest of his life. A woman with Maggie's background would probably always be snubbed by women like Eunice. And a man like Phineas could be hanged for the most minor of offenses, just as a woman like Daisy could be beaten and raped with no lawful reprisal. Aaron wondered in a world like this who could say what was right and what was wrong. A man did the best he could to take care of himself and the people he loved.

Aaron noticed Auntie Gem standing in the doorway looking out toward the barn. "He's putting up the horses."

"You both all right?" the old woman asked, a look of solemn knowledge crossing her aged face.

Aaron simply nodded affirmatively, realizing that Auntie Gem understood the situation better than any of them did. She had worked for Mathilda Gower for many years.

"Is Daisy still asleep?" Maggie asked.

"Yes'am, her and Miz Arnold. I checked on them both before I came out here. That laudanum got them resting easy."

"We can go inside," Aaron said. "Phineas will probably stay outside for a while."

Auntie Gem went inside first, the others following. The old woman poured a cup of hot coffee and handed it to Aaron. "You hold this while I fetch that bottle of whiskey out of the cabinet."

"Aaron, do Aunt Tilly and Uncle Chester know about Wesley?" Maggie asked as she sat down at the table between the two men and watched as Auntie Gem liberally laced Aaron's coffee with ninety-proof liquor.

"I don't know. We left before the marshal went to tell them. It'll be hard on Mrs. Gower, but she's better off believing her son died accidentally falling from his buggy than ever knowing the whole truth about him."

"You're right," Maggie agreed. Wesley's accidental death could protect a lot of people from some heartbreaking truths. It would destroy Aunt Tilly to know what a monster her son had been. She had always been so proud of him.

"Does the marshal plan on having any kind of investigation?" Thayer questioned. "Wesley Peterson was greatly admired in Tuscumbia."

"The marshal seems to think that because he was so greatly revered by the townsfolk, no one would ever question that his death could have been anything other than an accident."

"Reverend Peterson is dead?" Eunice Arnold stood in the bedroom doorway, her usually perfectly coiffed hair untidily falling from its bun, her green woolen dress terribly wrinkled.

"Land sakes, gal. I thought you was still asleep," Auntie Gem said, moving quickly to help steady the staggering woman.

Aaron got up and went to Eunice, helping Auntie Gem place her in a chair. "It's all right, Eunice. Peterson met with an accident on his way back to Tuscumbia. You need to put what happened to you and Maggie yesterday out of your mind."

"He . . . he was crazy, wasn't he?" Her brown eyes begged for confirmation as she stared up at Aaron.

"Yes, he was totally insane. But there's no need for us to burden his mother with that truth, is there?" He hoped he could persuade this self-centered woman to do something unselfish for once in her life.

"I won't say anything," Eunice promised. "Mrs. Gower is such a fine woman. Maggie?" The blond woman turned to see where she was.

Sitting across the table, Thayer beside her, Maggie answered, "I'm here."

"He would have killed us. He would have killed me if you hadn't gone with him." Eunice seemed stunned by the truth.

"Aaron's right," Maggie said. "We need to forget everything that happened. We have to keep it all to ourselves to protect Aunt Tilly and Uncle Chester." *And to protect Aaron and Phineas,* she added silently.

"I'd like to go home," Eunice told the others.

"I'll take you," Aaron said. "But first, I need to talk to Maggie."

"You don't have to take me, Aaron," the widow said, placing her slender hand over his. "Just send someone for Papa. He can come and get me."

"You could ride into town with us," Maggie said. "Thayer's going to take me to the Mobleys' as soon as it's good daylight."

"Dammit, Maggie, we need to talk," Aaron said. "After we talk, I'll drive both of you into town."

"You take Mrs. Arnold home," Maggie said, defeated. "I want Thayer to take me. There are some things that only he can help me arrange."

"Woman, you and I have got to talk. There's too much that needs to be said between us." He couldn't understand what was wrong with Maggie. She was acting as if everything between them was over. Had Wesley's death caused that much of a change in her feelings?

"I hardly think we can discuss anything with Eunice standing right here."

"Eunice knows the truth about everything now. Why the hell are you fighting me on this?"

Eunice tugged on Aaron's hand "We could all go in the other room while you two—"

"No!" Maggie said. "I don't want to talk now. I've got to get to Jude. She's bound to hear about Wesley's death before I can get to Tuscumbia."

"Then let me take you," Aaron said as he stood. "We can have our talk on the way into town."

"No. I can't deal with anything else now," Maggie cried as she ran to the door, flung it open, and rushed outside.

Aaron started to go after her, but both Thayer and Eunice called after him.

"There will be plenty of time later to tell her everything you want her to know," Eunice told him. "She's been through so much these last few days. I owe her my life. I . . . I feel badly about . . . well, about everything. Don't push her, Aaron. She loves you, and she'll still love you tomorrow and the day after that."

"Eunice is right," Thayer said. "I'll take her to town and keep an eye on her. Give her a day or so, then come to her if you can tell her what she wants to hear."

"You just remember that she belongs to me," Aaron warned.

Thayer looked from his friend's rugged face to Mrs. Arnold's knowing eyes. "Oh, I see. You get some rest and clean yourself up. I think Maggie will be ready to hear what you have to say by tomorrow." The young man laughed as he went out the door. Hesitating on the porch, he yelled back at Aaron, "Looks like I'll just have to wait for Jude to grow up if I want to marry a beautiful redheaded Campbell."

The sky was stacked with layer upon layer of thick, white clouds like a bed piled high with white cotton quilts. Although it was early afternoon, the dreary darkness caused by the rain clouds simulated early night. The day was warm and humid with an increasing hint of moisture in the air. The approaching rain lay southward, but its presence surrounded them.

Maggie stepped down from the buggy, knowing what she had to do, but dreading it all the same. In little over an hour, she and Jude would be on a train headed for Franklin, Tennessee. She had persuaded Thayer to telegraph his mother yesterday. He had tried to talk her out of going, insisting that she should talk to Aaron, but he had eventually stopped giving advice and simply did as she requested.

She did not want to see Aaron again; she didn't dare. She might not be strong enough to resist him if he asked her to stay. For her child's sake, she could not stay on here and be his mistress. Leaving was the only hope she had left.

"Maggie, you don't have to put yourself through this if you don't want to," Thayer said tenderly as he assisted her down, holding her arm securely.

"I have to give my condolences to Aunt Tilly and Uncle Chester. You can see for yourself that the crowd is beginning to break up. I can't leave without seeing them, without saying something."

"You could have sent a written message of sympathy." Thayer walked with her as she moved closer to the large crowd surrounding Wesley Peterson's grave.

The horse-drawn hearse still stood in front of a long procession of buggies and carriages and wagons. Every citizen in the town had made the trip to Oakwood Cemetery to pay their final respects to the good reverend. Maggie wondered how many of these people had known the man for the monster he had really been. Would any of them believe her if she were to scream out the truth? Poor Aunt Tilly. At least there was no reason why she should ever know.

Thayer led her slowly through the crowd, the two of them causing curious stares and hushed whispers. Gradually the mourners began to move backward, allowing the couple to make their way toward the graveside where Mathilda and Chester Gower stood speaking quietly with Brother Osborne.

This would only take a few minutes, then she could return to the Mobleys', fetch Jude, and board the three o'clock train. Her life in this town was over.

Everyone was staring at her, whispering about her, but she didn't care. She had come to lie to Aunt Tilly, to say that she was sorry Wesley was dead, when actually, she was relieved to know that he could never harm anyone ever again. If nothing else, his death had freed Daisy from her depression. When Maggie had told her, the young woman had fallen into her arms and cried for a long time. Then she had asked for her husband.

"How dare you come here, you harlot," Mathilda Gower screamed, her fat body shaking with rage when she spotted Maggie standing near the foot of her beloved son's open grave.

"Please, Aunt Tilly," Maggie said. "I had to come to tell you how sorry—"

"You . . . your treatment of my son caused his death as surely as the fall from his buggy. You could have been his wife, but you chose to disgrace us all with your sinful ways. I gave your family a home, and how did you repay me?"

"Let's go, Maggie," Thayer said, tugging on her arm.

"Please, Aunt Tilly. Uncle Chester, I'm so sorry." She pleaded. "I know how much . . . you both love—"

"Don't speak to me about love, you whore," Mathilda raged. "What do you know about love? My Wesley knew about the great love of God. He was far too good for you, but even after this whole town knew what you had done, he was still willing to offer you marriage. He was kind and forgiving. Your rejection destroyed him."

Aaron could hear Mrs. Gower's voice clearly above the whispered murmuring of the huge crowd surrounding the gravesite when he parked his carriage behind Thayer's. Thank God that his friend had sent word for him to get to town as quickly as possible, and that Jude had told him where Maggie had persuaded Thayer to take her. Damn, whatever had possessed her to come to the graveside services for the good reverend?

"We were shocked when your little sister came to Wesley to plead with him to marry you," Tilly shouted. "When she told him that you were carrying your lover's child, she might as well have stabbed him in the heart. He was wild with grief."

Crying, Maggie turned into Thayer's arms.

"Come on. Let's go." Thayer held her close as the whole town watched.

Maggie was carrying her lover's child, Aaron thought. My God, how long had she known and not told him? His child. His child growing inside of Maggie's beautiful body.

"Look at this sinful woman. She's a fornicator. She carries one man's child and lives in another man's house warming his bed," Mathilda accused, her silver eyes alight with hatred.

"The hell she does," Aaron Stone roared as he stepped into full view of the agitated crowd, all heads turning in his direction. "Maggie has never belonged to anyone but me. It's my child she carries and my bed she warms."

"Oh Lord," Maggie sighed against Thayer's chest. "It's Aaron."

"Indeed it is," the young man said, smiling. "And about time, I'd say."

The townfolk stood silently, amazed by the sight and sound of the giant of a man as he moved past them, straight toward Maggie Campbell.

Mathilda Gower, restrained by her husband's tenacious grasp, glared at the man making his way to the maligned redhead.

"I love you, Maggie Campbell," Aaron announced, his green eyes beseeching her forgiveness. "I want you to be my wife."

Thayer loosened his hold as Maggie raised her head and pulled away from him. "But what about Eunice?"

"I told her two days ago."

"That's why . . . that's why you sent for her?"

Aaron reached out and took Maggie in his arms, his lips raining tender kisses across her forehead. "Will you talk to me now, my love?"

She couldn't speak because tears filled her throat.

"Get her out of here. I'll go back to the Mobleys' and see after Jude until you two get things straightened out," Thayer said.

"Marrying her will change nothing," Mathilda yelled when Aaron picked Maggie up in his arms.

Brother Osborne placed a restraining hand on Mrs. Gower's shoulder. "Tilly, my dear, you must find it in your heart to forgive. It is what Wesley would have wanted."

Within minutes, Aaron had Maggie seated in his carriage beside him and was motioning the horse into movement. One big arm still held Maggie at his side as he drove them away from the cemetery while an astonished crowd gradually dispersed.

"Where are we going?" she asked, not really caring as long as she was with the man she loved.

"To Thayer's town house, so we can have some privacy."

An ample smile of anticipation formed on her mouth. No one existed tonight except her and Aaron. He would take away the hurt. He would make everything all right again.

A low, flickering fire burned in the massive fireplace. The mellow sound of autumn rain echoed in the stillness of the master bedroom.

"Sometimes, I feel as if I've always loved you," she said as she laid her head against his outstretched arm.

"I think I loved you from the first day we met," he whispered, his finger circling her ear. "Oh, sweet Maggie, let me love you."

"Aaron," she moaned as his mouth hungrily devoured hers. When his kiss deepened, she responded with a passionate cry. Never had she known such an intense arousal as when his hands moved slowly over her body, lovingly caressing every inch of her compliant figure. While he fondled her swelling breasts, her hands moved across the manliness of his hairy chest.

"Please, Aaron, please . . ." Her voice quivered as an unrestrained longing coursed through her.

"You're mine. You belong to me."

"Yes," she murmured, massaging the firmness of his muscular back. "I belong to you. I always have and I always will."

Sighs of acute pleasure chanted from her swollen lips as his hands stroked the soft sweetness of her thighs while his hot mouth tempted first one and then the other of her budding pink nipples.

"I want you. I've wanted you forever," he groaned.

She looked up into his face, which appeared as drugged with passion as she knew her own must have seemed. "I love you. I love you so."

"And I love you, with all my heart, sweet Maggie. And I love this child." He gently stroked the slight swell of her stomach. "Can you ever forgive me for being such a fool?"

Reminiscent of the first night they had made love, thunder echoed in the distance and blinding flashes of lightning illuminated the ebony sky outside, but Maggie and Aaron were aware only of each other. Naked in the dim radiance of the firelight, they eagerly succumbed to the mounting favor pulsating through their feverish bodies. His tender, persuasive lovemaking obliterated all the loneliness and pain, leaving only the knowledge that the final consummation of their passion was the only thing that mattered.

Even cocooned in a romantic stupor, Maggie knew Aaron's hands and lips had ceased their erotic homage. She whimpered, "Aaron?"

"It's all right," he assured her, his big hand lifting her small ones above her head, pinning them there as his somber eyes adoringly touched her body with an intimacy as arousing as the feel of his fingertips on her skin. "I want to look at you, my love. I want to see what's mine."

She shivered as he let his gaze move ever so slowly, thoroughly inspecting the silky fall of her long, red hair lying against the pearly smoothness of her neck and shoulders, carefully examining the large, firm thrust of her peach-tipped breasts, then, almost reverently, staring at the fiery thatch between her milky white thighs.

"You're the most beautiful woman in the world. Your body was made for my possession."

"Oh Aaron, I want to give you everything."

"You are everything," he told her, his fingers brushing across her lips, over her proud chin down her long creamy neck. "I'm starved for the feel of your body beneath mine, sweet Maggie, and tonight I'm going to have a feast."

"Yes. Yes." Her voice was an inaudible sigh, her mouth a recipient of his lustful kisses.

His hands cupped the womanly fullness of her breasts, the sensitive peaks stiffening at his touch. His lips plundered the inner sweetness of her mouth, his tongue exploring before stirring outward to lavishly torment every nerve ending in her lips and jaw and throat. When his tongue reached the upward tilt of her engorged breasts, her body instinctively arched into the bulging evidence of his arousal, pulsating with undeniable need.

His mouth moved over her breast, his tongue flickering repeatedly across the rosy crest before encompassing the fleshy halo. A cry of abandoned longing came from the depths of her very being.

He calmed her feverish cries, whispering little love words over and over as his mouth made a pilgrimage lower and lower, nibbling passionately along the shapely curve of her hips, placing ardent, petting nips on her inner thighs, having used his hands to persuade those limbs to separate in urgent expectancy.

When he lifted her hips in order to bring her femininity closer to his marauding lips, she cried out. He soothed her again with his words. "Let me love, my sweet, my darling."

She succumbed to his enticing words, leaving herself wantonly open to his rapturous nuzzling. It was as if tiny explosions were occurring throughout her body all at once, the intensity of her release was so great.

"Oh Aaron." She trembled beneath him, her senses raw with pleasure.

"Now, sweet Maggie," he said as he placed his massive body over hers, gradually impelling his manhood into her writhing body. "I'll be careful, my love. I won't hurt you or our baby."

When he completed his penetration with one triumphant stab she moaned with the ecstasy of his possession, clinging to him, imitating his masculine plunges with feminine actions of her own. First she and then he fell into the fiery vortex where mind and body divide, both into their own euphoric paradise.

The morning came enclosed in the gloomy dullness of a day doomed to continual drizzle, but, for Maggie, the day was as pure and sweet as if the sun were shining and a thousand songbirds filled the air with their sweet music.

Aaron looked down at the woman lying in his arms, the woman he had made love with all night long, the woman who was carrying his child. "When are you going to marry me?"

"As soon as possible," she laughed, patting her stomach.

"Do you want to move away from here, start over fresh somewhere else?"

"No. I love White Orchard. Besides, I think there are enough good people around here that we and our children can have a happy life."

"I agree," he said, then kissed her on the forehead. "I'm going to write Martha and tell her that I've finally become a man. I'm ready to accept the inheritance my father left me."

"You've forgiven your parents?"

"I understand my parents," he told her, his lips covering her flushed face with tender kisses. "If Richard Leander loved my mother as much as I love you, then I know why he could never give her up."

"Oh Aaron, we came so close to losing one another."

"That's all behind us. From now on, we'll always be together. My affair with you is going to last a lifetime."

"Yes, a lifetime and then some," she sighed as their lips met in a kiss filled with love and promise.

Epilogue

No place on earth could be as beautiful as Alabama in springtime, and no one on earth could be as happy as Maggie was on this glorious May morning. It had been almost a year since that fateful day she and Aaron Stone met at the Chattanooga depot.

So much had happened since the past October when Aaron had professed his love and claimed her and their unborn child. Life was so good that, sometimes, she had to pinch herself to make sure she wasn't dreaming. Yesterday's hopes and plans had died, but new and better ones had taken their place. She was married to a man who worshipped the ground she walked on. He had been treating her like fragile glass during the long winter months of her pregnancy and the six weeks since the birth of his son and heir. She was getting tired of it, and she intended to do something today to change things.

Master Richard Leander Stone had just been put down for his morning nap. She had spent well over an hour with her beautiful red-haired, green-eyed baby boy, nursing him, rocking him, singing to him. He was the joy of her life, but she had to admit that she wasn't any more a fool over the child than his proud papa.

The thought of what she had planned for her husband sent her pulse racing. It had been weeks since they'd made love, and she knew he was as ready as she was for a reaffirmation of their physical passion.

In October, they had married quickly in a very private ceremony. Aaron had insisted she wear white. He reminded her that she had come to him a virgin and therefore deserved a maiden bride's gown. They honeymooned aboard Aaron's steamboat, the *Chattanooga*

Belle, and spent a week at Chattanooga's Stanton Hotel where Maggie had been introduced to the mayor and other prominent Tennesseans at a party held in honor of the newlyweds.

When they returned to White Orchard, she helped her husband finish its restoration, soon becoming accustomed to the grandeur of her surroundings. The house she once thought so suitable for Eunice became her own, filled with an elegance worthy of the finest lady, and yet, every corner of every room was touched with Maggie's sweet magic, turning the mansion into a loving home.

Outside, flowers bloomed everywhere, and dozens of rosebushes sprouted new buds. In a few weeks, their magnificent colors and nectarous aroma would bless the land.

In a way, she had been able to keep her promise to Pa after all. Aaron had made her see how happy Micah was, how readily he'd taken to life on the river, and how his innate intelligence would eventually lead him to a better life. He didn't write often, but when he did, his letters were filled with censored tales of his many adventures.

And then there was Jude. She was in Tuscumbia attending the Deshler Female Institute with the Mobley twins. Her manner had greatly improved, but her stubbornness and curiosity were still the bane of Maggie's life. She was doing everything she could to make a lady out of her little sister. Only the good Lord knew if the task was impossible or not.

Maggie checked her appearance in the cheval mirror one more time before going downstairs. She had sent word for her husband to meet her in the pear orchard at noon, and it was almost that time now.

She smiled to herself, remembering that day so long ago when Aaron first brought her to White Orchard. He had held her and kissed her and touched her. They had almost made love. Today they would.

She tried not to rush, but her heart was filled with so much love and her body with so much pent-up longing that, by the time she reached the orchard, she was out of breath from running.

The orchard was like a gossamer fairyland, row after row of towering trees in full bloom surrounding her. When the gentle wind blew, soft, white blossoms cascaded downward, swirling about in the air. As she stood there, her fabulous titian hair piled on top of her head, her beautiful face aglow with health and vitality, pear flowers rained down on her like feathery snowflakes.

That's how Aaron saw her, standing in the orchard, blossoms dancing in the breeze around her, noontime sunshine turning her hair to flame. He tried not to think about what this life would have been like without this precious woman. He had been a fool to think that anything but love mattered. She was his life, and he spent every day thanking God for their happiness.

"I got your message." He smiled as he walked toward her.

"So I see." Loving the feel of his hard, masculine features, she reached out to touch his face.

"I told Phineas I might not be back all afternoon." He pulled her into his arms, his head bending to hers.

"And what did he say to that?" She snuggled closer, her full, milk-laden breasts nestled against his powerful chest.

"He said to enjoy myself," Aaron laughed, one big hand sliding down her back to cup her bottom.

"Did he tell you the good news?"

"Oh, yes. He was beaming with pride. Did Daisy tell you she was going to have a baby before she even told her husband?"

"I'll never tell."

Aaron covered her tempting mouth with his own, his tongue boldly thrusting into her warmth. After long moments, he raised his head and stared down at the woman he loved. "I need you so," he whispered into her ear.

"And I need you," she sighed.

"Here in the orchard?" He held her close, his hands moving caressingly over her body, one big hand stopping in her hair, releasing it to fall in long, lustrous curls down her back.

"Yes, my love. Here. Now. We can go to the house later."

Maggie slowly unbuttoned her dress, letting it fall to her waist. She was naked beneath it. Aaron couldn't take his eyes off of her swollen breasts. He reached out and touched one pointed tip. Tiny droplets of sweet mother's milk moistened his finger.

"My God, how I've envied my son," he groaned as he bent his head to take her breast into his mouth.

Maggie swayed against him, moaning her pleasure. He lowered her gently to the ground and removed the remainder of her clothing. He hovered above her, adoring her with his eyes while she helped him strip away his shirt. Soon his breeches followed.

There in the sunlit flowery grove, man took woman and woman took man, renewing a promise of devotion that would be theirs forever, bonding them into one entity, the fulfillment of their hearts' desire.

CPSIA information can be obtained at www.ICGtesting.com
Printed in the USA
LVOW10s1021200616

493326LV00001B/60/P